THE BILLIONAIRE
SHIFTER'S
Virgin Mate

DIANA SEERE

THE BILLIONAIRE SHIFTER'S VIRGIN MATE

McDermott "Derry" Stanton is an old-money playboy who sleeps his way through half the world, one willing woman at a time.

A bear shifter, he never hibernates alone. Sometimes even one woman isn't enough.

But when this irresistible billionaire meets Jessica Murphy, everything changes. The man who views life as a female feast suddenly acquires more discerning tastes. The only woman who can satisfy him now . . .

Is Jessica Murphy. He must have her. Immediately. Frequently.

Jess, however, doesn't want any man, least of all a spoiled playboy who's about to become her brother-in-law. A pre-med student with deep ambitions and a past filled with painful rejection, she's all business.

Too bad Derry Stanton *is* her business. A frequent customer at the Platinum Club where she waits tables, and now the best man to her maid of honor in her sister's wedding, the guy is everywhere.

And pretty soon, she finds herself everywhere, too.

In his arms, on his bed, between the sheets. . . .

But sex is the last thing she needs.

Or it was until she meets Derry and starts hearing the Beat. And feeling a connection she'd never imagined, never dreamed, never hoped for.

It's all too un*bear*ably good.

The Billionaire Shifter's Virgin Mate is the second book in the Billionaire Shifters Club series by Diana Seere, the paranormal pen name for two New York Times and USA Today bestselling romantic comedy authors. This book is a standalone within a series. Learn more about us on our Diana Seere Facebook page. ;)

One

J ess Murphy walked through the wide doors into the opulent lobby below the Platinum Club, surprised by the butterflies fluttering in her stomach. The building was more luxurious than she'd expected, every inch of glass, steel, and marble gleaming like freshly minted coins. Well-dressed men and women hurried around her over the shiny floors.

"Can I help you?" asked a man from behind a vast reception desk decorated with fruit and flowers. He wore a black suit, had gray hair, and sounded like a British butler in a classic film.

"I'm Jessica Murphy," she said. "I'm, uh, it's my first night working at the Platinum Club."

The man tapped something on his screen. "You are expected on eleven," he said. "You can take either the public or the service elevator."

She glanced at the posh lobby, the posh people. "I'll take the service one. Where is it?"

He gestured at a side door behind him.

"Thank you," she said, taking a deep breath as she walked across the marble floors.

Jess had to remind herself that this was only a waitressing job. There was no reason to be nervous; this wasn't an important career move for her, just a way to pay for medical school. Because the club's clientele was so elite, the job paid insanely well, and incoming staff members, at all levels, were screened meticulously.

In fact, she'd been hired almost a month ago, yet this was the first time she was stepping foot in the place. Instead of working tables right away, as she'd expected, she'd had to visit a notary and sign a dozen nondisclosure agreements—and then submit to a background check, personality test, and three phone interviews.

Now, finally, she could actually begin *working*.

She walked through a doorway into a space that looked older than the lobby, found a vintage-elevator call button, and popped a mint into her mouth as she waited for the car to arrive.

She could imagine her sister Lilah feeling exactly how Jess was feeling now, fighting her nerves on *her* first day as she thought of all the famous, powerful people upstairs.

Lilah had worked at the Platinum Club until last month, when she'd shacked up with her billionaire love god, Gavin Stanton. In fact, they were already planning their wedding. No more money worries for her.

No more worries of any kind, apparently.

The changes that had come over Lilah in the past couple of months made Jess uncomfortable. She was glad Lilah was happy, but it had happened much too fast. At one point, her sister had been so sex-crazed she'd claimed her rich boyfriend had turned into an *animal*.

Jess sighed. Lilah had always been too lusty for her own good, too easily enchanted by a pretty face.

Gavin Stanton certainly had that. And the rest of him wasn't bad either. Not Jess's type, but . . . not bad.

Shaking her head, Jess walked into the car—a gorgeous old thing with wood paneling—and pressed the button for the eleventh floor as instructed. Time to focus on the job at hand. Love was the last thing on her agenda. And sex was second to last. If she was going to survive the long slog through med school and internships to become a doctor, she couldn't get distracted with trivialities. She had to keep her eye on the prize. Work, school, work, school, work. And more work.

The elevator stopped, not on the eleventh floor, but the tenth. Jess looked down at herself, uneasy with the tight jeans and T-shirt she wore. They'd told her the club would provide a uniform when she arrived. Hopefully whoever joined her in the elevator was just another wage slave, not anyone important in management. She wanted to make a good impression on her first day. Her impressively curvy figure looked respectable in formal clothes, but in a T-shirt, her F-cup chest had a knack for distracting people.

Damn, I should've worn a jacket. But it had been so hot today. Autumn in Boston could still get steamy.

The doors slid open, revealing an extremely tall, thickly muscular man with long black hair and bright blue eyes that slid over her body so thoroughly she sucked in a breath.

Talk about steamy. Now *this* guy was her type. He was huge. Dark. Powerful.

Dangerous.

She felt beads of sweat form at the small of her back, under her breasts, her arms. What had he bathed in that morning—testosterone? She could smell it. She could *taste* it. She couldn't help sucking it in, breath after breath, eager for another hit.

A slow smile spread over his full, sensual lips. "Why, hello there," he said. Was that a British accent?

Every alarm bell she had was clamoring so loudly in her head, she was amazed she'd been able to hear him speak.

"Hi," she said, stepping aside instinctively. Getting too close to this man would be a mistake.

"I don't believe we've had the pleasure." Oh, crap. It *was* a British accent. He held out a hand. "McDermott Stanton. My intimates call me Derry." The way he said *intimates* made her toes curl.

Stanton? Her sister's new squeeze was a Stanton and a member of this fancy club. Gingerly she took his hand. "Any relation to Gavin Stanton?"

As he squeezed her hand between two massive palms, the wine-red birthmark on her neck, presently hidden under expensive concealer, began to tingle and burn.

"If you're here to see my brother," he said, his slanted brows coming together in a frown, "my condolences. He's recently become engaged." Then he grinned, white teeth flashing, as the elevator began to rise. "But I, as it happens, have not."

This flirting had to stop. She pulled her hand free. "Lilah's my sister."

His grin, however, only widened. "What good fortune, then, that we should meet."

"I'm going to be working here," she said. "You'll see me all the time."

"My fortune grows."

She fixed him with her best balls-shriveling stare. "I won't get personally involved with any of the members. I've signed a contract."

"Contracts don't apply to family members, surely," he said, looking wounded. "Even Eva wouldn't be so cruel."

Eva was the woman at the employment agency who had hired her. "We're not family yet," she said. Why was the elevator taking so long? They only had to go one floor, damn it. She moved past him and stabbed the button again. At last it began to rise. So did the temperature. Turning away from him, she took a deep breath and pretended her heart wasn't racing like a hummingbird on meth.

Being close to him made her feel strange, as if he'd sucked up all the oxygen.

"No," he agreed. "Not yet."

Him, a voice inside her said. She started, the word crystal clear, as if someone were standing behind her and whispering it straight to her soul.

The car came to a stop. She pressed the button to open the doors. Yeah, it was *him* all right—too much blue-eyed brawn for such a small, dark, enclosed space. His cologne filled her nose with an intoxicating blend of spice and leather, blanketing her brain in a rosy fog. She wasn't a fool; she knew she could be as hormonally affected as other people. The trick was not to trigger the hormones in the first place.

As soon as the doors were open wide enough, she strode off the car into a brightly lit hallway.

"Such a pleasure," Derry's voice rumbled behind her, rich and smooth as honey.

She waved but didn't turn around.

It had been pleasurable. Far too much.

Derry made a dismissive snort and shook his head twice, quickly, like a dog ridding itself of something annoying. That was quite the brush-off. He opened his hand and pressed the palm against a piece of stainless steel. Anyone who did not know about the ultraexclusive Novo Club eight floors beneath the ground would think nothing of the spot.

Derry, unlike most people, knew damn well. You had to be a bit of an animal to be a member.

Or more than a bit.

His phone buzzed in his pants. Funny how they were a little tighter than usual. That long brown hair. Those eyes. The slope of her cheekbone. The tightness at her throat as she struggled with her own arousal. He'd *smelled* it.

To his shock, upon entering the elevator he had felt the tingling in his nerves that signaled the beginning of a shift. Even now his tailored shirt strained against the expanding muscles in his shoulders and the hair that was thickening all over his body.

What the hell was wrong with him? He hadn't shifted involuntarily since the first flush of puberty decades ago. He shook his head again, more roughly this time, and struggled to free his phone from his tightening pocket.

The damn thing was like a child's dollhouse book in his giant hands. Fumbling, he finally slid the lock and barked into the mouthpiece.

"Stanton," he snapped.

"Stanton squared."

"Oh. It's you, Gavin. Just met your future sister-in-law. She's a . . . treat." He sniffed the air, catching the last of her scent. Mint, dog shampoo, roses, and rubbing alcohol. Now that was a combination. Was she a veterinarian?

That would be a bit serendipitous.

"Don't even think about it, Derry," his brother warned. The threat was implied.

The growl was real.

"Too late. I was thinking about it long before I laid eyes on her," Derry said airily. He loved taunting Gavin about as much as Gavin loved watching his precious football team, the New England Patriots.

"She's off limits."

Derry raised his eyebrows and held the phone away from his ear in mock shock. "You think that will stop me?"

"She's not your type."

"She has tits and a pussy, no? Then she's my type. In fact, she could have a secret penis and—"

"We are not going to rehash that Bangkok trip. My bank account still has flashbacks. You cost me a solid five figures in bribes to get you out," Gavin chided.

Derry sighed, Jess—Jessica?—Lilah's sister's scent permeating his thoughts. Something about her was appealing in a Jane Austen sort of way. She was closed off and rather prim. A career woman, he imagined. Someone who wouldn't give a playboy billionaire rake the time of day.

And yet . . . why did her scent bedevil him? It should have dissipated by now. And the itch to shift into his other form was still strong, nagging with a persistence that confounded him.

"Derry? You there?" Gavin sounded annoyed. Derry knew it was less about Lilah's sister and more about being ignored.

"Where else would I go?" Derry asked, looking around the tiny elevator. It felt like a coffin.

"You will not come on to her, make passes at her, brush up against her, kiss her, fondle her—"

"Are you reading from a contract, Gavin?" Derry asked in alarm. Gavin was the type to actually *have* a contract for this sort of thing.

"No. But I can have my lawyers draw one up if need be."

See?

"I get the picture," Derry mumbled. "Virgin sister-in-law is kryptonite. No touching."

"No *thinking*."

"You can't censor my fantasies," Derry insisted. *Thank God*.

"I would if I thought it would do any good."

Ding! The elevator stopped, and the doors slid open as if propelled by magic. Morgan, the Novo Club's stalwart master, stood holding a tray with Derry's favorite drink.

Home Sweet Club.

Her.

That damn woman's scent grew stronger. How could that be? She wasn't here. She wasn't a shifter.

"Derry?" Gavin's voice held a question, and it wasn't, *Are you there?*

"Fine, fine. I have hundreds of other women I can substitute for your future wife's sister. I'll console myself with the runners-up for Miss Universe."

"I'm sure you can find one to keep you occupied," his brother said as Derry took the drink and nodded thanks to Morgan, who disappeared.

Derry took a sip of fifty-year-old Glenfiddich scotch. The slightly woody taste of dark berries, almond, smoke, and warm oak made him relax and smolder at the same time. The scotch was infuriatingly delicious.

It tasted and smelled exactly like Jessica Murphy, damn it.

"One? Oh, you think so small, Gavin. I intend to have them *all*. Tonight. At the same time."

Gavin laughed and ended the call, leaving Derry with his scotch.

And the lingering scent of a woman he'd just promised he would never touch.

Two

J ess closed her eyes and took a head-clearing breath before setting out to find Molly Sloan, the woman who was going to fit her into a uniform for the evening. She hoped Molly, whoever she was, carried a wide range of sizes. It wasn't just her chest. She was large all over. From painful experience, any job or activity that required a uniform made her nervous.

She glanced back at the elevator. Not nervous the way the huge, delicious guy who would soon be her brother-in-law made her nervous. That was a hot, sticky, thrilling kind of nervous. The kind she was careful to avoid.

No, preparing for this job made her cold and careful. If they wouldn't accept her generous figure, tough. Lilah hadn't said anything, but Jess was a little larger than her sister, maybe just enough to be outside their range of cocktail-server uniforms. If that was the case, she was happy to wear her own clothes. She hoped they would be reasonable.

Whoever *they* were. Where was this Molly person she was supposed to meet? She walked over to a door across from the elevator, which was slightly ajar, and stuck her head inside. "Hello?"

A muffled voice reached her from the floor to the left. "Sorry! Just a minute!"

Jess opened the door and walked inside a bright, airy space that appeared to be a fashion boutique. Mirrors on one wall, tons of clothes artfully displayed on round racks and low tables, long shelves of shoes, a lounge area, and small doors in the back, apparently for changing.

"I'm Jess Murphy." She looked around for the source of the voice she'd heard but saw nobody.

"Oh shit," said the voice. Then more loudly, "I lost track of time."

A round rack began to shimmy and roll, and then a curvy woman in black crawled out from under it holding a screwdriver between her teeth. Breathing hard, she got to her feet and removed the screwdriver. "Stupid thing keeps falling over. Thought I could fix it myself." She grinned, a white thread clinging to her tight sweater, and held out a hand. "Damn, you're as beautiful as your sister." A petite brunette with impossibly large—and gorgeous—blue eyes, Molly made Jess relax instantly. She looked a little like her sister, Lilah. Maybe this would even be fun.

Instantly at ease with this friendly young woman, Jess shook her hand and returned the smile. "Thanks. That's quite a compliment. Are you Molly Sloan?"

The woman rolled her eyes. "Way to be professional, Mol," she muttered. Then, "Yes, I'm Molly. You're not, like, really early, are you?"

Jess took out her phone. "No. A few minutes late, actually." Because of the delay in the elevator. Silently she added another black mark to her Derry rating card. It was already largely filled in because of the way he'd unbalanced her right before her first day on the job. Now she might be late too.

"Then we'd better hurry." She rubbed her hands together. "Lilah said you were similar to her in size, but your style is all different. I put a few things together for you already to try on."

"I'm larger than Lilah."

Molly waved her hand as if this was of no importance. "I hope you like what I picked out for you. After we get you dressed, we'll do shoes."

"I wear a really unusual size . . ."

Molly laughed. "That's just what your sister said. I swear, you two are such pessimists. Have faith in the Magic of Molly." She walked over to one of the small doors in the back and opened up a small dressing room. "I've already put the outfits inside."

"But how could you possibly have the right size? You just met me."

"I told you. Lilah described you."

"But—she can't even buy me a sweater that fits me, and she's known me my whole life."

Molly gave her a cheerful frown and pulled her inside. "Molly Magic. You'll see."

With a sigh, Jess gave up, closed the door, and undressed to try on the first thing she saw, almost looking forward to proving Molly wrong.

But she couldn't. The cream silk blouse fit her perfectly. And then the vest with the silver buttons inlaid with some kind of red jewel, like fake rubies, hugged her curves like a tailored suit. With dread, she reached for the pants. Surely those couldn't fit—the inseam would be short, or the hips too narrow. But she slid them on, gasping as they fit her like a second skin.

She looked in the mirror. The clothes had men's styling but a woman's fit. Having expected an uncomfortable cocktail dress that would leave her inner thighs chafing and her tomboy soul annoyed, she was ridiculously happy.

"What do you think?" Molly called.

Not afraid to admit she was wrong, Jess flung the door open. "It's perfect. You *are* magic."

Molly's round cheeks flushed pink. She grinned. "You like it?"

"I love it. How did you—never mind. I got it. The Magic of Molly."

Bubbles of laughter trailed behind Molly as she led her over to the racks of shoes. "I was imagining something with a little color. I hope you agree."

Now that she was a believer, Jess didn't argue. "Whatever you say." She wiggled her toes into the plush rug near the shoes. "Size eleven, please."

Molly handed her a pair of tiny socks that felt like angel's wings, then a box.

"I left my clothes in the room," Jess said, sitting down and putting on the socks.

"They'll be there at the end of your shift when you go—"

"Oh my God." Jess drew out a pair of black slippers with ruby-red bows that somehow were both masculine and over-the-top girly-girl. "I was afraid you were going to make me wear heels."

"Not on your first night. We'll go easy on you."

Jess put them on, rolling her eyes. "They fit."

"Of course they do."

"You are—well, you're magic!"

Beaming, Molly clapped her hands together. "Let's do your hair and makeup, then you've got to book it upstairs. You don't want to get on Eva's bad side."

Jess nodded and sat patiently as Molly got out a box of creams and brushes and makeup, then began applying them.

"Let's put your hair in a tight ponytail," Molly said. "To go with the suit. If it bothers you, we'll leave it loose tomorrow."

"I'll be fine. I like it tied back."

Molly brushed and sprayed and made appreciative noises. Then she gestured for Jess to get to her feet and looked her up and down. "That looks even better than I'd hoped it would. Wow. You're going to have to beat them off with a stick." She frowned. "Which you will—did they mention that? No dating the members?"

As if that had worked for Lilah, Jess thought. But aloud she said, "That won't be a problem. I'm not interested in dating anyone."

"Really?" Molly sighed. "I am. I love getting out, doing things. It's ironic I'm stuck down here."

Jess felt a pang of sympathy. "Have you ever asked to work up in the club?"

"Oh, no thanks. I'd go crazy with all those gorgeous men all over the place. I'm safer down here."

"If I meet anyone, I'll be sure to introduce you," Jess said.

Blushing, Molly waved that idea aside. "I can't date members either. But thanks." She glanced at a clock on the far wall. "It's time! Come on, this elevator can be slow. I call it Old Ironsides. Swear it's even older."

Within three minutes, Jess was walking onto the service elevator, thankful her annoying future brother-in-law wasn't on board again.

"Thanks so much, Molly." She began to wave good-bye.

"My pleasure! But don't worry, I'm coming up with you to show you around." Molly scurried between the closing doors.

Jess smiled with gratitude. For some reason, the thought of being alone in that elevator made her even more nervous.

The move from the subterranean Novo Club to the upstairs Platinum Club had come at a price for Derry.

That price was annoyance. Unbridled frustration coursed through his veins like thousands of mosquitoes feasting off him from the inside out. Normally calm and breezy, he had come into this obnoxious state of unrest recently and was doing his best to drown it out.

One ounce of fine whisky at a time.

He looked at his watch, surprised by the bare skin. He forgot he didn't wear a watch any longer, as it was no longer stylish. Digging into his breast pocket, he looked at his phone.

Late. She was late.

Derry lounged in a chair two sizes too small for him with a glass of whisky that was also too small. He lifted his hand a few inches, the movement so subtle it might have been an accident.

A willowy figure, tall, blonde, and delicious, appeared at his side.

"Another drink, Mr. Stanton?" Gillian was one of the servers, a tall, Swedish morsel with eyes bluer than a Caribbean pool and tits that plastic surgeons used as a model for desperate patients. Too bad they were fake, but they were a work of art in their own right.

He'd had a sample. Or ten.

She winked, making it clear she knew what he was thinking. Or, rather, that she thought she knew.

He sighed and lifted the ice-filled glass. "Thank you. Yes. A double this time."

Her eyes narrowed imperceptibly, the movement of her face muscles bringing out one tiny dimple. She had those in her ass, too. That fine, upside-down, heart-shaped ass that seemed chiseled from marble covered in silk.

And . . . nothing.

His body wasn't responding.

She quirked one eyebrow and turned in a smooth gesture, as if she were warm caramel in human form, walking away with gracious efficiency. He was supposed to drool now. Think luscious thoughts of naked flesh and heated, hitched cries of ecstasy.

And . . . nothing.

Antsy and scattered, Derry's mind and body were unquenchable. For months he found nothing that could satisfy him. Entertainment was not a distraction. Women in his bed—in twos and threes—made him feel unfulfilled, even as he tested his own refractory period.

Clubs and dancing and the standard prowl of finding a bed partner, or just a pile of women to fuck, seemed too droll. Clichéd. Boring.

When had life become so boring?

Gillian delivered the double whiskey with a look that lasted two seconds too long. Derry gave her a pleasant, polite smile that was the equivalent of a rejection.

Unaccustomed to *that*, Gillian's resulting sour look conveyed her displeasure.

Which, oddly enough, made Derry glad.

"You look like someone stole your lollipop," Eva said, appearing in that slightly magical way that the woman possessed. Derry felt like an errant schoolboy around her. Always. She was more motherly than he wanted, and if he were honest with himself, he'd have to admit that he was worried that she considered him too shallow. Unlike his brother, Gavin, Derry had not made his own fortune. His other brothers Asher and Edward rarely set foot in the Platinum Club, preferring the family estate in Montana. Their sister Sophia came to the Platinum Club at odd times.

Mating season, mostly.

He looked at Eva with a sense of *Eureka!* "It is October, isn't it?"

She quirked an eyebrow. "Do you need a calendar? Have your international party escapades been such a distraction that you've lost count of the *months*?"

Zing! The arrow struck its target.

"No. I—It's just—" Derry didn't stammer. Ever. But Eva brought this out in him, and coupled with the existing feeling of ennui mixed with a buzzing, impulsive need to seek something he feared he would never find, his frustration grew.

Eva's face changed as if she suddenly understood something. "Ah. October. It's time to begin hibernating for . . . you."

She was about to say *your type*, wasn't she? Derry and his twin Sophia were bear shifters. Their older brothers, Gavin and

Asher, were wolves. Poor Edward, the youngest, was the only mountain lion.

Blended families made for some very strange siblings. They weren't exactly *The Brady Bunch*.

"It is indeed," he answered Eva, distracted. October. Of course. And that meant—

"Derry!" a female voice shouted as the elevator doors parted and three women emerged. His sister Sophia, bold and brash, was first. Tall, dark, and full figured, she gave him insight into how he would look if nature had made him a female. She'd just been acting as temporary nurse to his brother's future mother-in-law, who'd recently had some kind of medical procedure.

The recovering lady was also the mother of the next woman on the elevator. A woman who made him very glad to be a man.

Jessica Murphy strode into the Platinum Club with a cool, detached demeanor that he knew was as fake as Gillian's rack. Inside, she must be trembling with fear. Her sister, Lilah, had worked here for a few months until she'd mated with his brother, Gavin. And now they were engaged.

Derry had been told bits and pieces of what the human sisters knew about his family. The Stanton family was one of a handful of shifter families in America, and the Platinum Club was a front for the *really* exclusive club. The one built so deep beneath the ground floor, so old and hidden, that even Boston's subway system maps didn't chart it.

The Novo Club. The only requirement for membership: be a shifter. Derry longed to go back downstairs, but he never stood a woman up.

Gavin had told him that Jessica had ridiculed Lilah when she'd confessed to her sister that Gavin was a werewolf. Derry couldn't blame her—the truth was so unbelievable in human society that it was easier to think her sister had a touch of hysteria in her.

And yet the truth was the truth.

You can deny reality for only so long. But reality has a way of refusing to ignore *you*.

Just as Derry couldn't ignore her.

Her.

In the dim recesses of his mind, he played the good brother, giving Sophia a socially appropriate embrace, saying the right words to Eva, exchanging small talk and chitchat. His mind and senses were elsewhere, the ribbon of Jess's scent finding its way to him.

Tying him in knots.

Binding him.

"How drunk are you?" Sophia asked, her voice loud on purpose. She wanted attention. Every October, right before she slowed down for hibernating season, she came to the club looking for exactly what he had sought for years.

A fuck buddy. Sophia picked them in twos, always finding men who could satisfy her. One was never enough. And if her post-mating-season stories were true, two really didn't cut it either.

He could sympathize.

Right now he could fuck his way through a women's Olympic volleyball team and still feel this unquenched need for something unattainable. His sex drive should be slowing down this time of year, though. Not speeding up.

And involuntary shifting?

At no time of year.

"Not drunk. Just distracted," he muttered, slugging away his drink. He could feel the defensiveness in his words as cherries and heated oak sweat and musk, and a light bouquet of curiosity filled his nose.

What did Jess smell like when she came? An image of her, lips parted with abandon, hair draped over his fevered body, crying out his name as their sweat and flesh drove them to a place where true release gave him back his sense of wholeness, made him—

Where in the hell did *that* thought come from?

And now he was hard.

"Distracted by . . ." Sophia looked around the room with laser-sharp focus, eyes filled with an impish merriment that he knew would lead to trouble. He took every ounce of focus off Jess, who was being introduced to Carl and Gillian at the bar by a pert little curvy brunette who handled something with dresses and hair at the Plat. One of the few female staff members Derry hadn't managed to sink his cock into, as Gavin once noted.

Too bad you never will.

Derry shook his head fast, like knocking a black fly loose before it could bite, the movement quick and dirty. God dammit, he was losing it. What the hell were the bartenders putting in these drinks?

"Distracted by the lack of good pussy," he said, making Eva roll her eyes. If he couldn't please her, might as well shock her. "I need someone adventurous. The women here are more Hello Kitty and I need something more like Catwoman."

"You need good antibiotics," Eva said, walking away after her quiet comment, leaving Sophia prostrate with laughter and Derry annoyed. He lifted his glass.

No one appeared.

A ripe, lush sense of pleasure and fulfillment tortured his nose, the scent filling his mind with images of his fingers against her skin, his mouth slanted against hers, his cock buried so deep he could touch her soul, their bodies moving as one toward a gentle love that would make them one.

His.

He tipped his head up, nostrils twitching, needing to capture every molecule of her essence, sensing her uncertainty, her need, her strength.

Derry watched as Sophia found a man to target, barely registered Gillian's delivery of a new drink, scarcely noticed his own insistent stare as a cloud of want, need, desperation, and grounded truth enveloped him. Every hair on his body stood on end, every muscle began to twitch and turn, every tendon tensed as he became aligned with a singular realization:

He knew *exactly* what would meet his need.

And at that same moment, she looked up and caught his eye.

Her.

Three

The Platinum Club took Jess's breath away.

Movie stars. Senators. Football players, musicians, models. She recognized one of her former professors from night school, then was flattered when the woman remembered her—and admitted she'd worked at the Plat herself, long ago.

"Enjoy yourself," she told Jess, holding up her bourbon in a toast. Then, as she brought the drink to her lips, added, "Not too much, of course."

"Don't worry." Her nerves calming, Jess thanked her and hurried back to the bar to refill her tray. No money changed hands, no tabs needed to be tracked. Every member had already paid more than enough in their dues to cover all the amenities. They came to the Platinum to relax, network, play—not pull out their wallets. Eva told Jess to be invisible but present, quiet but friendly, unhurried but very, very fast. No member should ever look around in annoyance, wondering where the server was or why their drink hadn't arrived yet.

"You're a natural," Carl, the bartender, told her. Young and friendly, almost certainly gender fluid and maybe pansexual, he'd had her back all night. "Must run in the family."

"Without tracing the tab, it's easy."

"You *make* it look easy. You haven't served the wrong drink yet." He handed her a tray with two pint glasses of a local ale, a whiskey smash, and a dirty martini. "That's a first. Even Lilah screwed up a few drinks on her first night."

Jess smiled wickedly. "She did?"

"Served a Bloody Mary to a vegan." He shook his head in mock horror. "It was quite the scandal."

She laughed. "You're teasing me."

"Never." He put one more drink on the tray. "Get back to work. Show them how it's done, sunshine."

Still smiling, she lifted the tray and pivoted in her ruby slippers, which were as comfortable after two hours on her feet as they'd been the moment she'd put them on. And although she was the only woman server wearing pants, she had noticed a few appreciative glances from the men in the club. Nothing requiring a stick, but enough to make her feel beautiful, sexy, and confident.

She strode through her area, serving the drinks, noticing two good-looking guys in suits were giving her a few of those appreciative glances at that very moment.

What a perfect gig for her. It was understood she couldn't get involved romantically without losing her position, so she could turn them down without any of the awkwardness she struggled with in her daily life. She could be beautiful and sexy without getting into unwanted trouble. She could have fun.

"So nice to see the new girl enjoying herself," a low voice rumbled in her ear.

Electric pleasure shot through her, starting at the base of her scalp, spreading out to the tips of her toes and fingers, then back into a hot, deep pool between her legs.

Him.

Heart racing, she glanced in his direction without turning her head. "Can I get you anything, Mr. Stanton?"

He didn't reply, each moment of his silence loaded with

innuendo. Finally he said, "What do you have?"

She could have fun, she reminded herself. He was going to be family. He was a member of the club. Nothing could happen.

She turned and met his gaze. "What would you like?"

A grin spread from one ear to the other. "Such a wonderful question. Small, but loaded with potential." His gaze dropped, hiding his eyes beneath thick, dark lashes. "Like a delicious morsel."

What precisely was he staring at? Her mouth? Her breasts? She wondered—she couldn't help but wonder—what he liked. "A morsel, Mr. Stanton? Perhaps I should get you something from the restaurant. There's a wonderful sea bass and pumpkin curry tonight."

"I had a different kind of morsel in mind." He licked his lips. "But you knew that, Jess, didn't you? You may not play, but you certainly know the game."

Her face heated, which annoyed her because he'd be able to see that he'd unbalanced her. "I know that I need to get back to work." With unsteady fingers, she lifted the whiskey smash and looked around for the person who'd ordered it, suddenly going blank on who it had been. The cable news anchor? No, she was drinking vodka shots. One of the men at the congressman's table? No, no, they were sharing a bottle of some expensive French wine, and Carl had warned her to make time to get more in the cellar.

"I believe you're looking for the actor," Derry said in her ear, his low voice making her shiver.

Without thanking him, she hurried over to the man sitting by himself at a small table, reading on his phone. If he was annoyed by the delay, he didn't show it. Relieved, she returned to the bar.

Where Derry was leaning, long legs stretched out, now waiting for her.

"Not your type, then, if you could forget him so easily." Derry put an enormous hand over his heart. "I'm gratified beyond words."

She reached for her water bottle behind the bar and gulped down a long, soothing drink. She'd been wrong to think she'd be able to have fun with him. Very wrong. He wrecked her concentration. He could wreck everything.

"Jess, we need you to get another bottle of that cabernet now," Carl said, gesturing to someone behind her. "Gillian will show you how to get to the cellar. I'll get you another double, Mr. Stanton."

Jess met Carl's gaze, seeing from his expression that he was implementing a rescue mission. "Right away," Jess said.

Gillian appeared, cocked an eyebrow at Derry, and led Jess away with her long, bare arm entwined in hers. She was the type of woman Jess had expected to see at an elite club—tall, blonde, gravity-defying breasts.

"You're not ready for that one, darling," Gillian said, shaking her head. "If he bothers you, give me a signal. And he will bother you. It's in his DNA. Can't help it, poor little thing."

Jess snorted. They'd reached the service elevator behind the bar. "Him? Little?"

Gillian laughed, not entirely with pleasure, and punched the elevator button. "Inside he is little. A spoiled little boy with too many toys."

"You mean women."

"Yes, I mean women," Gillian said. "Not that he doesn't take care of his toys. Never that. It was a pleasure to be played with." A soft, girlish giggle escaped her.

They got onto the elevator, where Gillian showed her an unmarked button that would take them below the lobby to the wine cellar. Lilah had mentioned something about being careful down here but wouldn't explain what she'd meant. After the car sank down the dozen or so floors and the doors opened, Jess thought she understood. It was dark, and the ancient cobblestone floor was uneven. In the stilettos the other servers were wearing, this place *would* be hazardous. Unsteadily she stepped into a dark hallway that looked like the entrance to a medieval dungeon in a Hollywood movie. Unfinished stone walls with black iron sconces casting uneven light.

"I thought we weren't supposed to get involved with the members," Jess said. She didn't want to sound judgmental, making a bad first impression with a coworker, but Eva had been quite adamant on that point. What Lilah had done may have ended well, Eva had said, but it broke the rules.

"I swore I wouldn't, but I couldn't help myself." Gillian took a few careful steps into the hallway and turned, running a hand over her perfect body with a sigh. "There's just something about him."

Gritting her teeth, Jess walked past her to get the wine, wherever it was. She didn't care if there was something about him. She'd denied herself for years. Self-denial was her middle name. She'd keep on doing it, no problem.

Gillian opened an old, scarred wooden door in front of them. The letters TPC stood out. "You know what's really scary?" She laughed softly. "I'd do it again in a second. Eva could be standing there threatening to fire me, and I wouldn't care. He's that good."

With Gillian's laughter echoing in her soul, Jess got the wine. The two of them went back upstairs without another word about Derry Stanton.

Jess Self-Denial Murphy, she thought to herself. *No problem*.

Her scent was so overpowering and all-consuming he could taste her in the back of his throat. How could you taste someone you'd never kissed? No amount of whisky was washing the distinct flavor away. He suspected the only way to get rid of this taste was to actually lick her. Kiss her. Probe and lave and drink from her. The mystery of the forbidden was his only problem. That was all.

Derry just needed to satisfy his curiosity. Then he would go back to baseline and all would be well and right with his world.

Right?

Carl walked past him, carrying a neat little plastic container with handles that he clicked open. Pulling off the top, the bartender reached in and began lining up small little red, green, and white items on a small counter behind the bar.

Intrigued, Derry approached. In the dim light of the Platinum Club, it was hard to make out what Carl was doing, and Derry's shadow always preceded him. "A small mountain," Gavin nicknamed him as a tiny cub, his body big and muscled, barrel-chested and hirsute now as a man. Standing at more than six and a half feet, with the body of a lumberjack, Derry tended to block out light. Sometimes even the sun. Just as he reached the bar, a familiar pair of voices called his name.

"Derry!" One a baritone, one a soprano. He turned to find himself greeting his brother, Gavin, and his future sister-in-law, Lilah.

Jess's sister.

Gavin gave him a curt nod, but Lilah opened her arms and swooped up on tiptoes to give him a welcoming, warm embrace. He closed his eyes and inhaled deeply.

No. Her scent was distinctly different. Jess and Lilah may be sisters, but there was none of Jess's uniqueness in Lilah. As he pulled away from the embrace, he opened his eyes, startled to meet his brother's deathly glare.

Oh dear.

No missing the meaning of *that* look.

The background jazz caught his attention as the smooth slide of a saxophone played a familiar tune. Too familiar. Something about Santa and reindeer. He watched Gavin's ear twitch and an eyebrow go up in disgust.

"Already?" said his brother. "It's not even Halloween yet. Why on earth is Eva playing Christmas music now?"

Lilah giggled, her voice like glass chimes being played with silk-covered mallets. "I love holiday music!" Gavin's sour face went to neutral as she squeezed his arm and sighed. "I can't wait to go to Montana and have sleigh rides and hot chocolate by the fire and make cranberry and popcorn garland for the tree."

Derry bit back a laugh. Gavin's idea of celebrating Christmas was peppermint-flavored vodka and a trip to Australia for the duration.

Falling in love changed *everything*.

"And I'll knit us matching red sweaters!" she added. "With little colored ball ornaments you tuck into special loops. We could even do light-up sweaters, like the one my mom has!"

Derry's laugh could not be contained.

Gavin's glare sharpened.

"Did someone say Christmas?" Eva asked, reaching for one of the baubles Carl had just unpacked. It was, to Derry's surprise, a fresh sprig of mistletoe.

Gavin groaned. "How cliché," he ground out.

"How wonderful!" Lilah squeaked.

"I don't need an excuse to kiss you," Gavin growled and proved his point, dipping Lilah down to the ground with a kiss that literally curled the woman's toes. He could see them respond through her translucent, fashionable shoes.

Breathless, she came up from the tongue acrobatics and gave Gavin a thousand-watt smile. "We'll have mistletoe everywhere at the ranch, alongside all the Christmas decorations I have in storage at my mother's!"

Derry crossed his arms over his chest and stopped trying to hide his glee at Gavin's distress. Funny the things you learn about someone you fall in love with on a dime.

"Marry in haste, repent at leisure," he said under his breath so that only Gavin could hear it.

As Gavin opened his mouth to reply, Lilah handed Derry the sprig. "You're the tallest, Derry. Can you hang this?" She pointed to a small hook just over the walkway a few feet from the bar.

He did as told. She gave a cheerful, quiet clap and jumped up and down a few times, some members admiring the resulting jiggles from afar. He cut his own eyes. Time to think of Lilah as a sister.

Her sister, on the other hand, wasn't really family . . .

Eva spoke to Carl in muted tones, then turned to the group. "We normally don't decorate while guests are here, but a member survey indicates that people want to be part of the fun. If you move into the fireplace room, you can help with the tree and the mantle. We have hot toddies and peppermint margaritas available." She gave Gavin a wicked smile.

"A triple scotch, Carl," Gavin ordered. "Neat."

"Yes, sir," Carl said with a barely concealed smirk.

An image of Gavin and Lilah dragging toddlers to one of those mall Santas made Derry chuckle, the idea driving out thoughts of Jess for a split second. Good. He needed something to keep him from smelling her. To distract him from a body that began to throb for her. To make him stop the interminable dawning realization that these feelings, scents and sensations weren't going away.

"Jess!" Lilah said excitedly, reaching for her sister. So much beauty in one hug. He saw Gavin admiring Lilah and then noticing him looking, too.

Gavin frowned and pulled on Derry's arm. He didn't budge an inch.

"Jess is off limits," Gavin whispered.

Lilah took a step back from Jess and smiled, looking up. "Oh, look! Mistletoe!" Lilah's eyes flitted between her sister and—

Derry.

Could his future sister-in-law be any more obvious? Were they ten-year-olds playing spin the bottle? Derry's eyebrows rose with an insolent, languid look that he hoped covered for his eagerness to complete the silly ritual.

Even a fake excuse to kiss Jessica Murphy was better than no excuse.

Gavin shook his head slowly, giving Derry a stare that made him look remarkably like their bossy older brother, Asher.

Off limits, Gavin mouthed.

Jess gave a nervous laugh, her eyes shifting around the room with an endearing look of panic. You'd think she hadn't kissed a man before.

Time to fix that.

She was in his arms in half a second, his lips on hers, his hands sinking into the warm, luscious curves. This would be perfunctory. A social nicety. The completion of a seasonal ritual designed to elicit titters and smug smiles.

And then he was lost, sinking deeper and deeper into the sweet honey and cream of a woman he never knew existed. Now that he knew she did, he could never let her go.

And oh, that taste. She *was* the taste.

His. Only his.

Four

For Jess, it was as if the world had disappeared in a blast of red-hot fire. Lilah, Gavin, the club, the music, the conversation—gone. There was only him. She couldn't even remember his name. The big one, the strong one, the bad one. The one who was wrapping her in flames.

Knees buckling, Jess reached for his shoulders. She dug her fingers into muscle, and feeling his strength brought her some comfort. But it wasn't enough. Her hands wanted skin, warm flesh to match the blaze enveloping them. To match the wet, slick heat of his mouth.

It wasn't a kiss. It was a meal. He was consuming her in fire, engulfing her deepest places with the taste of him, this burning deliciousness.

She slid her hands up the side of his neck—finally, warm skin under her palms—and up into the soft, thick waves of his hair. She gripped his skull between her hands and held him where she wanted him. Feasting on her mouth. Bowing to her. Taking from her. Opening—

With a grunt of pain, not pleasure, he broke the kiss.

"While I admire the holiday spirit," Eva said loudly, "the cornerstone of pleasure is moderation, don't you think?"

Derry staggered back a step, pulling Jess, whose hands were still entwined in his hair, along with him. Realizing this in horror, she jerked away, stumbling without his support and feeling the blood rush to her face.

What had she just done? My God. It was like the time when she was little and had fallen off the swings. At first it had been fantastic to fly through the air, but then she'd landed and everything hurt and she couldn't breathe and everyone was yelling at her.

"Jess?" Lilah wasn't yelling, but her tone wasn't happy, either.

In a daze, she looked at the faces around her. Gavin had pulled Derry a few feet away and was still holding his arm, looking like he was about to tear it off and feed it to him. Lilah hovered between Jess and Derry like the landlord of an Old West saloon trying to prevent a gunfight.

And Eva . . .

Oh God. Her boss. There wasn't much on her face at all. It was a professional mask. What was left of Jess's stomach fell to the floor.

She was going to lose her job on her first day if she didn't spin this somehow. Like that childhood day in the playground, her lungs weren't filling with air and she ached all over. But she could fake it.

Laughing with as much bravado as she could muster, she pointed a finger at Derry. "They weren't kidding. You kiss like an industrial vacuum cleaner. You could get a second job doing tonsillectomies."

Silence. Then, after a moment, Lilah put a hand over her mouth, stifling a giggle.

"The club must like having you around," Jess continued. "Suction like that would be more effective than the Heimlich maneuver. If anybody's steak goes down wrong, you're the man to call."

Derry's mouth dropped. A flush rose up on his neck.

"I think you owe the lady an apology, brother," Gavin said.

"She—she—I was not alone—" Derry looked more confused than angry.

Jess grabbed her tray. There weren't any drinks on it, but the prop gave her confidence. "Perhaps alone time is just what you need, big guy." She turned to Carl. "Could you please hand me my water? I've got the funniest taste in my mouth."

Shooting Jess the faintest of smiles, Eva picked up a box from the bar. "I'll be in the fireplace room." She looked at Derry. "Neither your attendance nor participation is required."

After she had glided away, Jess relaxed slightly. She gulped the water Carl handed her and scanned her section, but another server had taken over for her while she was . . .

Indisposed.

Insane.

Gavin had released Derry and now seemed to find the situation hilarious. She'd compared him to a vacuum cleaner. She'd laughed at him. She'd humiliated him.

Good. Inside, she was a seething mess. She couldn't let him do anything like that ever again.

"Better get back to work. See you later, Lilah, Gavin, Dyson—" With a mock gasp, Jess put a hand over her mouth. "Derry, I mean."

Gavin and Lilah's laughter gave her the exit she needed. She dove back into the rhythm of serving drinks to the elite.

Although she didn't see him leave, she knew—she *felt*—the exact moment Derry was no longer nearby.

It felt awful.

Derry stormed out of the club humiliated and reeling, his skin buzzing like bees.

It wasn't the first time, but typically he was drunk and had done something to deserve those feelings. This was different.

He was dumbstruck and aching, like an adolescent fumbling through his first kiss.

That had been no child's kiss, though.

That had been eternity in the form of a woman.

How her body had yielded to his, those lips opening and taking him in, welcoming him with the sighs of a thousand years of *yeses*. Her scent embedded itself in his DNA and made him want to smell her for the rest of his days. To taste, to touch, to sniff, to devour. For a moment, like in the elevator, he'd felt his body strain to shift into its other shape, but the feel of her in his arms had given him the power to control it, to remain a man who could—who *would*—drive his body into this woman who was born for him.

And then.

The mockery.

As his mind raced through the past few minutes, replaying it like a television caught in an infinite loop, his blood doubled in volume, and he felt the familiar expansiveness settle into his cells, burning with the pre-shift frenzy that the prodromal warnings gave him.

Fuck.

Now?

Why *now*?

Derry jabbed the elevator button with a rising sense of panic, knowing the change was imminent. The Novo Club was achingly far, though deceptively close. If he couldn't get in the damn elevator in time and get his palm on that silver plate, he was screwed beyond belief.

And not in a good way.

Her scent consumed him as insipid modern techno-beat music cluttered his ears, each note acute and fiery, screaming with the echoes of the damned. Senses sharpening by the nanosecond, the scrape of his fingertip against the burnished metal of the elevator button felt like sandpaper. The sound of seltzer sprayed into a highball glass was Niagara Falls. Jess's shower gel was a field of lavender in Provence, the purple a swirling, swaying vision behind his closed eyes.

His chest swelled, his cock hardened, and he struggled to stop his skin from growing the fur that tipped him from man to animal, from one form to the other, neither more true.

Both just who he *was*.

A deep breath brought thousands of scents, a mix of despair and arousal, loathing and desperation, the pheromones and perfumes and chemicals all mingling into a kind of olfactory madness overridden by one scent:

Her.

"I'm supposed to be hibernating," he said to himself, his ears sharp and fully aware that his voice was morphing into something not human. "Not shifting."

The gravelly rumbles of vocal cords not designed for language made him begin to breathe hard, his muscles going rigid, his joints beginning to loosen as tendons slid and stretched. The pain was a sort of pressure that came with satisfaction, his metamorphosis a kind of destiny as he became more *ursus* than *humana*, more primal than prim.

Ding!

An empty elevator greeted him, and he thrust himself into it, pressing his palm against the secret steel panel for the Novo Club. A jumble of half-formed words assembled themselves into a primitive prayer in gratitude for his forefathers who built what he needed most right now.

Second to Jess, that is.

Eight floors below ground, he would find sanctuary from a world that could not know the truth about him. The flooding relief of pores that opened, the spiral, wiry release of fur from his skin as it thickened, the sharpening of his sight, and the scent of his own need made him fling his growing body against the wood-paneled wall over and over, the cables holding the elevator in its channel whipping around above like the crack of a coachman at the helm of a nineteenth-century carriage.

"Jess," he whispered, except the word came out without consonants, a vowel-filled call that meant his shift was nearing completion. The pain of torn muscle fiber muted itself under the emotional torture of losing control. He hadn't shifted involuntarily since that humiliating coming-of-age moment while in boarding school in England.

The last coherent thought McDermott Stanton had as the elevator doors opened to reveal Morgan, the secret club steward, standing before him with a welcome, somber expression, was the understanding that he no longer controlled any part of his world.

Not his body.

Not his mind.

And most certainly not his heart.

Five

A n hour later, he stood before the elevator, pushing the Up button so hard, over and over, that he was like a woodpecker. Morgan had, as always, taken care of him through and after the shift, providing a safe place for nature to take its course. The need to mate, oddly enough, had led him back to human form.

He was confused. Nothing his body did made sense. Shifting in October was rare. Losing his ability to control his change from human to animal was unheard of.

And living with the humiliation of being kissed, then turned into an object of ridicule by her—*Her!*—was an issue that needed to be fixed.

Now.

Blinking hard, he stopped, the dull roar of the blood in his ears subsiding just enough for him to realize he'd run away.

McDermott Stanton did not run away with his tail between his legs from anyone. Rather, he ran away to *chase* a piece of tail and find his way between her legs.

Fury pounded through him, but it brought a sense of clarity.

If his kiss had been so unsatisfying for Jess, he should find another whom he could satisfy. Or two.

Or three.

And do it right here, right now, under Miss Jessica Murphy's mocking eye. She thought he wasn't worth a kiss?

Oh, he'd show her.

He'd show her exactly who was in control.

With determination, he marched back into the lounge just as the public elevator dinged.

"Derry!" called a melodic voice. "How perfect!" The gentle tickle of a Spanish accent was music to his ears as he forced himself to stop and turn on his heel, his smile more and more real as he caught the full image of Isla Monroe. The actress was far better known in her native country of Chile, but her breakout role in the US had come this year. Her face was plastered everywhere.

And soon it would be atop his cock.

"Isla! So good to see you," he said, his voice booming loud as he swept her off her feet with a grin and a kiss on each cheek. She was hard and tight against his body, her face beautiful from about twenty paces, but up close, she was nothing but surgeon's putty, Botox, and cosmetics. As a companion, Isla was good for a few hours of diverting fun.

Like eating junk food: you crave it, you eat it, and then you regret it quickly.

But it tastes so sweet when it's in your mouth.

"Derry!" squealed another female voice. Oh, the luck. Fortune was smiling upon him this evening, as Frederica von Eisenthorpe launched herself at him, wrapping those never-ending legs around his waist and embracing him the way a small child greets a parent after a long absence.

Freddi was never one for decorum. When you're the sole heiress of a family that had owned land in the time of the Vikings and managed to hang on to it through feudalism to social democracy and beyond, you don't have to follow the rules.

He loved her for that.

"Ah, Freddi, you look absolutely divine," he said into her shoulder, his words muffled by a mouthful of hair extensions the perfect shade of auburn that can only come from a chemical factory in New Jersey. "I must have done something wonderful in a past life to get both of you to myself tonight."

Isla quirked one eyebrow. At least Derry thought she did. It was hard to tell. Her lip went up a few millimeters, and she looked like she was having a stroke.

"Both of us tonight, Derry?" Freddi said as he pulled her off him. She reminded him of an octopus strangling its dinner. "Only two?"

He gave her a lascivious smile. "Do you have another friend?"

"We have a playroom back at our suite."

Derry smiled until his teeth felt like white, polished rocks in his mouth. "You say the most delightful things, Freddi." He looped their arms in his and sauntered back to the bar, barely nudging his head to catch Carl's attention. The second the threesome was seated, Gillian appeared, wearing a tight smile.

Hmmm. Speaking of a possible third . . .

Jess appeared right behind her, all polished professionalism with a neutral, blank face.

"Mr. Stanton," Gillian said smoothly. "Ms. Monroe. And Lady von Eisenthorpe. Let me introduce you to our newest host, Jessica."

Isla and Freddi acted as if Gillian and Jess weren't there, whispering to each other and scanning the room.

"The usual?" Gillian asked. Jess looked anywhere but at him.

"Yes, the usual. And, Gillian . . . are you free after your shift?" he murmured, making certain Jess could hear him. He looked right at her rather than the woman he was propositioning. "Freddi and Isla and I would love to get acquainted."

Gillian's nose twitched with a pleased look as she seemed to struggle not to giggle. "Oh, yes," she whispered, trying to keep

Jess from hearing.

Derry waggled his eyebrows and said, "Bacchus always was my favorite god."

"Not Loki, Mr. Stanton? I would think he would be more your speed," Jess said in a clear voice, her face breaking into a cold, professional grin that said, *Could you be any more shallow?*

"More like Thor," Freddi said, paying attention to the conversation quite suddenly. "Derry is very good at hammering important things."

The three women cut Jess looks that made her swallow, hard. He knew she was struggling to maintain that neutral look.

Good. This bothered her.

He was doing something right.

After an hour of serving drinks to Derry and his female companions, Jess was more than ready for one of them to lose consciousness. They'd been continuously pouring cocktails down their lovely gullets, draining each one, yet still they sat upright, sometimes on Derry's knee, asking for more.

More, Derry, more. It made her want to vomit.

Clenching her teeth, Jess set more drinks on their table, dirty martinis this time. Each time she served a round, the women made loud sexual comments, for which Derry rewarded each of them with kisses, under-the-table groping, and banter of his own.

"Dirty drinks for dirty girls," he said, lifting one for each of them.

Jess suppressed a snort, but Derry must have noticed her involuntary eye roll and asked, "Don't you like to get dirty, Jessica?"

There was absolutely nothing she could say without risking her job or her cool, so she said nothing.

"Stop teasing her," said the tall, auburn-haired one in insincere, European tones. "Our conversation is too mature for her tender ears."

Jess managed to keep her face and voice expressionless. "Can I get you anything else?" Her gaze skittered across Derry's for a moment, just long enough to see an aggressive hunger there that made her legs wobble.

She wanted to fling up her hands to protect herself. Or reach for him.

The seconds ticked by in silence. She was beginning to understand why this job paid so much. She was beginning to wonder if it was worth it.

"No, we don't need you. Isn't that obvious?" That came from Isla Monroe, Hollywood's newest It Girl. Jess had seen her in a movie recently and vowed to never see her in another.

Jess spun away without a word, digging her nails into her palm to stop herself from crying. No, not tears. Violence. She'd never wanted to rip a woman's eyeballs out of her head as much as she did at that moment. Both women. And then drag Derry away by the ear.

She stopped in the middle of the club floor and stared into space. *Drag* him? Drag him where?

The answer struck her as a high-res, full-sensory fantasy, right between the eyes.

Right between the *legs*.

She saw him in her bed. That glorious physique, naked. His limbs, stretched wide. His eyes and voice, imploring. His cock, his huge, demanding, beautiful cock, hard and ready for her. Begging for her.

The psychological stimulus had a predictable but unwelcome effect on her body. She was short of breath. Covered with sweat. Quivering.

"You don't need to do overtime on your first night," Lilah said in her ear, taking the tray from her. "Did you realize what time it was? I've been waiting to talk to you."

Jess grabbed Lilah like the lifeline she was. "Thank God," she said.

"Are you all right? You're shaking."

Jess couldn't tell her. This guy was going to be her brother-in-law. "I forgot to eat earlier. I just need a sandwich or something."

Hauling her to the bar, where she handed Carl the tray, Lilah patted her arm. "You didn't forget. You were too nervous, weren't you?"

"Get me out of here, will you?" Jess whispered. "I'm about to fall over." That was true enough. Every time she came within twenty feet of Derry Stanton, her knees buckled.

"Of course."

In five minutes she'd changed out of the borrowed club outfit into her own comfortable clothes, accepted Molly's congratulatory hug, and was waiting with Lilah for the service elevator to bring them down to the ground floor.

"I was going to take you out for a drink to ask you," Lilah said, "but you're exhausted and I can't wait."

"Ask me what?"

Lilah licked her lips, her eyes pleading. "Will you be my maid of honor? At my wedding?"

The fact that she would worry about such a thing made Jess laugh. "Of course I will, stupid! Who else would do it?"

Lilah flung her arms around her and squeezed. "It means a lot to me."

"I might as well be in one wedding in my life," Jess said. "None of my friends would ever ask me. I'm much too cynical."

"You're just going through a phase."

"Get used to it, sis. It's going to be a long phase."

Lilah got that older-sister look on her face that said she knew better. "We'll see."

"You will," Jess said. But she was too tired to argue tonight.

Lilah pressed the button for the elevator again. "This thing gets slower every night. You'd think a club of billionaires could speed it up a little."

A whistling and creaking noise indicated the car was finally arriving. Then they heard voices. Or were those screams?

Just before the doors opened, Jess decided the sounds were feminine squeals of delight, and she braced herself for the sight that was about to unfold. Because she knew who it was. Before she saw him, she could sense his nearness.

Him.

Sure enough, the doors opened, revealing an orgy in progress. A tangle of bare limbs, an expensive skirt lifted above an even-more-expensive ass, two huge hands squeezing a breast on two women while a third, reaching around from behind, stroked the bulge between his legs.

"Derry," Lilah said. "Save it for later, will you?"

With his open mouth hovering an inch above a puckered nipple, Derry slid his gaze from the movie star's breast to his future sister-in-law. He promptly straightened, closing his mouth and moving his hands over a woman's ass cheeks to the prim curve of her waist. The third woman, frowning at the newcomers, stepped out from behind him. Gillian. She looked at Jess with a self-satisfied but tense expression, like she was afraid of getting caught but liked being afraid.

"Lilah," Derry said. "I beg your pardon. I forget myself."

"Not much to forget," Jess said, stomping onto the elevator in her own comfortable boots. They gave her another inch or two of height, which she appreciated around his hulking frame and the other women, one of whom she would have to work with on a regular basis.

As the doors shut, she felt, rather than saw, Derry's annoyance. Two feet behind her, three women in his grasp, he seethed.

"Come on, Derry, there's nothing wrong with a little kiss," Isla cooed.

"Not to happy, healthy women," he said.

Jess shot him a contemptuous glance. "You seem to be confused about why it's called a *service* elevator."

"Boy, it's been a long night," Lilah said, hitting the button for the ground floor.

Lowering his voice, Derry said, "It will be."

By the time they finally reached the lobby, the three women in his arms had renewed their efforts to procreate in public. Jess marched off the elevator and through the lobby, determined to reach the street before anybody saw the flush in her cheeks.

It wasn't arousal. It was fury. She pushed the rotating door around with both palms and sucked in the cool night air.

"Hold it," Lilah said on the sidewalk, tapping her arm. "My shoe came untied."

Helpless to flee while Lilah bent over to tie her laces, Jess had to stand there and watch Derry lead his harem out of the building into a waiting limo. A big, bald, suited driver nodded curtly at Derry, who gave him a drunken salute. The driver looked like he could double as a WWF wrestler. His face was as expressionless as a pancake.

Bodyguard? How could a guy like Derry—a veritable bear of a man—need a protector?

One by one, the women shot Jess amused, contemptuous glances as they climbed inside. Her last vision was the movie star's waxed vulva. And Derry's hand, sliding up her thigh in its direction, just as his driver slammed the door shut.

If she'd ever needed a reminder of why she kept her own panties on, she'd just had it.

One she'd never forget.

Six

The never-ending spread of hot flesh felt like a midnight chocolate-and-lobster buffet at a nudist resort. Add a few bottles of Chateau Lafite, and Derry would think he'd reached nirvana.

And yet his mind wandered.

Freddi's tongue was in his mouth. Then Isla's breast was against his lips. Gillian's masterful palm caressed him there, and there, and oh—*there*.

Yet it left him flat.

Not *flat*. The plumbing worked. It worked just fine.

But his heart wasn't in it.

As Manny directed the car down the city streets, the back of the limo filled with the heat of four sets of lungs, the scent of pussy and wine crowding out all others.

Including Jess.

He could feel his mouth and nose searching for the last remnants of her, like looking through a departing window on a plane until the person on the tarmac is real only in your mind. Isla's hand slipped under his waistband as Freddi dispatched with his belt and pants. Freed and hard, he took all the women in with his eyes.

His body relaxed into it.

His mind clenched.

God damn it. He doubled up his efforts, trying to unclench. He watched as Freddi dove between Isla's legs, the tangy scent of her so familiar and enticing. The buildup that came from wanton abandon was part of the thrill of so much flesh. Tumbling into a pile of limbs was about losing himself.

His mind, however, seemed to have found him.

Found *her*. Jess.

And wouldn't let go.

Isla tightened her thighs against Freddi's cheeks. It looked like two stretched pieces of hard taffy, cold and stripped. She moaned and moved in short thrusts upward until Freddi pulled back, as Derry watched, his stomach twisting like barbed wire in a tornado.

He couldn't.

He just . . . couldn't.

Gillian's offer of ministrations to his cock was pleasant enough. She looked up at him, coquettish and coy, her eyes on his as her hand reached down for his softening shaft, like slipping a chilled body into a hot springs in Iceland.

Freddi worked on Isla, giving pleasure with a lusty reverence that he could appreciate visually but could not match sensually. Not on the inside.

And not with his own, aching body.

The whole scene became surreal. He watched it all as if from a distance, though his own sweat dripped onto Gillian's arm as she looked at him with so many questions, the limo unbearably warm even in the New England autumn chill.

He felt like a wax statue from Madame Tussauds museum.

What the hell had happened to him?

Alcohol. He needed more alcohol.

He needed an ocean's worth of alcohol.

Barring that, he sought out the decanter of fine scotch that his staff always stocked in the limo. He found it.

Dry.

Freddi's mild snore from between Isla's legs gave him a clue as to how the decanter had come to be empty. Searching Isla's face, Derry expected disappointment. Outrage.

Instead, he found slumber.

Gillian's eyes tipped up in an eerily subservient expression as she bent down to suck on his unresponsive cock, her head moving up at the last second, sucking suggestively on his finger instead. The limo lurched to the right, and her lips were dislodged from him with an audible *pop!* that made him start to laugh.

It was a bitter, confused sound.

What in the hell was wrong with him?

"Derry?" Gillian said, her hand primping her mussed hair, her fingers searching for the bottle of Champagne propped between Freddi's calves. She gave him a look that said everything it needed to say as she tipped the bottle up, her throat working hard as she drained it.

"I'm . . . tired," he grunted. Tapping on the window, he got Manny's attention.

"I'd like to be dropped off at Gavin's, and then take these three lovely ladies home," he declared.

"Will do, Mr. Stanton," Manny replied.

Gillian gave him a pouty look, then took in the snoring women. "They're so fake."

He gave her a sardonic grin. Surprise—a staff member willing to be honest. Most were worried about losing their jobs. He reappraised Gillian with new eyes.

"No more or less fake than anyone else." His answer surprised him. He tucked his cock in his pants and dressed fully again. Gillian made no protest.

Ah. So it was like that.

She snorted at his words, then let out a small belch from the bubbly. "If you really think that's true, you're deluding yourself."

"I appear to be shockingly capable of extraordinary levels of self-delusion," he said sadly.

"Aren't we all."

"I have elevated it to an Olympic sport," he muttered under his breath. Blood throbbed everywhere, behind joints he'd taken for granted and in parts of his body that now craved the unfamiliar. He was done, three women splayed before him in various states, and while he wasn't a cad and would never sleep with a passed-out woman, he was completely dumbfounded.

Three. He had three women ready, willing, able, and horny. So many warm mouths. So many wet holes. So many inhibitions cast aside.

And all he wanted was one who wasn't here, and who had humiliated him for sport.

Self-delusion?

He just won the fucking Nobel Prize for it.

"We're here," Manny announced. Derry gave Gillian a curt nod and climbed out, his body unfolding as he stood. He felt like a deflated camping mattress that reinflates when granted space to spread out. Given his size, he'd learned to fold and curl, bend and slouch, yield to the vagaries of a world not designed for beings his size.

Molding his form to fit the spatial norms of human society was one thing.

Denying himself the pleasures of the flesh was quite another.

"Good night," he said to Gillian, the words a formality. She gave him a cold look as he shut the door. Manny took off.

Derry stared at the elevator in the parking garage. It would take him straight up to Gavin's penthouse.

Where the decanters were always full.

Jess was dreaming.

The best kind of dream. The sex kind.

In her waking hours, she controlled her body, her thoughts, even her fantasies. She never indulged. God knew, some of her fantasies she could *never* indulge.

But she wasn't awake. Because none of her fantasies, even the vanilla ones, were ever fulfilled, her subconscious liked to take revenge at night. When she slept, she lost control. When she slept, she couldn't stop herself from diving headfirst into her most secret desires.

Like tonight.

It began in an old elevator. *The* elevator, the same one where she'd been hours earlier. A massively powerful man stood behind her, his face hidden in shadow. But there was no mistaking who he was.

Him.

She smelled his skin, she tasted his sweat, she heard his heart-beat.

"It beats for you," he said, his voice so low and powerful, she could feel it vibrate in her cervix. "Jessica."

It was a dream, so she did the wrong thing. She always did the wrong thing in her dreams. Turning to him, she reached out and rested her hand against his broad, muscular chest. His heart thudded against her palm. Then she smiled and slid her hand down over his abdomen to the cold, hard metal of his belt buckle. "Just your heart?"

The moonlight—dream elevators had moonlight—lit up his dark, gleaming eyes, heavy-lidded and seductive. They looked hungry, amused.

"You're a very naughty girl," he said. "I can't wait to teach you a lesson."

Her dream body began to melt like ice cream in a supernova. "Are you sure you have the energy left for me? You've had so many pupils already. So many women. Maybe you're ready to retire from teaching. More than ready. Maybe you're burned out."

His hand, as big as a dinner plate, shot out and covered her mouth. Gently but firmly he pressed it against her lips and drew her close. His scent filled her lungs, her soul. "I'm burning, all right, Jessica Murphy." He rotated his palm and cupped her cheek. "And so are you."

"Maybe I am," she whispered. "What are you going to do about it?"

The elevator doors opened. In front of them was the lounge at the Platinum Club. Except now the sofas and chairs were empty, and the moon shone overhead in a clear, indigo sky. There was no ceiling to block the view.

"Whatever I want," he said, grabbing her hand and pulling her with him into the club.

It was pointless to resist. And she didn't want to. She wanted whatever he was going to do to her. "Don't make me wait too long," she said.

He pointed at the bar where there was a tray holding two glasses. "Those are for us." He released her, strode to the curved sofa where he'd sat that night in real life, and sank into it with surprising grace for such a large man. He stretched both arms along the back of the seat and gazed at her, his eyes drilling into her. "Nice outfit."

She looked down at herself, amused to discover she was wearing a push-up bra and thong, knee-highs, and shining silver stilettos. Every inch of her was on display. The moonlight lit her exposed curves in a hazy, shimmering blue.

The real Jess would have run screaming.

This wasn't the real Jess.

She sauntered to the bar—knowing he was studying her ass—and lifted the tray. Holding his gaze, she carried it over to him, her heart pounding. As she bent to set the tray on a table, he suddenly leaned forward and licked the hollow between her breasts, his rough jaw rubbing the tender swells of flesh on either side. His hands caught her waist, stroking and kneading her body, and she forgot the tray and the drinks and the world and climbed into his lap, knees spread, eager to ride him.

"Jess," he moaned, biting her nipple through her satin bra as his hand, following the tight band of the thong, reached around and stroked her wet vulva from behind.

His belt buckle was gone. His pants were gone. He was naked, a glorious male specimen, huge and powerful, broad shoulders, heavily muscled chest, and an erect cock thrusting up between them, seeking entry, hungry for her—

High, feminine laughter spiked into her consciousness. "Derry, what's the matter with you? Couldn't you wait for me?"

"Or me?" said another woman, also laughing.

A third chimed in. "You can't be *that* desperate."

It was the women from the club. The ones he went away with in the limo.

Suddenly they were there, surrounding them. Jess was completely naked now, but Derry wasn't holding her anymore. Now he was in a tuxedo, freshly shaved, holding a drink in one hand and leaning away from her as if she'd just fallen on him and he didn't want her to spill the fine liquor on his suit.

"Just kidding around," Derry said, pushing her aside. "Shall we go, ladies?"

She fell off his lap and never hit the ground, just kept falling. She fell and fell and fell, hearing the laughter pour down on her as she drowned in the darkness.

Her own stifled cry woke her. Damp with sweat, she shot up in bed and clutched her chest, struggling to catch her breath. Her dog, Smoky, the stray that she and Lilah had adopted after Gavin had run over the poor mutt the night he'd met Lilah, whined and nuzzled against her arm, trying to give her comfort. Lilah had been kind enough to leave him with her when she'd moved out. Jess needed to live with someone, even if it was an animal.

Arousal clung to her; she could feel it. The nightmare hadn't erased the pleasure that had come before.

"Damn it." She kicked the covers away and doubled over the edge of the bed, her heart still pounding. Smoky turned his nose down, resting it on his paws, just watching her.

This was why she hated dreams. You couldn't control them. And in the end, they only brought pain.

Seven

"This better be important," Gavin muttered as Derry entered the expansive penthouse. A warm glow from the living room indicated a roaring fire, and the room smelled heavenly, a mix of lavender and sage, of garlic and savory delights. Empty dishes dotted the countertop around the sink, and a scratchy blues record, something deep and old from New Orleans, tickled his ears.

And then he heard a very feminine snore from the couch.

Although Manny had dropped him off near the elevator in the garage downstairs, Derry had spent the past hour, possibly longer, pacing the Boston streets alone. Only when he'd regained his composure did he return to Gavin's and take the elevator up to his brother's penthouse.

Derry had questions. Questions only Gavin might be able to answer.

"Lilah's here?" Derry asked softly. He suppressed a sigh of frantic disappointment. He would leave. What he needed most was the comfort of his brother's company, but he was enough of an adult to step back.

"Of course she's here," Gavin said, a touch of irritation peppering his words. "She lives here."

"I'm sorry," Derry replied, starting for the door. "I would never have come if I'd—"

"It's fine. She's sleeping. We're . . . it's fine."

"Trouble in paradise?" Derry joked, taking Gavin at his word and walking into the kitchen, picking up and putting down several mostly empty wine bottles until he found a decent merlot with a few glasses' worth left inside. Without manners or any shred of grace, he upended the bottle and drank it in one long, glorious guzzle.

"You are treating my '92 La Mondotte like Gatorade, Derry."

Making a face as the slightly bitter red wine finished its path down his gullet, Derry answered, "I'm not exactly in need of electrolytes now. Besides, Gatorade does nothing for helping me achieve the state of oblivion I seek."

"Oblivion? I heard you left the club with three women. You can't get further away from reality than that, little brother."

Derry snorted. *Oh, how right you are*, he thought. *More right than you can imagine.*

He didn't answer Gavin, instead walking across the room, his eyes flitting over Lilah. She was gorgeous in repose, like a famous painting he couldn't quite name but that haunted his dreams.

Except darken her hair and make her look exactly like her sister.

Gavin's eyes narrowed. "This has to do with a woman."

Damn it.

"I've just been with three," Derry said, forced gaiety in his voice. He wasn't sure why he bothered. Gavin could always see through him. "Can you smell them on me?"

Gavin sniffed. "The only scent I detect from you is desperation."

Derry groaned at the pathetic little joke, but some part of his gut tightened. Dancing around the truth with Gavin was always a losing strategy.

"I'm here because I'm bored."

"Bored after being with three women?" Gavin sniffed again. "Except . . ." His eyes tightened to blue triangles, then widened as his older brother tilted his head, studying Derry. "You didn't. Sleep with them, I mean."

"I had my fun." Derry couldn't keep the gruff, defensive tone out of his voice, and Gavin picked up on it, his laughter overriding Derry's single-shoulder shrug. Derry found an unopened bottle of whisky and slit the paper seal with his thumbnail, the hiss of the bottle as he unscrewed it so faint it was like a fairy's whisper.

And then he guzzled enough Glenfiddich to cover any desperation that prowled in his cells.

"Jesus, Derry, you're drinking that like it's mineral water."

"Might as well be," he answered, wiping the back of his hand across his wet mouth.

Gavin crossed his arms over his broad chest and stared. "This *is* about a woman."

Derry's eyes flickered to the couch, then floated back to Gavin. "You could definitely say that."

A tight sense of alarm filled Gavin's face, giving him a sudden, menacing look. Derry's inner warning system tickled his extremities, making the muscles vibrate as if he were about to shift. *Danger*, every fiber of his being called out.

Danger.

"I've said it more than once, so quit stalling. Spit it out." Gavin's words felt like grenades being cradled in his brother's hands, unpinned and ready to be dropped. Perhaps he should have gone back to his loft. Visiting Gavin may have been a mistake.

"Spit *what* out?" The entire night's activities, from early cocktails to the intoxicating kiss with Jess and so much more piled up inside him. Add in the rush of adrenaline that came from Gavin's alarming tone change, and he was nothing but a live wire.

An intoxicated, increasingly frustrated, live wire.

"Are you in love with Lilah?"

Struck dumb, Derry gaped at his brother.

"Excuse me?" His deep laugh echoed through the quiet apartment, making Lilah stir. He shut down his reaction instantly, giving Gavin a very sober, sincere look. "God, no."

Gavin's shoulders relaxed. "Good."

"Why in the hell would you think that?"

"You looked at her when you mentioned that your troubles involved a woman." Gavin's eyebrow arched. He looked exactly like their late father. Derry felt like an errant schoolboy being dressed down for a bad grade.

"Because she looks so much like—"

Damn.

Gavin frowned. "Just like . . ." His voice trailed off to a husky sound that faded into something less than words. He scrubbed his face with one palm, the skin from his hand against stubble making a *swish skrit swish skrit* sound that felt like a rat running laps around the inside of Derry's skull.

And then his eyes lit up with understanding, going dark quickly.

"Oh, for God's sake, Derry. Not *Jess*," Gavin groaned, Lilah's sister's name invoked like it was a crime Derry had committed.

In essence, it was.

"Of course not."

"Don't lie."

"I'm not—oh, bloody hell," Derry spat.

"The only thing that's bloody here is your face in two seconds if you don't promise me you'll stay the hell away from Jess," Gavin said.

"Tell her to stay away from *me*! She kissed me under the mistletoe!"

"And insulted your manhood."

"Which is why I have no interest in her, Gavin."

"That's exactly why you're interested in Jess, Derry. Women who reject you become forbidden fruit. She might as well have hung a target on her back, with your cock the weapon of choice."

Derry couldn't even argue. Damn his brother for being right.

"I had an uncontrollable shift tonight," Derry confessed under his breath.

Gavin's face tightened as he twitched in surprise. "That's not funny," he said in a low voice. "Just because you know it happened to me when I met Lilah does not mean it's acceptable fodder for jokes. Don't you dare equate what I went through with your little dick dipping."

As Derry opened his mouth to protest, a shuffling sound from behind the kitchen bar interrupted them.

"She's not interested in you anyhow," said a sleepy, feminine voice. Lilah's blonde curls spilled over one shoulder as she sat up, rubbing the cheek that had rested against the pillow on the cushion.

Derry took her in, eyes combing over her as he pretended to drink more whisky from the bottle. She was magnificent. He had to give Gavin that. And yet Lilah did nothing for him.

She was a fabulous conversationalist, and a genuinely pleasant person to spend time with, but when he looked at her, he saw Gavin. Sister.

Shifter.

When he even thought about Jess, he felt his heart expand all the way to the root of his cock and up through the basal ganglia into all the important emotion centers in his brain.

Parts deactivated for so long he'd simply replaced them with sex. Lots of sex.

Too much sex.

Lilah's words felt like daggers being jabbed into his ribs. "She's . . . w-what?" Derry stammered. Stall, he told himself.

"We rode home together. I dropped her off at her apartment. She told me the kiss under the mistletoe had been a mistake. She shouldn't have done it, but the pressure at the club made her think it was expected. She was being . . ." Lilah yawned, her neck stretching in the moonlight as if it were a piece of performance art. Creamy skin glowed in the night and Derry found himself transfixed as if watching a private performance by one of the world's master artists. He ached to paint that neck.

"Nice." Gavin finished Lilah's sentence for her with a tone so mismatched Derry started slightly. "She was being nice." His brother managed to make such a benevolent word sound like an insult.

"Nice girls don't kiss like that," Derry muttered. But the really naughty ones do.

"Jess doesn't kiss *anyone* like that," Lilah said earnestly. She scooted her shapely ass to one side as Gavin sat next to her, his arm wrapping about her shoulders, his lips planting a kiss on her temple.

A tiny bubble inside Derry's chest popped, the feeling so light and feathery he might not have noticed it under any other circumstances.

But he did. And it reverberated like a gong. The want. The need. The pure desire for the kind of deep love Gavin and Lilah had found was one treasure no bank account could ever buy. No inheritance could provide it.

"She kissed *me* like that," he finally ground out, his words almost an afterthought.

Gavin glared at him, the room spinning with an icy chill that made Derry realize, even in his emotional, boozy haze, that he was a third wheel.

"A formality," Lilah said, smiling until dimples showed. "You were a formality."

If Lilah had sucker punched him, she couldn't have done more damage.

Gavin's tight jaw and slightly tilted head carried the nonverbal stance of a threat.

"Indeed," Derry conceded, playing the game, covering for the breathless feeling that turned his lungs into wet tissue paper. Perhaps Jess had really said as much to Lilah, but Derry had felt what he'd felt when he'd kissed Jess. That kiss was anything but formal. Definitely not a performance.

Denial was a powerful force, but love was more powerful.

He jolted.

Love?

"What in the bloody hell is wrong with me?" he murmured as Gavin stood and guided him to the exit.

"I don't have enough time to list it all," Gavin said flatly. The elevator doors opened, and Gavin came in close, his hot breath like iron shavings against Derry's ear. "And you're going home. The limo's downstairs. No crashing at my place tonight."

"That's it? You're turning me out in my time of need?" he joked, but the sudden plume of emotion in his chest told him he wasn't joking.

"You can grab three women anytime you want," Gavin said, clearing his throat. "Your needs are met elsewhere. Just any woman but Jess. Are we clear?"

The doors closed before Derry could answer.

But I shifted, he wanted to call out. *I couldn't help myself.*

I can't help myself.

It's all about her.

Her.

Help.

⎯⎯⎯⎯⎯

The next night at the club, Jess was closed up tight. Cold and tight. Like a bank vault without a door, a block of ice, a woman in total, absolute control.

Dreams couldn't touch her here. Even at the Platinum Club, which was designed to satisfy the wildest dreams of so many. But she wasn't a member. She was one of the cocktail waitresses, and their only dreams were to make other people happy.

People like that movie star chick, Isla, the one Derry had fucked last night. Isla apparently hadn't gotten nearly enough of her dreams satisfied, because tonight she was drinking glass after glass of the club's best Chilean wine, complaining about the temperature before sucking it down and demanding another. And Jess had to serve her with a smile, quiet competence, patience, and every outward indication of pleasure.

No problem. Tonight, Jess was a woman in control. An ice woman. She brought the beautiful movie star her drinks, confident she wasn't betraying a speck of discomfort or burning, seething, loathing disapproval. Isla never even glanced at her.

Gillian, however, was acting strange, perhaps because she was afraid Jess would squeal about her sleeping with a member. She kept shooting Jess tight-lipped glances, eyes tracking her as she moved from bar to patron. After about an hour, Jess got tired of the surveillance and confronted her coworker near the back of the bar.

"Is there a problem?" Jess asked her.

"I don't know," Gillian said. "Is there?"

Jess studied her, only now noticing that she wore no lipstick, had shadows under her eyes, and displayed only one pair of tiny studs in her ears. For Gillian, that was like being butt-naked.

Feeling unexpected compassion for her, Jess lowered her voice. "Don't worry, I'm not going to say anything." Why shouldn't she feel compassion? What did she care what Gillian did in her free time? Even if it was with her future brother-in-law?

Why would she possibly care?

Ice woman.

"There's nothing to say," Gillian said, looking away. "He couldn't get it up."

The sudden vision of Derry's enormous cock made Jess flush.

(Why wouldn't it be enormous? It wasn't wishful thinking or anything, just a sensible assumption.) Then she realized what Gillian had said. Enormous and flaccid? "He couldn't . . ."

"Maybe he's gay. I offered to suck him off and—pfft! Nothing."

Jess's mouth went dry. Although it wouldn't have been if she'd been the one sucking—

No, damn it. ICE WOMAN.

"He's not gay," Jess said. "Just because he lost interest in . . . in having sex at that moment."

"Before you blame *me*," Gillian said coldly, narrow-eyed gaze turning to the brooding, boozing Isla in the lounge, "remember I wasn't the only woman who gave it her all. The only one with a brain, but his cock doesn't care about brains."

"But *he* does." The words popped out of Jess's mouth before she could remind herself about the ice-woman thing again. She felt herself flush, cursing her fair complexion that would suggest she gave a fig about Derry and his gigantic, unsatisfied cock or how he felt about women with or without a functioning cerebral cortex. "Never mind, I guess you're right. He's gay. Obviously."

Now Gillian's narrow gaze was fixed on Jess. "Or wanting someone else," she said slowly, raising an unusually natural eyebrow. "Someone who's playing hard to get."

Jess's heart felt like it was beating in the back of her throat, cutting off her airflow. Was Gillian suggesting Derry wanted *her*? And that she was manipulating him, trying to fan the flames?

"I'm not playing," Jess said in a low, hard voice.

"Maybe that's exactly what he needs." And after pulling that pin from the grenade, Gillian adjusted her tray on her forearm and sauntered away.

Jess's legs felt unsteady, remembering the groping in the elevator, the orgiastic display en route to the limo.

All that, and he'd failed to follow through? But why would he do all that if he hadn't really wanted—

He'd known you were watching.

No, no, no. It wasn't about her. It couldn't be. Not the way Gillian had implied. If Derry had put on a show of his sexual perversions, appetites, and popularity, it was only to soothe his pride after she'd humiliated him under the mistletoe.

Then why hadn't he taken advantage of the situation later? Once he'd freed his colossal cock from his pants, why turn . . . soft?

Alcohol. It had to be the alcohol. Gillian was screwing with her head. It wasn't anything to do with Jess. Men who drank as much as Derry had that night simply couldn't expect their sexual organs to perform. It was biologically impossible. She turned back to the bar, rotating her tray in her unsteady hands, struggling to remember her drink orders.

No, it was all right. She'd served everyone already. All she had to do was check on her tables, see if anyone new had sat down—

Before she pivoted on her heel to face the lounge, she felt him arrive. Like a breeze, an embrace, a song. Her entire body hummed as if his powerful hands were playing every string in her soul.

Get a fucking grip. Ice woman. For God's sake.

Holding her shoulders back, she sucked in an empowering breath and strode over to him. "Good evening, Mr. Stanton," she said, managing to sound impressively calm. "The usual?" Which would be whisky if he was alone, and then, a few minutes later, whatever his female companion was ordering, since the alone time never lasted longer than one drink.

"Gatorade," he growled, not looking at her.

She thought she'd misheard. Perhaps it was a Chilean vintage she was unfamiliar with. "Could you repeat that?"

His head snapped up. Dark eyes locked her in place. "Gatorade. Red. No ice."

Professionalism came to her rescue. "Diet or regular?"

"Are you playing with me?"

Her stupid cheeks got warm again. "There's more than one kind," she said. Because there was, and she couldn't help but say so.

"Are you saying I need to go on a diet?" he asked, smiling at her with his mouth but not, definitely not, his eyes.

"I beg your pardon, sir. You'd like the one with fifty-six grams of sugar. Of course. Any particular varietal of 'red', or shall I assume anything will do?"

His voice dropped another octave. "As it so happens, not just anything *will* do," he said. "Do I seem like the type of man eager to consume whatever throws itself in front of him?"

Given they were only talking about flavored sugar water, her heart was beating much too hard. He could probably see its imprint through the fabric of her blouse.

She wanted to tell him that, because he was a man whore, she *did* expect him to consume whomever threw herself at him.

But he was a club member, and almost-family member, and it didn't matter how gargantuan his own member—

She lost her train of thought. Where was she? Her heart was bumping her blouse again. That was all wrong. If she said that, he might interpret it as playing hard to get. Not to mention unprofessional.

"Was there a particular flavor you had in mind?" she asked, flinching inwardly as she heard sexual undertones in her words. It was impossible with this man not to hear sexual undertones in everything. It wasn't her, it was him. Not her fault. She tried to think about ice again.

He crossed his arms over his massive chest and stared at her. After a long pause, he finally said, "No, I apologize. You were right. I'm not particular. I enjoy all kinds. It's a gift, really, to be so . . . flexible."

Now go and get the drink, she told herself. The server doesn't need to say anything else. *Go go go.*

Her feet didn't move. His gravitational pull was too strong.

She took a step closer. His eyes widened. Darkened. She thought that beneath his crossed arms, she could see his chest begin to rise and fall more deeply.

Would he . . . Did he really . . .

He'd been with the most beautiful, most coveted women in the world. And now he was turning to *her* to slake that unquenchable thirst.

If Gillian could risk it, why not her?

Just as he uncrossed his arms and began to reach a hand out to her, a buried memory dragged her back into the past.

Rich, good-looking guys. A party. There was laughter. Horrible laughter.

Hadn't one of them said something like what Derry had just said? *I'm not particular.* But he'd been joking. It had all been a joke.

Taking a step back, then another one, she moved away, bumping into somebody. The movie star, who recoiled in disgust, then continued her journey to Derry's lap.

"Be careful," Isla snapped, never looking at her.

"Thank you," Jess said. "I will." She spun around and hurried away to get the Gatorade.

Gatorade? What the hell was he thinking? Red sugar water wouldn't quench this thirst. Not when he was parched for Jess. He needed to taste her again, to run his tongue across those soft, lush lips, to be invited into the divine sanctuary of her mouth, to worship at the altar between her thighs.

"You need to replace your neck with a swivel chair, Derry," Isla said in her bored voice. Or, rather, just her voice. She always sounded bored.

"What?" She made even less sense than usual. How much of that wine had she been drinking?

"You twist your neck any further watching that waitress, and it will snap off. Unless it's nice and soft like your cock was last night." She reached between his legs and grabbed his junk.

His junk tried to crawl away from her.

"See? Useless. You're getting *boooooooring*, Derry." Isla flung the sentence at him like a monkey at the zoo, throwing feces.

And, in return, he felt a sense of primal disgust rise up in his throat.

What was he doing?

What the *fuck* was he doing?

"If I'm so boring, Isla dear, go find someone who will titillate you." He tweaked one of her nipples and fumbled as his fingers caught metal. Her nipple-clamp fetish. Ah.

"You're wearing those?" he said in a harsh voice meant to mock. Her eyes flew open in alarm.

"What?"

"Must be Friday. You're so . . . predictable, Isla." He added the same condescending huff she and Freddi attached to every third sentence out of their mouth at most nightclubs.

She jumped to her feet and grabbed her clutch. "How dare you speak to me like this!"

Her raised voice turned a few heads. Not a single server or bartender watched them, though. Eva had trained them all very, very well. Never react. Be discreet. Let the patrons preserve as much dignity as possible.

"And your limp dick has turned you into a joke!" Isla yelled, emphasizing the two words she most wanted others to hear.

The staff might be discreet.

Isla? Not so much.

If the gloves were off, and Isla's claws certainly were showing, might as well go for the jugular.

He stood, towering over her. "Whose fault was that, Isla? Too many lip treatments and enough Botox to freeze the stock market will cause a downturn." He looked at his crotch, then wagged a finger in her face. *"Tsk tsk tsk."*

A patron guffawed, his baritone triggering an avalanche of mocking laughter. Women tittered.

Isla turned into a burning fury.

A burning, Botoxed fury. Her face was fifty shades of red, but she couldn't express anything beyond a fish face and a look of constipation.

Out of nowhere, a bucket of red sugar water flew into his face, blinding and drenching him.

"Ms. Monroe!"

He couldn't see. Could barely speak, and was that crushed ice caught in his outer ear? But he knew that voice. "I am so sorry that Mr. Stanton is mistreating you like this! Are you OK?"

Jess.

He opened his eyes to see a livid Isla, half-covered in red Gatorade, turning her head to and fro to spread her rage-filled, pinched expression between the two of them.

"And Mr. Stanton, you should know better!" Jess added. "Ms. Monroe is a member here, and no one should treat members with the kind of disdain you've shown her."

"You certainly don't apply that same principle to me!" he barked, surprising himself.

Isla faced Jess and took her empty hand in both of hers. "Thank you. He's been beastly. An absolute beast!"

You don't know the half of it, he thought.

Isla played the room perfectly, the laughter dying out into murmurs as opinion swept in its inevitable pendulum. She looked around and began to pretend to cry as she reached for the bottle of wine and upended it, guzzling it like, well—

Gatorade.

Her face looked like it was melting, and no tears came out, but two men approached with linen handkerchiefs, neatly ironed. She took them with gratitude, dropping Jess's hand like a hot potato and walking away with what Derry knew—and Isla certainly knew—were two oil billionaires from Russia.

"Derry!" Eva's hiss was as controlled as possible under the circumstances. Thank God the club had a strict no-cell-phone-video rule. "Why on earth are you belittling and berating poor Ms. Monroe?"

"Excuse me?" He felt like Thor himself spoke the words from Asgard via his throat.

"Shhhhh." Jess and Eva tried to quell him.

"I will not be shushed!" he thundered. "Isla started it!"

"You sound like a petulant child." Eva's words were spears to the psyche. He reached up and was greeted by a series of red drops, all falling from the coils of his wavy, dark hair.

"And you look like you're doing your best Carrie imitation," Jess said under her breath. She shot him a tight, professional smile that made it very clear that she was having a delightful time pretending to rescue one patron while utterly humiliating him.

Again.

Control. He needed to establish control over this mess. When in doubt, turn into a rake. A lecherous playboy. A man with uncontrollable erotic urges.

A perfect beast of a man.

He ostentatiously took her in, eyes raking over the fine swells of her hips embraced by the tight black satin of her thigh-length cocktail dress. Her flesh was a vision of cream and curve in his mind that his big paws could grasp and hold on to while she rode him. His breathing slowed as his eyes focused only on her, the sticky red mess of his face nothing compared to the roar of red blood that flushed his cock upright and hard, tight and full, pressing against the zipper of his pants and begging for release.

The curl of her delicate skin between neck and ear begged for his tongue, just like the sweet parting of her thighs would give him an ambrosia he could imagine now, as he took in the contoured flesh of her exposed calf, his own fantasies forced to fill in the blanks of her body.

When he finally—finally, with an aching slowness that made him nearly come in his pants like an untrained teenager in the throes of hormones and frenzy—looked at her face, he saw his own hunger mirrored there. No mocking. No humiliation. Just the naked, raw awareness that he was reading her soul, her flesh, her mind, and her divine, tender heart.

And then—

The slap made him lose eye contact, the pain of Isla's palm against his cheekbone barely registering, and nothing in comparison to the inner pain of having the moment shattered by her petty gesture.

"I want you out," Isla said in her accented voice, the words like nails on a chalkboard, dragging until they drew blood from places where it should be impossible. She was back, like a bad disease. Too bad there was no antibiotic to eradicate her. The two Russians bookended her, turning her back to the hallway where some private rooms held delightful secrets. Derry should know. He'd had sex in every single one of them.

Before.

Before *her*.

He ignored Isla, not bothering to rub the spot she'd hit, knowing it would just give her satisfaction, sure she was watching him even as she left. Instead, he looked to Eva for his exit.

"I'll need a change of clothes delivered to me in one of the lounges," he declared. He smelled like a kindergartner at snack time.

"Of course," Eva said tightly. She turned to Jess. "Please help Mr. Stanton to restore himself to decency."

"I don't think that's possible," Jess said, deadpan. Her hand still clutched the damn highball glass that, he assumed, once held the Gatorade that covered him.

Derry snorted in spite of himself.

"That was not a request, Ms. Murphy," Eva said. Isla shot Jess an evil glare from across the room. Either that, or a contact lens went astray. It was hard to tell with Isla's face these days. Why was she still here?

"Me?" Jess squeaked. "You're serious?"

Not one to answer rhetorical questions, Eva pointed her attentions toward Isla and left Jess and Derry standing there, him dripping, her blinking, with one order:

To get him out of these clothes and into something more comfortable.

Eight

Wishing her hands would stop shaking, Jess gave the empty glass to the quiet staff guy who was already on his knees cleaning up the sticky mess. She was supposed to help Derry get naked? Had she heard that right?

She wanted him with parts of herself she hadn't even known she possessed.

"Where—which lounge—" she began. There were private rooms on this floor, but Isla had just marched that way with the two Russians, and it didn't seem like a good idea to be within fifty feet of them right now.

"Downstairs," Derry growled, still watching her in that way that made her toes curl, her insides try to go outside.

She turned toward the elevator. "Follow me."

"Try and stop me." His voice was so low it could've been the bass line snaking through the lounge from the dance floor.

A shiver danced down her spine, settling between her legs, where she was aching for him with sweet, wet need. And he knew it. She'd seen the knowledge in his eyes.

If he'd made fun of her, if he'd curled that generous lip and teased—she could've slapped him down like Isla had. Harder. She would have, too, even at the cost of her job. Laughter would've been unbearable at any price.

But he hadn't laughed. And the sober, serious intensity of his expression had shocked her. She'd never seen him look like that before. It was as if underneath all the debauchery and mindless, immature blather, he was actually an intelligent, sensitive, compassionate man.

Good one, Jess, she told herself. It was incredible what hormones could make you believe. Luckily for her, she had enough sense to recognize the delusion for what it was: lust.

The elevator, thank God, was already on their floor. The door opened immediately, and he followed her inside, his breath seducing her like a song. She could feel him even when he was two steps behind her. She shivered, sensing him everywhere, wanting him deeper.

When the door shut, he closed the space between them and crowded her from behind against the wall of the elevator car. Strong fingers splayed along the nape of her neck, brushing her hair to one side. She felt his hot breath on the back of her neck just as the elevator lurched, and she lost her balance.

"Easy," he said, catching her from behind. His arms came around her waist, shoving up her breasts as he held her close. His pelvis pushed into her hips.

He was hard as steel.

"Apparently I am," she said, not putting up any struggle whatsoever. She closed her eyes, uncontrollably aroused by the feel of the erection he'd failed to muster for the other women. Her neck throbbed where his breath caressed her, right on her wine-red birthmark. The throbbing became a pulse. The same pulse that beat between her legs.

Him.

"It must be *hard*," he said as he ground deeper into her, "to be so beautiful."

"I've learned to endure," she whispered.

Suddenly he pulled his hand away, a few strands of her hair clinging to his fingers. "Christ," he said. "I need to bathe. I'm sticking to you. That damn Gatorade."

"Oh, sure. Blame it on *that*."

His voice rumbled near her ear. "You did this to me. You made me like this." His lips found the pulse under her ear. She felt pressure, a kiss, a tongue.

And, incredibly, an even stiffer erection grinding into her.

She was tempted to mention how hard he was, ask him why he'd had trouble last night, why he didn't now. But she knew it had to be the lack of alcohol and couldn't bear to hear him lie to her.

With a chuckle, he wiped a strand of wet, sticky hair out of his eyes. "Most servers choose to hand the members their drinks. Not throw it in their faces."

"Eva told me to do it."

"But you enjoyed it." Teeth dragged across her skin. "Didn't you?"

"Maybe a little," she said.

The elevator bounced to a stop. Derry released her abruptly and turned away, facing the doors as they opened.

"I'll require a change of clothes," he said. "My own. If there aren't any here at the club, send someone to retrieve them from my home."

The abrupt shift from being treated like a seductress to a servant was a slap in the face. She was just about to tell him to get his own damn clothes when she stepped off the elevator and saw a guy in the all-black Platinum uniform nod and stride away through a green-curtained doorway.

He'd been talking to a male staffer, not her. But it was an important reminder of her station in this place. She took a deep breath and counted to five.

The floor was unfamiliar to her. Dark wood flooring, frosted glass doors, dim lighting. It smelled of sandalwood, candle wax, oiled leather. Modern instrumental music played softly from invisible speakers.

"Three is my favorite," he said, shooting her a smoky look before stepping forward and grabbing the handle of the third door down the hallway. "Let's hope the number brings me more luck tonight than last."

Did he assume she was going to jump in where the other women had failed, just because tonight his equipment was functioning?

When she followed him inside and saw that the space was only a bathroom with a luxurious but tiny dressing room attached, she froze. She'd imagined it would be larger, more like an apartment. This was much too intimate.

And he was already unbuttoning his shirt.

"I'll go get your clothes," she said, sounding breathless even to herself. "While you shower."

In two strides, he was between her and the door, his hands now unbuttoning the last button over his abdomen. Dark hair peeked out from beneath the crisp, red-stained dress shirt.

She swallowed over the lump in her throat. There was nowhere safe to look—his eyes, his chest, below his belt, which he was now unbuckling—no place was safe.

"I will not be found in here with you," she said firmly. "Do you understand?"

"Eva wanted you to assist me. Your boss wants you to please me."

"Not like that. She knew you'd never leave Isla up there without another woman to lure you away," she said. "She trusted me to disengage when you were no longer in danger of humiliating one of the members, especially a loud and famous one who could damage the club's reputation."

He moved away from the door but was still only inches away from her. "Are you saying she used you as bait?"

"Yes. Now go take a shower before you start attracting ants."

His expression darkened. "Has she done this before? Used you to remove misbehaving men from the lounge?"

"No, but—"

"If she does, I want to hear about it immediately. It's not safe. I won't stand for it."

She laughed. Suddenly he wanted to protect her? The only man she was in danger from was *him*. Jabbing him in the chest with her manicured index finger, she wiggled past him and opened the door. "Take a shower. I'll check on your clothes."

She was halfway down the hall when he shouted to her from the doorway. "Ms. Murphy!"

Reluctantly she stopped. "Yes, Mr. Stanton?" she asked, turning around.

God help her. He'd taken off his shirt. She'd always appreciated a little breadth in the pectoral muscles. The sight of his massive, well-defined, dark-haired chest, the broad shoulders, the happy trail over his rippling abdomen into his trousers, knocked the wind out of her.

"I'd like a bottle of '94 Novo brought to me here," he said. "Others will see to my clothes."

She managed to suck in a breath. "Ninety-Four Novo?"

"It's quite rare, but I find that I have an undeniable taste for it this evening."

She wasn't familiar with the vintage. Carl would know. "Yes, sir. I'll take care of it."

"I'm very glad to hear that, Ms. Murphy." He turned on his heel and strode back into the private room. Mouth dry, she stood still and watched him disappear, bewitched by his thickly muscled shoulders, the hint of dimples low on his back.

She was as attracted to him as ants to Gatorade.

Derry slumped against the back of the closed door, his barrel chest filling to the brim with air and fire, with desire and her scent, nose detecting every deliciously aroused atom on Jessica Murphy's tantalizing body. Dear God. He swallowed, the barest hint of her taste on the edge of his lips from the kiss he'd planted on that succulent skin, an erotic tease of the feast he needed most.

He was a starving man right now.

As he pulled away from the back of the door, strands of his long black hair stuck to the polished oak. He chuckled, the laughter a deep rumble that felt timeless. Ancient. Infinite.

How he felt every second he was within arm's reach of her.

Her.

Gatorade. The woman had doused him in electrolytes. On Eva's orders, no less. Later he would have words with Eva. Angry words. Using Jess as bait to manage the miscreants in the club was utterly unacceptable. Abominable.

Intolerable.

No more. It wouldn't be easy to convince Eva of her wrongdoing, but he would hold the line on this. Jess was his. His and his alone.

He throbbed for her as he disrobed, every feather touch of his own fingers against his skin like a whisper from her lips. Rock hard and straining for release, his cock reminded him of the ache to be in her. Rubbing his body against that sweet swell of her lush ass had been torture. A pleasant torture, mind you, but one that could only be cultivated if it ended with Derry above her, buried in her wet heat, her mouth screaming his name, her face flushed with the primal, carnal knowledge that only his hands, his mouth, his body could provide.

Her.

Her.

Mine.

As he pulled off his socks and padded to the shower naked, he turned on the six-headed shower and waited for the water to heat up, the steam soon pouring over the glass walls. Hot needles assaulted his back with what should have been a delightful relief.

Instead, he found himself quite mad with need.

Closing his eyes, he saw her honey-shaded hair spread over his face as she rode him. Reaching for the soap, he swam in the pool of those passion-filled, catlike eyes that begged him for sanctuary and love. Lathering up, the sugary drink washing off his skin, he imagined his own touch, so inadequate, was hers instead, those feminine hands touching the swell of his hardness, her knees dropping to the ground, her lips wrapping around his thickness and—

Damn it. He felt the tightening of tendon and bone that began a shift into his animal shape. Bloody hell. What curse was this? He was so close, so close to release. With unprecedented difficulty, he finally regained his control of his human form.

Just in time to lose it.

Neck straining and body leaping forward with the familiar pleasure of climax, he came, shuddering with an intensity that rode through his body like an electromagnetic pulse, his seed washing down the wall. He didn't even have time to say a word, no sound, no groan. Wave after wave of craven desire pulsed through him, and then he gasped, her name the only word he knew, her face branded behind closed eyelids as the water washed over him like a holy ritual that had no name.

Yes, it did.

Jess.

Her.

For the second time in less than ten minutes, he slumped against a door, only this time, he was weakened by the betrayal of his own damned body. When had he become a horny teenage boy with no self-control?

"Fuck," he muttered aloud, breathless and panting, chasing his own mind in circles around a heart that knew what he needed.

And, for the first time in his entire life, he was filled with an emotion that was new.

He was *afraid*.

What if she really didn't want him? Jess did this to him. Brought him to this point of vulnerability, where the mere thought of her made him come in a damn club shower.

She had invaded his soul.

How?

Sorceress. She must be a sorceress. How else? His lips twitched at the thought.

His cock twitched, too, making him stare at it with a look of incredulity. Already? While he prided himself on his stamina, this was a record for . . . recovery.

He disappeared into a vague sort of haze for a moment, a combination of endorphins and overwhelm, and came to only when he realized, to his grinding shock, that he was painfully hard.

Again.

Already.

Dispensing with the necessaries, he washed up, rinsed, and shoved himself into the minimal amount of clothing needed to go and hunt Jess Murphy down.

And find a way to invade her right back.

Nine

"What bottle did he ask for?" Carl asked.

"A '94 Novo," Jess said. "I hope I got that right. He said it was rare."

Carl put down a bottle of vodka and looked at her with a raised eyebrow. After a pause, he said, "Very. You'll have to go into the special cellar for it." Lifting a cocktail shaker in the air, he nodded at the crowd in the lounge. Busy night. "I can't spare anyone right now. You'll have to get it yourself."

Jess assured him she'd hurry back to help serve, then returned to the service elevator. The elevator passed the floor where she imagined that Derry was, at that moment, soaping up his naked, powerful, glistening body, all alone and still hard for her. Aching for her. Under the hot spray, he was rubbing and lathering his cock, back arched, teeth clenched, shouting her name as he—

The elevator came to a sudden halt. She was there. Out of her mind, but present.

She tried to distract herself by wondering about the ancient wine cellar. She hadn't realized how old the original building must have been. She loved historical sites. Later she'd have to ask Eva about it. Or even her future brother-in-law—would he know? Hadn't he been a member of the club for a long time?

Thoughts of Gavin inevitably brought her back to Derry. But thoughts of Derry were never far away. She touched her neck, biting her lip as she relived the feel of his kiss. She walked toward the cellar door in a daze, only half-awake, her mind spinning with thoughts of him in the shower, then stepping out and patting himself dry with a towel, rubbing here and there, stretching, flexing.

He wanted her. How could she resist that?

She couldn't. There wasn't enough ice in the world to cool her down when she got thinking about Derry.

She'd have to make sure they were never alone. Relying on her own willpower wasn't going to work. There would have to be situational remedies. Avoiding him. Chaperones. A blindfold, if necessary, so she couldn't look at him and get obsessed with the cut of his upper shoulders.

She needed to conveniently forget that they would be in their respective siblings' wedding soon.

Oh God.

The cellar was cool and dark, but smelled clean. It might look like a dungeon, but there was no moldering garbage and scurrying vermin here. She flicked on the light and began scanning the shelves for France. Many of the bottles looked ancient, foreign, with handwritten labels.

There. The entire back wall was devoted to French wines. The poor lighting slowed her down, and she felt bad about how long it was going to take her to get back to the bar to help Carl and the other servers during the rush. Even after she'd found the wine, she'd still have to deliver it to Derry's room. Her body warmed at the thought.

No. She'd ask somebody else to bring it to him. Or invite a chaperone. A situational remedy.

"It's on the bottom row, two paces to your right."

Jess's heart leapt into her throat. That voice. It struck chords she'd never heard before she'd met him.

He was a few steps behind her. She was bent over, her ass in the air, her hands braced on her shins, and God help her—she didn't want to move. She wanted him to take her right there, just like that, before she could change her mind and stop him.

For a moment she indulged in the feel of him seeing her with her legs spread a little, her skirt hitched up, exposing the backs of her thighs, inviting him closer . . .

With supernatural willpower, she raised herself to standing, smoothed her skirt down, and turned with every intention of thanking him for his help and then running like hell.

But then she saw him.

His hair was damp, tousled. His eyes were blazing. And his shirt—a fresh one, but just like the last—was unbuttoned. Torn, faded jeans hugged his hips and well-muscled thighs. And he was barefoot.

"Nobody will find us down here," he said roughly, reaching for her. "Nobody will know."

"I'll—" she began, but he swallowed her protest with a kiss.

Tasting his mouth, inhaling his scent, hearing the growl of desire in his throat—her fortress of self-denial crumbled.

She wrapped her arms around his neck and melted. She wanted all of him, every massive inch, on her and in her. Now. It would be impossible to stop now. Her arms were trembling. Her knees were buckling. She was like the survivor of a car accident, except the accident hadn't happened yet. The crash was coming, and she didn't want to stop it.

"Derry," she cried, kissing his face over and over, clinging to him, shaking.

"Jess, my darling," he said, his voice like a kiss. His hands stroked the back of her head, the curve of her waist, her breasts. "It's all right. I'm here. I'm here."

She couldn't talk. She'd held back for too long. She didn't know how to do this. She felt like crying. She *was* crying.

Making soothing noises as he caressed her, Derry lifted her in his arms. Before she could respond to this impossibility—he looked strong, but come on—he was laying her down on an ancient oak table and climbing on top of her. She felt smooth, flat planks under her shoulders, her back, her bottom. Derry's hands were everywhere else, exploring her inner thighs, her ankles, her hair.

"You're trembling," he said. He loomed over her but was careful to support his own weight. "Are you cold?"

She shook her head. Closed her eyes.

"What then?" he asked.

She tried to tell him.

His lips traced her cheekbone. "I can't hear you, darling. Would you mind terribly saying that again?"

"Afraid," she whispered, opening her eyes to find his arctic-blue eyes piercing her soul. His eyes were wide with surprise, then narrowed, his head tilting slightly to the left as he studied her.

Cataloged her.

Owned her.

"Then," he said, kissing her once on each cheek, "we will be afraid together." His mouth took hers with a breathless movement that filled her with heat, her trembling vanquished instantly as his entire body covered hers with a pressure that drove all doubt from her in one swift second.

The slide of his palms along her skin drove her mad, her hands buried in the lush wetness of his long black hair. He was so big. Enormous. And his cock pressed against her thigh, so close yet so far, but then receded as he bent his head, pulling her shirt down roughly to expose one nipple and devouring it with his hot mouth.

"Oh, Derry!" she cried out, arching up, begging for more. The touch of his lips, the gentle sucking that intensified, the rhythm of his measured teasing made the pulse between her legs quicken. She was wet, soaking for him, every nerve in ecstasy even as a tiny voice inside her told her to stop.

She banished that voice to stand in the corner like a misbe-having child.

Derry nuzzled the space between her breasts, then moved on to the other, pulling her shirt down so she was exposed, the chilled air in the cool wine cellar no match for their heat. By the time he'd kissed her navel and moved down, she realized time had disappeared. She was floating, living in a space she didn't know she could inhabit, her legs on either side of his broad, muscled shoulders, now unclothed as his open shirt slid to the ground, pooling beneath her feet at the end of the table, and his palms slid under her skirt, seeking the tender skin between her thighs. She felt a tug, heard a faint snap, a shredding of fabric, and then the confounding cool heat of his breath.

"Ah, you're wet for me, Jess," he said, that British accent making the words seem naughtier than they were, making her wish he would do unspeakable acts. She wasn't quite sure what those would be, but if anyone could do them, she was certain Derry was up to the task.

His hair was silk and onyx, thick and wild, her fingers frolicking in the sensual glory of this man who had so much to explore. He was a world, a mountain range, a continent, and as one hand stayed in his hair, the other traversed the terrain of his hot back, the wide muscles radiating lust.

All *man*.

A sudden flash of self-consciousness immobilized her as he dove between her legs, planting the lightest of kisses on a trail headed for her wet, wanting pussy.

Then he paused, and she could hear the raggedness of his breath as he stared at her most private places. Moments passed. Long, hot moments during which he neither spoke nor moved. Her awkwardness returned, strengthened. She tasted fear again.

"What's the matter?" she asked. "Is something wrong?"

"Nothing is wrong," he said, his voice like gravel. "And you are the matter. You are everything that matters." He spread her thighs apart and began to devour her.

"Oh my God," she breathed. The earth fell away. She was flying.

"You're delicious," he said between licks, between kisses. "And beautiful. My Jess, my Jess." He dove his hands beneath her ass and lifted her higher, opening her wider.

She leaned back, gave in, let go.

How hadn't she known it could be like this? There had only been that time in college, the fumbling and the giggling, the premature ejaculation, the snoring, the forgetting and moving on. Hookups. Friends with benefits, but the friendships weren't much and neither were the perks.

Jess remained a virgin, and not for lack of trying. More like lack of will to *keep* trying.

But this. This.

Him.

He was so confident. So firm. He acted like he knew his way around her own body better than she did.

Fingers. Tongue. All choreographed to the second, to her breath, to the beat of her heart.

She unwound completely, like the last piece of thread falling off the spool. Pleasure washed over her like rain. For the first time in her life, she submitted to the demands of her own body. It had been an eternity. How could she live without ever being touched like this? Without ever letting herself be touched?

His tongue slipped between her folds and caressed her in long, wicked strokes. Her clit was hard and aching, despairing for him. She arched her back to satisfy herself, to get closer. He indulged her with more pressure, a deeper kiss.

"Derry," she gasped. "Derry."

"Let go, my love." His thumb danced at the base of her clit, pushing her into madness. "Jess. Jess."

His voice sounded far away, but she felt him right there with her, flying into the stars. Then the tension shattered and she kept going higher, spiraling, spinning, dying.

With him. He was there, he had sent her, he would send her again. With him, she would never be alone.

Slowly, inevitably, she fell back to earth. She landed in his arms, dazed and spent, unable to hold a coherent thought. He was holding her, cooing to her, caressing her, saying her name.

"Derry," she replied, just wanting to shape his name with her lips. She opened her eyes and saw the cellar's shadowed ceiling, reminding her of where she was. She'd forgotten. The table was hard under her back, but Derry still cradled her hips in his arms.

She looked down at him, and their eyes met over the curves of her body. Energy crackled between them. Suddenly sensing his unsated hunger, she sucked in a breath, her pulse waking from its temporary rest.

It was his turn now. For all the pleasure he'd given her, she wanted more. She was hungry to have him inside her. She needed all of him.

"Jess," he said, rising to his knees, fully aroused, seizing her ass with one hand. Digging her heels into the table, she lifted her hips to meet him.

"Jess," said another voice. This one a woman's, from a slight distance. "Have you gotten lost?"

Oh my God. Eva.

Derry didn't seem to hear her. He was stroking his erect cock, hungrily eyeing her pussy.

Jess snapped her knees together and twisted to one side. Where were her clothes? Could she hide under the table? What the hell had Derry done with her panties?

"Jess?"

This time, Eva's voice got through to Derry, who jolted at her words, tucking himself in his open jeans, Jess absentmindedly noting the absence of underwear on him. *We're a pair*, she thought.

Jumping off the table, she smoothed her hair, raking it with her fingers, hoping she didn't look as fuzzy and scattered as she felt. The air reeked of sex, her own musk like the bouquet of one of the thousands of fine wines stored in this cavernous, anachronistic room.

Derry caught her eye, and his mouth spread into a smile so predatory she nearly climbed back on the table and opened her legs for him. He shoved his arms into his shirtsleeves and buttoned up fast, then stroked her cheek with one finger.

"I smell like you," he whispered, just as Eva made an appearance.

"Again? Does it run in the family?" Eva snapped at Jess, who exchanged a genuinely bewildered look with Derry.

She must be referring to Gavin, Jess thought, and made a note to ask Lilah what the hell that was about. Jess felt the creeping flush crawl up her breasts, the sensation of being caught being naughty a new one for her.

It felt . . . good.

Straightening her spine, she spoke up. "I was, um, doing what Der—Mr. Stanton requested."

Eva sniffed, then pursed her lips. "I can tell."

Jess's blush deepened. "I meant finding the wine."

"You go back upstairs and tend to your section, Jess." Eva's stare was like a laser, boring into her. "And remember the rules."

Oh, she remembered the rules, all right.

Except that the red birthmark on her neck pounded so hard she could only think of one rule, one order that biology and destiny seemed to make her fate.

Him. She had to have him.

Derry started as the thought flowed through her, and their eyes met.

He knew.

How did he know? Could he read her mind?

"Go," Eva barked.

Jess fled.

How the hell are you doing?" Derry and Eva said simultaneously as the door to the wine cellar clicked shut with Jess's departure.

"Me?" Eva retorted, clearly offended. "I didn't turn one of the club staff members into a snack bar, Derry!"

"In a manner of speaking, you have!" he roared, bearing down on her, towering over the woman who acted like an older sister to him. She'd been his first crush as a small little cub-boy, and he'd never quite gotten over having his little six-year-old heart broken by the news that they couldn't marry, for she'd already been promised.

But that was long ago, before her betrothed had died, before Asher's wife, before so much pain and—

He shook his head to clear the sudden rush of nostalgic memory that came unbidden.

He was going mad.

"What the hell are you talking about? And your buttons are off." One perfectly manicured finger tickled his chest with a poke. He looked down, distracted from his protective rage, to find she was right.

Damn it.

"You're serving up Jess as bait when you have a problem member!" he growled, unbuttoning his shirt and turning away, as if exposing his naked chest to her would be a crime. When did he, of all people, become modest?

And yet with Eva, he was.

"*You're* the problem member, Derry," Eva shot back.

Her ire surprised him. Nothing rattled Eva. Why was she so upset about this?

"Isla's been a pain in the ass for years, Eva. She's nothing but trouble."

"The same can be said about you."

Ouch.

"But I am charming and know how to make the perfect apple caramel tart that you love," he teased, trying to change the mood. The need to escape poured over him like a sudden, violent rainstorm.

He was still hard, throbbing for Jess, and her name pounded in his head like a heartbeat. She was upstairs somewhere now, serving men, bending and reaching, her cleavage and calves on display, the inner skin of her knees and the edge of the same thighs he'd just licked out there, in public, being ogled by men who had no right to even breathe the same air.

A radioactive cloud of possession filled him.

"You're playing with fire, Derry. Gavin told me to make sure you leave Jess alone."

Ah. So that's what this was about.

"As if Gavin knows how to leave the staff untouched," Derry said. "Such a fine role model, my big brother."

"Older brother. Not bigger," Eva said, her voice back to the sophisticated, unflappable tone he knew.

"True. In more ways than one." He shot her a jaunty smile and waggled his eyebrows. *Play the clown*, he told himself. *That's what you know.*

"Your penis size is nothing compared to your ego," Eva said, selecting the bottle of wine he'd asked Jess to retrieve. She handed it to him without looking at the label.

"You've never sampled the merchandise, Eva. How would you know?" He wasn't flirting. There was no attraction between them. Too many years, too many layers of loyalty and shared grief, and the ingrained distance of something so close to kinship that blood connection wasn't required.

As she sauntered away, she called back over her shoulder:

"I don't need to visit hell to know it's a place that I would find thoroughly unpleasant. The same is true of your bed, Derry."

"My bed is like Disneyland!"

"Everyone is fake, and the bathrooms are clean?"

He growled, trying to defend his manhood at the same time he suppressed his laughter. Sharp wit, that woman. Derry idly wondered why she'd never found a mate since . . .

None of his business, he reminded himself.

So why was his choice of a mate any of Eva's concern?

"Keep Jess away from the jerks in the club."

"Then *you* stay away from Jess, Derry."

His hands curled into fists, chest expanding, his body wide and thick. As blood pumped through him, hard and pounding for Jess, he envisioned her delivering cocktails to yet another asshole who wanted to fuck her for his scorecard.

No.

And yet, a few weeks ago he himself had a scorecard to fill. Was he so different?

"This isn't a joke." His voice dropped, going deeper than the hidden Novo Club, deep into the earth's core, finding a timbre that vibrated with an ancient sound that made his blood turn to hot lava.

She turned around and their eyes locked.

"Love never is."

Ten

I t was her day off.

Not her day to *get* off.

Walking up the stairs into the biology building, Jess put a hand over her mouth to hide her involuntary smile. The morning was cold with a hint of frost, and she wore her favorite black leather gloves, the ones Lilah had given her for her twenty-first birthday. Soon Jess would have to find Lilah a present for her wedding. Hard to believe it was only weeks away.

She yawned, exhausted, thinking of all the work to be done. She'd only slept four hours the night before, but the quality had almost made up for the quantity. The best dreams, like a sexual drug trip, had enthralled her unconscious mind.

And her body. She'd woken up wet and feverish for him, her hands between her legs. Like sleepwalking except . . .

Biting her lip to hide another smile, she pulled open the heavy door to the old building.

Sleep-sexing. Slexing. She wondered if her professor had ever done a study or written a journal article about such a thing. Guys had wet dreams, but what about women? Could she actually climax in her sleep if the dream was good enough?

Feeling flushed, she had to pause and turn to a bulletin board to get ahold of herself. Finger by finger, she took off her gloves and shoved them in her purse. Then she took out her compact and checked her lipstick.

She needed to make a good impression today. In three minutes, the professor whose expertise in human sexuality had led cable news stations to frequently invite her on air, making her a household name across the English-speaking world, was interviewing Jess to be her research assistant.

Well, one of many. Professor Jane Lethbridge already had quite a few assistants, most of them postdocs. But the job listing she'd read had said she was looking for an undergraduate, preferably premed but not required. Since Jess had first enrolled through the night school, and was older than most undergrads, she knew the regular students looked down on her. Those privileged kids who had gone to Andover and Deerfield, who took weekend ski trips to the Alps, who ate caviar for breakfast—she could only imagine what their lives were like, but they hadn't been like hers, and she knew it showed. Working for a famous professor would help her prove she fit in. And improve her odds of getting into a decent med school.

She felt strange as she walked down the hallway, surrounded on all sides by the centuries of elite academia. Last night she'd been stripped bare in the wine cellar of an exclusive private club, and now she was here, in a different kind of club, almost as nervous as she'd been last night.

In a way, she was more nervous. This was real life. This was her future.

I'm your future too, a low voice rumbled in her mind.

This time she didn't smile. She couldn't think about Derry right now. The only way to cope was to compartmentalize her life at the club and her life—her real life—at school. The reason she worked at the club was to pay for her education, not enjoy herself in the basement.

Eva hadn't called to fire her, so she seemed to still have a job. But if she and Derry did something crazy again—

She shook her head and turned her attention to the room numbers. She could *not* think about him right now. Her interview with the beautiful and brilliant Professor Lethbridge was in two and a half minutes, and she couldn't show up with dilated pupils and a sex flush.

Room sixteen. Her office should be the next one, seventeen. But her door was blocked by a cluster of chattering students, male and female, all with perfect hair and perfect clothes and perfect bodies.

Too nervous to look at any of them closely, she strode up and gestured at the door. "Excuse me."

Their conversation didn't falter. A tall, lanky guy with a full beard was telling a story, and apparently it was hilarious, because when he finished, they all broke out laughing.

"Excuse me," she said again, more loudly. "I have an appointment."

Their smiles faded. One by one, they turned and stared at her.

"With Professor Lethbridge," Jess said, attempting a smile.

"She's busy," the bearded guy said. His voice reminded her of someone. Maybe it was just the accent. Faintly Midwestern.

"Are you waiting for her too?" she asked, suddenly alarmed at the idea of having to wait out here with these people. Some professors were notoriously oblivious about time. Professor Lethbridge could be running hours behind.

"We're not waiting," Beard said, flashing a grin. "We're working." He put an arm around a brunette who sported a dragon tattoo on her flat abdomen, visible because she was only wearing a jog bra under her unzipped hoodie. He bent down and licked her temple.

The group laughed again, but the brunette stomped on his instep to free herself and put her arm around the guy to her left.

The others only laughed harder.

The door flung open. Professor Lethbridge stood there in a black pantsuit, waves of black hair loose around her face, a turquoise scarf around her neck. "For God's sake, children, keep it down. The grown-ups are trying to think." She saw Jess and pointed a finger at her. "Jessica?"

She put on her best game face. "Everyone calls me Jess."

"I'm not everyone," the professor said. "Come on in."

The others barreled through the door, but Jess hung back, unsure if she was supposed to wait or join the crowd.

"Chop-chop, Jessica," Professor Lethbridge called out from inside. "No time to waste. I'll be on the *Today* show tomorrow. As much as I prefer my maturing face to be *au naturel*, Middle America doesn't. I'm getting my eyebrows threaded in half an hour."

Jess entered the cluttered office, lined with bookshelves and paintings of Renaissance nudes, and took the chair the professor indicated. Unfortunately, the gang of other students made themselves at home, crowding together on the small sofa, pouring themselves coffee from a pot in the corner, adjusting the thermostat. It was as if they lived there.

"Jessica." Professor Lethbridge sat on the edge of her desk and crossed her long, lean legs. "I would love to participate in the evolution and blossoming of an Extension School student. I'm nothing if not open-minded."

"Extension?" a voice queried behind her. Jess could feel the sneer without seeing it.

"How about you, Jessica," the professor continued. "Are you open-minded?"

Jess sensed a trap. "It depends."

"On what?"

"On how cute he is," a woman whispered.

More laughter.

"Honestly, children. If you can't shut up, you'll have to leave."

But Professor Lethbridge didn't look angry, only amused. She obviously enjoyed being the center of attention.

"It depends on the situation," Jess said.

"What kind of personal sexual boundaries do you have?" the professor asked. "Pardon me for asking, but if you can't discuss sex here in the friendly environment of your peers, I won't be able to use you."

"My sexual boundaries are that I won't discuss my sexual boundaries," Jess said. She'd had a lot of experience telling people to leave her alone about her nonexistent sex life. Just because she'd had one night with Derry didn't mean she was suddenly a different person. They hadn't even had sex, not really.

Unless she counted her dreams last night.

She hoped the professor attributed her flush to the excessive warmth in the room. The furnace was blasting out of a vent over her head.

"Is that what you tell your partners?" Professor Lethbridge asked. "That you won't talk about sex?"

She suddenly realized how absurd it was that she, perennial virgin, was applying for a research position with this woman. She'd assumed it would be mostly photocopying and emails, not this.

There would be other jobs. This was obviously not going to help her fit in with the rest of the student body—quite the opposite. "I'm sorry, but I don't think I'm right for this position after all," she said, getting to her feet. "Thank you for your time. I think I should be going." Without making eye contact with any of the others, she walked to the door.

"Archie, don't let her out of the room," Professor Lethbridge said.

To Jess's surprise, the bearded guy jumped and got to the door before she did.

"I'm intrigued by her," the professor continued, speaking with a voice that could reach the back row of the largest lecture hall.

"She's obviously repressed. None of you can offer that perspective. Jessica may be unique."

The guy blocking the door grinned at her. Something about the hard glint in his green eyes triggered another memory. A large house, a party, loud music, laughter—

Archie.

Oh my fucking God. It was Archibald Rumsey. The senator's son, from one of those far off, western states. She hadn't recognized him behind the beard.

The bastard. The evil, scum-sucking bastard.

"Get out of my way," she said, "or I'll kick your balls into your throat."

Archie drew back and looked at the others with shocked amusement. "Did you hear what she said?"

She clenched her teeth. "I'm not joking."

"Somebody's a little tense," he said, still pretending to be afraid.

"Somebody's a shitstain who needs to get the fuck out of my way," Jess said.

For the first time, he looked at her, really looked at her. "Do I know you?"

He didn't even recognize her. But why would a binge-drinking frat boy like him remember anything from two years ago? Why remember a young woman you had humiliated? Why carry that guilt around with you when it might spoil the unlimited good times you were entitled to?

"No," Jess said. "You don't know me." It was the truth. Two years ago, he'd only seen her as an object to be paraded around for fun.

Fun. *His* fun, and those of his sadistic, privileged, sociopathic cronies. For her, that one night had brought unforgettable humiliation and pain.

She'd been in her first year at community college, planning to transfer the next term to a four-year university. She'd been working the register at Trader Joe's, a job she'd loved because of the fun, playful atmosphere, when a cute guy with a basket overflowing with junk food asked if she was busy that night.

Because she'd been stupid enough to think a handsome Harvard student would find a plus-sized local girl attractive enough to invite to a party, she'd agreed to go. A few hours later, wearing her sexiest dress, she'd rung the doorbell of the house he'd told her about. The throbbing music from the stereo and the shouts and laughter of the party were spilling out onto the street, making her smile, ready to have the time of her life.

Instead, she'd learned what a "pig party" was.

The challenge: find the ugliest girl you could. The "pig." Convince her you really liked her. Bring her to the party. Vote on the ugliest "pig." The winner got—what? Jess never found out.

Not that it mattered.

Shame washed over her, flooding her with hot rage. Remembering the way she'd flushed with pleasure at his invitation, flattered by his attention, she wanted to vomit. She shouldered past him, pushed open the door, and marched out into the hallway, not caring if she'd made a bad impression on the professor. That wasn't the kind of life she wanted to lead, the kind of people she wanted to work with, the kind of medicine she wanted to practice. If she became a clinician, and private research was looking more and more appealing every day, she would treat her patients with respect. Discretion. Kindness.

What was wrong with wanting a little privacy? What was wrong with being reserved?

Nothing.

Besides, she wasn't repressed. She was *careful*. For good reason.

Archibald Rumsey was one of those reasons. The world was full of men like that. Worthless, selfish shitstains like that. Men who took and took, consumed, and spit out whatever was left. Men who never thought about anything but their own pleasure, their own amusement. Privileged, good-looking men who never had to worry about the pain they caused, about the broken hearts they left in their wake.

Men like Derry Stanton.

Fool me once, shame on Derry.

Fool me twice, blame his older brother.

Gavin's penthouse was becoming a tiresome destination these days, only because it seemed to be the first place Derry thought of when he experienced the overwhelming sense of debilitation that this single-minded need for Jessica *Damn Her* Murphy generated in him.

Last night had confirmed so much.

Last night he'd tasted the sweet nectar at the fountain of *her*.

And that taste would never be enough. Ten years between her legs, beneath her, above her, behind her—in proximity of her blinding beauty and the wet wonderland of her body still wouldn't be enough.

And ten years was a blink of the eye for Derry's kind.

Fuck Gavin. Fuck him and his smarmy smirk and flared-nostril, overprotective, fake brother crap when it came to being an obstacle in Derry's way as he pursued Jess.

If Gavin thought he could prevent Derry from being with Jess, it was time to set the record straight. No one could stop him.

No one.

Manny pulled the limo into the exclusive garage entrance, and before the wheels were at a full stop, Derry was out the door and in the elevator, foot tapping with impatience as the silver box took him toward a confrontation he was itching to start.

Between Eva and her judgmental, overly involved, pseudo-maternal treatment of him and Gavin's puffed-up bad-boy routine, Derry was sick of his network of friends and family.

Time to stop avoiding conflict.

And start a little.

As the elevator doors opened, Derry burst into Gavin's penthouse, ready to go for the jugular, his long, thick legs carrying him fast through the enormous, glass-lined living room. Heart hammering, sending blood everywhere it needed to go for the pumped-up verbal thrashing he was about to deliver, Derry came to a dead halt as he heard:

"Oh, my God, Gavin! Again! Again! Right there! Oooooooooooo-hhhhhhhh."

Instinct made him turn toward the delectable female voice.

Decency made him turn away.

"What the fuck are you doing here?" Gavin shouted from the kitchen, where Lilah was, apparently, his lunch. Sprawled before his brother on the kitchen counter, she was a study in creamy flesh, ripe, full breasts like divine, warm mountains, her blonde hair like spun sugar in ribbons across the dark countertop. Gavin's nude form was a muscled study in Greek sculpture, though Derry knew his own body was considerably more aesthetically pleasing, of course. Gavin was a bit scrawny next to him.

"These open-concept apartments really do have their downsides," Derry muttered, eyes averted, though his nose told him everything he needed to know. Lilah's scent created a war within him, her feral, yet delicate musk mingling with Gavin's wolf scent, the two as layered and intriguing from the perspective of smell as an original Monet on exhibit is a visual wonder.

And Derry was, after all, a mammal. His body responded to the scent whether he liked it or not, his mind choosing the fortress of safe images.

Jess.

Gavin reached for a kitchen towel and covered Lilah's breasts. The gesture was as effective as using a matchbook to cover Derry's cock.

"Get the hell out of here!" Gavin shouted.

Frozen in place, amused and horrified, pulsing for the fight he'd come here to win, Derry didn't respond. *Couldn't* respond.

With anything other than laughter.

Wrong response.

Gavin pulled out of Lilah, who began to giggle, and grabbed the nearest piece of cloth he could find, whipping the bright-red apron around his waist.

It read:

My Meat is Hand Pulled

All the fight drained out of Derry and was replaced by a hysterical, boisterous sound that grounded him. He heard Lilah join him and turned to find her wrapped in a couch throw, staring at Gavin's crotch.

"I—gave that to—Gavin as a—joke last week," she gasped.

"He doesn't cook!" Derry hooted.

"I know!" she answered, the two of them in convulsive fits as Gavin glowered, marching away from them both in disgust, ass muscles lean and stark against the ridiculous red fabric.

SLAM!

A bedroom door announced Gavin's reaction.

"I am so, so sorry, Lilah," Derry said in earnest. His face burned with an embarrassment he didn't think he was capable of experiencing. "I barged in here, unthinking, and need to remember that this is your home now. Your and Gavin's home."

"It's fine, Derry."

"It is anything *but* fine."

Silence greeted him. He caught her eye and realized that she had read a message in his words he'd never meant.

"No, no, Lilah, *you're* fine. You are more than fine. In fact, I can see exactly why Gavin finds you so attractive."

One eyebrow arched up, and Lilah clutched the throw a little tighter around her body.

"Jesus Christ, Derry!" he heard Gavin call out from afar.

"I—" Smooth, suave McDermott Stanton had devolved into his twelve-year-old self. All he needed was a slight stammer, a tent in his pants, and the inability to make eye contact with her, and his regression would be complete.

Lilah frowned. "Apology accepted. I think."

"That was no apology!" Gavin yelled, walking back into the kitchen in jeans, barefoot and shirtless, carrying a lovely robe for Lilah. "Turn away, you pig!" he ordered Derry.

"Bear," Derry murmured.

"Asshole."

"That's more accurate," he conceded.

"Why in the hell are you storming into my apartment—my apartment! not yours!—in the middle of the afternoon and interrupting me while I make love to my future wife?" Gavin demanded.

"How was I supposed to know you'd turned your kitchen counter into a sexual playground? Glad I got here before the chocolate sauce and whipped cream made its debut."

"Bugger off! You could call. Text. Knock. Send a carrier pigeon."

Gavin shooed Lilah into the bedroom to get dressed. Derry saw a flash of her worried, flushed face before she closed the bedroom door. She was right to be worried. Once the profanities started flying from his older brother's mouth, he knew what would fly next.

Fists.

Gavin had a remarkable sense of control. Supernatural, almost. And yet once that line was crossed, watch out.

The grip on his arm was hot steel. "You bloody little shit!" Gavin hissed, gloves off as Lilah couldn't hear them. "I'm balls deep in her, and you walk in and make jokes about her body?"

"That's not what I was—"

The blow that hit his jaw was not entirely unexpected.

But thoroughly welcomed.

Days of repressed fury rippled through bone and sinew, and Derry was more than ready to let primal instinct kick in and kick his brother's ass. The only danger was in shifting; if both changed into their animal form, Derry would likely kill Gavin in a true fight. While their father had encouraged such skirmishes when they were younger, to gain a feel for the animal world and the limits of physical power driven by instinct and feral drives, as fully mature adults, they could commit mortal damage upon each other.

Derry had the upper hand as a bear.

Gavin, however, got in an uppercut while he was distracted.

The punch dazed him, giving him a split second to register the sound of Lilah screaming for them to stop, standing on the periphery of their circle of violence, Gavin muttering obscenities between pained grunts, Derry wondering if a good embrace of Gavin's midsection combined with a tackle would make his pecker fall off.

Never fight fair, their father had said, unless you're in a gentleman's duel. Maintain the pretense of honor in public.

In private?

Fight dirty.

A shower of ice made Derry's heart stop midbeat. Howls of rage poured into the space as Gavin crouched on the floor behind a chair, drenched, flecks of crushed ice resting in his hair like diamonds.

Lilah held a large container from the automatic ice dispenser.

"You two are ridiculous!" she screamed. Pointing the bucket at Gavin, she added, "I expected more from you!"

Derry had the presence of mind to be offended.

"And less of *me*?"

"The lesser man," Gavin spat out, a bit of blood on the corner of his mouth.

Derry's jaw set in anger, bile rising in his throat.

"You two come in here right now or I'll call Sophia and have her figure this all out!"

"She'll take my side!" Derry called out in triumph. Humph. If Lilah was going to join the family, she needed to learn to threaten with something far worse than—

"I'll call Asher!" she declared.

Perhaps he'd misjudged her as much as she'd underestimated him. No one wanted their eldest brother Asher involved in this mess. No one.

United in their displeasure at that, Gavin and Derry stopped the fight and glared at each other.

"What the hell are you doing here?" Gavin asked reluctantly, gingerly touching his face to check for damage.

"To talk about Jess," Derry blurted out, surprised by his own words. Lilah's expression went from interest to shock to amusement.

"Why would you come here to talk to Gavin," she said to Derry, "because you think she's the One?"

"The One?" he and Gavin shouted in unison.

Lilah's giggle made it clear she thought this was all a joke.

A bolt of energy shot from the base of Derry's cock to the backs of his eyes.

The One. How in the hell did Lilah know? She was laughing, yet she was *right*.

The tip of his tongue ran across the bottom of his top teeth. A rawness greeted him. Not quite blood, as he saw on the back of Gavin's hand as he smeared it, wiping his mouth, but close. The sucker punch had hurt, but it was a good kind of hurt.

The kind of pain that knocked you out of the misery of being a walking hormone.

Clarity emerged, and as Derry took a deep breath, he looked

first at Lilah, then at Gavin.

"You're both crazy," he said bluntly.

Lilah's face lit up. "Improvement! We're talking!" She turned to Gavin. "Derry told us how he feels. Now it's your turn."

Gavin looked scandalized. "My turn to what?"

"Emote."

"I would rather wear a Christmas sweater with Scottie dogs and blinking lights on it."

"That can be arranged!" she chirped.

"And nothing else."

"That," she said, her voice going smoky, "can definitely be arranged."

Gavin cringed in horror.

"What, exactly, am I supposed to emote about, my dear? Other than my blue balls." He shot Derry a flared-nostril death stare. "You are a master of *coitus interruptus*."

Derry looked pointedly at the discarded apron. "You mean your meat wasn't pulled?"

Gavin lunged, and Derry, laughing, deftly stepped aside, leaving Gavin to bang into the counter next to Lilah, who closed her eyes and sighed.

"You're both deflecting so you don't have to deal with the underlying issue here."

Derry was starting to enjoy this. He looked at Gavin. "I had no idea you were marrying Dr. Phil."

Gavin cocked one eyebrow and gave Lilah a bemused look. "I'm learning more about her every day."

"You two need to talk about how you feel. Gavin's overly protective because Jess is my virginal sister, and Derry's—"

"Virginal?" Derry asked, taken aback.

Lilah rolled her eyes. "As if you couldn't tell."

What was that supposed to mean? How could he tell? Did virgins taste different?

Virgin.

Dear God.

The enormity of the stakes in this situation hit him.

Jess was a virgin. No wonder she'd been so reserved. What he'd assumed was a cynical coyness had been . . . genuine?

A twenty-one-year-old virgin in twenty-first century America? Had she been raised in a convent?

Gavin gave Lilah the hairy eyeball, then shared a bit of it with Derry. "Great. You might as well wave a nice, juicy tenderloin in front of a starving pit bull's nose, Lilah," Gavin groaned.

Lilah frowned. "I know I shouldn't break Jess's trust, and this is private information, but—"

Gavin crossed the room in seconds, one finger poking the V at Derry's shirt. "She really, truly is off limits."

"No."

"She isn't some notch on your belt! Another maidenhead for you to claim, like an ivory tusk or a set of antlers!"

"You collect *maidenheads*?" Lilah asked, gawking.

"He's speaking metaphorically."

"Actually, I wasn't."

"I'm not drawn to virgins, for fuck's sake, Gavin. I'm drawn to pussy. Any pussy. Except that's not true any longer!" He slammed his fist into the granite counter, a container of wooden spoons overturning, spilling onto the ground like toothpicks.

"You like men now?" Lilah asked, perplexed.

"I like *Jess* now. And only Jess. I—" He rubbed his eyes, pinched the bridge of his nose, and scrubbed his jaw with his hands. "I can't get her out of my head. When I close my eyes, I see her. The taste of her is on my tongue."

Gavin shot him a withering look. "You haven't."

Derry gave a one-shouldered shrug that said more than he should have.

"Oh, Derry," Gavin groaned.

"You slept with Jess?" Lilah squeaked.

"No." His eyes darted anywhere but on their faces.

"But you . . ."

Derry pressed his lips together, suppressing the instinct to bite them. The less said, the better.

"But you got really close," Lilah said, finishing Gavin's unspoken thought.

Derry raised his eyebrows and tried to think of what to say. Being tongue-tied did not come naturally for him.

And yet here he was.

Lilah said, "Listen, Derry," her voice threading a string of fear through his body. "Jess isn't interested in you."

"Then she has a funny way of showing it," he replied, thinking of the feel of Jess's lush thighs pressed against his ears.

"She's . . . . . . she's really, really serious about school. Being a doctor. Being self-contained and in control."

Derry had found long rake marks on his shoulders this morning while showering.

Right.

"*Et tu*, Lilah? You're telling me your little sister is off limits?"

"No. I just don't want to see her heart broken." She frowned, really studying Derry. "Or, maybe," she added in a speculative voice, "yours?" Her little huffing laugh made it clear she didn't know what to think.

Gavin did a double take and looked at Lilah like she was shifting into a salamander before his eyes. "You're worried about Derry's *heart*?"

"I am."

"I'm more worried about his cock!"

"That's less likely to be broken," Lilah mused.

"Only because Sir Alexander Fleming discovered penicillin right before Derry's sexual maturity," Gavin muttered.

"And," Lilah said archly, pointedly ignoring her husband-to-be, "if anyone will get hurt, it's Jess." Compassionate, warm eyes met his, so much like Jess's and yet more open. Vulnerable. Unafraid of the world and its many dangers. "Derry's made is very clear he has no problem with casual relationships. Jess is the opposite of casual. She's not a notch on someone's belt."

With great determination, his future sister-in-law's face set with a steely look. By God, for a flicker of a moment there, she looked like Asher.

Somehow, Lilah's gentleness upset him more than if she'd been angry, like Gavin.

He'd had enough, and clearly, Lilah and Gavin had not.

"I'll take my leave," he said, invoking the formal language of their oldest brother, Asher.

"See yourself out!" Gavin shouted.

Derry did.

The limo drive home was considerably quieter than the one earlier in the night but also more dismal than the short jaunt from the club to Gavin's place. The night was winding down, and he was alone.

By choice.

When the hell had he done this before?

Oh. Yes. That's right. Now he remembered.

Never.

His loft greeted him like an old friend. Designed by one of the delectable young granddaughters of an old shifter family, the taste ran toward decadent Renaissance.

Or maybe that had been her body . . .

The old warehouse had once been a slaughterhouse that had hidden a speakeasy in the 1920s. Novo Club members told the tale of raucous Irish mob parties, hot flappers, and an environment where being part of a shadow world could pay dividends.

Derry also chose the building for another reason.

The safe room in the basement.

Not *that* kind of safe room. A shifter safe room. The shifter immigrants who had established the Novo Club in the 1880s had decided that redundancy was their friend. While the Novo was the only club of its kind, Boston and Cambridge were dotted with little bunkers, safe houses for hiding should another great purge come, as in the European witch hunts.

You couldn't trust mankind.

Ever.

At best, though, you could work around them.

The high ceilings and enormous windows, coupled with exposed brick and painted beams and ductwork, allowed for a tremendous amount of natural light to fill the wide-planked room. A series of paintings, all using light in Dutch Golden Age style, framed the walls. His own studio was tucked away in a corner, his painting a hobby he hid from everyone. Antiques, all bold and large, designed for a man of his size to stretch out and relax, reminded him of wonderful memories.

The red velvet chaise: doggy style.

The purple baroque settee: she was on top.

The leather Morris chair—

He burst out laughing at the memory of the threesome he'd engineered, with one under him and one over him.

And then his laughter died in his throat as memory played a trick on him, turning two women into one.

One with the face, breasts, and ass of Miss Jessica Murphy.

"Humph." His grunt echoed through the cavernous main room, the tall windows flanked by thick velvet curtains, the city lights pouring into the loft as if they were from a bottle of the finest vintage.

Exhaustion racked him. His half-complete painting mocked him, begging for his hand.

Like his cock.

"Now you want attention?" he ground out, frustrated and

THE BILLIONAIRE SHIFTER'S *Virgin Mate*   105

angry and resentful and hurt—yes, hurt. Jessica Murphy turned him into a twisted, hormonal mess, and as he stripped naked and crawled under the covers of his pitifully empty bed, he hoped that sleep would purge him of these maddening thoughts about her.

He fell asleep only to awaken with his hand wrapped around himself, seed pouring onto the fine Egyptian cotton, his body covered in sweat.

And her scent invading the very root of his essence.

Eleven

J ess hauled her backpack and roller suitcase off the plane in
Billings, Montana, exhausted from a delay in Minneapolis, the
cramped seats, the junk food, her own worries.

Lilah hadn't understood why she'd rejected the offer of taking Gavin's private jet. As she dragged her suitcase through the
airport, trying to figure out where to find the rental cars, she
questioned her own stubbornness. It's not like it would've been
Derry's plane. It was her soon-to-be brother-in-law's.

But in the weeks since the incident—she called it an incident,
like a cop describing a crime—she'd had to be aggressive about
defending her personal space. Her one concession: she'd dropped
Smoky off at her mom's house, where some Dog Whisperer of
Gavin's would whisk Smoky away to a doggy resort where he'd
have a blast.

Gavin had not been amused when she'd asked if she and
Smoky could trade places.

Derry had expected for them to continue what they'd begun
in the cellar. The next night, he'd sat at his seat in the club and
smiled at her, sober and irresistible, looking like a schoolboy
anticipating a special treat if he behaved himself.

Jess had switched sections with another server. After work,

Derry met her on the sidewalk outside with a single rose in his hand.

"I need some time," she'd told him.

"Of course," he'd said. "We'll go slow. I'm famous for my stamina." He'd caught her hand and kissed it, dragging his tongue across her knuckles, almost making her forget what she'd decided.

"I can't do this."

"I'll teach you," he'd said.

"I don't mean I can't . . . Oh, you know what I meant!"

He'd grinned. Delighted with her, with his life. Such a happy, fun-loving man, not a care in the world.

It would never work.

"Give me some space, Derry. Please."

Gazing up at her, his lips still pressed against her fingers, his mirth faded. His laughing eyes lost some of their joy. She'd braced herself for a flash of anger, perhaps an insult—men like him didn't like to be denied, they weren't used to it—but he'd squeezed her hand and gently let go. He almost seemed pensive, as if he'd expected this.

"Your wish is my command, my love," he said, ducking his head in a bow.

Love. *Him*.

"I need to be alone," she'd told him, fighting the sudden urge to cry. The birthmark on her neck had begun to sting like a sunburn.

Even tonight, in the airport weeks later, thousands of miles away, the spot still hurt. She couldn't wear a scarf and had stopped wearing her favorite gold necklace. Ice packs and lotions didn't soothe the pain.

Maybe she was being stupid. Why not sleep with him? The damage had been done. She was completely obsessed with him, finding it impossible to concentrate on her schoolwork, which was why she'd had to bring so much of it with her in a desperate hope she could catch up during the wedding. Well, not during the wedding itself. The days before and after, when everyone else was hiking and getting massages and facials and dancing and drinking and eating and having sex, hot sex, wild sex—

Her dreams hadn't gotten any more G-rated. And strange, bizarre images kept interrupting the climax. It was always Derry, of course, but he wasn't always himself. Sometimes—

Well, she wasn't going to think about that. She had to get the car and find the Stanton's ranch out there in the wilderness. The sun had set long ago, and she'd need the GPS to guide her through the dark, unfamiliar roads. If she kept imagining Derry as an animal, it was only because Lilah had put the idea in her head, raving about Gavin being a wolf.

She knew Derry wasn't a wolf. If he were anything, he was something larger, stronger, cuddlier, more playful . . .

And she was insane. She turned her full attention to getting the rental car. Since the plane ticket hadn't been cheap, and her small savings should be going toward school, she took the least expensive economy car they had. It was only slightly larger than her suitcase. Not petite herself, she had some trouble getting comfortable, even with the seat all the way back, but she soon forgot about physical discomforts as her mind returned to the big, handsome dilemma that was Derry. It was too dark to admire the unspoiled mountain view, so she was stuck with her own thoughts during the long, lonely drive.

"I was so worried about you!" Lilah crushed Jess in a bear hug, knocking the backpack off her shoulder.

"I told you I was on my way," Jess said, giving her a quick squeeze. She noticed a man in a white jacket who'd just stolen her suitcase. "Hey!"

"He's bringing it to your room, you nerd," Lilah said, laughing. Her cheeks were rosy, her eyes bright. She'd looked happy two weeks ago, but now she was shining with an inner light. It hurt to look at her, the joy burned so bright. "I picked the room out just for you. It's got the best view of the lake."

"There's a lake?"

"Oh, Jess. Wait until you see. Why did you come so late? I'll take you on a tour in the morning. The mountains are so gorgeous in the morning. And the afternoon. It's unbelievable. I remember the first time I came here, I just stood gaping out the window. I was supposed to be serving drinks, but I just couldn't believe how beautiful it is here."

"And now it's all yours," Jess said.

A funny smile curved Lilah's lips. "Not all mine," she said, eyes twinkling. "We share it. The family shares it."

"I'm welcome anytime, is that what you're saying?" Jess asked. "Thanks, but I wouldn't want to crash your love nest, at least not so soon in your marriage. I'm sure Gavin doesn't want his sister-in-law barging in when he's trying to romance his bride."

Flushing pink, Lilah put a hand over her mouth and looked at her feet. She started to say something, then burst out laughing and turned a darker shade of red.

Jess was no idiot. She grinned. "Somebody already walked in on you?"

"You see, before me, Gavin's apartment was kind of a home base for his brothers. They would come and go as they pleased." Jess cleared her throat. "Let's just say Gavin put a new lock on the door last week."

Jess's humor faded, realizing who it must've been. "Derry saw you naked?" A completely unreasonable jealousy washed over her. Lilah was even more beautiful in her birthday suit than fully clothed. Had Derry been turned on? Maybe he couldn't help but make comparisons between the two of them, noticing Lilah's perfect skin, her slightly less-outrageous breast size . . .

Lilah recovered her composure and gave her another hug.

"Don't you dare worry about being unwelcome here. Gavin and I have our own little cabin up there." She pointed at a dim path through the woods beyond the circular drive. "You couldn't possibly bother us. There's plenty of room. All the brothers have their own places here. We even got Mom her own little place, a guest cottage near the sauna building. It's quite the compound."

If their mother had her own building, then Derry certainly would. That was a relief. Jess had been afraid of being cramped into a small country cabin with Derry, seeing him in the hall, the bathroom. But this was like a luxurious vacation resort. When Lilah led her inside, Jess gaped at the vaulted ceiling, the stone fireplace, the full wet bar and leather lounge. Uniformed staff were running here and there, offering cocktails and hors d'oeuvres on black trays to the two dozen well-dressed guests that socialized in the vast great room.

"Is Mom here yet?" Jess asked, gaping in awe. She'd known the Stantons were rich, but . . . this was something else.

"First thing tomorrow. Gavin sent his best guy back to escort her on the plane so she doesn't have to lift a thing." Their mom was mostly recovered from her hip surgery but still needed a little help with heavy objects.

Unfortunately, as Jess looked around the lavish home, she recognized a few faces from the club, wealthy, connected people she'd had to serve as a waitress. She'd known, as maid of honor, she'd have to socialize, but tonight she'd rather curl up in bed and catch up on her chemistry homework.

"You're tired," Lilah said, hooking her arm through Jess's and guiding her away from the crowd. "You don't have to deal with all this tonight. I want you to enjoy yourself. The Stantons are connected to the rich and powerful in a way I'll never get used to. There's no need to stress yourself out making small talk with strangers."

"Doesn't it stress *you* out?" Jess asked.

"Sometimes. But Gavin's great. He keeps the really annoying ones far away from me."

"It's like you've married into the royal family or something," Jess said. "Do you have a tiara?"

"Don't be a brat." Lilah led her through a plain, nondescript door to a quiet hallway. "Yours is the last one on the left. Your bags are already there. We put a little card with menus next to the phone—all you have to do is text your request to have food and drink or whatever brought to you. If you forgot your bathing suit, you can ask for one of those too. The spa is amazing."

"Is this a house or a hotel? You've got room service?"

"It's heaven, Jess," Lilah said, giving her a final squeeze. "Enjoy yourself!"

Derry could smell her when she landed in Billings.

Perhaps that was an exaggeration, but if it was, the exaggeration was slight, for her pending arrival obliterated every other element of the universe. He had no appetite. Coffee made him nervous. Wine tasted like vinegar. His clothes constricted, scratchy cloth designed as a social convention that was just a polite form of torture.

And scents.

Oh great God, the scents.

Jess's rose above the cacophony of olfactory chaos this wedding represented. Three days to go, and already thousands of tendrils of perfume, cologne, makeup, deodorant, wine, beer, coffee, arousal, desperation, manipulation and more assaulted him like bullets and daggers, like fists and feet, like rocks hurled from a short distance straight at his teeth.

How had he never, in all his years, been so crowded by the

dissonance of competing odors? The world smelled like a tuning fork struck by a second one, the two out of frequency, driving his nerves to an insanity from which no one could recover.

He used to find solace in parties and crowds, the joyful unraveling of men and women plied with wine and song a bath of humanity he could dip into at will.

Now it was a primordial soup of odious irritation.

Derry found himself twitching at the slightest unexpected movement, leg tapping incessantly, his impatience living on the surface of his skin and yet—why? He had nowhere else to go. As best man, he had three jobs: a bachelor party, a toast, and to offer the ring during the ceremony.

A fourth, he reminded himself: to dance with the maid of honor.

Jess.

Her name rippled through his subconscious mind a thousand times, as necessary for his survival as oxygen and water.

The cute little server from the club, the one who'd joined him, Freddi, and Isla in the limo, walked past with a tray of crudités in tiny shot glasses, dipped in guacamole.

She approached him where he sat, in a lounge chair two sizes too small, and dipped her sweet cleavage so that he caught an eyeful.

"Care for a taste?" she asked, her voice seductive.

Of Jess.

Gillian—that was her name—flinched as if slapped.

He'd said that aloud, hadn't he?

"Of just . . . a little," he mumbled, trying to cover his slip. He grabbed two of the little appetizers and took one to his mouth, upending the vegetable sticks and dip as if doing a shot of tequila.

As he chewed, she gave him a skeptical look.

"Is she here?"

"Who?"

"Jess."

"Jess who?"

The skeptical look deepened to disgust.

"Jess Murphy. You know. The woman you kissed under the mistletoe at the club. The woman who threw Gatorade all over you at the club. The woman you fucked in the wine cellar at the—"

His hand was around her wrist, gripping hard, the other about her waist as he pulled Gillian in close.

"Stop talking, please."

"Huh. So I was right. The rumor's true." He heard the sneer in her voice. Damn it. She was guessing. And he'd handed her the answer. "Poor girl."

He simmered, emotion turning into a boil. The crisp November air did nothing to quell the spark that had ignited his change. He wasn't in true danger of shifting. Not yet. And yet . . .

"Men like you never change," Gillian said, glancing to the left. Derry could tell she was like Isla, fishing for an audience, trying to catch someone's eye to validate herself.

She had to define herself by how others saw her. So different from Jess.

So much like him.

The old him.

"Men like me are none of your concern."

"Considering it's my job to serve nothing but men like you, I'd say you're wrong."

"If all you ever plan to do is serve men like me, Gillian, then you might want to ask yourself why you're working for people you so clearly disdain."

"It's that easy, is it, Mr. Stanton? Just go out and change my life because I want something different?" Her tone became more vicious. "I tried that. A few weeks ago. You might remember that night? The one where you ditched me with your two little friends."

"What does that have to do with—"

"Women like me sleep with men like you so we don't have to continue *serving* men like you."

Stunned into silence, he stared at her.

"You use us. We use you. I'm going to find a man who understands this, a man who can give me more than you ever could. You've missed your chance. You'll never see me again."

He clenched his jaw. "How lovely for both of us. I wish you every success in realizing your dreams."

"I know what you think, but Jess Murphy isn't any different from me, or Isla Monroe, or Freddi von Eisenthorpe. She's just better at playing the innocent virgin. You fell for it hook, line and sinker."

He kept his face impassive, but inside, he reeled. Could Lilah have been wrong about her sister? That Jess was more experienced than she pretended? She wouldn't be the first little sibling to hide secrets from an older one.

A cold, cruel smile twisted Gillian's face. How had he ever found her attractive?

Words failed him. What was the point of this conversation? His nose detected her bitterness, an acrid scent of tangy fear that she exuded. Every word out of her mouth was true—in her mind. And that nasty terror seeped out of her pores like poison.

"Maybe she'll have better luck than me, Derry." The use of his first name was like being lashed with a whip. Gillian's whisper was a garrote, her face inches from his, her lips pressed against his cheek before she added, softly:

"I hope you can get it up for *her.*"

And with that, Gillian walked away, and in her absence rushed a swirling rage that crested the dam of his human body like a scene from a disaster movie.

She's just better at playing the virgin.

You fell for it.

Maybe she'll have better luck.

I hope you can get it up for her.

What if Jess's sharp words after the mistletoe kiss had been real? Her own sister had warned him. Lilah's words thrummed through him like a gong:

Jess isn't interested in you.

I just don't want to see her heart broken.

His chest cracked in two, the rush of air and need and despair filling the void. What if Lilah had *really* been warning him away? Did she think he was that grossly shallow?

Did everyone?

What if it had been genuine? What if Lilah had been telling the truth about her feelings?

The world tightened into a tiny dot.

And then it imploded into fur and bone and roars and the sudden rush of trees and light, the scent of sun and ozone, as he raced into the woods to become the other half of himself.

Being human had become unbearable.

Twelve

Enjoy myself, Jess thought. *Yeah, right.*

With a yawn, she dropped her tablet containing the unfinished chemistry problems onto the bed. It was a four-poster, big enough for a king, solid as granite. An elephant could do Zumba on the mattress, and it wouldn't wobble a centimeter.

That gave her ideas. Had Derry slept in this bed? It seemed like it was designed for him. She closed her eyes, drifting into another dream about a big man with big hands and a big appetite. A shiver rippled through her, tightening her nipples into erect points.

Chewing her lip, she slipped her hand under her sweatpants. She was already wet. God, since that night in the wine cellar, she'd been continuously aroused. She was like a walking girl-erection.

When would she see him? Was he close?

He was the most attractive man she'd ever laid eyes on. Not just in real life—anywhere. Paintings or sculptures, TV, online, movies, amateur or professional porn. Every preference she'd ever had for a man, he satisfied it. And surpassed it.

The sensual curve of his lips, the thick band of muscles between his neck and shoulder, his silky dark hair, the dimples above his ass . . . Well, she was just imagining those since she hadn't gotten a good enough look before, but what she'd seen was mouthwatering. There was no point denying it. When she closed her eyes, she saw him.

Right now, she saw him shuddering his release as his thick cock pounded into her and he shouted her name: *Jess, Jess, Jess.*

Her breath caught, overwhelmed by the forbidden fantasy.

Night after night, she'd stopped herself from indulging in this . . . in this natural biological act of self-love.

And then broke down and did it anyway.

Maybe, if pleasuring herself while she imagined Derry kept her away from the real man, it was the right thing to do. She pressed her palm over her aching vulva and tried to imitate what he'd done to her. She'd never felt anything like that before—or since, no matter how hard she tried. The climax had been far beyond any orgasm she'd ever had, and for all that she was a virgin, she'd had many. She'd been alone a long time. She'd always been alone.

It wasn't just his looks. If only it were. He was funny, dangerously smart, quick with his tongue.

Oh, his tongue . . .

She spread her knees wider, wriggling down into the luxurious sheets, and cast her mind back to the dark, quiet cellar where the only sound was his flesh against hers, his rumbling voice, their fevered breath, her pounding heart.

What else could he do to her? She tried to imagine . . .

No.

She sat up, pulling her hand away.

No. She couldn't do this. She had to stop thinking about him, especially when she was in bed with her hand down her pants.

She kicked off the down comforter. What she needed was fresh air. Cold, bracing fresh air that cleared her mind. Then she'd finish her chemistry. Because she was a student and she had dreams. Impressive, admirable dreams, not the kind she'd be ashamed to share with anyone. If she continued to lie around masturbating like a teenage boy with his first private internet connection, she'd never get to med school, never be a doctor, never demand the respect she craved.

That's what it was about, wasn't it? Proving to the rest of the world that she was good enough? All her life, she'd been dismissed at a glance. She was the checker at the grocery store, the girl with secondhand, unfashionable, plus-sized jeans, the night-school wannabe who wasn't good enough to mingle with the *real* undergrads.

Tonight, however, she pulled on her sexiest, most trendy jeans, and a designer parka with fur trim, and strode out of her room like a woman who knew she was worth something. Why was she doubting herself so much lately? She hadn't felt this way since—

Well, since the frat party. That public humiliation, when she'd been so young, naïve, and vulnerable, had been the lowest point of her life. It had taken months to recover.

Sometimes she wondered if she ever had.

Not wanting to run into the crowd in the great room, she ducked out a door at the end of the hall. She found herself standing on a wraparound deck overlooking a small lake that shimmered in the moonlight. A silhouette of mountain peaks framed the lake and house, and above everything, a white dusting of stars, more than she'd ever seen in her life.

She already felt better, just to be outside and breathe. She was in control of herself again. All she needed was oxygen, exercise, and fully zipped jeans.

It was too dark to explore the wilderness to the right of the lake, but she remembered the path Lilah had shown her to the cabins in the woods. Jess wasn't going to knock on any doors, just explore a little, stretch her legs.

She took the steps down from the deck to a wide path around the lake, its boundary marked by low box lanterns flickering every few feet in the ground. Soon she reached the edge of the windows of the great room, where dozens of guests were still loudly enjoying themselves. Now she saw that her path led directly to a pair of French doors into the house, into the party, the last place she wanted to go.

Just as she was turning to go back the way she'd come, she saw the bottom step of a long rocky stairway that led up the hillside. The path lanterns came to a stop at its base. The steps looked older than the house, the mortar spread by hand, the stones uneven and covered largely by tree roots and fallen leaves.

But it seemed to lead in the direction that Lilah had pointed, into the woods where she and Gavin had their cabin. After a brief pause, Jess left the lit path and began climbing the steps into the wooded darkness.

It smelled rich, clean, earthy. Nothing like the city back home. This was pine bark and lake frost and crisp, glacial air. She drew it into her lungs and held it, savored it. No wonder Lilah was eager to share this place with her. Jess looked forward to coming again when there weren't so many people around.

Although there seemed to be plenty of privacy *here*. The steps climbed higher than she'd expected. Had the driveway been that far above the lake? It was too dark to see more than a few feet in front of her, and the woods had thickened around her, blocking her view of the well-lit house.

She smiled, powerfully drawn to the mysterious staircase. This was just what she'd wanted to find, a place to distract her from how badly she needed to get laid, once and for all.

Well, more than once, and that wouldn't be all.

Him.

Oh damn. She was still thinking about him. If anything, being out here in the woods was making her feel more turned on. So alive. Just one more biological organism in the vast, eternal universe.

As she reached the top rocky step, she discovered another

manicured path lit with lanterns curving to the left. This must be the one Lilah had pointed to. The woods had thinned out, letting her see the stars again, and she was amazed that they were bright enough to illuminate the tops of the trees. To the right, the path snaked into the dark forest, no lanterns illuminating it. To the left must be the main house.

But going back there didn't appeal to her right now. What was there except chemistry homework and a big, empty bed?

She turned and went the other way. It was dark, but the path was flat and inviting.

She had no idea how that small decision would utterly transform her life.

***

As she walked, the path curved steeply uphill. She took out her phone and aimed it at her feet, using it as a flashlight. The trees began to grow closer, their long branches crowding her from either side, but she continued, irresistibly drawn forward.

Something she needed was ahead of her, something that needed her. It was strange but undeniable. With each step, reality fell behind her like an unread book. What she wanted was out there.

She was still hiking ten minutes later, even more desperate to get . . . *there*. To find it, whatever it was. The effort was making her sweat, so she unzipped her parka and paused for a moment to catch her breath and listen to the sounds of the forest. No sirens, no honking taxis, no shouting drug dealers, no gunfire, no traffic—just nature.

And something else.

Like music, it had a beat, deep and throbbing.

And a scent. She inhaled, tasting it on her tongue, drawing it into her lungs.

Irresistible. Caramel? Cinnamon? No, something more masculine, like coffee. Cedar?

She dragged her tongue across her upper lip, trying to place it. She licked her bottom lip, hungry for more.

And then she realized it was Derry.

Him.

She was hearing and tasting and wanting him, not like a lonely, obsessive girl, but like a wild animal acting on instinct. Every one of her senses was tense and alert, fixed on his presence ahead of her in the darkness, not more than fifty paces away. Thirty-seven. She could feel it, feel the distance that separated them as if it were a physical object, feel him.

Derry.

But something was wrong. He was thrashing about, moaning, upset. Sudden terror for his safety burned through her like an acid cocktail. He was hurt, she could feel it. She could feel his suffering.

Without a thought, she sprinted into the darkness. "Derry!" she cried. "It's Jess! Are you all right?"

Twenty-three paces to go. She'd been tired a minute ago, but now she was filled with boundless energy. She could run for miles.

"Derry!"

She heard the sound of cracking branches and rustling leaves. Had he fallen? Was somebody hurting him? She had to run faster.

Still a dozen paces remaining. The cracking sounds had stopped, but she could feel him there just outside the short beam of her cell phone flashlight. "Derry, why aren't you answering?" Heedless of the unknown dangers in the shadows, she strode off the path to close the gap between them. Anxiety tightened her chest, making her lungs burn with the strain.

There! There he was!

But—

Not pausing to question what she saw, Jess rushed forward and put her hands on his fur.

Yes, *fur.*

"Are you all right?" she asked, feeling the sloped shoulders for broken bones, grabbing his paw to search for thorns or blood.

Paws. He had *paws*. She held the phone up to his face to see his eyes.

Ah, yes. Those were the same. Dark blue, intelligent, gentle. He was looking right at her, right into her soul. A brown bear with blue eyes.

And then he jerked away and lumbered into the shadows. She chased after him, light lifted, wanting to see it all. Needing to see it.

Her panic had faded, but the urgency remained.

She wasn't thinking about how this was as impossible as Gavin being a wolf. Her brain wasn't propelling her into the forest. She was running on instinct, hungry to learn everything about him. Now. She had to see him now.

No longer running, he was huddled behind the splintered remains of a tree that seemed to have been broken in half. A low growl from his throat didn't scare her away; she knew he wouldn't hurt her. From the look of the tree, he was in far more risk of hurting himself.

He cried out, his voice more like a man's, and then began to change. Hand trembling, she held the phone over her head to see it all.

The shift into his human form was swift but seemed painful. He shouted and gasped, arching his back, shaking his fists at the sky. Then he doubled over. Broad human shoulders strained outward, leading to bicep and elbow and forearm. Bunching quadriceps appeared. Knees, calves. Paws became arches and toes.

Fur and claw had faded into dream. Now there was only a man. *Him*.

He was magnificent. She didn't know how he did it, how he could survive such a change, but she didn't care. Later, maybe, her scientific brain would obsess over it, but at that moment in the forest, all she wanted was to touch him. It had hurt him, going through that. It hurt to watch.

She climbed over the fallen tree and captured his face in her hands. The phone was in her pocket now, so she couldn't see him. The touch of his warm skin was enough.

"Are you all right?" she asked again. Maybe this time he would answer.

He pulled his face out of her grasp. "What are you doing here?" He straightened so that he was looming over her. "You—you—you saw. Me." His voice was shaking with anger.

"I did. I'm glad I did."

"You're not upset." It sounded like an accusation.

She held up her trembling arms. "I wouldn't say that. If you could see how I'm shaking—"

"I can see." His voice was gravelly.

"You can?" She tried to move closer, but her foot caught on a branch.

"Easy," he said, gripping her upper arms.

His touch, even through the thick parka, made her suck in a breath. All she wanted was to be close to him.

Without the parka. Without anything. Pulse tripping over itself, she reached out a hand and rested it on his chest, searching to see if his heart pounded as hard as her own. Then she began to trace the muscles of his chest, stroke the curls down the middle, over his navel . . .

"Hey," he said, grabbing her hand. He held it in the air between them.

She smiled. "Hey," she said seductively.

"I need to get dressed." Dropping her hand, he twisted away. She heard the crunch of sticks and dried leaves. They grew fainter.

He was leaving her there.

"Hey!" she called out. "Where are you going?"

His voice shot through the dark. "Not so missish now, are you?"

"What's that supposed to mean?"

"What kind of innocent virgin would see a bear change into a fully naked man without screaming and running away in terror?"

"What does being a virgin have to do with it?" She climbed over the fallen tree trunk and followed his voice into the woods. "Are you telling me everyone who has sex turns into an animal? Because that I can believe."

"I'm telling you I know you're not what you seem."

"You're one to talk!" she cried. "You were just lumbering around here on all fours, Yogi!"

His crunching footsteps stopped. His voice lowered another half octave. "I am *Ursus arctos horribilis.* Otherwise known—in this vulgar English language—as a grizzly bear. And while I *am* smarter than the average bear, don't call me Yogi."

"Better than being called a liar. And did you say 'horrible'? Because that sounds about right."

"I only said you're not what you seem. But as you've pointed out, I'm the bear calling the virgin a—well—I concede your point and most humbly request you excuse me. I prefer the pleasure of my company and my company alone right now."

She ran after him, incensed. "I never said I was a virgin."

"Then you admit your scheme?"

"To what, sleep with you? Fine, yes. That's my scheme. Now slow down so I can get what I came here for, you big idiot."

He'd led them to a path, finally, and the ground underfoot was flat and clear. Dark, but at least there weren't any torn-up trees strewn about. She watched him storm down the path, clearly ignoring her request, his glutes moving with a fluid motion, liquid grace and primal power all rolling and animated before her, his naked body a mountain she wished she could climb. As her eyes roved over his enormous, nude limbs, taking in the coordination, determination, and completely uninhibited way he moved, she felt her core begin to throb, her body aroused, her pussy wet and wanting, an ache that only he could satisfy.

I was already attracted to him before I knew he was a bear, she thought to herself. *I'm not attracted to him* because *he's a bear.*

The birthmark on her neck stopped hurting abruptly, a warm, pleasant sensation replacing the annoying rawness that had nagged her for weeks.

"Derry!" she called out. "Please stop!"

He halted, shoulders so broad she wasn't sure her arm span was wide enough to touch both tips of his shoulders, his chest moving with a breathlessness not caused by exertion. Long black hair rolled down his back like a raven's feather, pieces of leaf caught in his wavy locks. His shoulder muscles moved, a constant kinetic symphony that she swore she could hear in her bones.

A long, measured inhale made his back rise up, his skin swell, the artistic perfection of coiled strength so beautiful to watch she forgot what she was going to say.

"I stopped," he finally said in a low, clipped voice, that damned British accent so intimidating. "What do you want?"

"You."

Thirteen

S he *knew.*

She'd seen him. Caught him. Viewed him in bear form. And she still wanted him.

Derry resumed walking, needing the sanctuary of his cabin even more as her words became increasingly ridiculous. She might as well have just admitted that she was the charlatan Gillian had described. While Derry was all for using people in a bid to gain pleasure, a hedonistic abandon that left everyone satisfied, he turned stone cold at the idea that Jess, of all people, should have a piece of him.

Too late.

The man he'd once been was no more.

And now she'd seen the animal.

Why wasn't she horrified? Eyes wide, mouth open, face flushed with terror, limbs numb and shaking? Screaming at him, telling him he was an abomination, a freak, something to be eradicated and destroyed, caged and contained at best?

He'd only heard the rumors about the many ways humans responded to seeing a shifter make the transition from one form to another. Discreet to the point of obsessiveness when it came to his changes, Derry had never exposed himself to that most intimate of moments when he put his DNA on display. Although he was young and fortunate enough to be born in a more enlightened era, he was still so careful.

Every shifter, from childhood, was told the stories about the old days. The witch hunts and the torches, the stabbings and hangings, how the townspeople in cities and rural villages would gather in hunting parties and kill, heedless of the shifter's age, mammal, or state.

They killed shifters when they were in human form sometimes.

Who was the dangerous animal again?

Asher would have to be told about Jess's knowledge. All of his brothers, and Sophia, of course. Any breach must be reported and dealt with. Perhaps Jess already knew, he mused, his heartbeat picking up speed. Gavin had assured him that Lilah would never reveal their secret, but the bonds of sisterhood were strong.

Just how strong?

Lilah. Her words came back to him, all the ways she'd tried to dissuade him from thinking Jess would ever truly be with him. Her truth.

The truth.

Jessica didn't really want him. Not after what she'd just witnessed. *Stupid, stupid, stupid*, he chided himself. How had she crept up on him? He could hear a chipmunk on bare ground. In bear form, his senses were sharper than usual, yet she'd gotten so close undetected.

How?

He reached the edge of his private courtyard, the stone-lined ground making it easier to walk barefoot. Steam rose up from the hot springs-fed pool each individual cottage possessed, and the lights embedded beneath the water gave off a supernatural glow.

Supernatural.

He snorted.

Her touch seared him. Halted him in his tracks, her palm

laid slowly at the base of his shoulder blade. She must have been on tiptoes to reach even that high. The ends of his hair brushed against her hand, the strands catching. He felt the resistance.

Go.

He knew that walking away was the safest approach.

His toes gripped the stone beneath them, unwilling to move.

"Derry, I've never done this before." A second hand joined the first, electrifying the nerves in his back, sending hot current through the base of his cock.

"I should hope not," he said tightly, fighting his arousal, enraged at the idea of her chasing a naked man who wasn't him to his private home in the woods.

"Don't reject me. I couldn't bear it." Suddenly she giggled. "So to speak."

She was hysterical. He couldn't abandon her like this. Under normal circumstances, it wasn't safe for her to be so far from the house in the dark. The route between his cabin and the main building was, as he'd insisted, hidden from the main path. When he came out to Montana to spend time at the family compound, he came to be alone. A literal and figurative hibernation. Having women stumble into his sanctuary was the last thing he'd wanted.

But now, after what she'd seen—he could hardly just leave her here. He'd have to get dressed and call for a servant to lead her back.

"You've caught me at a disadvantage, my dear. For all my skills, seducing women when I'm in this state isn't one of them."

"You've already accomplished the seducing part. Now you can reap the rewards." Maneuvering around him, she lifted her shirt, grabbed his hand, and crushed it over her breast, loosely contained in a soft bra. "Don't you want to?"

Trying to ignore the feel of her plump, silky flesh under his fingers, he gaped at her, speechless. She was so insecure. Clumsy. Ridiculous.

Her voice shriveled to a peep. "Please?"

Sincere.

His blood heated. And the depths of his soul sang out in triumph, in recognition.

Her.

She was no charlatan. This bright angel of his dreams really was a virgin, as impossible as it was. Meryl Streep wouldn't have been able to fake this. She was smashing his hand to her other breast now, kneading it around like a baker with a ball of dough. An unlikely laugh began to build in his chest, one that he certainly couldn't let her hear, for it would hurt her, this lonely girl, his love.

For the first time since their meeting in the elevator, he felt completely in control of his body. The overwhelming compulsion to shift into his animal form was gone. She'd seen him as a bear and accepted him. She'd opened herself to him, exposing her own vulnerabilities, and her honesty and humility and bravery humbled him.

I have to make this good for her. He cursed himself for the setting. Out here at his cabin, he didn't have any of the usual props he enjoyed using during a seduction—vibrators, costumes, feathers, ticklers, crops, oils, clamps, blindfolds, chocolate syrup, chocolate truffles, chocolate ice cream, chocolate lube—honestly, chocolate was usually all any woman wanted . . .

How he would love to introduce her to such pleasures, her sweet body flushing under his ministrations, her ruby lips learning to touch him just the way he liked, her climax coming again and again, at his command, during hours, days, weeks of teasing and erotic play.

But he had none of his toys here. Only himself.

Slowly he looked down her body and dragged a thumb across her full, round, luscious breast.

He'd just have to make the best of it.

Jess's face was hot with shame. She was making a fool of herself. After all these weeks, all these years, she'd finally decided to go for it—and the man who'd famously fucked his way across New England every weekend wasn't interested. He was even naked, for God's sake. And erect! The degree of *not* wanting her was so extreme, he wouldn't even relieve himself on her. In her. With her.

"Jess," he said apologetically.

Apologetically! She could hear the regret in his voice. The pity.

"Just kidding," she said, trying to step back, but his hand was clamped over her breast, caught under her shirt, right where she'd shoved it. How unbearably awful. "I can find my way back."

His hand slid around her waist and hauled her up against him, his hard cock digging into her belly. "You're not going back."

Now she was confused. Damn it. "Why not?"

"Do you want me or don't you?" he asked.

"Is that a trick question?"

Arm tightening, he lifted her off the ground and regarded her eye to eye as her feet dangled in the air. "Maybe we should stop talking. It ruins things." And then he bent his head and kissed her.

Ah.

The kiss was gentle, but when she snaked her arms around his neck and parted her lips, he thrust his tongue into her mouth and made her forget everything that had ever separated them.

He was right. They really should stop talking.

Hungry to get closer, she spread her legs and hooked them around his hips. His hands grabbed her ass and held her, stroked her, inflamed her.

The kiss stopped being gentle. They feasted, moaning into each other's mouths, nipping and sucking. She rode him, squeezed him between her thighs, desperate to satisfy a million fantasies of all those miserable nights.

"Unzip my jeans," she gasped.

His hand wiggled between their bodies, finding the button as easily as if it were his own. No doubt he'd had some experience with that maneuver. "Are you a good swimmer?" he asked.

"What?"

"I wouldn't want you to drown." His huge hands pushed under the waistband of her jeans and shoved them down her thighs. "You can be on top."

Just as easily as the button removal, he popped off her shoes one by one and then flung the jeans, with panties, into the forest.

Distracted by his fingers now stroking her wet folds, she clung to him and nodded. Whatever. Whatever he wanted.

"Jess," he whispered, carrying her across the courtyard. The bouncing footsteps only heightened her pleasure. His thumb was right below her clit, rubbing in rhythm to his steps.

Oh God. She might come right here.

"I do have a bed, but this is more fun." He held her under the arms and set her gently on the ground near a bubbling, steaming pool. A mountain hot springs. "You should enjoy your first time."

Lilah must've told him about her inexperience. She was too excited to be angry right now, but later, she and her sister would have a word. Before she found a way to get even.

He was already gloriously naked, but she still wore the parka of all things. As she reached up to remove it, he put a hand on her shoulder to stop her.

"Aren't we getting in the water?" she asked.

Nodding, he stepped back and dragged his burning gaze over her. "I want to remember you like this."

"Naked from the waist down, wearing a ski jacket?"

He didn't smile. "So beautiful," he said hoarsely.

Breathing fast, she wriggled out of the parka and lifted her shirt over her head. Then she pulled off the bra and let it all fall at her feet.

Now they were even. Both naked, both exposed.

Letting him look at her like this, even after the night in the cellar, even in the weak starlight, made her tremble. He'd seen so many women. No man had seen her, not like this.

Did it make it easier knowing he had his own secrets? His own vulnerabilities?

Holding his gaze, she licked her finger, then dragged it across her own nipple, making it pucker more tightly.

Yes, it did make it easier. They both had to tear down sturdy, well-guarded walls.

She drew her finger into her mouth again. This time, she brought its wet tip over to his chest. When she began circle his nipple, he sucked in a breath and captured her wrist in his powerful grasp.

"I must beg you to be more careful," he said tightly. "Too much improvisation on your part will make it impossible for me to, ah, extend your pleasure. As much as every strand of my unusual DNA is screaming for me to drive my cock into your lovely pussy while you gasp and beg for more, I mustn't."

"You mustn't?" she teased, thrilled again by the accent. Smiling, she leaned forward and licked the bunching muscles of his abs like a kitten tasting her first saucer of cream.

He hauled her up into his arms and smashed his lips against hers. He plundered her mouth, drove his tongue deep inside, claiming every inch as his own.

But then he drew his head back and pinned her with that midnight-blue gaze. "Not the first time," he said. "That needs to be gentle."

"How about the second time?" She wasn't teasing. She really wanted to know. Moving her hands around his waist, she explored the contours of his hips and ass, wild with the feel of their bare flesh making contact from chin to toe. His erection rose between them, hard and ready.

"The second time will be for me," he said, devouring her mouth again for a moment before releasing her to the ground. He inhaled raggedly, rubbing his hands over his face, and then pivoted to face the pool.

My God, he had a beautiful backside. Each cheek of his ass demanded its own moment of worship. Or an hour. She reached out to feel the right one, but he flexed and stepped into the water, his muscled arms held to either side like a testosterone airplane.

Or a god. Could he be a god? What normal man could transform himself into a bear with blue eyes?

Her knees trembled with desire. Tonight was going to be like a pagan ritual, with the moon, stars, and mountains silently watching her give her hot, aching, hungry flesh over to the unknown. To Derry, a man as massive as the mystery of his nature.

The steam rose up around his muscled chest and shoulders, forming droplets on the dark, wavy locks of his hair. He extended a hand. "Jess."

She walked to the edge of the pool and ran her hand over her heavy breasts, her rounded belly, her soft thighs, the pleasure tightening inside her like a spring. Nobody had ever looked at her like that before. When her fingers traced her mound, he flinched as if in pain, tightening his jaw, uttering the soft growl of an animal—which, she remembered with a forbidden thrill, he had been only moments ago.

Her heart pounded against her ribs, terrified of where she'd brought them.

"Catch me." She closed her eyes and let herself fall into the water.

For a moment she panicked, thinking she'd finally gone too far, but then his arms came around her and eased her into the steaming water with him, where his lap waited for her, hard but soft. She reached for his cock because how could she not satisfy that most embarrassing of dreams, even the ones she had when she was sitting on the bus staring out the window, shifting in her seat, chewing on the inside of her cheek in frustration?

She wasn't going to be frustrated tonight. Tonight she was going to take it all and revel it in like a starving lottery winner at a Las Vegas buffet. No, unfair comparison. He was no cheap mass-appeal smorgie. Derry was a mystical dream come to life, a shadowy fantasy who knew her body better than she did and desired nothing but her own happiness.

His cock was hard, velvety, thick, and when she squeezed it and pulled, he threw back his head on his sinewy neck and groaned in delicious pain. High on power, she did it again, and as she pumped, she stuck her tongue in his mouth and tried to claim him as he'd done her a moment ago, sweeping along his teeth, dancing with his tongue, grinding her pelvis into his balls.

"Jess, wait," he gasped. "I can't go slow if you—"

"Fuck slow." She straddled him, bobbing in the hot water, moving his cock between her legs. Her breasts jiggled on the surface, skimming his chest. Each electric brush of her nipples against the thick hair made her more determined for him to be inside her. "Now. I need you now."

"Darling—"

She slid the head of his cock between her folds, not caring how she'd totally lost control of herself and was showing absolutely no dignity whatsoever. Floating in the water, she clutched his shoulders with one hand while the other aimed the cock into her pussy.

"Jesus," Derry breathed. "I can't stop you."

"Why would you want to?"

"What about protection?"

"You need a security team?"

He chuckled. "I meant birth control."

Oh.

"I'm on the pill." She'd been on it since high school for cramps and skin problems. This was the first time she was grateful for its original purpose.

"Ah. And I assure you I test regularly—at Gavin's lab, as it happens—and am fine. No shifter has yet tested positive for any of the unpleasant contagions." He cleared his throat. "Not even the most active of us."

She frowned. What did he—*ohhhhhhh*.

"It'll hurt, sweetheart," he added. "It's supposed to hurt. I don't have much experience with your kind—"

"My kind? You make me sound like some sort of supernatural creature you've never met before." She ignored every delay he was making and sank lower on his shaft, feeling a deep interior resistance that she'd expected him to break through without her having to beg for it. "Come on, do I have to do this all myself?"

"I warned you," he said roughly, clamping his hands onto her hips. "Remember that."

She smiled, triumphant. "I'll remember."

"Put your tongue in my mouth."

Breathless, she did as she was told. While he feasted on her mouth, one hand left her hips and found her clit, just above the shaft of his cock. She began to bounce up and down, trying to go for it.

"You're not ready—"

But she was about to explode. She felt a rushing in her ears, the urge to weep. "The hell I'm not," she said. "Do it, damn it!"

He stroked her. "Almost."

"Now," she said.

"My love," he cooed. "You're so beautiful."

But she was beyond speech. She clung to him, head dropping to his shoulder to bite that thick band of muscle, to make him give her what she needed.

Just as her teeth pressed flesh, he thrust up into her, snapping her into pieces, putting her back together, filling her with the rich, heady taste of sex, love, and dreams.

"I'm sorry," he was whispering, "I'm sorry."

She realized that he misinterpreted her cries. "Don't be. It's wonderful," she whispered. She cupped his cheek, glorying in the feel of him inside her, her inside him, their union.

With a groan of his own, he grabbed her hips again and lifted her, removing himself from her, then hauling her back down. Thank God she was on the pill, she thought idly, breaking the wonder of the moment just as he—

"Oh my G—" She swallowed her own cry as he did it again.

And again.

He filled her, impaled her, claimed her.

The pieces of her life that she had carried around like bits of broken glass suddenly fit together in a seamless whole. The anxiety clinging to her back fell off and drowned in the hot water. Doubt and fear drifted away in the steam, floating out of sight and memory.

All that remained was tight, hot, brittle, spiraling pressure. She had to relieve that pressure. With each thrust of his cock, the tension increased, unbearable tension. Nobody could survive it, not even a god.

Driving into her again, he met her tortured gaze with one of his own over the rising steam. "My love," he said, voice strained. "I can't—wait—so—s-sorry—"

All at once, she came around him and with him, shattering into pieces that would never be broken again.

Fourteen

I n his dream, Derry had waded waist deep into the warmest, wettest pool of delightful water. Tendrils from a soft, silky water fairy's hair tickled his belly, the feel of sweet, spun cotton caressing his abdomen.

He groaned, nirvana enveloping him in an eternal embrace, his cock surrounded by melted butter and hot sunshine, the gentle strokes of Mother Nature a kind of heaven on earth. His hips rode up, demanding more, more, more as his body responded to the powerful ministrations of an ambrosia that made him stir in his sleep, waking sharply and nearly sitting up, but unable, pinned in place by a very eager, very naked bed partner with her head bobbing up and down at his very thick, very aroused, pole.

This was no dream.

This was the *best* dream come to life.

"Jess," he moaned, her name on his tongue evoking her taste, which was embedded in his mouth, his throat, on his skin and in the whorls of his fingertips. At the sound of her name, she looked up, coquettish and coy. The sight of her lips wrapped around his cock made an internal rhythm push him up, his body begging for release but his mind catching up to it just in time to stop himself from spilling his seed down the same throat that had cried out his name in ecstasy last night until she'd gone mute.

"Is this . . . OK? Am I doing it right?" she asked, looking away from him and turning her gaze to the tender, vulnerable flesh she manipulated. "It's so . . . fascinating."

Derry sat up on his elbows and looked down at her. Given his height, it was a fair distance. Her hair was a tangled honey-brown mess, matted in places from the friction of their third (or was it fourth?) time last night.

Once unleashed, her sexual desire had been utterly insatiable. Apparently.

"Fascinating? Tell me more. Every man dreams of being told how amazing that part of his body is."

"It's softer than I thought." She lightly dragged the tip of one fingernail against his foreskin. "And you're not circumcised."

He shuddered. "Why would I be?"

She laughed, the vibration of her movement making her breasts bob a bit, triggering more blood to flow into his erection, making the thin thread of restraint that allowed him to have this conversation and not bury himself deep in her right this second unravel that much more.

"Most men your age are."

"I thought you were a virgin." *And you underestimate my age*, he wanted to add, but wisely stayed silent. There would be time to explain. She was twenty-one and likely assumed he was in his late twenties. She'd experienced the shock of seeing him in bear form last night. Learning he was more than four decades older—in human years, but only slightly older in shifter years—would come at a different time.

"Doesn't mean I haven't seen one or two of these."

A cloud of jealousy ripped through his organs. The idea of Jess touching another man intimately made him want to tear apart this cabin plank by plank, stone by stone, and stuff each piece down the guy's throat.

Jess wrapped her palm around his shaft. Her fingers couldn't touch each other, the girth so great. As she rose up, he sucked air between his back teeth, the combination of her curiosity, fascination, and damned fine naked splendor shattering his mind.

And then she dipped her head down and gave him her mouth, throat opening to take him in, the gag making its expected entrance at the very end, her movement up and look of apology triggering his smile.

"I need more practice."

"Music to my ears."

Her eyes roved over him, the covers kicked off, their bodies musky and spent, yet awake for a morning filled with erotic delights.

"You're so beautiful," she declared.

"That's my line." No woman had ever said such a thing to him, and he felt a stirring within, pleased with her words. Mornings after typically involved walks of shame, the chauffeur called to bring the woman (or, often, *women*) home. Rare was the bedmate who spent the night and had a morning romp with him, much less *this*.

Crawling up his body, she made sure her nipples traced a line up his midsection until they were pressed together, chest to chest, her cheek snuggling into the crook of his neck.

"You're so warm," she marveled, playing with the thick hair on his chest.

"And you're so exquisite, Jessica."

She went silent. Pensive. He felt her heartbeat sync with his, smelled her hesitation. Then she ran one hand from the top of his shoulder, slowly moving down his ribs as if counting them, claiming them, the slow, steady march of her skin against his a tactile warmth that made him tingle by the time she reached his hip, fingers contouring to his ass, her delicious inventorying more than an invitation.

It was the touch of fate.

Mine, said that connection of skin against skin.

Mine.

She kissed his neck, then flicked her tongue against his nipple, making him shiver.

He flipped her onto her back, the motion swift and intentional, leaving her breathlessly squealing as he opened her legs with one knee, his hands busy with those mesmerizing breasts.

"What are you doing?"

"You got to be fascinated. My turn to be captivated."

"But I—we—I need to wash up! We haven't showered. It's . . ." She covered her face with her hands in a gesture of endearing embarrassment, the way she bit her lower lip so sweet he almost laughed.

"It's what, Jess?"

"It's . . . I . . . The scent. I must, you know, women have that smell." Her nose wrinkled.

His face split with a leer. "Oh, yes," he growled, inhaling deeply. "And it is a testament to our merciful Mother creator that you do. How boring this would be without your imprint."

"Imprint?" A red, racing blush covered her chest, neck and cheeks. He wanted to eat her up.

But first things first . . .

"Your unique scent. Musk. Pheromones. Whatever. It's what makes you, you. It's how I mark you."

"Mark me?"

"Note you. How I know who you are."

"You can tell that by my scent?"

"Yes." He nudged her thighs farther apart with his nose, one hand sliding up the creamy expanse of her belly, finding a rosy, tight nipple. She gasped and arched up. Ah, she wanted more.

Thank God *she* wanted more.

"But I thought guys didn't like the—" She shut her mouth

quickly, turning away slightly. The fascinated young woman who'd just been staring at his dick like it was an archaeological masterpiece was shutting down before his very eyes.

He studied her. "You had no problem with this at the Plat in the wine cellar. Why now?"

She frowned, then blushed, her flustered appearance endearing. "I don't know. I just—"

"Men who cannot appreciate the scent and taste of a natural woman aren't worthy of the title 'men.' They are little boys. Little, selfish boys who focus purely on their own pleasure and who deprive themselves of the joy that comes from the fine bouquet of an aroused woman's juices."

"Derry!" she gasped, now deeply embarrassed, yet—intrigued.

Sunlight streaked through the layered curtains in his bedroom, highlighting the delicate, pink folds of her womanhood. He bent at the holy V between her legs and looked up.

"Jess."

She stayed quiet, though her body exuded excitement.

"Look at me, Jess." His voice held a demand that he be obeyed. She did.

"You have a choice, my dear. You can believe the utter bullshit that society implants into the minds of women about standards. What true men find beautiful bears—no pun intended—little resemblance to what society claims men find beautiful."

Jess swallowed, the delicate skin of her throat making him wish he had two mouths.

"This scar," he said, pointing to a crooked, pale line on her knee. "What is that from?"

"A bike accident in second grade," she said with a smile.

"And this," he asked, cupping her breast, his hand not quite big enough for her bountiful flesh, a condition which pleased him to no end. "You've been told they're imperfect, have you not?"

She nodded, eyes still wide, her expression unreadable.

"Wrong. They're perfect." He sucked one nipple into his mouth, rolling the sweet pebble on his tongue, enthralled by how the heat on her skin made her break out into a light sweat, her scent morphing.

"You," he said, regretfully letting go of her breast and cradling her face in his hands, "are perfect as nature made you. *I* am imperfection personified. And still I rejoice in life, lived in two very different worlds."

"I've been living in two worlds too, Derry," she said with a sigh. "The same society that draws tight lines I can't live within, and my own, lonely world where it's easier to keep everyone out so I won't feel rejection. I thought it was easier that way." Her doe eyes met his. "Until now."

Her openness made him feel more naked than being nude could ever achieve. Her reserved facade was just that—a shell she used to keep the vagaries of the word at bay. Tenderness consumed him, replacing the rutting need that had built at his wakening, and he pulled her to him, too desperate to be connected to her to care that he was dropping his own shell, too.

Her mouth tasted like ambrosia as he kissed her, pulling her up into his lap, curling her body to mold with his as he sought out her tongue, dancing with the same abandon he'd felt last night.

That his feelings had only deepened in the hours since sleep had overcome him was a disturbing realization, one that gave him pause. As his hands filled with the warm, buttery feel of her waist, her breasts pressed against his chest, her body squirming to center herself over him, he stopped.

"What is it about you, Jessica?" he asked, his voice hoarse with the craven need for a true answer. "No woman has ever made me feel so . . . so . . . so *this*."

She did not smile, instead brushing his long locks off his face, the gesture tender and intimate. Eyes the color of amber with rich cocoa swirled in the irises met his own. She did not answer with words, eyes raking over his face, her neck tilting as she took him in, searching him for the answer to his own question.

Suspended above him, now resting her weight on her knees, she took her hands and pressed them flat against the base of his torso, sliding up, fingers threading through the thick hair at his waist, moving toward his pecs and shoulders as she skimmed him like a blind woman reading Braille.

"I don't know," she answered truthfully, mouth trying but failing to smile, eyes wide and open like the sun. Her slow, deep inhale was music, a melody made for him, a heart song shared only by the two of them.

The sunlight made the room so bright, and as he sat up and stretched over her, moving his hand to her breasts to imitate her own motions, he nudged her legs open once more with his hands, then nose, burrowing into her scent, covering himself in it.

Branding him.

He was becoming hers with each kiss, each stroke, every thrust, and all the sounds and scents.

Hers.

"Oh, Derry," she moaned, her hands on his shoulders, fingers digging in as his tongue found the soft flesh that he knew would drive pleasure through her body. Last night she had wanted him inside her, heedless of the pain he knew it must have caused, finding ecstasy in the ache of a new self being born.

He was privileged to be her guide on this journey of self-exploration, and he damn well knew it, her blood pounding in his ears, his own rushing to his groin as she writhed above him, one hand seeking his, her fingers intertwining, sharing her intensity.

Every touch made him crave more. Every hitched breath made him need a thousand like it. The endless capacity for the enjoyment of time spent with her, for the rush of hunger that seemed insatiable, for the sense of mourning that they were not immortal and could not spend eternity together, made all his earlier years on this earth feel trivial. Child's play.

Mere practice for this moment, this gasp, this climax that roared from his lovely, beautiful soul mate as his tongue drove her to new heights, her hips grinding into his face, embedding her scent in his pores, on his taste buds, in his cells.

His.

She was his, now and forever.

And God help him, that was all he ever wanted. The choice had been made for him.

Jess sat up and kissed him, her tongue seeking the forbidden taste of her own juices. She began to kiss his neck, his shoulders, coming around to his back and tracing fine lines along his shoulder blades, making him shiver. She delighted in his body, as if it were a new playground to inhabit.

Let her tour the grounds.

As she touched him, leaving his shivers and groans in her wake, Derry understood that he'd thought himself a free man, one who could roam the buffet of life and sample from hundreds of dishes at whim, but in the end his gentle teasing of his brother for settling for Lilah—"Only one woman? That's like eating only one food for the rest of your life. Better make it a good one"— could come back to bite him in the ass.

Which, at this very moment, was exactly what Jess was doing.

"That's new," he growled as he spun around and pinned her to the mussed bed, her wrists captive, his body looming, her legs opening and wrapping about his waist with a surprising agility.

"Again?" he asked, clearing his throat to remove the incredulity.

"More," she whispered, angling just so. He sank into her, warm velvet embracing his pulsing erection, the world deepening yet again, layer by layer, into the divine.

She was sleek and silky, so wet and ready for him, primed by his mouth and the unbridled enthusiasm of repression unleashed. He thrust into her, gentle but deep, rooting himself in her. Over and over, stroke by stroke, the concert of flesh and fire crescendoed, their scents mingling to form a new identity, one he could find in a crowd of thousands.

One that would haunt him to his dying day, centuries from now.

Old and new fused as she let go, screaming his name, calling to him for more, to the point where he had no more to give, and it was only then that he felt it, too—the burning cry of the ancients, a mark like no other, a third voice between them that called out to him without words, without sound, without form.

It just was.

Just *them*.

He thrust one last time as her heels dug into his ass, her fingernails clawing him until he bled, her neck muscles tight as she thrashed and arched up against him, begging for him to go deeper, until he made love to her soul with a body whose limits he only found now, in this very moment, his seed spilling into her and filling her with the heat of a thousand dying suns. He was her moon, in orbit about her, and as he kissed her neck, the shudders and twitches of the last attempts to cling to pleasure wracking their conjoined bodies, he paused, puzzled.

As he pulled back a few inches, his eyes focusing, he saw it.

Or, rather, saw *nothing*.

For Jess's birthmark on her neck was gone.

<hr />

Jess kissed him good-bye at the door of his cabin for the tenth time. He was adorable in sweats and a T-shirt, an outfit he'd of course never worn to the club.

"I really need to go," she said again, loving the way his morning whiskers felt against her cheek. And the way his neck felt under her fingers. And the way all the beautiful things he'd said felt in her heart. "They'll ask me why I'm late."

In less than an hour, she had to attend a private bridal luncheon with Lilah and—this was the scary part—Derry's twin sister, Sophia.

"Tell them you were in bed," Derry said, smiling against her cheekbone as his hand explored her ass.

"Mmm." Her mind splintered again, paralyzed by the sensation of being touched with so much strength and passion after a lifetime of none at all. The things they'd done together . . .

And all the things they hadn't and would as soon as they were alone again.

"What if they guess the truth?" he asked.

"Truth about what?" She slipped her hands under the elastic waistband of his sweatpants, remembering she'd done the same thing to herself just the night before, a lifetime ago.

He nibbled the tip of her nose and gently removed her hand from his cock. How was it he didn't sit around playing with himself all day? Seriously, she would if it were hers. But it *was* hers now, wasn't it? Grinning, she reached for him again.

But he caught her by the shoulders, stopping her at arm's length. "Who's 'they'?" he asked. "I thought it was just your sister."

"And yours," she said with a sigh.

His grip tightened. "*My* sister?"

"Sophia. You've only got one, right?"

A scowl darkened his face. "But why?"

"The sisters of both families. Bridal thing, you know how it goes."

"I do not know. Since when is this a requirement?"

"Since women love weddings and do things to draw it out in every way they can," she said. "My mother suggested it, even though she won't be here until tonight."

"But surely," he said, rubbing his jaw, "you can't include my sister in those activities. She's not—she's—Sophia isn't—"

"She is your sister, is she not?"

"Look at her," he said. "Can there be any doubt?" Sophia's build was almost as impressive as Derry's, and her affection for sexual pleasures just as infamous.

"And the groom is your brother. We have to invite her." She was glad to finally have the strength to open the door and step out of the range of his kisses. "And we want to. We're going to be family." And she would be sleeping with family. Not to mention sleeping with a member of the club where she worked, which could cost her a job.

She'd lost her mind. Losing her job along with her mind would be too much.

Maybe he was also thinking about complications, because he fell silent. They both stared at the heavy planks of his front step under their feet. With a start, she realized the gashes in the wood were claw marks.

On that bright, sunny morning, her memory of seeing his other form seemed dreamlike, insubstantial, unreal. But there were the claw marks to prove it. This man, so human and articulate, lived part of his life as a bear. A fucking *bear*. Oh, just because he did. Who knew why? She certainly didn't. And hadn't even asked him.

In her defense, she'd been busy.

If he was a bear, then his sister might be something too. God, it was crazy, but she'd seen it and, somehow, felt it. The explanations would have to come later. "Is Sophia . . ."

"Like me. In every way."

"A bear?"

He held her gaze. "Yes. And she'll—well, she won't be supportive of us and our entertainments."

"So I shouldn't tell her?"

"Were you planning on making an announcement?" he asked dryly.

She smacked him in the chest, smiling, and turned away. Again.

"I'm out of here, funny guy. I've got hair to wash. The minerals in that hot springs are giving me split ends, I can feel it."

"Next time you should use the lovely conditioner Eva gave me," he said. "She'd seemed to feel I should stop stealing it from the Platinum Club during my longer visits."

With a pang, she realized what he meant: longer visits where he found a private room to have sex with a woman, or several, touching them the way he'd touched her, perhaps even saying some of the same beautiful, romantic things he'd said to her.

It shouldn't have hurt—she'd known who he was, what he'd done and how often—but it *did* hurt, like a broken beer bottle stabbing her in the guts.

"What's wrong?" he asked, ever perceptive, always watching.

She couldn't bring up his sordid past and her own insecurities right now. "I'm nervous about meeting your sister, I suppose. And facing Lilah, knowing I probably have major sex-face."

"It might be helpful to wear a perfume you aren't presently wearing," he said, studying his bare toe—so to speak—as he brushed it along the gash on the step.

"I'm not wearing any perfume right now," she said. "Were you afraid she'd smell it on you? Even after you took a shower?"

Not meeting her eyes, he coughed into his fist, shrugged those enormous shoulders, and waved her along. "Don't want to be late. Remember, just walk back the way you came. It'll be easier in the daylight."

Not that she'd had any trouble finding him in the dark. "Right." Knowing she'd never leave if she touched him again or even lingered another moment, she spun around and jogged down the steps, past the courtyard and pool where he'd changed her forever, and all the way through the woods back to the main house.

Following last night's steps exactly, she slipped into the rear door facing the lake, a sapphire oval reflecting the mountain peaks like a cheesy oil painting, and got to her room without having to talk to anyone. Keeping Derry's comment about perfume in mind, she scrubbed her body extra vigorously, lathering up her hair, her underarms, her butt, her toes, everywhere, noting with amusement and alarm how many marks she bore on her skin of their lovemaking. Welts, swelling, scratches, abrasions, love bites, handprints on her hips. It was as if she'd been in battle, except nothing hurt in a bad way, not even the soreness between her legs.

And every brush of the washcloth reminded her of something he'd done to her. The twirly move with his tongue. That thing with his pinkie finger. With a groan, she leaned against the wall of the shower and turned off the water.

She wanted him again. Even more than before. Her legs were weak with wanting him. They had time to be together one more time before lunch, didn't they? Just a quickie? He didn't have to do that thing with his pinkie finger . . .

The sound of her phone ringing broke through her latest lust fever. Dripping on the Italian tile, she walked to the bedroom and picked up her phone, not surprised to see Lilah's face.

"I'm sorry," Jess said quickly, staving off her sister's complaints. "I'll be right there. Just got out of the shower. I overslept. I'm sorry, don't hate me."

"Stop apologizing," Lilah said. "You're not late. I just wanted to ask if what I'm wearing says slutty waitress or sexy bride or sophisticated events planner or desperate—"

"Wear whatever you want," Jess said, patting the towel over her tender privates as she dried herself. "You always look beautiful."

"Some of these people own their own countries. I heard one guy say he'd bought a planet, that if you give NASA enough money, they'll send you a deed with a photo shot from a Hawaiian telescope that says, basically, congratulations, you've got a planet, Mr. Rich Dude—"

"Sounds like bullshit to me. But even so, what does this have to do with what you're wearing?"

"I can't look like a slutty waitress in front of these people!" Lilah cried.

"What if you *are* a slutty waitress?" Jess grinned, enjoying teasing her sister until she realized that *she* was the slutty waitress now.

And Lilah didn't even know it.

Lilah's voice turned pleading. "Can I come by and show you, and you'll tell me if it's OK?"

Jess looked down at herself and flinched. The hot water had made all the scratches and love bites even redder and more pronounced. She couldn't let Lilah see her right now. "I'm not a good judge. Where's Gavin? Can't you ask him?"

"He's useless. He'll just say I'm beautiful no matter what I wear."

"Which is exactly what I said."

Lilah's exhaled loudly. "Never mind. Forget it. Who cares what they think? I don't. I don't care."

"That's the spirit," Jess said, but her sister had already hung up.

Now it occurred to Jess to worry about her own outfit, which was certainly not the clothing of a woman who owned any planets, or whose father had, or—

Did Derry own any planets? The man could turn into a bear. What else didn't she know about him?

She pulled on her tight black skirt and turquoise sweater, one of four outfits she'd brought with her back when she'd been thinking about Derry in the abstract, imagining what he might do to her if she sauntered past him in a skirt that hugged her ass, or leaned into him wearing a sweater cut so low she'd had to buy a special bra.

She went over and studied herself in the mirror.

Slutty waitress.

Ah well, she'd own it. That's what the members thought of her anyway, so she might as well play the part.

Fifteen minutes later, hair still damp after a quick blow-dry,

Jess hurried down the hallway to the great room, where she was meeting Lilah and Sophia before they headed down to an enclosed porch over the boathouse. The cocktail party of the night before had dispersed, replaced by a few quiet people here and there sipping coffee and looking at their phones. Jess only vaguely noticed them, however, the majority of her attention fixated immediately on the Amazon—as in legendary female warrior, not free, two-day shipping—who stood, legs hip-width apart, hands on hips, gaping at Jess as she walked in.

Her stunned expression only intensified as Jess drew closer. Jess's hope that Sophia had been listening to some shocking story, or staring at a bad play in a game on the TV behind her, faded into dust.

"I don't believe it," Sophia said, giving Jess a slow head-to-toe once-over that would've made a seasoned stripper blush. Tall and physically large, with a rolling curviness that made Jess seem like a toothpick, Sophia was intimidating. The golden-brown eyes that examined her were sharp and searching. Whatever she found was not appealing, either.

Jess could barely get the words out. "Don't believe what?" There wasn't any way Sophia could know about her and Derry so soon. Could she? Glancing down at herself, Jess searched for some sign of unbelievable-ness. Maybe the scarf and concealer hadn't done nearly enough to cover the love bites and scratches. Why hadn't she packed a turtleneck? Or a nun's habit?

Just then Lilah popped up from behind a leather club chair, her blond hair pulled up into a messy updo, hourglass figure wrapped in a tight purple sweater and black skirt.

Too funny: they'd worn almost identical outfits. As different as they were from one another, every once in a blue moon they acted like the close sisters that they were.

"You're both here!" Lilah exclaimed. "Why didn't you guys say something? I was only playing Candy Crush." Moving around the chair, she shoved her phone in her pocket and flung her arms around Jess. "Hi, sis," she said, then moved on to Sophia. "New sis." Her eyes were bright and smiling again.

For the first time, Jess thought she might understand why her sister was so happy. If Lilah believed this was going to last forever, then maybe she was justified. But how could it? What goes up must come down.

Shoving aside that unwelcome thought, Jess returned the hug and met Sophia's disapproving stare over Lilah's shoulder. "Is the boathouse far?"

Sophia crossed her arms over her chest. "Didn't Derry show it to you? I'd figured he'd given you the *full private tour*," she said, drawing out the words. "Or did you run out of time?"

Releasing Jess, Lilah turned to her future sister-in-law with a frown. "Is something wrong?"

Sophia paused, studying Lilah for a long moment before sliding her gaze over to Jess. "Let's just say I have a *nose* for *trouble*."

Oh God, Jess thought. Derry had anticipated this. And she'd used a gallon of scented products, too.

Well, if Sophia knew, she knew. Nothing to be done about it now but hold her head up high and keep her composure. She and Derry were both adults, and whatever they wanted to do, however long and hard and wet they wanted to do it, with or without pinkie fingers, was their own business. Their own sweaty, sticky, exhausting, *delicious* business.

Arousal swept over her again. She put a hand over her mouth to cover the sudden panting. Accelerated heart rate, flushed skin, tingling clitoris—all kicked in just from thinking about him. A single thought brought her near the edge of climax.

She couldn't sit through a bridal luncheon feeling like this. She had to slip away for a moment and get a grip on herself.

I'll help you with the gripping.

Jess twirled on one heel, gratified to see Derry was only a few feet away, gulping from a coffee mug and stuffing a bagel into his mouth in two bites.

But if he was eating, how had she heard him?

Lilah's voice spoke at her ear. "The boathouse isn't far. We'll go out the back door. It's just east of the lake, above the pier." Lilah tapped her on the arm. "Jess?"

Jess spun back to the two women. Both were staring: Lilah with dawning amusement, Sophia with open hostility.

It was crazy, but she couldn't wait.

"I need to powder my nose. I'll meet you there." Without waiting for permission, or even acknowledgment, Jess strode away from her lunch companions, floating past Derry with her heart thundering in her ears. *My room*, she thought urgently.

Somehow, she knew he would hear her.

Fifteen

Every late autumn, Derry's ritual before hibernation included two steps: eat an extraordinary amount of food and wind down on the wild sex.

Somehow, he'd managed neither this year.

While he didn't hibernate in the traditional sense that a full bear might go into winter seclusion, he found himself spending his winters in an indolent, sloth-like state, his libido diminished and his waistline enhanced. In childhood, his brothers Gavin, Edward, and Asher had teased him mercilessly, leaving his twin sister alone. While she, too, hibernated in this half-bear, half-human state, she'd always escaped their ridicule.

My room.

Jess's voice rippled through his mind, and he swallowed his bagel in one final bite, swigging the coffee in spite of its temperature. Last night took a toll on him, and not just emotionally. He'd woken starving for food, and now he shoveled the nourishment in, drinking a second cup of hot, black coffee as fast as possible before following Jess.

Pure, unfiltered desire coursed through him, the scent of her overpowering, drawing him to her like a magnet. She was halfway to her room when he caught up to her, grabbed her by the waist as she yelped, and pulled her into a tiny changing room outside the pool.

"You want me," he rasped into her ear, clutching her from behind, her gorgeous legs revealed as he pulled her skirt up, insanely intoxicated to find her wearing no panties at all, bare legs smooth and so lickable he nearly dropped to his knees, tongue extended.

Her ass pushed back, pelvis arching, rubbing against his hot, thick cock.

"I can't stop thinking about you, Derry," she moaned, her tiny hands flat against the changing room wall, the sound of people outside the slotted door a muted audience. She bit the back of her hand as his fingers found her swollen clit under her skirt. One hand fingered her with torturous, wet circles using the pad of his thumb, his other hand unbuttoning his pants. Within seconds, he was sliding home.

She sucked him into her, then clamped down, her pussy walls begging for more. The effect was like greased lightning as he rode her, plunging in and pulling back out as she begged him for more.

"Fill me," she gasped. "I can't get enough. I need to come. God, Derry, I need you to make me come now!"

Wild heat drove him senseless, his abs slamming against the bunched edges of her skirt, hiked up around her waist, the white, sweet globes of her luscious ass calling out for a smack.

"Oh!" she called out as he spanked her, just once, the sound like erotic music. In the second after, she cried his name, biting the hand he had braced against the wall, her body shuddering with the first of a wave of orgasms she rode, her legs buckling as he held her up without effort, her face flushed, hair in sweat-soaked tendrils along the delicate line of her neck.

Derry's mind splintered as she claimed and released, clamped and let go, pulling him in and milking him as his own orgasm drove out every shred of self-control he thought he possessed as a sophisticated lover and turned him into a, well . . .

An animal.

Not literally, but metaphorically speaking, and as their bodies resumed normal heart rates, and they realized they'd just rutted like beasts in heat with wedding guests not five feet away, chatting around the pool, Derry's coarse voice, ragged from holding back his sounds of passion, cut through their breathing.

"Where the hell have you been all my life?" he asked. Close enough to see individual pores on her skin, he realized he was facing the spot where her birthmark had been.

Had.

It was still gone.

He opened his mouth to say something about it, an uneasy tingling inside his mind spreading like a wildfire.

Just as he was about to speak, she straightened her skirts, turned around, stood on tiptoes, and kissed his cheek.

"That was great. See you after lunch."

Without another word, Jess the Virgin slipped out of the changing room and left him surrounded by her scent, a spent member, a thousand questions—

And a huge grin on his face.

———

She couldn't stop. Not wouldn't.

Couldn't.

Even now, slick and throbbing, Jess knew she could ride him for another hour, her folds swollen with the need for more release, her body primed and ready for orgasm after orgasm after orgasm. Nothing she had experienced in her entire twenty-one years came close to this. No word adequately described what Jess had become.

Horny? No.

Aroused? Nope.

Excited? Not quite.

Insatiable? Close.

Pretty damn close.

She could have Derry fuck her nine times a day, and still her body would ache for a tenth climax. This was insane.

She was insane.

And loving every minute of it.

That smack on her ass had opened up a whole world she'd never considered before. Like expecting the sky always to be blue and then seeing your first sunset. Obviously she knew some people went in for that, but she hadn't expected her body to respond so urgently to a little spanking.

Oh God, just the word made her wet. Again.

She paused in the hallway that led to her room, her mind empty. What was she doing again?

With a start, she remembered the luncheon. With his sister, who'd already made that snide comment about smelling trouble. Jess could only imagine what she smelled like now. If she'd been wearing panties, they would've been soaked.

Fuck it. Some girls had to make up for lost time. If other people didn't like it, they could kiss her ass.

Her big pink aroused ass.

Taking calming breaths, she ducked into a powder room for a quick cleanup before making her way through the house, out the back door to the lake, and scanned the shore for the boathouse. It sat to her right, a sloping walk past the outdoor pool area—because of course they had both an indoor and outdoor pool, a lake, and several private hot springs. Of course they did. The one percent. The one one-hundredth of a percent.

And soon Lilah was going to be one of them. Whether she was ready for it or not, Jess's life was going to change, too. No more counting spare change to buy a container of store-brand yogurt, no more clutching the pepper spray in her pocket as she walked through her own neighborhood in the middle of the day. As Lilah's sister, she would never have to be that poor again.

And as Derry's girlfriend . . .

She tripped over the flagstone. No, that's not what she was. She caught her balance and hurried past the pool deck to a flagstone path snaking its way through the manicured, rolling turf. She knew what this thing was with Derry, and it began and ended with soggy underwear. If she told herself that often enough, she might believe it. She had to believe it, because the longest Derry had ever dated a woman was probably twenty-four hours. The fact that he was still interested in her this morning didn't mean he was in love with her, no matter how many outrageously sweet words he moaned in her ear while he gave her yet another orgasm.

A waiter met her at the top-floor entrance of the boathouse, a narrow building perched on the shore with stairs leading down one side. The roof was converted into a glassed-in porch, where Lilah and Sophia reclined in white wicker chairs that were padded with floral cushions. As Jess walked in, they each held a champagne flute and were talking in animated, hushed tones that fell silent the second they saw her standing there.

"Mimosa?" the waiter asked.

Jess looked at him, a short guy in his sixties whose red hair was going white. In a flash of paranoia, she wondered if *he* knew as well—because from the looks Lilah and Sophia were giving her, they'd known everything at a glance, so she was obviously doing a crap job of hiding her feelings.

"Two, please," Jess said. One for each ovary.

The skilled waiter did as she asked without a flicker of surprise or disapproval, and in seconds Jess was sitting in the third chair, mimosas in hands, staring down two women who obviously had very different feelings about her sex life.

"It's none of your business," Jess said by way of an icebreaker. Then she tipped her head back and drained her first mimosa.

Sophia snorted. "Is that the only congratulations you can offer your sister two days before her wedding?"

The bitch was right. Jess got up and bent over to hug Lilah. "Forgive me. Congratulations." Then she sat down again and gulped her second drink.

"Lilah and Gavin are fated to be together," Sophia said, crossing her long legs.

Lilah put a hand over her chest and sighed. "That's so sweet of you, Sophia. It means a lot to me to know you think that."

"It's the sort of love that strikes once in a generation," Sophia continued, watching Jess through narrowed eyes over the rim of her glass. "And in our family, that's longer than it sounds. Had you heard our family is a little unusual, Jessica?"

Appetizers covered a small, round table between them. Jess reached forward and selected a cheese straw. "I'd heard."

"You told her, Lilah?" Sophia sounded mildly disappointed, like a teacher with a nine-year-old who hadn't done her homework.

Lilah seized her own cheese straw and looked down at it. "She was living with me when I—when I found out."

"You freaked out and told her," Sophia said.

"For what it's worth, she didn't believe me," Lilah said.

Sophia turned to Jess. "But you do now, don't you?" She sipped her Champagne. "I wonder why that is?"

Would Derry get in trouble for letting her see him? Jess fidgeted in her seat, consuming her cheese straw, then reached for two more.

All the lovemaking had given her one hell of an appetite; she glanced around for the rest of the meal, relieved to see the waiter laying out dishes on a buffet table behind them. "As you so thoughtfully pointed out," she told Sophia, "this lunch is to celebrate Lilah, which means we should be trying to make her happy. I don't think interrogating her sister is going to make her happy, do you? Can't you find something else to talk about?"

"Oh look," Lilah said brightly. "The food is ready. Let's eat."

She shot to her feet and gestured for them to follow.

Sophia's nose twitched. "They've just put out the mahimahi with a manchego crust and grilled sirloin. Oh, and butternut squash muffins with extra nutmeg." The first real smile of the day spread across her face.

"Did my mother tell you about the menu?" Lilah asked.

"No, I can smell it." Sophia's rubbed her stomach. "I'm famished. This time of year, I'm always starving. There's never enough food to satisfy me."

"This time of year? Why—" Lilah began. "Oh. Right."

Jess made a mental note to ask her later what *that* was about.

Lilah handed her a plate and motioned for her to go ahead of her. "Mom must've told them you love fish."

"I'm rather partial to freshwater fish myself," Sophia said, loading up her plate with muffins, mashed sweet potatoes, half a cow, grilled green beans, and two large pieces of the mahimahi. "But I'll eat other things when I'm desperate."

Since both Sophia and Jess were apparently hungry, the awkward conversation halted while they sat at a dining table and inhaled the delicious array of gourmet delights. Lilah only picked at hers, admitting she was too nervous to eat.

"Just wait until your honeymoon," Sophia said. "Gavin's taking you to Paris, right? I could spend months there, just eating day and night. What's your favorite café?"

"I don't have one. I've never been there before," Lilah said, smiling as she twisted the rock on her finger.

Sophia gaped at her. "What? But . . . that's impossible. How could you live this long without ever visiting Paris? Although I suppose you're a bit younger than me. I can't imagine how I'd survive without ever eating in Paris." She put her hand over Lilah's, her face twisted in genuine grief. "I'm so sorry for you."

Lilah laughed. "It's all right. I'll be there in a few days." She turned to Jess. "We'll have to plan a time for you to get over there."

"You've never been either?" Sophia's expression was a vision in horror.

"It's really expensive to fly to Europe," Jess said. "Some of us weren't born rich."

"Is that why you're sleeping with Derry?" Sophia looked down her long nose at her, lip slightly curled. "I suppose I shouldn't blame you. I've slept with worse for far less." She fell into a meditative silence, chewing the last of her sirloin. Then she looked down, saw her plate was empty, and got up with it, heading to the buffet for another mountain of food.

Jess stared at her back and wished that looks really *could* kill.

"She's actually nice," Lilah whispered.

"I've got good ears too," Sophia said, chomping on a muffin as she poured gravy over the second half of the cow.

Lilah flushed, shrugging. "We'll talk later."

While Sophia dug in to her second and then third plate of food, Lilah and Jess talked about the dress, the flowers at the rehearsal dinner, the flowers at the ceremony, the band and the musicians, the guest list, what their mother was going to wear, how beautiful the lake was out the window. This continued through dessert, a selection of assorted chocolates and gelato that had been flown in from Belgium and Italy, respectively, just that morning. It was when they were sipping their coffee that Sophia yawned loud enough to startle the waiter, who rushed over and asked if there was anything he could do for Ms. Sophia.

"I'm about to pass out, Ewan," she said, yawning again. "You know how it is."

"Abe and Don will help you get back to your cabin," Ewan said, snapping his fingers at out-of-sight minions behind him.

"Forgive me, Lilah, it was lovely." Sophia's eyelids fluttered. She barely offered Jess a glance. "But I'm falling into one hell of a food coma. Don't worry, I just need a little nap to recover."

Two large, handsome men approached the table with their

arms outstretched. Sophia fell into them with a grin, waved to Lilah and Jess, and staggered away from the table.

"She must've had way more to drink than I thought," Jess said under her breath.

But she'd forgotten about Sophia's acute senses. Twisting around to shoot her a glance over her shoulder, Sophia asked, "Derry hasn't told you much, has he?"

Pushed to her limit, Jess jumped to her feet. "What's your problem? What do you—"

"Stop. Please." Lilah pulled her back down into her seat. "Let her go. She's upset, that's all. She just needs a little time."

"She must spend a lot of time being upset if this is how she feels whenever her brother has sex with somebody, because—"

"Sophia doesn't feel this way whenever her brother has sex with somebody," Lilah said. "Only with you."

"Because I'm your sister?"

"No, I don't think so," Lilah said. "I'm just guessing, but I think she sees what I see."

Involuntarily, Jess put her hand on her neck, where the scarf had fallen down, probably exposing the constellation of hickeys. "I tried to cover it all."

"Metaphorically speaking. I know you"—Lilah scooped up a large spoonful of cherry gelato—"and she knows Derry. Which is why we're both worried."

"We're fine."

"Well," Lilah said. "*Derry* is fine. It's you everyone's worried about."

"Don't worry about me. You're getting married the day after tomorrow. You need to focus on your own issues."

"I don't have any other issues but you," Lilah said with a smile. "That's why I'm so happy."

This time, Jess expressed her annoyance. She didn't want to be anyone's project. "Congratulations."

"I can see the appeal," Lilah continued, "given his size and his charm, his skills in bed—don't look like that, I'm talking about his reputation, not firsthand experience—I can understand why you made him your first. But Jess, in all the months I've known him, I've never, ever seen him see a woman as more than a quick roll in the hay. Not once. He doesn't mean to be shallow, but—"

Jess's voice was like steel. "He's not shallow." She remembered the agony she'd felt coming off him in the forest. Derry had more depth than Gavin's pinkie finger.

No, don't think about pinkie fingers.

"I'm sure he has his moments—" Lilah began.

Jess stood up. "I'm really happy for you, I really am, but I can't talk about this with you." She gave Lilah a big hug over the coffee and leaned back, offering the nicest smile she could, even though she'd just told her to fuck off.

"You might want to keep it a secret," Lilah said. "Whatever it is you're doing with him. Sophia is a cakewalk compared to his brothers. Seriously, Jess. You really, *really* don't want Asher to find out. Take it from me. Personal experience."

"He won't find out. We'll cool it from now on," Jess said. "We haven't totally lost our minds."

"Have you lost your fucking mind?" Sophia roared, barging into Derry's cabin, interrupting him as he was buttoning up after lunch. A dreary affair it had been, sitting with Gavin and a bunch of investors in methane crystal technology and alternative energy sources. He'd stuffed himself silly on the smoked reindeer that had been flown in, then come back to his cabin for a nap that ended with a hard-on, a shower and a quick yank, and now, apparently, a lecture.

"If I have, I'm sure you'll find it. Perhaps it's with your manners?"

"You're screwing Lilah's sister? The mousy little brain?"

"Don't talk about her like that."

Hysterical, mocking laughter poured out of his twin's mouth like ribbons of cruelty. "You're hopeless."

Jess must not have heeded his warnings about perfumes and covering her scent. Then again, the way he'd ravaged her against the changing room wall an hour ago, how could she—

Damn it.

He was hard.

Again.

"Derry, you might as well bathe in her quim juices."

He started at the old-fashioned word. Asher used it from time to time when he was at the Novo Club, on those rare occasions he allowed himself a third whisky. Such an antiquated term for a woman. A sense of dread filled him.

"You're beyond obvious. Asher is going to kill you," Sophia said with a sneer.

And there it was.

"Asher doesn't need to know. He has the worst sense of smell of all of us."

"Listen to yourself!" Accustomed to having her rants accommodated by three other brothers who found their little sister "cute," Sophia had never quite dropped her belief that Derry, too, would humor her someday. "You aren't even trying to deny it."

"With you? Of course not."

"And when you're done with her? You'll ruin the family. Gavin will hate you forever. Lilah is a marshmallow who has a steel backbone when it comes to The Brain."

"The *what?*"

She waved a dismissive hand. "Her. Jess. Your magic pussy."

Derry clutched his sister's wrist in his hand, unaware he'd crossed the room, his nose inches from hers, temper at the ready.

"You will not speak of her like this."

Sophia had never been intimidated by him. If anything, being the only girl in a gaggle of boys had made her a fierce woman, willing to go toe-to-toe, or nose-to-nose, in an argument.

"You reek of her." Her chin jutted up in defiance.

"So what?"

"And *only* her." A tone of despair tinged her words, those eyes so much like his going wide until the irises no longer touched her eyelids, pure white encircling the brown.

In opposition, his own eyes narrowed as he took in her words.

And then he snorted with incredulous disgust, dropping her arm.

"You're berating me for sleeping with only one woman?"

"You've gone *monogamous*, Derry!" Sophia spat out the word like she'd discovered he was a serial killer who cooked live babies and fed them to Buddhist monks. "I can't let you do this to yourself!"

"What?" His voice rose an octave.

Sophia sniffed him, circling around him, taking her time. "Normally you smell like so many different women I can't tell them apart after a while. I've identified some standard threesome scents."

"You've—huh?" His words devolved into grunts. He was speechless. This was new territory with his sister. While he, too, could smell various men on her, he'd never taken inventory. Never cataloged them. Never given them names, like a botanist identifying genus and species.

"You're so . . . flat. Dead. My nose finds you so boring now. One scent. One!"

"You realize that where I stick my cock is absolutely, positively none of your business."

"It's my business when I am watching you ruin your life!"

"I'm ruining my life by spending less than twenty-four hours sleeping with the same woman?"

"Lilah can tell the difference, too." Sophia said this with the declarative air of a woman using her final option to negotiate.

"Lilah knows?" His throat went dry. Fuck. That meant Gavin knew, or would.

Soon.

Sophia rolled her wide eyes. "Of course. She's become one of us. Plus, she's The Brain's sister. She figured it out quickly."

At least Sophia wasn't using the term Magic Pussy, even if he had to admit it held a certain charm.

And truth.

He looked down and saw to the final button on his shirt, finished dressing, and tucked his shirttails into his waist. The casual gestures didn't bother Sophia, who had seen him in every state of dress and undress. As shifters, being nude was the norm half the time. In human form, though, she conformed to societal standards.

As he buckled his belt and threw a tie around his neck, she paced, her long legs eating the floor, thick, dark hair wild and untamed around her agitated face. Then she halted before him, grabbing each end of the loose tie, and tied it for him.

He half thought she only did it for the opportunity to legally strangle him, even if only for a few moments as she tightened, then loosened, the noose.

"Our kind is not meant to be monogamous," she declared.

"Some of us do find the One," he said slowly. "Look at Gavin. That means we pick one and stick with one."

"Gavin is a wolf! We're bears! We don't mate for life, Derry. When it's my time for breeding, I'll go out and find as many men as I can . . ." Her eyes went dreamy at the thought. "And you are supposed to spread your seed."

He twitched slightly, not exactly enamored with hearing his sister talk about her sex life and most certainly not about his seed.

"We are part human," he pointed out. "They tend to be monogamous." Why was he so defensive? He wanted this conversation to end.

Time to end it.

"But the human side of us doesn't have to be so . . . staid. Sad. Depressing. Once you pick just one, all the variety is gone. Then you might as well cut off your dick and become Asher."

The comment jarred him. "Asher cut off his . . . ?" He cocked his head to the side and peered at her, waiting for a satisfactory answer.

"I was speaking metaphorically."

"Thank God." He breathed a sigh of relief.

"Asher has spent his best years pining away for the One. Once you pick a 'one,' that's it. You're toast. As in, all you get is toast. One kind of toast. The same kind, over and over, forever and ever, and—"

This conversation felt familiar. He frowned. Why?

Oh. Yes. Because he'd berated Gavin in exactly the same way just a few months ago.

Ah, karma.

His stomach growled. "Speaking of toast."

Her stomach growled back. "Yes?"

"There must be a ridiculously overattended reception somewhere on the ranch. With food. And minimal conversation."

She smiled. "Two out of three, yes. I'm afraid the conversation is what you have to suffer in order to stuff yourself."

The storm had moved on. Hot tempers, the both of them—but they always cooled off quickly. With the deep understanding that came from being womb mates, they left Derry's cabin and went out in search of food.

The place was filled with people Derry didn't recognize, mostly businessmen from Gavin's extensive circle of associates. A handful of wealthy, old-school shifter family members were here. He saw a Rosini jaguar shifter, and good old Ragnar Jensen and his sons, with their fine, aquiline noses—all male, of course, for that bloodline had not produced a female in five generations, a running joke in the shifter world. Gavin had invited very few shifters, and Derry knew why.

Lilah. Gavin was protecting her from undue scrutiny, preserving the sanctity of their special day.

It was cute.

But Gavin couldn't hide her forever.

His mind created a map of personalities and families in the crowd, a kind of sorting that started with shifter or non-shifter, then known or unknown, and finally—male or female.

As a waiter offered bacon-wrapped scallops with lavender sprigs and lemon zest, he took five in a row, barely chewing, just hungry enough to register the bloom of flavor on his tongue. As he waved the young man off with an empty tray, he searched the room with a scanning precision, an involuntary reflex that kicked in before his conscious mind recognized it.

Fuckability.

Who, in the room, could he seduce?

As he looked around, observing and calculating, something was off. Different. Strange and unnerving.

He was not attracted to a single woman in the room, and by his quick count, there were forty-seven present.

The odds of not being attracted to at least one woman out of forty-seven were about as likely as choosing Boone's Strawberry Wine over Screaming Eagle Cabernet Sauvignon.

His brow creased.

"Fish taco, sir?" asked a barely legal, leggy blonde waitress with tits like cream puffs and skin like velvet. Big, bright green eyes framed by long, black, gleaming lashes met his, her flirtation obvious.

He took one, and as he put it in his mouth in one bite, the flavor turned from a burst of savory to the bitterness of confusion. His eyes zeroed in on her high, round rack, and he willed himself to feel . . . something.

Anything.

He was dead below the waist.

"You like the taste of fish?" she tried again. Derry just cocked an eyebrow, an anemic laugh escaping between his lips, his look chasing her off. Sophia was in a corner by the bar, a crowd of three men surrounding her. He scanned the room again. Eleven of the women were old bedmates, so this wasn't a stale room for him. Once, he'd been at a party and realized there wasn't a single piece of fresh meat among the female attendees.

Out of twenty-three women.

But here? This was . . . What was going on? It wasn't as if he were going to sleep with anyone other than Jess.

Jess.

As her name ripped through his mind, his blood began to race, then pool quite neatly, filling him with an engorgement that made him flex his thigh muscles in a feeble attempt to adjust himself without the vulgar display of reaching down and moving his erection into a more comfortable arrangement.

It wasn't quite the Beat of shifter lore, but it was damn close.

The most comfortable arrangement for his cock, though, wasn't in his pants.

It was buried deep inside her hot, tight, curvaceous body.

He had to find her.

Marching past the throngs of women who once had been colorful and delicious, their scents like ripe fruit begging to be plucked and devoured, he found them gray and dismal, no more interesting than a pile of gravel.

Her.

He had to have her.

Now.

Again.

Forever.

Sixteen

J ess stole one of her mother's french fries and popped it in her
mouth. Marilyn Murphy had arrived just a couple of hours
earlier and was enjoying a quiet evening in her private quar-
ters near the pool, just a short walk from Jess, with a massage
and room service.

Naturally, the Stantons had an on-site, full-time massage ther-
apist. And although Marilyn wasn't a health nut—she was eating a
bacon cheeseburger and fries with a tumbler of grape Fanta—she
did like a nice back rub. With Jess's encouragement, Marilyn had
typed in the number in the phone by the bed, and handsome Ron
had appeared in a black sweat suit with a folded massage table
under his arm. Now, an hour later, he was just packing it up as
the food arrived.

"Are you sure you wouldn't like a session, Ms. Murphy?" he
asked Jess.

She could only imagine how he and her mother would react
to the signs of wild lovemaking on her body. "I'm sure. Thanks."

"Call me anytime," he said. "That's what I'm here for."

Jess saw him out and went back to the table to steal another fry.

"Why didn't you order your own food?" Marilyn wore her
yellow bathrobe from home, an ancient fleece thing from T.J.

Maxx that needed to be retired to the great rag pile in the sky.

Making a mental note to get her a new one for Christmas, Jess turned her gaze to the burger, which smelled incredible. "I did. I don't know why I'm so hungry." She had a suspicion that the marathon sex burned a lot of calories.

"Do you think they'd mind if we asked for more?" Marilyn licked her fingers. "This is a really good burger. I don't want to share."

"Mind? Are you kidding? They've got more money than God. It makes them feel good to use it."

With a happy sigh, Marilyn took another bite. "And to think Lilah is marrying into all of this. I just can't believe it."

Jess sipped the grape soda. Their mother had no idea just how much her daughter was marrying into. "I know, right?"

"I was thinking, sweetie. This would be a great place to meet somebody."

Inhaling suddenly, Jess accidentally snorted soda into her nose. Her mother had always felt bad about not giving them as much as she'd like, and a few dozen rich, single men must look like a bonanza of opportunity. "No. It isn't," Jess said. "Lots of these guys are members at the club. And I hate rich guys."

"You don't hate Gavin, surely."

"No, he's great. He's different." And so was Derry.

"So, there are other men that are different. You just have to search for them. Don't be so quick to dismiss people based on their looks. You can't judge a book by its cover, that's what I always say."

You can't judge this family by its cover, that's for sure, Jess thought. You might miss the detail about them being shape-shifters.

For the first time, it occurred to her that the Stantons might not be the only family like it.

The thought struck her like a baseball bat to the head. Why hadn't she thought about it before? If one family could have shifters, there must be others. And it would be natural for them to know each other, seek out each other socially, professionally, perhaps even marry each other.

In fact, the Platinum Club might be just the kind of place where a secret society could form, where supernatural beings could meet and congregate with some protection from outside exposure.

Who else was a shifter? Was Eva? Sweet, lonely Molly? Carl? Her mind spun.

"Are you all right, dear?" her mother asked. "You look funny. Did you get enough sleep last night?"

"I slept all afternoon, actually." After lunch, she'd crawled into bed for a nap, only waking when her mother arrived.

The hours apart from Derry were like a century of solitary confinement in the deepest cell of a medieval dungeon.

Well, she thought, stealing yet another french fry, perhaps that was a slight overstatement. But her body felt that way, tingling all over, cold then hot, itchy, restless. Diagnosis: sex fiend. If she concentrated, she could feel Derry moving around the house, as unsettled as she was.

Marilyn reached across the table and put a hand on her forehead. "Maybe you're sick."

Jess started to disagree, nudging her mother's hand away, but realized it gave her the excuse she needed. Feigning a yawn, she wiped her greasy fingers on her mom's napkin and got to her feet. "Maybe you're right. I should go back to bed so I'm feeling good for the bachelorette party and rehearsal and everything."

"I think that would be a good idea. Your face is definitely flushed."

"Is it?" Jess lifted her hands to her cheeks. "You'll be all right without me tonight?"

"Absolutely. I told Lilah I'd rather rest in my room tonight. She tried to get me to join that big party out there, as if I could relax with all those rich and famous people."

"But that's just what you want me to do," Jess said, exasperated. "You're single."

"So are you," Jess shot back.

"And lonely. Don't argue, I've always seen it, and it breaks my heart," Marilyn said.

Mom was right. Jess felt extremely lonely. Painfully, breathlessly, unbearably lonely.

Where are you?

She heard the words in her mind, not knowing if they were hers or Derry's.

Come to me.

It was Derry.

"Good night, Mom." In a daze, she kissed her mom's cheek and moved to the door. "See you in the morning." If Marilyn said anything else, she didn't hear it. Her feet were moving automatically, propelling her out the door into the open courtyard that led to the wing that held her own bedroom, through a hallway she'd never been in before, into a full commercial kitchen—she waved hello to a dozen white-coated staff—but didn't slow down until she was standing outside in a covered driveway.

Come to me.

Shivering in the cold, she looked down at herself and realized she was barefoot, wearing only the T-shirt and yoga pants she'd slept in that afternoon. But the voice was coming from up ahead, down the drive in one of the large, semidetached garages. Going back for a jacket or a cocktail dress or sexy lingerie was out of the question. She had to continue. Nipples puckering in the chill, she jogged out into the driveway, rising on tiptoe when bits of gravel and ice dug into her heels. A snowflake landed on her cheek, sizzling as it melted.

She paused at the first garage, but it wasn't the right one. The feeling was coming from the next one.

Come to me, said the voice.

"I'm coming," she whispered, walking around the side of the next garage to a small door. To her frustration, the doorknob didn't turn. The delay felt like a tragedy she'd never survive. Heart racing, she knocked on the door, tentatively at first, then banging with all her strength.

The door swung open, and a massive figure swept her off her feet. "What took you so long?" he asked, his deep voice setting her on fire. Crushing his mouth against hers, he carried her into the garage, kicking the door shut, enclosing them inside the dark, quiet space. Before she could draw a second breath, he was pushing her against the door and she was lifting her legs to straddle his hips. They greeted each other with sighs, moans, caresses, tangled tongues, fumbling hands.

"Jess, I can't stop—I want you. I want you." He kept saying those words over and over, against her ears, her throat, her mouth.

"I heard you," she gasped. "I felt you."

He pushed the hard bulge under his trousers into her pelvis. "Feel me?"

"Not enough." She reached down to unbuckle his belt, unbutton his pants, unzip his fly, free his cock—so many damn steps, and she was coming at it from a bad angle—but he stopped her and set her gently on the floor.

"Good," she said, lunging for his belt. "Now I can reach you better."

"Easy, love. I have an idea." He took her hand in his, brought it to his lips, tongue tracing her knuckles in that way that drove her crazy, and pulled her through the dark garage. She bumped into something hard and, reaching down, felt a canvas cover over what she assumed was a car, but it seemed lumpy and small for that.

"Ow," she said, rubbing her shin.

"Sorry." He reached up and pulled a chain for a bulb on the ceiling, lighting the cavernous garage in a faint yellow glow. "I forget you can't see the way I can."

Around them, vehicles slept under white covers.

"Asher's collection," Derry said. "That car there is older than I am."

Lots of cars were older than they were. Just how old was he?

Later, she told herself, she'd wonder why he'd said that. Later. She put her hands on his belly and slid them around to his back, tugging his shirttails out of his trousers, all conscious thought falling away. His skin was warm, so warm. And she loved the curls, the way they felt springy under her palms, her cheek, her lips.

"Not here," Derry said, kissing her as he captured her hands. "You called me here."

"Just over there." His palm came up behind the back of her neck, stroking her nape, digging into her hair. He stopped and bent down to kiss her. "Or here is good."

"No, you're too tall. Is there somewhere we can get horizontal?"

"Too tall?" He recoiled, sounding wounded.

Smiling, she stroked his hard cock through the wool of his trousers. "For what I want to do."

"I'm too tall. Or too short. Depends how you look at it."

She rubbed harder. "Where?"

"The big one," he gasped.

"It really is. I don't understand how it fits, honestly."

He looked down at her with a grin. "I meant the Rolls. Come on." Hooking an arm around her waist, he led her over to the longest vehicle, then released her just long enough to tear off the cover. Stretching out in front of them was the type of car she'd only seen in old movies, the kind of luxury automobile that was designed for a man with a chauffeur and a fortune in early twentieth-century British pounds.

"What is it?"

Derry reached in and opened the door. "Rolls-Royce Phantom. Asher brought it over from England ages ago. Do you like it?"

Sighing, she came up behind him and, pressing her breasts into his back, reached around and stroked his abs. "I like this."

He climbed into the backseat, having to fold in the middle like Ron's massage table to fit inside. "I remember it being bigger than this. I must've been a cu—child the last time I was in here."

She crawled in after him, stroking the cheeks of his ass as he bent over. "We'll make it work." She slid her hands between his legs from behind and tickled his balls.

With a cry, he fell onto the leather seat and pulled her on top of him. "Twenty-four hours ago, you never would've dared to do that," he said, palming her breasts under her T-shirt, his voice lowering to a growl when he discovered she wasn't wearing a bra. He swept the shirt over her head, then pulled her down to suckle her breast.

Fire shot through her from nipple to clit, making her too clumsy to manage his pants. She arched her back and rode him, the top of her head brushing the car's ceiling, wriggling her pants and panties over her hips and off, to invite him inside, flinging the clothes over the edge of the car.

His hands pushed between their hips and just as swiftly fit them together.

He entered her with a shout. Filled, stretching with him inside her, Jess dug her fingernails into his shoulders and bore down harder, deliciously painful, terribly satisfying, she invited him in deeper and deeper.

The ecstasy began to build in a familiar way, like when she was alone but harder, softer, faster, more, and she let go of the last fragments of her self-consciousness and began vocalizing with wild abandon, squealing louder and louder with each thrust.

"What the hell are you doing in Asher's car?"

The unfamiliar voice, so male and so angry, snapped her out of her madness. She looked up and saw a long, bearded face with angry green eyes glaring at them through the back window.

Derry pulled her down and rolled her under him, crouching over her body to shield her as he looked up. "For fuck's sake, Edward, would you give us some privacy!" he shouted.

Of all the times for his own brother to find him and Jess *in flagrante delicto*.

And he hadn't even come yet. So close, and yet . . . so far.

So very, painfully, blue-ballishly far.

"Derry?" Edward sounded so scandalized he began to laugh, which only increased the look of mortification on poor Jessica's face. "You're having one of your orgies in the garage? In the Rolls?"

He abruptly stopped, the chuckles dead in his chest as Jess's expression hardened, then tightened.

"He doesn't know," Derry murmured to him. "He has no idea there's only you."

Her look of deep skepticism made his heart physically hurt.

"And there is only you," he whispered, kissing her cheek.

She gave him a weak smile.

"I am not having an orgy!" Derry shouted to Edward. "And do you mind? We're naked."

"I see that. I don't *want* to see that, but I do."

"Then turn around and have some decency!"

Edward pitched Derry's clothes at him through the tiny window.

"Get dressed. Asher is going to kill you. I hope you didn't stain the leather."

"Oh, good God, Edward. Don't talk about issues in which you have no interest."

The angry flush in Edward's bare cheeks above the neatly trimmed beard made Derry feel some sense of satisfaction. The youngest of the Stanton family, and the only mountain lion shifter, Edward lived in solitary misery. At least that was how Derry assumed it must feel. Derry felt a sting of regret as he watched Edward lose his composure, turning away to gather himself. Only last year, in a rare moment of drunkenness, his young brother had admitted to being celibate. Edward had refused to explain why he had chosen to live such a perverted lifestyle.

Derry had sworn to himself not to use that against him.

Then again, that orgy comment wasn't exactly fair, either.

"I'll be back," Derry murmured to Jess, whose face had gone blank as she disguised her emotions. Shielding her from view, he backed out of the car and faced Edward. They weren't eye to eye, for Edward was smaller, but he was whip-strong, muscles forged by years of mountain firefighting.

Derry painfully tucked his shirt in, avoiding brushing against various swollen parts. "Care to explain why you're barging in on me in an intimate moment?"

Edward pointed to his motorcycle, a vintage Norton he treated like the girlfriend he didn't have. "I was fixing a spark plug. I assure you, I never expected to come in here and find you in the middle of fireworks."

Derry's eye roll was as menacing as possible. Edward was not intimidated.

"Only one?" Edward said in a soft, cultured voice. All the Stanton children had been raised by British nannies in the States before being sent to England for boarding school, even Edward, whose mother had wanted to keep him in America. She had died while he was abroad, a devastating loss that had brought Edward home early to finish school in the States. Perhaps because of this, his British accent was lighter than the rest of the Stanton siblings, yet he carried himself with an old-fashioned formality more in keeping with Asher's personality.

"My sex life is none of your business."

"Your love life is quite often covered by no fewer than two hundred media outlets after a particularly spectacular playboy moment, Derry," Edward said with a wry grin. He worried his hands, rubbing them, the only sign of nervousness.

"No more."

Jess scrambled out of the Rolls, showing more leg than Derry liked Edward to see, her T-shirt her only garment. Glittering green eyes took her in, Edward's obvious appraisal of her concluding with approval.

A green flame roared inside Derry.

"Here," Edward said, bending down to retrieve her pants and panties, handing them to her with a respectful modesty that even Derry could sense. As Jess grabbed them, Derry noticed how soaked the panties were.

He bit back a self-congratulatory chuckle.

"You can leave now," he said coldly to Edward, reaching for his forearm and pulling him a few feet from Jess, who was hobbling on one foot in an effort to finish dressing.

"I can't leave my bike in that shape!" Edward argued, looking pointedly over Derry's shoulder. He turned and followed Edward's gaze.

The bike was partly dismantled. Derry felt a strange oily sensation on his palm and looked down to find Edward's wrist covered with streaks of grease.

"We haven't met yet," Jess said, suddenly at his side. Her hand outstretched for a social nicety, she tried to shake Edward's hand. "I'm Jess Murphy. Lilah's sister."

Edward's eyes went anywhere but on her as he shook her hand and mumbled, "Nice to meet you. I'm Edward."

Derry's nose shifted into overdrive, picking up on subtexts only scent could communicate. Jess was horrified. Edward was mildly aroused, but then again, he'd been sexually starving himself for God knew how long—he would be. Some other element lingered beneath the surface, a dull sort of dread that Derry could not identify.

"You don't look like Derry," Jess said, tilting her head to one side, studying Edward's face.

Floom! There went the green flame.

Wrapping his arm around Jess's shoulders in a gesture that went far beyond an animal's claim, Derry gave Edward an unequivocal look.

Mine.

Don't even fucking think about it.

Edward's eyes flashed, the same color as Derry's jealousy, and then the flame extinguished.

"We're half-siblings," Edward explained, his voice controlled now, his standoffish personality kicking in. "We share the same father."

"Is that why you look so different?" Jess replied with a smile. She hugged Derry as if the three of them were at a church potluck, making conversation. "And are you a bear, too?"

All sense of composure drained out of Edward as if he'd been exsanguinated.

Derry felt his body tense, primed and coiled for some fight he couldn't understand, yet felt coming. The fact that his balls ached and throbbed, begging for release, didn't help either.

Absolute horror poured blood back into Edward's skin, making him redden and pale at the same time, a strange paradox that Derry could not reconcile. He continued to stare at Jess, but his words were for Derry. "You, you . . . you told her?"

"It's a long story."

Edward finally turned to look at Derry, eyes dark and bleak. "Asher really *is* going to kill you."

Seventeen

J ess let Derry escort her out of the garage into the dark, cold night. Wearing only the T-shirt and yoga pants, she felt naked and vulnerable. Unseemly. Her bare breasts were tingling from foreplay and eager for more, but she stopped him when they reached the door to the kitchen. There she slid her hand out of his grasp and turned to face him under the house lights. "We've been really stupid. We have to stop." Edward's words about Asher had upset her even more than the look on his face when he'd caught her screaming and naked on top of his brother's cock.

"Stop?" Derry asked sharply. In his expensive dress shirt and dark wool trousers, he didn't look unseemly at all, although he was a little rumpled. Deliciously so.

But she would have to be strong for both of them. "The stupid has to stop," she said.

"Perhaps you could do me the favor of being more specific."

The house lights were behind him, so she couldn't see his expression clearly, but she heard the tension in his voice. "We have to be more discreet. We can't keep having sex all over the place."

A smile crept into his voice. "But we can keep having sex in some places."

God help her, she wasn't willing to give that up. To wait so long and then have to stop after her first day of having a sex life—no. "Private places."

"I love private places." He palmed her breast, kneading it, stroking her nipple.

She smacked his hand away and gestured at the outdoor floodlights shining from each corner of the house. "This isn't private. There are probably security cameras recording us right this minute."

"No. Not at a Stanton property. Never."

Stepping out of groping range, she crossed her arms over her chest, vowing to never walk out of her room without a bra ever again. "I thought rich people loved surveillance."

"But shifters don't."

Of course, that would make one hell of a viral video. "All right, but somebody could see us. There are dozens of guests milling about."

"I'll come to your room," he said.

"No, you can't. I'm sorry, Derry, but we have to get ahold of ourselves." When he lunged for her again, she hopped away. "Not that kind of holding. Listen, my mother might come by. Servants are everywhere. Somebody would see you. You're pretty hard to miss."

"Would you not miss me, lovely Jess?"

"I'd miss you like crazy," she said with a sigh. "But I don't want you to get in trouble with that brother of yours that everyone's so afraid of. Asher. Edward was really worried for you. Even Lilah warned me about him."

Derry ducked his head and mumbled, "It would be preferable to keep our activities unknown to my eldest sibling."

"Why? What can he do?"

"Come to think if it, I believe you're right. This isn't a safe place for us to congregate," he said, gesturing to the door to the kitchen. "You go on ahead, pretend you were searching for a glass of milk and a bowl of cookies, just a little midnight snack, and retire to your room."

So he didn't want to talk about Asher. She'd find a better time to make him open up. "People don't usually eat entire bowls of cookies," she said, smiling.

"I'm not like other people. Hadn't you noticed?" His fingers brushed across her nipple in a good-bye grope as he strode away.

After a moment to catch her breath, Jess opened the door and slipped inside, took his advice about the milk and cookies, and retreated to her room, frustrated and alone. The urge to chase Derry down, wherever he was, was so powerful she had to curl up in a ball in bed and force herself to remember the moment in the Rolls when she'd looked up, mid-squeal, and seen Edward's shocked face.

The stupid had to stop.

Stop the stupid.

They could wait a few days until they were back in Boston to enjoy themselves. There they could find privacy, anonymity, king-size beds, and long nights without interruption. She imagined his apartment must be huge and opulent, the opposite of hers. The faucets probably didn't drip, and the windows didn't need a stick to prop open in the summer. The appliances would be from her lifetime, and she didn't need to guess that he wouldn't have to fight junkies off while keying into her foyer.

They could wait.

If their relationship lasted that long . . .

It was still dark when she woke in a cold sweat. Heart pounding, she squinted at the clock on the nightstand.

Just after five. Too early to have breakfast, too late to go back to sleep.

What had she been dreaming? She felt terrible, like her bones had frozen. She couldn't stop shivering. On the window she heard hard rain tapping the glass. Wrapping a quilt around her shoulders, she got out of bed and walked over to look outside. It wasn't rain, it was sleet. No wonder she was cold. Hours ago, when she hadn't been able to sleep because she was burning with lust again, she'd turned down the thermostat.

Her breath fogged the glass. Winter was coming. She pressed her fingertip to the window and drew a heart. When she began to write two pair of initials with a plus sign between them, she wiped it away abruptly and turned her back to the window.

Stop the stupid.

A fragment of her dream came back to her. She'd been naked at the club again, serving drinks to a jeering crowd. Had Derry been there? She couldn't remember and, if he had been there, didn't want to.

Dropping the quilt on a chair, she went into the bathroom and tried to shake off the lingering bad feelings. If she could just get warm . . . She knew who could warm her up real good, but she'd turned over a new leaf, like a New Year's resolution, and she wasn't going to cave in so quickly.

She remembered the sauna Lilah had told her about, next to the outdoor pool. Apparently, when they were much younger, the two eldest Stanton brothers had enjoyed jumping into the lake in February—through a hole in the ice—after heating up in the sauna.

It had been years since she'd sat in a sauna. This was the perfect morning for it, an ideal setting. She pulled on a swimsuit, sweats, and her parka, and went out to look for it, exploring through the empty halls, seeing herself reflected in the glass doors as she walked out onto the back landing and down the steps to the pool.

At the path that led around the lake, she paused, tempted, so tempted, to turn left, to find the old stairs up into the woods and surprise Derry with breakfast in bed. That's what she'd say, flinging off her clothes and jumping on top of him, that she was his to consume, his to devour.

She took several steps in his direction before sanity returned. Her phone, with its built-in flashlight, was sitting in her room; for her to stumble around in the freezing predawn would not only be unpleasant, but might attract unwanted attention when she got lost or tripped in the dark and almost killed herself.

With a long sigh, she pivoted on her heel and marched to the pool. A floodlight shining from the main house illuminated the tendrils of steam rising up from the surface, telling her that the water, in spite of the sleet, was heated and ready for use.

The sauna was what she needed right now. She walked through a gate to the pool deck and maneuvered around lounge chairs to the small building at the end. Next to a dial and thermostat was a bulky wood door. She pulled it open a crack and felt a rush of heat. If there was a light, she couldn't find it; after a minute of fruitless searching, she tore off her clothes, huffing in the cold, and scurried blind into the hot room, pulling the door shut behind her.

Dry heat stabbed her lungs, making her gasp. Coals glowed in a grate in one corner, faintly lighting a few feet around it. Fumbling in the shadows, she spread out her towel on the lower bench at the wall farthest from the door, not sure why her pulse was racing. Must be the sudden rise in temperature. She was having trouble catching a full breath.

"I can't tell you how pleased I am to learn this is a private place," Derry's voice whispered in her ear.

She screamed and jumped to her feet. "Derry!" She pressed her hand over her pounding heart. He'd been lying on the higher bench right behind her. "What are you doing here?"

"Me? I would ask you the same thing, except my manners forbid it." He sat up and grinned, his white teeth reflecting the glow from the coals.

"How did you know I was here? I mean, how did you know

I was going to come here?"

"I didn't. Or, rather, I knew it the way I know everything about you."

"Which is how?"

"I have no idea, but I'm rather learning to enjoy it." He patted the wooden bench next to him. "Have a seat."

"I can't. We'll start fooling around. You know we will." The heat was making it hard to breathe. Whatever chill she'd had earlier was long gone. "I'll go back to my room."

He stood. Only now did she see he was completely naked. And erect. "I'll join you."

"Not like that, you won't," she said, waving at his erection.

His voice dropped. "You could help me get rid of it first." While she stared, praying for willpower, he took his cock in hand and began slowly pumping, never moving his gaze away from hers. "Have you ever watched a man pleasure himself?"

"The entire history of the world is men pleasuring themselves." It would've been a more effective put-down if she hadn't sounded like a flirtatious bimbo as she'd said it, all squeaky and breathless.

He strode over to the door and flicked on a light. "There. Now you can see everything." Leaning back against the bench, he stroked faster, watching her. His cock swelled hard and long in his hand, which was quite nice, but it was the hungry look in his eye that made her grab a bottle of water she'd seen on the bench and pour it over her head.

It dripped down her cheeks and soaked her breasts through her bikini top, bringing a second of relief. Even hot water was cooler than her flesh.

"I should complain about your wasting the refreshments that I brought, but it looks much better on you than it would've tasted in me." His gaze dropped to her chest, where her aching nipples were pressing through the wet nylon of her suit. "Looking at you makes me so hard, Jess. See what you do to me? This is for you.

This is because of you."

His heavily muscled physique flexed with each stroke of his hand. Mouth falling open, he stared at her under heavy lids as he squeezed and pumped, moving harder and faster.

She was going to combust. Right now, right here, she was going to burst into flames. An hour ago she was freezing, and now she was burning.

With more self-control than she'd ever thought possible, she turned, opened the door, and fled out into the dawn. The first dim light of day shimmered on the far surface of the lake, though the shore closer to them was still shadowed by the house. The freezing rain had stopped, but the sky was still a cool gray.

Not cool enough. Jess jogged past the deck chairs, down the stairs to the path, and then over the lawn to the lake. Not stopping, she charged ahead until she was submerged up to her waist, gasping as the cold water surrounded her skin and tried to turn her blood to ice.

Just as she was about to crawl back out onto dry land and save herself, she saw Derry's naked figure running across the lawn, headed at full speed directly toward her.

She stopped moving, paralyzed by the sight of him. Ancient gay Olympians would've passed out in awe. He was magnificent.

No! She couldn't let this happen. Here they were even more exposed than before. Without giving herself time to think—a familiar problem lately—she sucked in a breath and fully submerged herself. If icy water didn't knock some sense into her, nothing would.

The cold struck her with such force, she wondered if she'd die before she could learn some self-control. She'd never realized how *painful* water could be. It was like being in space. Not that she knew what it was like to be in space, since she wasn't an astronaut, although wouldn't that be awesome? Being in space? Better than here in this lake which was making her feel very weird, like she was awake and asleep at the same time.

Somebody was lifting her out of the water. And then it was even colder, because air was slapping at her bare arms and shoulders and everywhere she had a body.

"Jess, talk to me. Are you all right?" Derry was holding her. He was like a giant hot water bottle.

Clinging to him, she tried to speak through her chattering teeth. "T-t-t-t-owel?"

"Why'd you do that? You could give yourself a heart attack doing that." He sounded furious. His grip on her arms as he rubbed her was a little too rough, although she appreciated the friction.

"What the hell is going on?" another man's voice cried. "Derry, by all that is holy, why are you trying to drown the maid of honor? And why are you *naked?*"

Eighteen

Did his siblings have a secret schedule of some sort, a rotation for making certain to walk in on him while he was having sex with Jess? Not one to believe in conspiracy theories by nature, Derry was increasingly suspicious about the string of coincidences that continued to interrupt this budding romance.

Plus, those blue balls hadn't been blue because of the cold.

"I'm rescuing her, you idiot!" he screamed at Gavin, lifting Jess over one shoulder like a sack of rice and marching out of the water, completely unfazed by Gavin's look of rage-filled horror.

"Put me down!" Jess shouted, pounding his back with her cute little ineffective punches. She might as well pelt him with marshmallows.

Without a word to either of them, he stormed back up the snow-speckled lawn, up the stairs, and over to the pool deck, dropping Jess into the water like a child finding the perfect rock to plunk into a river, delighted by the sound. Compared to the lake, the heated pool felt like bathwater.

She shot back up by pushing her feet against the pool's bottom, her face rocketing to the surface with a blustery sputter, and gasped, "You asshole!"

"At least she has some sense of perspective left," Gavin growled from behind Derry.

And then a mighty shove in the middle of his back—and it had to be mighty, to move a man Derry's size—catapulted him right into the water next to her. Pivoting midair to see what had hit him, he watched Gavin lower his leg just before sinking below the water. Hah. He knew his brother took martial arts, but . . .

Jess was treading water a few feet from him when he popped over the water's edge, his own limbs instinctively mimicking hers.

"If you two are going to rut like animals, at least have the decency to do it indoors," Gavin said in a low, threatening voice that made Jess's eyes widen with fear, but Derry just laughed.

"We can't rut anywhere at all, Gavin. Between Sophia and Edward and now you, my own siblings have nicely subverted my sex life. How much is Asher paying you?"

Gavin's eyebrows drew together like two battle-axes over glowing sapphires. "Consider yourself fortunate that Asher has no idea about any of this." He waved his hand toward Jess with a dismissiveness that made Derry's nostrils flare. "You were told she's off limits. And now you're fucking her in public and running around naked on the ranch, with hundreds of guests here? Derry, what on earth are you—"

Derry opened his mouth to reply, but Jess beat him to it.

"Off limits!" Jess made her way to the edge of the pool and pulled herself out, the movement so sleek and athletic, his view of her ample, shapely ass only making his cock harder, damn it.

She wiped the pool water from her face and walked up to Gavin, stopping two feet away, looking up. Planting her hands on her barely-clad hips, she tightened her face and squared off against Gavin.

"You don't get to dictate what anyone can and cannot do with me!" Her slow cadence, the steel behind her words, made Derry's stomach drop slightly.

Gavin paled but did not break eye contact with her. Didn't blink. He remained impassive, his face as frozen as a stone gargoyle's.

"I am my own person. Derry is his own person. My sister may be marrying you, and you are about to become my brother-in-law, but that does not make you my keeper!"

Derry's heart split into two hands and applauded.

"If telling him—or anyone, for that matter—that I am off limits is a reflection of some sick, perverted idea of yours about your role in my life, then wipe it out. Now. You have zero control over what I do, Gavin."

Derry snickered at the word "perverted," the sound making Gavin squint one eye at him, the gesture familiar. In childhood, it had meant he was going to get a thrashing later from his displeased big brother.

Who knew what it meant in adulthood, but whatever it was wouldn't be good.

"And you!" She turned and pointed at Derry, who felt the full force of her self-righteous rage like she was holding a fire hose aimed at his face. "You think you can just waltz into my life and take my virginity and—"

"WHAT?" Gavin finally spoke. This time it was Derry who felt all the blood rush out of his face. Oh God. What was she going to say next?

"—and not tell your family what's going on? I told Lilah about us, Derry, and she—"

"You told Lilah? Lilah's known about you two?" Gavin's incredulity made it abundantly clear that his anger and shock over finding them in the lake in various stages of undress had been genuine. He'd had no idea. Derry had wanted to keep it that way.

"Yes," Jess said, continuing her tirade, her ire focused once again on Derry, who looked at her and just took it. "But you're slinking around, angry when Sophia figured it out by smell, and when Edward found us making love in Asher's car, and—"

"You had sex in Asher's Phantom?" Gavin roared. "By God, Derry, you're a dead man!"

"Would you stop interrupting me?" Jess screamed at Gavin, now in his face, finger wagging, her normally feminine voice now low and so menacing it sounded almost demonic.

Even Gavin shrank back, however slightly.

"What is going on?" interrupted another female voice. Long, silky blonde waves caught the pool lights as Lilah appeared, wearing a parka and suede boots, entering the situation with an iron rod in her backbone and looks that could kill. "You're making a huge scene. Eva texted me and—"

Gavin whipped around, aggressive in his stance, curling his body around hers with a sneer that made Derry recoil. "You knew Derry was fucking your sister and didn't tell me?"

"What the hell does that have to do with anything?" Jess said, inserting herself physically between the two, her protective stance evident. Derry watched with a morbid fascination as he realized that while Lilah may be the big sister in the family, Jess was overpowering instinct right now.

She was defying the laws of animal behavior.

And taking on his big brother, Gavin.

"Enough!" Derry leapt out of the water and grabbed Gavin's arm, turning him away from the women. Lilah gasped as she took in his state of undress. Either that, or his cock was so enormous she couldn't help but react. He rather liked the idea of the latter.

"I can sleep with whomever I choose," he said.

"We all know that," Gavin said with a sneer.

"And so can I!" Jess added, through gritted teeth.

"Of course you can," Lilah said, putting her arm around Jess, who had begun to shake in the cold. Derry held back an impulse to replace Lilah's arm. He sensed the need for sister solidarity.

"But not with him!" Gavin countered, getting in Derry's face, teeth bared as if showing fangs. Steam rose off Derry's skin like coiled heat, rising up to the early morning sky, the familiar tingle beginning.

My God.

They were about to shift.

Lilah's eyes cut over to his with an alertness, a fear that understood the immediacy of the situation. Or, it suddenly occurred to him, she was about to shift, too. Could she feel it? How did humans who went through The Change learn to read the subtle signals of the body when they'd not experienced it all their lives?

Time for musings later.

The chlorine nearly made him lose consciousness, the scent overpowering. Gavin's skin teemed with sweat and a lime verbena soap he'd used in a recent shower, while Lilah smelled like aluminum and coconut. Jess's fear poured off her like an infusion, but there was more. Anger. Fury. The musk of frustration and the relief of having a target.

Gavin.

Right now, Derry had to find a way to defuse what was about to become an incredibly volatile, and potentially violent, situation.

"Lilah? Jess?" In the distance, a hushed voice called out. A distinctly feminine, human voice. Derry's ears perked. It was coming from behind the pool house.

Before he could move, a woman he had never met, yet felt he knew, appeared.

Jess gawked as the woman, old enough to be the sisters' mother, took in Derry's naked form. He felt her eyes crawl over him, cataloging his wet skin, his curves and planes, the hard muscle and thick hair. Her eyes settled on his midsection, and quickly she turned, modesty prevailing, curiosity sated.

In profile, he saw it. The resemblance, the bone lines, the high cheekbones and—

Oh dear God.

"Mom?" Lilah and Jess said in unison.

This was not how Derry had imagined meeting his future mother-in-law.

Oh shit. Her mom. Looking at Derry.

At least he wasn't erect anymore.

Jess was tempted for only a moment to help him find a towel—a large one—to cover himself and salvage some pride, but then she remembered how he was the one who had brought them to this, where strangers and family caught them at their worst. Lilah might understand, but her mother wouldn't. Jess's cautious, prudish streak had come from her.

Let Derry be embarrassed. Not that he felt any shame, the giant manwhore. Countless women had seen him naked because he liked showing off that sexy body of his.

But for a second there, when he'd been facing off with Gavin, he'd seemed to change, get even bigger. Gavin, too, had become truly menacing, his teeth bared like—well, a wolf. She'd never seen him as a wolf. Since it defied her previous understanding of the world, she hadn't quite believed it, not truly. Until now. Something had changed, or almost had.

Had they begun to shift just then? Even Lilah had acted strangely, digging her fingernails into Jess's shoulder, hard enough to hurt.

Jess put up a hand to the sore flesh, realizing she was still shaking from cold, shock, and adrenaline. Catching sight of her clothes in a pile outside the sauna, she pulled away from Lilah, whose grip had softened, and strode away from the little party. She picked up her sweats, shoving her damp limbs into the pillowy fleece as fast as she could.

Her mother was still staring at Derry. Jess sympathized. It was hard not to.

When Jess returned to the group, Gavin was wrapping his own

shirt around Derry's midsection, cursing him under his breath.

"My apologies," Gavin said to Marilyn. "I'll take care of this." Then he grabbed Derry by the shoulders and frog-marched him away.

Derry's head twisted around, trying to catch Jess's eye, but she quickly looked away.

Just because he'd known she would be in the sauna didn't mean he'd had to meet her there. And then to try to drive her insane, touching his body, watching her watch him, putting himself on display—it wasn't fair. He didn't play fair.

"You're up early," Jess said to Marilyn, plastering on a smile. "Did you sleep well?"

"You think this is a joke?" Lilah asked tightly.

"Better to laugh than to cry," Jess said. How could she ever live this down?

"Do you realize why I came out here?" Lilah's voice was soft but terrifying. "Because I got a text from Eva. You know why Eva texted me? Because *she* got a call from Edward. He was afraid a certain member of the Stanton family was going to hear a rumor about Derry's antics and then kill him, which would kind of spoil our wedding tomorrow, don't you think?"

Jess's shivering got worse. Edward, Eva, Lilah, Gavin, and her own mother had seen her and Derry acting like insane, hormonally deranged teenagers. If she hadn't turned down that thermostat last night, she'd be in bed, safe and cozy, her reputation (somewhat) intact. And the reason she'd had to turn down the thermostat was because she'd been feverish for Derry.

Derry again. It was always Derry.

"Is Eva going to fire me?" Jess asked. Her teeth were chattering.

Lilah's tone turned as cold as the icy lake. "That's what you're worried about? Your job?"

"Let's talk about this inside." Marilyn said, putting an arm around Jess, rubbing her upper arms. "You need a hot drink. We all do. My cabin has a little kitchen. And it's *private.*" She pursed her lips at that last word, giving the windows of the big house behind them the side-eye.

Feeling even worse, Jess hung her head and let her mother and Lilah lead her away. Her first thought had been about her job, when here was her sister, who'd done everything for her, having to worry about being humiliated at her own wedding. How many people had seen her and Derry running around naked?

They reached Marilyn's little cabin and went inside.

"Lilah, I'm s-s-s-so sor-r-ry," Jess said. The chattering had gotten worse. "Your wedding. I'm ruining it." Lilah's face softened.

"Hot shower," Marilyn said, pointing at the bathroom. "I'll make tea."

"I d-d-don't want to get wet ag-g-gain," Jess said.

Lilah and Marilyn both glared at her. Jess realized, belatedly, she was in no position to argue. Deflating, she walked away to the small bathroom, thinking it was nice to be alone for a minute. Maybe she could stay in here for a few days. For the rest of her life, she'd be wondering who else had seen her jump in that lake and get hauled around over Derry's shoulder like a cavewoman in a pre-historically inaccurate melodrama.

The shower helped drive out the chill but couldn't do anything for her ego. When she was done and dressed again in her sweats with a towel wrapped around her damp hair, she rejoined her mother and sister, hoping the lecture wouldn't last too long. More than anything, she wanted to curl up in bed and sleep. Maybe cry a little.

"That was Gavin's little brother, I understand?" Marilyn handed her a steaming mug of tea and ushered her into the small sitting area overlooking the lake. "Sophia's twin?"

When Marilyn had been recovering from surgery, Sophia had helped her out at the house, playing nurse. The two had become unlikely friends. "Yes," Jess said, sinking into a deep, overstuffed chair. "That's him."

"I take it you two haven't been seeing each other very long," Marilyn said.

Looking into her tea, Jess shook her head.

"Speaking of 'seeing,'" Lilah said. "I'm afraid you were in full view of half the guests in this house."

"I was trying to get away from him," Jess said.

"Has he forced himself on you?" Marilyn asked in alarm.

"No, no," Jess said quickly. "Not the way you mean. I-I- was willing enough. But this morning, after what happened last night, I told him we had to cool it. But then he was there in the sauna."

"What were you doing in the sauna wearing a bikini at five in the morning?" Marilyn asked.

"Trying to warm up."

Marilyn shook her head. "But then you jumped in a frozen lake."

"Well, Derry was in the sauna. He surprised me. So I had to leave."

Lilah let out a loud sigh. "Jess, why didn't you just go to your room?" Lifting her hand to her head, she tugged at her hair in big clumps the way she did under stress.

"I-I—" What could she say? That she'd been burning with lust because Derry had started an exhibitionist sex show and, under the circumstances, the lake had seemed like the best option at the time? "I wish I had," she said finally. "I'm sorry, Lilah. It's your wedding, and—"

"At least you were wearing a swimsuit," Lilah said. "And you guys weren't actually, you know, going at it."

"Oh, Lilah, please," Marilyn said, sitting up straighter, the prim Puritan that she was. "Let's get the story straight. Jess, you entered the sauna, not knowing Gavin's brother was already sitting there in his birthday suit, and you were so traumatized to be alone with him, you fled, not knowing where you were going, out of your head, and ended up in the lake. Fearing for your life, and perhaps your sanity, he risked his own modesty by jumping in and rescuing you."

Lilah snorted at the word "modesty," then caught Jess's glare and covered her mouth.

"Thanks, Mom," Jess said. "That's exactly how it went."

"Oh, you're not fooling *me*. I'm just giving you ideas about what you can tell everyone else," Marilyn said. "Don't think for a minute that *I* don't know you've been very naughty."

If only she knew. Jess lifted the mug to her lips to hide her involuntary smile.

"And I wouldn't blame Lilah one second for being angry with you," Marilyn added. "It's her special day."

"Oh, it's all right," Lilah said. "As long as this is the end of it."

Jess slammed the mug on the table. "Now hold on one minute. You don't have any right to tell me to end anything."

"You really can't control yourself for two more days?" Lilah asked.

"Oh." Jess sank back into her chair. "I thought you meant *ever*. Of course I can control myself for a couple days. Here. And there. Anywhere. I'm like that green eggs and ham guy."

"Except in reverse, since you seem to be jumping him all over the place," Lilah said. "I'm going to start calling you Sam-I-am."

In spite of her shame, Jess laughed.

Marilyn frowned at her. "You know what I think?"

Jess's humor vanished. She could imagine what her mother thought of her right now. Virgin to slut in sixty seconds.

Lilah stood up and cleared the cups away. "You know, Mom, I think Jess would love to rest in her room for the rest of the morning. The rehearsal's this afternoon and—"

"Let me tell you what I think, and then you can run away," Marilyn said.

Giving Jess a sympathetic smile, Lilah sat back down. Jess's heart squeezed, grateful to have such a wonderful sister.

Marilyn crossed her arms over her chest and lifted her chin the way she did when she was going to begin a lecture. "Lilah is marrying a very rich, very handsome man. Gavin is like a prince in a fairy tale, and Lilah's the princess." She gestured broadly, as if encompassing the cabin, the house, the lake, the private jet, everything. "The beautiful people have come to watch and celebrate the biggest wedding of the year. No expense has been spared, and everyone will be looking at Lilah, wondering what she's got that caught the most famous bachelor in the world."

"He is not famous," Lilah said, laughing. "He's always been careful to avoid publicity."

"He would be if people knew more about him," Marilyn said.

"All right, Mom," Jess said, "what's your point?"

Marilyn sucked in a breath and went in for the kill. "It can't be easy to have your older sister at the center of all that attention," she said, "when you're not."

Jess recoiled in genuine shock. "No, that's not true. This has nothing to do with me being . . . *jealous.*"

"Mom, I'm sure that's not why Jess—did what she did." Lilah leaned closer to Jess and muttered, "Repeatedly."

"I'm just telling it how I see it." Marilyn looked away, chin in the air. "I hope I'm wrong."

"You are wrong," Jess said, standing up. "Gavin's a nice guy, I suppose, but I wouldn't want to marry him in a million years."

"But maybe you like the idea of everything he's got, and why not try his younger brother?" her mother asked.

"I can't believe you think I'm . . . such a . . ." Jess couldn't use the word she wanted in front of her mother. "I like Derry. Not his money, not his connections. I think he's really gentle and sweet and smart, under all the stupid he lays on so thick, and he's been nicer to me than any guy I've ever—I've ever—" She had to stop talking before she started to cry. Blinking hard, she turned away and strode to the door. How could her own mother understand her so poorly? Attention was the last thing she'd ever wanted.

She yanked the door open and hurried away from her mother's cabin, not caring that the sleet had turned to snow or that the dusting on the lawn was rather lovely.

Her own mother . . .

"Jess! Wait!" Lilah was running up behind her.

Given what Jess had put her through, she stopped and waited for her to catch up. But her temper was still flying too high to speak.

"Don't let her get to you," Lilah said. "She doesn't know how you feel."

"How I feel?"

Lilah gave her a knowing look.

"Why don't you go back to Gavin?" Jess said. "Have breakfast in bed, whatever. I'm going to lock myself in my room and stay there."

"I'll come with you."

"No, please. I—" Jess began.

"Just for a few minutes. Then you can hibernate." Lilah's eyes widened. "I mean sleep. Rest. Prepare yourself for later."

Jess had to laugh. It was too crazy. They were making bear jokes. "I knew what you meant. Sure, if it'll make you feel better."

"I'll have some fresh croissants sent to us. I'm starving."

Jess's appetite should've been nonexistent, but the thought of pastry made her stomach growl. "Whatever makes you happy. I owe you."

Fifteen minutes later, they were curled up on Jess's big bed with almond and chocolate croissants and a fresh pot of coffee on a silver tray.

"When did you first think you were in love with him?" Lilah asked abruptly.

After groaning at the trap she'd fallen into, Jess carefully put her cup down and buried her face in a pillow.

Lilah put her hand on her back. "Or maybe you haven't admitted it to yourself?"

Face submerged in down, Jess shook her head.

After a long moment, Lilah patted her on the shoulder. "You know why I'm concerned?"

Of course Jess knew. With a sigh, she sat up. "Don't worry. I know it can't last."

"You do?"

"Yes," Jess said. She did. Of course she did. This was *Derry Stanton*. "That's why I'm binging on him."

"Like eating an entire pizza before going on a diet?"

Jess nodded. "Except he's much more than a pizza. Hell, if that's all he was, I'd be fine. But he's more like tiramisu and truffles and a Costco-sized jar of Nutella."

"I wish you'd met Edward first," Lilah said wistfully.

"It's not like I needed one of Gavin's brothers to have sex with."

"I know, I know, but Edward's like you, well, like you used to be, and he's so sweet and really good-looking, and—"

"What do you mean, like I *used to be*?"

"I shouldn't say." Lilah rolled her eyes. "But I guess I already did. He's, you know, celibate. By choice, the way you were."

"Really? Edward's celibate. Why?"

Lilah looked uncomfortable. "Uh . . . not sure. Something that happened a long time ago. Gavin wouldn't tell me. I don't think he could've ever had much experience with women though. He's the youngest in the family."

"You thought the nun and the priest should hook up," Jess said.

"It crossed my mind."

"The blind leading the blind."

"It would be sweet," Lilah said.

"Would've been. I'm not blind anymore." Flushing to the tips of her toes, Jess remembered a particularly educational moment with Derry. That crazy pinkie finger.

"Yeah, too late now," Lilah said. "Derry would never allow it."

"Excuse me? Derry's not the boss of me," Jess said.

"But he's the boss of Edward," Lilah said. "They've got a very clear pecking order, these brothers. Asher, Gavin, Derry, Edward. That's how they see themselves, that's how they behave. If Derry wouldn't want you to sleep with Edward—and I think it's pretty obvious he'd rather cut off his own penis—Edward will stay far away from you. No matter how desperately he wants you."

"Edward wants me?" Jess asked, shocked. Had he wanted her *before* seeing her humping Derry in the Rolls?

"Theoretically," Lilah said.

"Oh. Meaning he doesn't."

"But he would have, I'm sure of it, if you hadn't gotten mixed up with Derry first." Holding her coffee, Lilah climbed off the bed. "I should go, let you rest. I'll see you at—"

"Just for the record, I didn't admit to that thing you said."

"Sure." Lilah drained her cup and set it on the tray. "Should I have them send more croissants?"

"You don't believe me."

Lilah paused for a moment, then sat on the edge of the bed again and gave her a serious look. "I'm going to tell you something I wasn't going to tell you, at least not yet. But it might help you."

A chill ran down Jess's spine. "What?"

"If Derry were the One for you, you'd know." Lilah fell silent as if this explained everything. Her expression was pitying.

In spite of the way her own heart was pounding, Jess rolled her eyes. "Great. Thanks for the tip."

"And if *you* were the One for Derry, he would know," Lilah continued.

"Then I won't hold my breath, since Derry is famous for his four-ways, not his one-ways." Jess tried to keep her voice light, but she felt sick.

Lilah stood up. "Exactly. That's why I'm so worried about you."

Nineteen

"Do you mind? You're holding me closer than a Bangkok hooker trying to convince a client to buy her for a twenty-four-hour whirl."

"You would know," Gavin muttered.

"For the record, I've never paid for sex," Derry answered airily, pulling out his Oscar Wilde voice, the touch of condescension and devil-may-care easy to access.

Too easy.

The sound that Gavin made was decidedly contrary.

Derry didn't appreciate having his arm twisting behind him but let Gavin do it for the sake of decorum. It gave him an excuse to escape the mortifying scene back there. He turned to catch Jess's eye, but she avoided him.

I'm sorry.

Me too.

The words floated through his mind, then disappeared like a swarm that comes together for a brief moment from instinct, parting for no reason at all.

Derry shut his mouth until he found himself in the sauna again, tossed against the bench by his wolf brother, who exhibited a surprising level of strength for such a weak species. They weren't adolescents any longer, though. Both knew who had the upper hand when it came to sheer physical power.

And the near shift back there rested just under Derry's skin, waiting to be unleashed when safe.

Safe.

Whatever that meant.

"Spit it out," Gavin demanded, hands on hips, chest wide, shoulders braced for a fight. The room held a small bit of steam that cleared fairly quickly, yet Gavin's eyes glowed through the obscurity.

"Spit what out?"

"Why you're doing this."

"Why I'm doing what?"

"Why you're fucking Lilah's sister."

Derry's laugh built in his throat as he stretched himself out on the cedar planks that made up the sauna's bench. Taking his time, he positioned his body in the most relaxed pose possible, knees up, balls resting gently on the wood. He was far too tall to truly stretch out, and besides, he needed the time to think.

How in the hell could he rationally explain what he'd just done with—no, *to*—Jess?

Perhaps that was the problem.

There was no rational explanation.

What he felt was entirely, irrevocably, unbelievably and painfully irrational.

It was love.

His skin melted into the cedar, eyes open and drying out, the revelation like being set on fire. When he'd seen Jess and Lilah's mother, he'd thought of her as his own mother-in-law. Not Gavin's. When Jess had needed to be protected from Edward's roving eyes, he'd curled himself into a ball to shield her.

When she'd humiliated him at the club, he'd pursued her. When he'd taken her virginity—freely, and lusciously offered—he'd accepted the gift not as a present but as an exchange. A power distribution between equals.

Here, she'd seemed to say. Please have this. And in return, all I ask is that you give me your heart right back.

By God.

He had. *Forever.*

The room began to spin, the heat overpowering.

"Derry," Gavin said, his voice carrying the implied requirement of an answer.

Before he slipped into unconsciousness, Derry stood, shoving past Gavin, who had tried to block the door. The force of Derry's push made Gavin slam into the wall, but Derry ignored his indignant shouts. Running, taking on speed, the shock of frigid air snapped him back into his own mind.

It was torture.

Footsteps, far too swift to be mere human, caught up from behind.

"This is one hell of a way to show your jealousy, Derry," Gavin said, not at all winded as he ran beside him. Derry sprinted for his cottage, knowing the grounds so well that he zigged and zagged past bushes and trees, stone retainer walls and side stairs, until he opened the slider to his courtyard and darted into the house.

Gavin followed.

"So you admit it," Gavin said casually, as if they hadn't just spent ninety seconds sprinting faster than most Olympians.

"Silence does not equal agreement," Derry countered.

"But your lack of denial does."

Fuck.

"I'm not jealous," Derry groaned, walking past Gavin, who shoved him in retaliation for Derry's earlier push. Ignoring the immature move with but an eye roll, Derry walked into his bathroom and turned on the hot water in the shower.

"I'm not leaving!" Gavin called out as Derry stepped into the glass and stone enclosure, his showerheads aimed perfectly for his height and build. "I'm making coffee!"

Derry looked out the tiny bathroom window at the low sun over the mountains.

Still morning.

Already his day had gone to shit, and noon was hours away.

As he soaped himself, he inevitably stroked his cock, which stirred at the display of basic biology. Touch that skin, and blood flowed forth. Stroke it a few times, and semen spurted. Ignore it long enough, and blue balls developed.

And, Derry supposed, as he rinsed off, choosing not to relieve the agony building up within, the same formula could be applied to human behavior.

It seemed so simple to Gavin. He was getting married, and Derry was jealous, so his manwhore brother was targeting the sweet, weak little gazelle sister of the bride.

Nothing could be further from the truth.

A barking laugh poured out of Derry, short and bitter.

The truth was so unbelievable that Gavin would never accept it. And why should he?

Derry threw on business casual pants, a turtleneck, and a V-neck cashmere sweater in a heather gray that Sophia had once told him showcased his blue eyes. As he rounded the corner between the hallway and his kitchen, Gavin sat at the countertop, on a high stool, sipping freshly brewed coffee as if they were meeting for book club and not in verbal battle.

"I'm not jealous," Derry said simply.

"Then what are you?"

"In love."

Gavin's howl of laughter made his hand twitch, coffee sloshing all over the granite countertop. "You asshole. Quit stalling. You need to come up with some excuse better than that to explain why you've been all over her for the past few days, now of all times, my wedding, so provocatively inconsiderate and improper . . ." Gavin's words slowed, like a child's spinning top losing its coiled power, and his brow turned down.

Gavin looked at him and sniffed. Over and over until the laughter drained entirely from his throat, his glowing eyes filled with a disastrous sense of horror that made Derry's oversized testicles crawl up into his groin.

"You—Derry! You don't smell at all like yourself!"

He let out a chuckle of relief. Oh. That.

"I smell like English lavender, don't I? The maid appears to have filled my cottage with nothing but Father's old soap."

"You know exactly what I mean. My powers of scent might be less than yours, but you smell like you and Jessica. And no other woman." Gavin's voice dropped half an octave with each word of that final sentence, his head tilting, face twisting into a befuddled look that would have made him look like an old archivist at Derry's alma mater if only his brother were one hundred fifty years older and wore spectacles.

And smelled like mothballs.

"Right."

Gavin approached him, and his look changed to sympathy. "Are you ill?"

Lovesick, Derry thought bitterly. The word was on the tip of his tongue, but he bit it back, breaking eye contact with his brother and turning to prepare a triple shot of espresso. He would need ten of these to get through the day. He'd teased Gavin mercilessly about forsaking his bachelor party, but now he understood. Understood all too well. Why dabble with fluff when you can have the authentic in your bed, loving you?

The wedding rehearsal was this afternoon, followed by a dinner, and then tomorrow—the wedding.

Jess, he thought. *Jess.*

I'm here.

He closed his eyes, and his hand jumped with surprise, dumping coffee beans across the counter. They skittered like a rain stick turned upside down, the sound shattering his mental contact with her.

"You really are *only* sleeping with her. For how long?"

Forever.

"A few days," Derry muttered, cleaning up the mess. The ritual of plucking each coffee bean from the ground with his thick fingers made for slow work, but right now he needed distraction.

"You've gone a few days with only one woman? You must be in love, Derry," Gavin joked, the laugh dying in his throat as Derry stood and whirled around, his face burning from Gavin's words.

They stared at each other.

Thousands of words passed without voice.

Finally, Derry found his.

"I think she's the One, Gavin."

Gavin's eyebrows shot to his hairline, hands back on his hips, face flushing with a surprising anger that put Derry on guard.

"Nonsense! You're a bear. Bears don't mate for life."

"I know!" Derry groaned, throwing away the dirty coffee beans, cradling his head in his hands and leaning his hip against the counter. "It makes no sense! But women are nothing to me now! It's as if the world of pussy has gone from a rich tapestry of shades of pink to nothing but a dull, dreary gray! Their scents are gone. Women are nothing but cardboard to me. Sexually, I mean. I can speak with them. Converse and joke but not flirt. I . . . It's as if . . . I don't know!" He threw his hands up in the air in frustration, glaring at his brother as if demanding an answer.

Gavin gaped at him.

Not much of an answer.

Finally his brother's face spread into a sly smile, one nostril widening as a corner of his mouth twisted into a leer. "Good one, Derry. You almost had me."

"Had you what?" Derry's head spun. The lack of coffee didn't help.

"The joke. You can't have a 'One.' This is a prank, right?" The smile went dead, Gavin's voice cold. "And you're using Lilah's sister for the joke, which is absolutely unacceptable."

"I'm not joking!" Derry roared, throwing the coffee bean container at Gavin's head. Taken utterly by surprise, Gavin didn't dodge in time, the ceramic jar grazing his ear.

Violence unleashed now, inertia took hold. It was a relief to throw the coffeemaker next, then a copper pot, and finally, Derry picked up the microwave, lifting it up over his head, blood pumping with a frenzy that made him so savage he could tell that love had driven him mad. No one believed him. No one would ever believe him. They all categorized him as a rake, a shallow, callow asshole who fucked his way through life, living on the old money from his ancient family's treasure.

He was nothing but that image to the world.

Did Jess feel the same?

If his own brother couldn't believe he was capable of love, then why not prove that he had a different kind of power?

"Jesus, Derry! Stop!" Edward's voice cut through the hormone-driven chaos in his mind. Barely able to contain the impulse to cast the appliance as far as possible through Gavin's head, he turned to see his baby brother standing at the slider, hands up in a gesture of supplication, eyes pleading.

Gavin moved to a point of safety behind a couch.

"What's going on here?" Edward asked in horror.

Slowly, with an ache that made his chest hurt, his heart torn into millions of tiny threads that had all come unwoven with Gavin's disbelief that he could have a One, Derry lowered the microwave.

He looked first at Edward, then at Gavin's hard, guarded face. What was he doing? His heart tried to pry itself out of his chest, thumping hard as if it struck a pickaxe against his ribs. The violence was hard to restrain, the beat of anger a powerful impulse, Gavin's cruel implication that he wasn't worthy of the same love everyone else experienced his worst fear.

With a painful dawning that made him want to curl into a ball and hide, to shred his clothing and run free, to escape and explode at the same time, he composed himself.

Barely.

And finally he said:

"You know me. I'm such a bear before I've had my morning coffee."

Late that afternoon, Jess looked around the space Lilah had called "the family room." No family room Jess had ever seen included a mural on the vaulted ceiling or stained-glass windows, but she was willing to indulge the bride and keep the cherub jokes to herself. Tomorrow, Lilah and Gavin would be married here. And in only a few minutes, the wedding party would begin the rehearsal.

Jess ducked behind a large potted plant before adjusting her bra under her sweater. The room was too warm; she was sweating. She'd worn a thick, bulky sweater instead of something more feminine, not wanting to trigger anything sexual with Derry or look like she wanted it.

No matter how badly she *did* want it.

Every hour she spent without touching Derry now felt like a year. Did that mean she knew he was the only one for her, destined to be hers for the rest of her life? Or did she just want to get laid and was afraid that her chances of feeling so good again were fading with each moment? Derry had already given her more time than he gave to most women. For all his enthusiasm now, the odds were he'd forget her within a day or two.

It was her brain that was calculating the odds. But her heart felt differently. What the two of them had was something special, something other people couldn't understand.

And then her brain slapped her heart silly. She was enjoying Derry's company and his body and everything, but she couldn't believe it would last forever. Her whole life, she'd prided herself on being smart; she wasn't going to get stupid now.

Or so she told herself. This, as much as her affection for her sister, kept her from sneaking off to see Derry privately, if just for a little kiss or two.

"If you think that garment will have any chilling effect on me whatsoever," Derry's voice rumbled softly in her ear, "you're even more of an innocent than you were a few weeks ago."

Jess froze, just savoring the feel of his nearness, the scent of him in her nose. "I thought it might help."

"Kind of you, darling. But we're way past that now, aren't we?"

Then she did turn, taking a step back as she did so, out of reach. "Yes," she said, smiling, "I guess we are."

He wore a heather-gray sweater and a blue turtleneck that made his blue eyes shine like a summer sky. Or maybe it was because he'd tied back his thick hair, exaggerating his clean-shaven cheekbones. She'd never seen him without a shadow on his jaw before, and she was intrigued. Her fingers itched to cup his cheek and feel the soft skin over broad bone, the hint of stubble she couldn't see.

But she didn't. She'd promised.

"You look nice," she said, clearing her throat.

Running a hand down his chest, he ducked his head. Was he blushing? "Generous of you to say so. This is how my mother would dress me when I was little. I thought, perhaps, Gavin would see it as evidence of my good intentions." A grin flickered for only a moment. "If my appearance does not reflect my true nature, at least it demonstrates my desire to emulate a good one for the occasion."

Jess glanced beyond the potted plant at the rows of seating and a preliminary altar, where Lilah and Gavin were greeting the rest of the family and their closest friends.

"I've promised to stay away from you for the next couple of days," she said softly.

"An eternity."

She searched him for any sign of mockery, finding none. "We'll have to be together, of course, for the ceremony and tonight's rehearsal," she said.

"I understand we'll be seated together at dinner as well."

Her heart expanded in her chest. Just talking to him made her happy. "Nobody could blame us for talking to one another," she said. "Right?"

"It would be improper not to. I've been remiss in hearing more about your life in your own words." Giving her a bow, he offered his elbow. "Shall we?"

Feeling like it was the two of them against the world, she took his arm, maintaining plenty of air between their bodies, and let him escort her over to Lilah and Gavin. They were talking to Edward and Marilyn, all bubbles and smiles—until they saw Jess and Derry arrive together.

After giving her hand a brief squeeze, Derry released Jess's arm. "Felicitations to the lovely couple," he said, then turned and gave Marilyn a deep bow. "But first I must offer my sincere apologies for my sunrise indecency, Mrs. Murphy."

Nervously Jess watched her mom absorb the apology, leaning in to let Derry kiss her on the cheek.

"We won't talk about that," Marilyn said. "Although I should probably thank you for pulling Jess out of the water before she got hypothermic."

"It was my, ah, pleasure," Derry said.

Jess dug her fingernails into her palms to stop herself from giggling.

"Not many lifeguards could carry a Murphy woman around like that," Marilyn continued. "I can definitely see the appeal." Her appreciative gaze danced over Derry's body.

Oh no, Jess thought. *Please don't tell me my mother is flirting with him.* At the first hint of flattery, Derry's manwhore instincts would take over, embarrassing everyone.

But Derry glided over the bait with a polite smile. "I believe you know my sister, Sophia? I hope she behaved herself while she was living with you. We are twins, you know, in more ways than one."

"She was such a help. It's so nice to see her again." Marilyn's eyes widened, looking past them. "Speak of the devil."

Jess turned to see Sophia talking to Molly and also to Natalie Mercado, an old high school friend of Lilah's, chatting near the windows, which looked out on the lake. The four of them were the bridesmaids. Each had purchased their own gown separately, all in the same lovely shade of purple Lilah had always preferred. Jess doubted any of the other three had stressed out the bride as much as she had. No matter how tantalizing Derry was in his cashmere sweater, she was going to behave. She had to redeem herself.

"When does the rehearsal start?" Jess asked.

Lilah scanned the room. "We can start any minute if we're all here." She began counting on her fingers. "Molly and Edward, Nat and Asher, Sophia and Carl, Jess and Derry. That's it!"

Jess and Derry. A pair. It sounded nice; it sounded right. Involuntarily she glanced at him and caught him staring. His expression was serious, not teasing or seductive, and it knocked the wind out of her.

In unison, they both looked away.

"I don't see Asher," Derry said carefully.

"Don't get your hopes up." Gavin slapped Derry on the back. "He's in his garage. Eva wanted to see his newest acquisition.

Just had it delivered. Not the Bugatti he'd wanted, but he seems pleased with another Morris."

Jess was careful not to look at Derry at the mention of his big brother's vintage car collection.

"Will Eva be here tonight?" She tried to keep the dread out of her voice. Her boss had seen her and Derry making fools of themselves that morning, and Jess wasn't in any hurry to face her.

"She'd better be. She's marrying us." Gavin already had his arm around Lilah, and now he slid his arm down around her waist, pulled her closer, and buried his face in her hair as if none of them were standing there watching. Or, as in their mother's case, sighing and clapping her hands together.

Lilah melted against Gavin for a long, hot minute before breaking away and offering the rest of them apologetic smiles. "It turns out that as the manager of the Platinum, Eva found it convenient to marry people, so she became an ordained minister. Now she marries everyone in the family."

"Eva's a minister," Jess said. "I can see that. She's got that vibe about her."

"She does so enjoy telling people what to do," Derry muttered. "Putting the fear of God into them, as it were."

"Here they are," Gavin said.

Behind them, Eva stood with a man who sucked all the air out of the room, like a broken window in a spaceship. Stony-faced and straight-backed, he had to be Asher Stanton, the oldest brother and *de facto* patriarch of the family. He bore a superficial resemblance to Derry—dark hair, blue eyes—but he was older, his build was smaller, and his reserved expression was totally unlike his fun-loving, exuberant, hedonistic younger brother.

Jess hated him instantly.

While Asher went over to greet his wedding partner, Natalie, who seemed oblivious to his domineering aura, Eva joined Jess and the others at the altar.

"Lilah, why don't you and your mother wait over there like we talked about," Eva said. "You'll be the last to enter, of course."

With a cheerful wave, Lilah and Marilyn walked across the room and disappeared behind the potted plant. Jess wished she could go with them, but she had to face Eva, who was now staring directly at her.

"Nice to see you," Jess said.

"Ah, that's right," Eva said. "I've already seen you, but of course you were busy."

Derry took a step, putting himself between Jess and Eva. "That was my fault. Entirely. And it won't happen again."

"I've heard that before," Eva said, but she was smiling as she studied the clipboard in her hand. "But perhaps it's better if we continue this discussion when your older brother isn't in the room."

"Either one of them," Gavin growled.

"I'm happy to defer the conversation indefinitely," Derry said.

Eva tapped Jess, then Derry, with a pencil. "You two will go first. I trust, my young McDermott, that you won't forget the ring?"

"I assure you I will not," Derry said.

"I have several extra in my pocket, just in case he does," Gavin said.

Derry sniffed. "That won't be necessary."

"Nevertheless. The ring is merely a token. I might as well have a spare." Gavin adjusted his tie, inhaling deeply and licking his lips, and for the first time, Jess realized he was nervous.

How cute.

"Who walks down the aisle after Jess and Derry?" Sophia asked. Everyone in the room was now clustered around Eva.

Once again, hearing her name paired with his, from a family member, his own twin, sent shockwaves through Jess's body and soul. It felt right. It felt . . . inevitable. She was swept up in an overwhelming urge to just let go, just let it happen . . .

The feeling lingered, distracting her from the instructions that Eva gave to the Stantons and their friends in the same voice she used when issuing orders to waitstaff at the Platinum. As everyone scurried off, doing as she'd told them, Derry had to take her hand—which he squeezed before putting on his arm—and led her to the far end of the narrow carpet leading up the aisle.

Music began to play from wall speakers. Jess's grip tightened on Derry's sleeve, drawing a handful of the cashmere into her fist.

"Are you all right?" he asked softly.

"I'm nervous," she said. "Isn't that silly?"

His enormous hand came over hers. "No, my dear. It's not silly at all." He didn't say anything else, or grin seductively, or stroke her skin in places she'd never known she had—but his understanding silence made her weak in the knees. Here, if only he could take her here. Right now.

I want you, she thought.

With a swift chop of her hand, Eva signaled for them to proceed up the aisle.

I love you.

The voice drifted in between the notes of the music, blending with the wedding march but, she knew, audible only to her.

Her toe caught on the thick carpet.

"Lean on me," Derry said under his breath. "I'm too big to fall over."

Biting back a smile, she patted his elbow. "Thanks."

"That's what I'm here for."

They reached the podium that marked the altar, which Jess knew would be decorated lavishly tomorrow for the actual wedding. For months, Lilah had been sending her emails loaded with sample wedding pictures, music, and video, demanding she share her opinion. So much work had gone into the big day.

Derry and I will elope so we don't have to do all this, she thought.

And then flinched. What was the matter with her? Was she trying to torture herself?

"Jess?" Eva asked, coming over. "What's the problem?"

Derry squeezed. "There's no problem." He was watching her intently. "None at all."

"I forgot which side to go to," Jess managed to say, although she felt dizzy.

"Over here," Eva said, gesturing to the left. "Derry, here with Gavin."

Derry felt every disparate part of his entire being coalesce as he watched Jess, her hand on his arm peeling off like ivy from an old brick wall, walk to the bride's side as the rehearsal continued. Gavin's eyes were on him, ever-observant, but with a keen cunning that made Derry's skin crawl with something far more dangerous than a mere threat.

Gavin was cataloging him, taking inventory of his every move. If nothing else, Derry was the consummate social chameleon, able to take on whatever graces (or lack thereof) were required in any given setting.

He knew this would be difficult. Not the mindless niceties and small talk, but the proximity to Jess without permission to truly be with her. Ruses were fun to create and keep up when they didn't involve real feelings.

This? This went beyond torture.

Their easygoing conversation made the situation worse. He liked her. Genuinely enjoyed her company. By the time Jess had taken her place beside Lilah, turned in profile to listen to Eva's instructions, Derry's stomach was in knots. His heart sped up to triple time without any movement on his part. A warm glow suffused him, the sensation so wholly original that he didn't realize he was experiencing it until Gavin nudged him, finally, and whispered, "Had too much to drink?"

"What are you talking about?" Derry could tell from Gavin's tone that his brother didn't really believe he'd imbibed too much.

"You're turning red. A flush from the wrong wine or . . . you're nervous?"

Derry cast a bit of shade at Gavin. "You should talk. If you continue licking your lips like that, you'll need to borrow some of that makeup girl's lip balm," he replied, nodding at Molly, who caught the gesture and gave him a dazzling, friendly grin and a wave.

Nothing.

He felt nothing beyond basic pleasantness. He smiled back, a bland movement of his mouth that was yet another formality in a room where the only person who counted was Jess.

And he could not have her.

Yet.

"Shut up," Gavin groused, the tip of his tongue poking between his lips, halting, then retreating. If Gavin were in wolf form, his fangs would show through his sneer.

"Why on earth would you be anxious, Gavin?" Derry asked, all teasing gone from his voice. "Lilah is a stunning, intelligent, compassionate woman who is utterly devoted to you in every way. Fate brought you together. Destiny makes it clear she's your One. Why the worry?"

Gavin went still as the words poured out of Derry, his eyes going unfocused as he let the message sink in. Derry's own heart quickened. Every word he said about Lilah and Gavin was true. A green fist of jealousy gripped his heart and squeezed it, halting the beating.

Would he ever have what his brother had?

Without thought, his eyes darted toward Jess.

Her.

At that moment, Eva told everyone to relax for a few minutes while she left to handle some problem with the music.

With the rehearsal temporarily paused, Gavin let out his breath. He looked Derry up and down. "You're sweating like a pig."

"If there is a family of pig shifters, and I'm most certainly not of their bloodline," Derry said, his voice filled with arch disdain. His heart lightened slightly, and his mind cleared.

Sarcasm: the refuge of the socially damned.

Gavin's eyebrow quirked, his eyes jumping to Lilah then back to Derry. "No. I have to give you that. You aren't five feet tall at best and albino."

"Besides, pigs barely sweat. Whoever invented that saying was a dolt." Derry's huff was more forlorn than he expected, and alarm flooded his veins. He couldn't stop looking at Jess, who was now animatedly talking about flowers with Lilah and the other bridesmaids, whose names escaped him for the moment as Jess brushed one long, honey-colored lock of hair behind the curve of her perfect ear.

He nearly groaned. A pang of emotion vibrated through him, and he reached for Gavin's arm, the connection so needed. Gavin gave him a puzzled look as Derry opened his mouth to say so many words attached to feelings he couldn't possibly describe. How do you share the truth with someone who isn't the object of your desire about falling in love? How do you put into words the all-consuming sense that your world has changed forever?

While he knew he would say this to Jess, and soon, he needed the wise counsel of his brother, yet another new experience for him. Turning to anyone for emotional reasons was like learning a foreign language.

Derry opened his mouth, and before he could say the words, Gavin said in a low voice only he could hear:

"You look like you're about to come in your pants, Derry. Do we need to go to the stables and get a set of horse blinders for you to get you through my wedding rehearsal?"

A wind tunnel sucked all the vulnerability off Derry's skin, and he shot back, "You look like you ate tainted sushi, Gavin. Need a bucket?"

Where the hell was Eva? Could they please get on with it and release him from this torture?

"Aren't you two a sweaty, flushed, nervous pair," their oldest brother, Asher, said in his low, controlled voice, moving closer to them. "If it were five decades ago, I would think you'd been responsible for putting the live frog down Nanny Maisie's trousers."

"Actually, that was me," Derry confessed, relieved to move from the dizzying emotional moment into safer territory. Jokes and sardonic barbs were safer than these chaotic feelings.

Asher's mouth twitched at the corner. "Tell me something I don't already know."

I am hopelessly in love with a human.

The thought shot through Derry's conscious mind like a cannon released in a battlefield. Asher's body twitched as if a ghost had brushed against him in a hallway in passing. His eyes went troubled but turned to Gavin, not Derry.

Who stood there, sweating more, picking at his tie knot like an anxious gangster.

Asher's steady hand went to Gavin's shoulder. "Every groom has a moment of doubt."

Gavin's sharp look had no effect on Asher. "I do not have any doubt about my love for Lilah."

"Then why the worry?"

"He's human, Asher. We aren't all blessed to have ice water running through our veins like you," Derry said with a tight smile.

"Gavin is partly human, as am I. And you," Asher said, his eyebrow barely moving, eyes on Gavin as he addressed Derry. A cloud of uncertainty surrounded every inch of Derry's body whenever he conversed with his oldest brother, who was a mixture of a father, prison warden, and banker to him. Their relationship could be best described as distant, yet Derry had a reluctant dependence on Asher, and—if he let himself be truthful—a need for validation.

Validation that never came.

Gavin was the worldly success. Sophia was the girl. Edward was the baby. Asher was the patriarch. And Derry?

He was the court jester. The rake. The joke.

When Asher finally gave him his eyes, the look he saw in his brother's face confirmed it.

Might as well play the part he was assigned.

"Part human?" Derry said, voice rippling low. "You would never know, Asher. I thought you were carved from the devil's toenail and brought to life by—"

The joke died in his throat as Eva reappeared, clapping her hands to command everyone's attention, her brow turned down as those intelligent eyes glowed with observation of the trio. She gave Derry a questioning glance, then said:

"Let us continue."

Twenty

Eva joined them all at the mock altar, and music began to play, but Jess barely noticed. What she wanted to do was curl up with Derry and tune out the world. And even if she wasn't looking at him, he still dominated her thoughts. With effort, she smiled stupidly at everyone and tried to act like the sentimental sister. It was easier when Lilah and Marilyn finally appeared, laughing as her sister pretended to throw aside her imaginary veil. Even in a hunter-green pantsuit, which she'd chosen because it vaguely resembled a man's tuxedo, Lilah was stunning. Everyone stared and sighed.

And then Eva said, "Blah, blah, blah," pretending to do the ceremony, and they filed out again. The sentimental words had washed over her, racing like a poem at a poetry slam, the cadence turning into a throbbing beat in her head that said just one word.

Him.

A thousand times him.

Derry was as charming and sturdy walking up the aisle as he'd been walking down it, and soon they were standing together behind the potted plant again, the sound of the drumbeat coursing through her veins louder than any doubt.

"I must release you," he said under his breath. "Much to my

regret." His eyes seemed darker under those thick brows. Troubled. She ached to ask him what was wrong, to soothe whatever stirred up the storm inside, and in that moment his face cleared. Oh, he was good. She saw the deliberate facade form like a force field around his heart, and she was both inside it and at a distance, watching.

They were a pair, all right. She knew exactly what he was doing.

And later she would ask him why and be there for him and make sure he knew that.

They stepped away from each other. "You're a good escort," she said. *And a good person*, she thought, the pulsing beat inside her fading the longer he remained near.

His smile reflected emotion beyond the surface. "My skills as a dining companion are even better."

"I can't wait to see it for myself," she said.

Molly, the dresser from the club, joined them. Lilah had become instant friends with her, and while Jess liked her just fine, they weren't close. "They said it's time for us to walk over to Gavin and Lilah's for dinner." She tilted her head back. "Can you believe the ceiling in this place? It's like the Sistine Chapel."

"We're having dinner at Gavin's cabin?" Jess asked.

"Lilah thought it would be more private than the main house," Molly said. "So many guests here, you know?"

"It's not far," Derry said. "Not as far as—as *my* cabin."

"That's what Ethan was telling me," Molly said. "He has a house of his own, too."

"Who's Ethan?" Jess asked.

"Isn't Ethan your—oh God, I did it again. I'm terrible with names," Molly said. "I mean your youngest brother."

"Edward," Derry said, laughter booming out of him. "Always such a charmer with the ladies." More laughter.

"Please don't tell him I forgot his name," Molly said, clinging to Derry in a way that wiped the smile off Jess's face. "He doesn't come to the club, so I'd never met him before. Please don't tell him?"

Derry looked like this would be a difficult promise to make.

"Please?" Molly repeated.

With a sigh, Derry relented. "Just this once."

Jess wanted to push Molly away from Derry's side; she was much too clingy. "Shall we get our coats? It's snowing outside."

"I didn't even think of that." Molly turned to Jess. "We'd better. Are you staying in that wing off the pool?"

"Yes, but—" *But I want to walk with Derry*. No, she couldn't say that. She couldn't be alone with him in the dark, snowy night. "Yes, I am. We can get our coats and walk together."

Derry looked like he was about to argue, then ran a hand through his hair, loosening the tie in back. "I'll see what Ethan's up to."

"You promised!" Molly said.

"So I did. I will not share your error with my forgettable sibling," Derry said. "Comments between the two of us, however, are open season." After a slight pause, he bowed to both of them and departed.

"I always thought he was a total babe," Molly said.

Hands off, you hussy, Jess thought, then cringed inwardly, ashamed of her jealousy. "He sure is," she said with a sigh.

Molly wasn't stupid. Much to Jess's surprise, she pursed her lips, looked at Jess, then at Derry's retreating form, and said, "You two are an item."

It wasn't a question.

"Yes." Jess's answer came out before she could think. Eyeing Molly carefully, she found herself relieved to see excitement in her coworker's eyes.

"Beauty has tamed the beast?" Molly whispered, a friendly, conspirator's tone exactly what Jess needed to hear, even if she hadn't realized it until this exact second.

"No one can tame him," Jess said with a giggle. It felt good to have a friend to talk to. Lilah was completely consumed with the wedding, surrounded by their mother, Gavin, Eva, the bridesmaids, and a bunch of wedding planners with last-minute questions. Turning to her to talk about this crazy, whirlwind romance with Derry was selfish.

Her mother's accusing words came back to her. Before she let them take over, she grabbed Molly's arm and gave her a squeeze.

Molly reached for a glass of wine on a tray held by one of the servers, a young woman Jess didn't recognize, and handed it off to Jess. She took it, grateful, suddenly parched.

"If anyone can, it's you." Molly's words echoed in her mind as she lifted her own wine glass and gave Jess a meaningful look, one manicured finger pointed to the doorway where Derry stood, covered in a thick navy wool coat that made his eyes glow, eyes that sought out Jess.

And only Jess.

He winked, then left the room, a draft of cool air trailing behind him, lifting a lock of Jess's loose hair like a kiss blown by a lover saying good-bye.

Molly cleared her throat meaningfully and smiled, then drank her wine. Jess looked down at her own glass, bringing it to her lips and taking a sip, then lifting her eyes to scan the room.

And found Asher Stanton staring at her with a look that made her turn to stone.

"Cat got your tongue?" Molly asked, sensing the change.

More like a wolf, Jess thought, but shook off the cold dread and smiled at Molly, ignoring the creepy older Stanton brother. With relief, she and Molly left the "living room" to get their coats out of their rooms.

During the stroll up the path to Gavin's cabin for dinner, Molly chattered about how flattered she was Lilah had invited her to the wedding and how embarrassed she was about forgetting

Edward's name.

"Do you think Derry will tell him?" she asked Jess for the third time, just as they were approaching the bubbling hot-springs pool outside Gavin's cabin. Snow was starting to cling to the branches overhead, glistening in the moonlight.

"He said he wouldn't," Jess said.

"Yeah, I know. You're right. I'm being stupid. I just got the feeling Edward was kind of shy. I'd hate to embarrass him in front of everyone."

Jess remembered him discovering them inside the Rolls. "He's not that shy."

"He hardly said two words to me at the rehearsal."

"Maybe beautiful women make him nervous," Jess said, nudging Molly in the ribs.

"Yeah, right! That's a good one. Next to you and your sister, I'm invisible."

At the door, Jess paused with her hand on the knocker and looked Molly over. Even in a faux-fur coat, Molly managed to look ready for a lingerie photo shoot, with a plunging neckline that showed off her tight white blouse, and under it, a black lace camisole barely containing her generous cleavage, now dotted with melting snowflakes. Below the white blouse, she wore black leather pants tucked into high-heeled red boots.

Jess seriously doubted Molly suffered from the same kind of shyness as Edward.

"You're not invisible and you know it," Jess said, laughing.

"I do try." With a grin, Molly reached over her and swung the knocker herself. "Sometimes I hate being hidden away in the dressing rooms at the club. But it's what I'm good at. I'd be a terrible waitress or bartender."

"Any other dreams?" Jess asked.

Molly laughed again. "Like going to med school with you?"

"No, I mean anything."

"Well, I'd love to travel. This is the first time I've been out of Boston in years. I didn't realize how sick of the place I was."

Jess was speechless, unable to imagine tiring of her favorite city, her home.

The door swung open to reveal Derry, breathlessly elegant in a gray suit and midnight-blue tie that was the same color as his eyes.

How delicious. He'd changed for dinner like some old-fashioned British aristocrat. She lost herself in a deep appreciation for his style, a breathtaking display that made her knees go weak.

Waves of glossy, inky hair framed his face, the contrast between the wild abandon of warrior hair and the cool sophistication of the suit turning her into a throbbing mess.

"Sick of what?" he asked.

Molly yelped softly and stepped back, her sharp heel digging into Jess's toe. "Nothing!"

"Watch what you say in front of Gavin," Derry said. "He's as jumpy as a cat on hot bricks tonight. You'd think he'd be happy about getting married." After stepping aside to usher them in, he closed the door and took Molly's coat, his polite smile too friendly for Jess, who was discovering she was capable of shocking levels of possessiveness.

"She was talking about Boston," Jess said. "She's enjoying getting out of the city."

"Ah," Derry said. "I rather miss it already."

Jess took off her parka and held it out to him, feeling herself flushing hot to be so close to him again. "I do too."

Molly was already grabbing a glass of wine from a tray and striding over to greet Eva, her tight pants showing every curve of her ass and thighs. Fearing what she'd see in his face, Jess turned to look at Derry.

His gaze was pinned on her, not Molly. "Jess," he said, the word sliding over her like a kiss.

"This is going to be hard," she whispered. Her fingers itched to grab his lapel and hitch her legs around his hips.

A pinched look came into his expression. "It's already hard," he muttered.

She laughed, and after a long moment, he chuckled and ducked his head. "We'll think of it as a game," he said. "With fantastic prizes at the end for the winners."

Others were watching them. She turned, waved at Lilah, Eva, Gavin, and her mother, then said to Derry under her breath, "I feel faint. Get me a drink?"

He bowed. "At once, Jessica Murphy. Perhaps you should sit down while I retrieve it. If you stumbled, I'd have no choice but to lift you in my arms, and we both know where that would lead."

They sure did. "White wine, please."

"As you wish."

Jess walked over to her mother, who was standing behind Lilah with a huge smile on her face, just beaming at everyone as she nibbled on a puff pastry.

But when Marilyn saw Jess, her lips pressed together in a flat line. "You two," she said under her breath, dripping with disapproval.

"What? We didn't do anything," Jess said.

Marilyn rolled her eyes. "I could see the steam rising from way over here."

"We can't help that."

"I suppose not." Sighing, Marilyn shoved the rest of the pastry in her mouth. "At least you're trying."

Appearing with two wine glasses, Derry handed them each one. "There is no try, only do." When Marilyn took the glass, he kissed her on the cheek, and she flushed.

Jess smiled into her glass.

"So, Derry," Marilyn began, a fake smile on her face. "What is it you do, actually? For a living?"

His eyes darted to Jess for a split second. She could see the moment he turned into the charming but stupid playboy, as if flipping a switch. "Me?" He pointed a thick finger at his heart.

"Yes, you," Marilyn said. "I suppose you don't need the money, but you must do something to keep busy."

Choking down nervous laughter, Jess looked down at her feet, searching for holes in the floorboards to crawl through.

"I've devoted my energies to areas where I excel best," he said. "Enjoying myself and sharing that enjoyment with others."

"Aren't you getting a bit old to party all the time?" Marilyn asked.

Jess's head snapped up. "Mom, please. Enough with the inquisition. This isn't the time or the place."

"Then when?" her mother asked.

Jess glared. "Nev—"

"Whenever you'd like," Derry said. "Although perhaps it would be best to defer it until after the current celebration."

"You'd come over for dinner?" Marilyn asked. "My house isn't anything fancy."

Fearing her mother was going to annoy Derry with her assumptions about the future, Jess grabbed her arm and tried to pull her away. "Oh look. Everyone's starting to sit down for dinner."

But Derry took one long step and blocked their way. "It would be an honor to be welcome in your home," he said with a bow.

"Jesus, Mary, and Joseph, you Stanton men sure have a way about you," Marilyn said.

They sure did. Jess plastered a smile on her face. "Let's sit. Lilah told me your seat is near Asher." With fake enthusiasm, she propelled her mother across the room to a chair at the far end of the table. She parked her there and fled to her own seat, blissfully several chairs away and out of sight.

"What cruelty is this?" Derry's voice rumbled in her ear, tickling the fine hairs at her temple. "To be sitting so close to such a forbidden fruit?" Plucking the card with his name in fancy script off the plate next to hers, he pulled out the chair and sat, his knee brushing hers before jerking away.

She lowered her voice. "What kind of fruit?"

Fixing his gaze on his wine glass, his lips twitched. "Plum, I think. You're too spicy to be a peach."

"You know what my favorite fruit is?"

"Ah, good. Such simple, harmless conversation. Tell me, what is your favorite fruit?"

"Don't you want to guess?"

"Certainly, if you like," he said. "Apple, perhaps?"

"Nope."

He swirled the wine in his glass. "Grapes?"

"Come on, you're not even trying."

"My apologies. Perhaps the delicious pear?"

She shook her head. "Banana," she said, licking a droplet of wine off the rim of her glass.

Scowling, he ran a hand through his hair. "You torture me. You insist I behave, and then you torture me."

She giggled into her napkin. He looked so uncomfortable. Just wait until she started playing footsies under the table—

Oh no. She was doing it again.

No, no, no. She'd promised Lilah. She'd *promised*.

"I'm sorry," she said, inhaling deeply, trying to regain her composure. Sitting up taller, she exchanged hellos with Edward, who was sitting across from her, before draining her water glass.

Derry leaned forward and gave his little brother a dark look. "No plaid tonight?"

In a perfectly tailored dark suit with his full beard neatly trimmed, Edward looked like a rich lumberjack. *Not a bad look at all*, Jess thought.

Offering a sarcastic smile, Edward glanced at Molly to his left, who was pink-cheeked as she gazed across the table at Derry. "Hello again."

Molly turned. "Evan! Hi!"

Above his beard, Edward's own cheeks turned red.

Derry's mirth tumbled out of him in low, throaty laughter. Not wanting Molly to be embarrassed further, Jess kicked him under the table.

He shot her a smoldering look. Perhaps even violence to his shins was too seductive.

"It's Edward, actually," the poor man said apologetically.

"Oh my God, I did it again." Molly flung her head back and sighed. "This is why they keep me hidden away in the dressing room."

"I can't imagine why anyone would ever want *you* to hide," Edward said. His voice had dropped in pitch, almost softening to a purr.

Derry's laughter turned into a chuckle. "Good one, little brother."

Edward turned to Molly. "Ignore him. Tell me about yourself." He seemed awkward, as if the words had been rehearsed. Large social events were clearly not his thing.

While Molly launched into a summary of her job dressing the staff and assisting the members with their own personal style, Jess and Derry fell silent. Edward, eyes fixed on Molly, seemed transfixed and said little. Lilah herself came by with salads for everyone, laughing about Gavin getting tomato sauce on his jacket in the kitchen because he'd bumped into the chef carrying the lasagna.

Then Molly asked Jess about applying to med school, her ambitions to be a doctor or a researcher, and Jess found herself blushing under Derry's steady stare as she talked. They hadn't talked much about themselves, had they? It had all gone too fast, been too hot for conversation.

When Edward abruptly asked Molly about her boots—he didn't understand the point of them since high heels were so impractical—Jess softly asked Derry, "Do you have any hobbies?"

"You know what my hobbies are," he said.

"Seriously. That's it?"

"You wound me," he said, placing a hand over his heart. "Have I ever pretended to be anything other than what you see?"

"No. Which is why I'm suspicious. Maybe you've got something to hide."

He lowered his voice. "You know I do."

"Other than that."

"What are you imagining, my dear?" he asked. "I assure you I am not married. Nor have I fathered any offspring. My adventures with women are well publicized—"

"I'm not talking about anything like that," she said. "Never mind. Forget it."

They finished their salads in silence. When the plates were taken away, Jess talked to Carl, seated at her right, about how nice it was to be waited on for a change.

After a few minutes, Derry's elbow nudged hers.

"I was just trying to make conversation," she said.

Instead of replying, he took his phone out of his pocket.

"You want to text?" she asked. "That's easier for you?"

"Calm down, tigress," he said softly. "I'm giving you what you want. As I am wont to do." He held out the phone, tilting the screen toward her.

It was a picture of a naked woman. A photo of a painting, she realized. The woman was dark-haired and voluptuous, reclining on a white sofa.

Derry swiped the screen and revealed a second photo, this time of a different painting, a different woman. Then a third.

When she reached up to take the phone and see more for herself, he pulled it away and shoved it back into his pocket.

Making sure nobody was watching, she asked, "Did you do those?"

"Define 'do,'" he said.

"Paint," she said, torn between tears and laughter.

"Would you be bothered if I had?"

"I don't understand," she said. "Why would I be?"

"Some women would be uncomfortable."

"Posing might be," she said. "Especially if the room was too drafty."

"I keep it quite warm in my studio for that reason."

"You have a studio?"

Nodding, he drained his glass and signaled for the waiter. When his glass was refilled, he drained it again. "It's part of my loft."

"It's hard for you to talk about, isn't it?" she asked softly. They were careening into deep, personal territory. Jess loved it.

"Please don't . . . share . . . this with anyone. I'd be eternally grateful. Desperately grateful, in fact."

"Your family doesn't know?"

Shooting a glance at Edward, who was still talking to Molly, he shook his head. The tension in his expression made her realize how hard it had been to share his secret with her.

"They're really good," she said softly. "You're an artist."

The look he gave her was so grateful, so searching, she wanted to climb into his lap and hold him forever.

Derry had detected a change in Jess as soon as she'd walked into Gavin's cabin, where the rehearsal participants had all convened, ready to be wined and dined and to make small chat that would grate at him, each second of it time he could not spend talking with Jess.

As she'd made her way across the room, there had been an edge to her, her scent tinged with fear and a hunger for acceptance that had made him ache. Fear. Why fear? It had been no normal scent. His nose discerned layers in every person's emotional states, like the microexpressions muscles created in giving visual cues to a person's inner mood. Derry could find the finely tuned nuance of emotion in a person's odor.

Jess's had just migrated from a typical nervousness to a deeper, more complex fear that had put him on alert. It had nothing to do with basic nervousness or even her mother's obligatory questioning.

Some other issue was troubling her.

And he'd vowed to make it go away.

His worry had turned to unadulterated joy as he'd watched her, animatedly speaking with Molly and Edward, her hair coated in the scent of sunshine and foliage, her skin radiating fresh desire that intensified when her eyes met his.

And then he'd revealed his secret. His painting—his lifeblood. And now he, too, was nervous.

You're an artist.

My God, this woman. This perfect, ripe goddess.

"I'm sorry we couldn't walk here in the moonlight together. I missed you," he murmured, struggling to remain courtly and restrained, wanting only to paint her nude, gorgeous form for the rest of his life.

With his tongue.

"We were apart for fifteen minutes."

"An eternity."

"You're recycling your own pickup lines," she joked, tossing her long, honeyed waves behind one shoulder, making him sigh in carefully layered hitches lest he groan.

"No, my dear. I miss you so much that I feel the need to say it twice." He reached under the tablecloth for her knee.

He received her hand instead, fingers entwining with his, a sweet domestic gesture that quelled him.

"Is something wrong?" he whispered. "You don't seem

yourself." Perhaps his paintings bothered her. A tremor of vulnerability rippled through him, incongruous and foreign. Did she dislike what she saw? Was she being polite in calling him an artist? Had he misjudged her reaction?

Jess opened her mouth to explain just as he felt it. Felt her fear, the skin on his back prickling with the cool heat of animal instinct.

Before he looked up, he knew exactly what he would see.

Asher. Watching them from the head of the table.

He knows.

Jess's voiceless words slammed through his head like a lightning bolt, so swift and hard he flinched, crushing the small bones of her hand with his squeeze. She gasped. He let go.

I'm so sorry, he said silently.

But it wasn't her hand that hurt, for she rubbed her own brow as well.

"How can I hear your thoughts?" she asked, her voice trembling, her words spilling off her tongue.

Just then, he noticed Lilah standing behind them, tapping on Jess's back, her eyes widening as it became all too clear that she'd heard Jess's question.

Lilah paled. "You can *hear* him? In your mind?" Lilah's voice was so low Derry could feel it in his bones. But his future sister-in-law's eyes weren't on Jess.

They were on him.

Flustered, Jess stood abruptly, the glass of Chardonnay that rested between her and Derry's table settings upending, pouring a cool six ounces of white wine right into his lap. He felt the liquid but did not react, for Lilah's piercing gaze could not be escaped.

And then he felt Jess's hand on his cock.

"I'm such a klutz!" Jess said, patting at his crotch with a napkin twisted in the shape of a swan. "I am so sorry!"

Lilah gaped at the sight of her sister's hand pumping up and down in his lap. Derry snapped up Jess's wrist in his grasp. He could've easily held both her wrists in one hand and still have room in his palm.

The image made him woozy.

And hard.

"Oh my God!" Jess gasped, realizing what she was doing. "I-I'm so sorry! I can't do anything right, can I?" Biting her lower lip, she dropped the napkin, her face aflame. She looked up, behind Derry, and froze. He didn't have to turn to see why.

He felt him.

Asher. Still watching from his seat.

"May I have a word with you?" Lilah asked, her voice tight, blonde waves framing a very angry face.

"Of course!" Jess murmured, wiggling around the chair, breathing hard with anxiety. Derry's limbs filled with blood, ready to jump up and help, to intervene, to rescue her.

"Not you. Him." Lilah's words squeezed between tightly gritted teeth as she pulled Derry's arm, her fingers bunching his suit jacket, the effort useless if she truly thought she could move him by force.

He stood, obeying her request, following Lilah's tiny, quick steps made in beautiful turquoise high heels that showcased legs that reminded him of her sister. These Murphy women were damned enchanting. What special magic did they possess that made them so irresistible to Stanton men?

Deep in his thoughts, he didn't realize Lilah had stopped suddenly and turned to face him. Too late to stop his momentum, Derry bowled into her full-on, knocking her backward, making her shoes clatter on the marbled floor. Quick thinking allowed him to break her fall, hands on her waist, one snaking up behind her back as his palm opened against the space between her shoulder blades.

"Are you all right?" he whispered into her hair, their bodies smashed together as he released her, unharmed and still upright.

Self-conscious and worried, he flooded with relief at the fact that Lilah hadn't been hurt.

"You can hear each other's thoughts?" Lilah gasped, her face going a ghastly white.

"Lilah, what's wrong?" Gavin asked, then glared at Derry as if he'd made her unhappy.

Gavin and Lilah's words felt like bullets peppering his body, each causing more damage than the last. "I didn't—I don't know what's going on!" he protested.

"Can you hear my sister?" Lilah demanded. "In your mind?"

He reeled back. "How did you know?"

Derry watched in abject horror as she slumped against his brother in a dead faint.

Before he could react, Gavin had Lilah on the ground and Jess was bending over her, ripping her dark sweater over her head and bunching it under Lilah's feet, barking orders to Gavin involving water, air, and a pillow.

"What the hell happened?" Jess snapped, her focus on Lilah.

"Nothing!" Derry assured her as Gavin dashed out of the room to get the items Jess ordered.

Derry watched Jess reach for the soft skin under Lilah's jaw and feel for a pulse as she closed her eyes and appeared to count. Clad only in a light chemise and her skirt, Jess's skin broke out in gooseflesh from the cold.

Ignoring him, Jess continued to minister to Lilah, moving with a precision and professionalism that made Derry stand back and observe with a deep respect. Jess was a premed student, he knew.

Now he could see it in her.

Lilah's eyelids fluttered as Jess stroked her cheek. Unfocused but gaining consciousness, Lilah sat up, then promptly fell back. Jess caught her before she slammed her head into the marbled floor.

"Jess," Lilah gasped. "Jess, you can't. You can't change."

Derry went numb.

Jess chuckled, the sound carrying the tone of someone who is humoring another person. "I'll always be here for you. I'll never change."

"No, no," Lilah murmured. "I mean—" Her words faded off as she took a deep breath, clearly centering herself.

Derry knew *exactly* what she meant even if Jess didn't.

The murmur of voices behind them made him turn. A crowd, led by Eva, came toward them. Derry looked at Jess, dressed only in her thin piece of silk lingerie, and shrugged out of his suit jacket, slipping it about her shoulders. She gave him a surprised look.

He leaned forward, speaking through lips that weren't quite his. "While your state of undress is absolutely enchanting to me, there's no need to share that much beauty with the public right now, my dear."

She gave him a grateful look and returned her attention to Lilah, who now had Gavin next to her, stroking her hand. Jess offered Lilah some water and took her pulse.

"I'm fine. Fine!" Lilah insisted, waving off the attention. "I just think I went too long without eating and then drank wine on an empty stomach."

Gavin frowned but recovered quickly, glaring at Derry, who looked away. Lilah stood, legs shaky but gaining strength as the crowd made polite sounds of relief and Jess and Gavin helped her back to the large party table, leaving Derry alone.

Numb. Derry was numb. Lilah didn't want Jess to experience The Change.

Which meant Lilah didn't want him to be with her sister at all.

Twenty-One

After dinner, Jess refused to go back to the main house until Lilah agreed to talk to her privately. Something had happened—Lilah had never fainted before in her life—and Jess was determined to understand what. Since the fainting, Derry had withdrawn into himself, plastering that fake playboy shtick of his on the outside, charming everyone with compliments and a steady stream of bawdy jokes.

But whenever Jess had caught his eye, his humor had faded, and above his rakish smile, his eyes were sad.

What had Lilah said to him? Or was it something *he* had said to *her*?

When the family gathered at the door to leave, Jess hung back, half expecting Derry to do the same so he could flirt with her or escort her back to the main house—but he only gave her a nod as he walked out with the others.

"Can't this wait, Jess?" Lilah asked quietly, rubbing her temples. She was putting on her coat to sleep in a private room in the main house, avoiding Gavin until the ceremony the next day. "I still feel weird from fainting like that. Tomorrow's kind of a big day."

Gavin, also in his coat, strode over and put a protective arm around his bride, giving Jess a stern look. "Don't you think you've done enough? Walk over with us but don't upset Lilah."

Jess felt both guilty and annoyed. "She's already upset. I want to know why." She opened the door. "I'll walk with her, Gavin. You stay here. You have the rest of your lives to be together." The sweet, simple truth of this lodged deep into her bones. It was what she wanted for herself, what she was beginning to think she was close to having.

"I need to be there in case she faints again," Gavin said, hugging Lilah closer. "I can carry her—"

Touching his face, Lilah twisted out of his embrace. "No, she's right. I have to talk to her. We'd have trouble separating tonight anyway, and you know it. Without Jess, you'd probably end up spending the night with me in the house."

Gavin's mouth curved into a wicked smile. "So?"

"Tomorrow," Lilah whispered, going up on tiptoe to kiss him. "Then forever."

"Always," Gavin growled, closing his eyes.

Flushing from the heat the bride and groom were generating, Jess stepped outside and waited another minute for Lilah to join her.

Finally the two sisters were alone, walking together in the darkness.

"What happened in there?" Jess demanded.

"Well, I kissed him, he kissed me, I grabbed his—"

"Not *that*. God. As if I couldn't guess," Jess said. "The *fainting*. What did you say to Derry?"

Lilah paused. "I didn't. Everything went dark, and the next thing I knew, you were half-naked, looking down at me on the floor."

"Why did you want to talk to him in the first place?"

Lilah tugged her collar up around her face. "I don't remember," she mumbled.

"Quit stonewalling. Tell me." Jess grabbed her elbow. "Please.

Something huge is happening, but I don't know enough. You're marrying a guy who turns into a wolf, but you're more upset about me sleeping with his brother, who by the way can turn into a bear, but that's not what made you so upset, and now you won't explain!"

Lilah's mouth dropped so low her chin nearly hit the floor. "You know they're shifters?"

"You told me!"

"And you ridiculed me!" Lilah shrieked. She grabbed her head and moaned, flinching, looking around in case anyone else heard.

"It was a pretty ridiculous statement to make, Lilah! No one would believe it." Her voice went soft, vision blurring with over-whelm. "I still can't quite believe it, but I saw."

"Saw?" Lilah looked horrified. "Saw *what*?" She clutched the neck of her own shirt like she was holding on to the earth.

"Saw Derry . . . change. So yeah, I believe it now."

"Oh, Jess." Lilah reached over and gripped her forearm, her shoulders dropping with relief. "I see."

"Why . . . why are you so upset then? Because I know?"

"No."

"Because I'm with Derry?" If being with a wolf was good enough for Lilah, being with a bear shouldn't raise any eyebrows, least of all her sister's.

"I didn't realize. I couldn't believe that *Derry* . . . I mean, I assumed it was just sex for him. Derry was just being Derry, not caring how he was going to hurt you," Lilah said. "But now . . . if you've seen him shift, if you can . . . hear him . . . I can't interfere. I think that's why I fainted. I was trying to interfere with fate."

"What? That's nuts."

"This is bigger than me," Lilah said. "Bigger than you. It's dangerous to try to stop it. We don't know enough."

Jess felt her sister's forehead. "You must've struck your head when you fainted. That headache could be signs of a concussion."

"They're shifters," Lilah said. "You believe that now because you saw it for yourself. Nothing I said could've convinced you, but now you understand, somehow, that it's true and possible and real. You can *feel* it. Like faith. Or love." She spoke that last word like a caress.

"You thought I was falling in love with Derry? Is that what upset you?"

"I already knew you were falling in love with him. I was afraid he was going to break your heart."

Jess cast her mind back to the dinner. Suddenly she remembered. "You freaked out when you heard me ask why I could hear Derry's thoughts."

"Then you *can* hear him?"

"Yes," Jess breathed. "What does it mean?"

Lilah pressed her thumbs to her temples. "I don't know. I thought I did, but I'm not sure."

"Is your scar bothering you again?"

Lilah had an old scar that had given her piercing headaches for most of her life. "It's been hurting ever since I tried to talk to Derry," Lilah said. "I don't think I'm supposed to get involved. You two have to figure this out for yourselves."

"Can you and Gavin hear each other's thoughts?"

"Yes," Lilah said.

"From early on? Before . . . you were really close?"

"From the first moment. I knew, and he knew, from the moment we met."

Jess hadn't known anything when she met Derry except that he was dangerously, impossibly sexy.

Holding Jess by the shoulders, Lilah continued. "There are shifter legends about love and fate. About finding the One for you. Gavin is mine. I am his. I could hear this in my mind from very early on. It was magnetic and undeniable. Not all the shifters believe the legend, but it's ancient, and I've seen a book—"

She dropped Jess's shoulders and clutched her skull. "I can't talk anymore."

Seeing her sway, Jess quickly embraced her. "You need to get in bed. Gavin was right. I was selfish to keep you out here in the cold."

As she helped her sister down the path to the house and then escorted her to a quiet suite far from any of the other guests, Jess thought about how *certain* Lilah was about Gavin, love and fate, everything.

Jess hadn't felt anything like that. She doubted everything— herself, Derry, their future. Had Derry looked so unhappy because he'd known they didn't have what Lilah and Gavin did?

After getting Lilah into bed with a hot wrap and a kiss on the cheek, Jess returned to her own room, more confused than ever.

⸻

The next day, Jess stood with the other bridesmaids at the altar in their glamorous gowns, waiting for Lilah to appear at the top of the white carpet. She had butterflies in her stomach and a tissue in her fist and kept sneaking glances at Derry, hopelessly trying to read his mind.

Are you the One? she wondered.

Silence. And his face over the impeccable tuxedo was stony and unreadable, a stranger's face. He'd withdrawn behind his fortress, and she wished she could do the same.

The room had been impressive the day before, but now it was staggeringly beautiful. Like an arctic fairyland, everything was in shades of white—the roses, the aisle carpet, the silk-cushioned chairs, the billowing curtains hung from the painted ceiling, the hundreds of candles in crystal vases lining the aisle, and the trees.

Yes, trees.

Rising out of stone pillars and clouds of cotton, two dozen trees, leafless and snowy-branched, arched over the aisle. She and

Derry had promenaded between them, not sharing any jokes or comments this time, both of them perhaps overwhelmed by the moment.

Everything was breathtaking. Unreal. Magical.

And then Lilah had appeared, as beautiful as a dream, her gown the same white as the trees but trimmed with a shade of gold that perfectly matched her gleaming hair. The guests gasped and fell silent, watching her pass with awe.

Gavin clasped Lilah's hand, and they turned together to Eva to begin their future.

As Eva read the vows, each word made Jess think of Derry.

Love. Honor. Forever.

Jess stared at a single rose in Lilah's bouquet, trying not to listen anymore, because if she heard too much, she'd cry or jog across the room in her silver heels to fling herself into Derry's arms.

"I now declare you are married," Eva said.

When Gavin took Lilah in his arms and kissed her, the guests sighed as one being, then burst into applause. It was done.

Thinking it was finally safe to look at Derry, Jess broke her gaze from Lilah's bouquet and searched for the black hair, the blue eyes, the slanted brows.

Him.

It was as if he, too, had been waiting for this moment to look at her. Their gazes slid together and held. Frozen in place, heart pounding, she drank in the sight of him and thought of every kiss, every embrace, his laugh, his kindness, his love.

I love you.

She didn't know who said it. It rang in her mind and echoed in every atom of her body.

I love you.

A soft nudge from behind reminded her of where she was: standing like an idiot in front of hundreds of people who were waiting for her to follow Lilah and Gavin down the white, rose-petal-dotted aisle.

She was supposed to touch him again, but she didn't dare. Although Derry held out an elbow, she ignored it and hoped her teary smile would distract people from seeing she hadn't taken her partner's arm. Without arguing, he walked beside her, not touching. Perhaps he, too, was afraid to risk any contact right now, when their emotions were so high.

Artificial snow began falling from the ceiling, dusting the bride and groom, as well as the trees, flowers, candles, and guests, with delicate fluff. Everyone laughed in delighted surprise, lifting their faces to the tiny flakes. It was like swimming in heaven, where everything was clean and bright and happy, and even the snow was warm.

This, Jess thought. *This is what I want. This happiness.*

Ahead of them, Lilah and Gavin disappeared into a private room, where they would have a moment alone before greeting everyone. The wedding party broke apart and faded into the crowd to find a glass of Champagne or a friend before walking downstairs to the reception.

She felt Derry's presence behind her—large, strong, and familiar. She'd never wanted to hold him so badly.

"Jess," he said roughly.

"We can't. Not yet."

"I know. Asher is watching."

She was so tired of that man. "I don't care about him. I care about Lilah."

"He knows," Derry said. "We should be careful."

The crowd jostled them apart for a few long moments. They reunited in the hallway as the current of people flowed toward the staircase.

Jess glanced over her shoulder at the family patriarch. He *was* watching. "Who cares what he knows or doesn't know?"

"I care." Derry smiled at a stranger, then waved at another

woman who was winking at him.

It was too much. She let the current pull him away from her and decided to get drunk with Molly.

He wished he could swallow his tongue. Reverse time. Turn back the hands by thirty seconds and reboot. As Jess let the crowd take her from him, a sour, questioning expression on her beautiful face, he kicked himself.

She was right. Who cared what Asher thought?

"Do you know what I think?" said an ominous voice from behind him.

Fuck. The devil himself.

"I do not know what you think, Asher," Derry said in his best, breezy voice. "You are not my One. I cannot fathom what goes on in that tight little closed drum of a mind that you possess. Nor would I want to." He flicked his wrist with a gesture meant to condescend as he turned toward the bar.

"I think you want a piece of Gavin's life, and you've stooped to an all-time low in rutting with Lilah's sister."

Asher never was one to mince words.

"Pigs rut. I am not a pig." Second time in two days he was compared to a pig. Funny, that.

"Bears rut too, Derry. You just can't see it because she's a human, and humans do not have rutting times."

"You sound like a nature documentary filmmaker, Asher. What's next? Will you quote me facts about parasites that take over grasshoppers and turn them into zombies?"

"I feel like one half the time, Derry."

"A zombie grasshopper?" Derry peered at him in mock appraisal. "I can see the resemblance."

Asher, as he so often did, ignored the joke. "All I seem to do is watch animals make fools of themselves, clean up their messes, and observe it."

A flame of pure rage set his blood on fire, removing all humor from his body in one cold snap. "She's not a mess."

"You've made so many. How could you possibly know?"

Because she's the One.

The words should have poured out from him, in anger or passion or some semblance of righteous indignation, but they caught in his throat like long hair in a thistle patch. He made eye contact with his eldest brother, seeing coloring so similar to his own but on a body with sleeker bones, wiry and preternaturally calm. Asher carried himself like a leader. Dry and standoffish, he triggered instant self-consciousness in most people. He expected obedience and respect. While Derry was inclined to find such expectations to be pure folly, his entire life he'd extended both to Asher.

No more.

He wouldn't dare give an inch of emotional vulnerability to the person who represented the greatest threat to his lifelong happiness. And when you lived a life that stretched into multiple centuries, the stakes were high.

"My private life has never been the subject of inquiry from you before, Asher. Why the sudden interest?" Derry gripped a side table, his fingers pressing hard enough to leave marks in the wood. His vision sharpened, nose a thousand times more sensitive, senses bristling. A fluke of their physical environment had them in a corner to themselves, shielded by a long hors d'oeuvres table.

Asher's voice felt like a lethal kiss as he said, "It's bad enough that Gavin has decided to marry a human."

"She's not just any human." Derry meant Lilah, but the statement applied to Jess as well.

"She's an exception, yes." Asher's eyes gleamed with a repressed resentment, as if he wished his own words weren't true. "But an exception. Not a rule."

Derry remained silent. Asher was accustomed to Derry's blathering, a nervous chatter he used in social settings to get away from pesky interrogations. As his blood pounded through him, nearly boiling, rushing against the walls of his veins and arteries like thousands of tsunamis, he knew that this was no mere conversation.

Not a simple argument.

With words, right now, Derry was fighting for his life.

He nudged his head to the left, motioning toward a set of sliders that took them out into an enclosed courtyard, a small patio used for private dinners. Two tables with four wrought iron chairs at each were balanced perfectly on alternating slate and obsidian landscaping stones, the slate dusted with a fine powder of snow that had fallen this morning.

Everything was black or white.

As the door made a *snick* sound, indicating its closure, Derry whirled around, pulse throbbing, self-consciousness long gone. He took in Asher's features in the sunlight, combing over him as if seeing him for the first time. Dark hair. Blue eyes. Long face. Aquiline nose.

He was a man. Just a man. A shifter, yes, but one who was no more or less possessed of intrinsic power than any other. Not the monolithic, all-powerful brooding patriarch Derry had subsumed himself to all these years.

Just a man.

And a smaller one than Derry, at that.

"Get to the point," he snapped, sounding so much like Gavin that he surprised himself, Asher's tiny flinch a confirmation.

Asher made a derisive sound. "I have. Repeatedly. The fact that you're too enchanted with a piece of quim to—"

The crunch came with the acrid scent of wet copper, his knuckles registering the pain long, long after he found the odor, nostrils twitching. Asher's body did not move; only his head snapped sharply to the left as Derry's right hook took out the bridge of his nose.

As the reality of punching his brother seeped into his barely functioning brain, a tiny voice inside cheered. It sounded remarkably like Gavin.

Asher dipped his head down, his silence eerie. Derry stopped breathing, every hair follicle on his body tingling, ready to shift.

Blood began to drip from Asher's nose, marring the perfect white of the new-fallen snow.

"You will never speak of Jess that way. Are we clear?" The pain he should have felt in his hand—for hitting Asher was much like striking an ancient standing stone—dissipated as his words took on strength.

Asher's chin stayed down as he calmly, coolly reached into his jacket, the breast pocket containing the ever-present ironed handkerchief that Derry knew so well, being the recipient of its use during much of his childhood. Dabbing his nose, Asher looked up and took Derry's eyes captive.

"My deepest apologies for calling your latest conquest a quim. Is there another word you prefer?"

Yes, he thought.

Wife.

"Derry! Asher!" Edward's outraged voice pierced the moment before he could open his mouth in reply. "What in the hell are you doing?" His voice shook, hand going to the buttons of his tuxedo, mouth dropped open, leaving the end of his beard covering his tie.

"We were having a brotherly conversation," Asher said drolly. "Derry was just telling me about his new love."

"It's official, then?" Edward said, turning to Derry. "You and Jess?"

Asher's right eyebrow quirked up.

"You know too?" he asked, the words not quite forming a question.

"I found them in the garage in your—um, uh . . . in, well . . ." Edward's eyes flashed with panic as it became evident to Derry that his little brother knew damn well the consequences of confessing to Asher what Derry and Jess had been doing in his beloved Rolls-Royce.

Asher faced off against Derry, sniffing just once. He must have swallowed the blood.

Derry reeled. Taking on Asher was supposed to be harder than this. Standing up to the person who had controlled him—even out of his presence—for so many years should be more difficult. Had it really been so easy all along, and he hadn't known?

"Jessica Murphy and I are officially together," he declared, shoulders squaring, pulling himself to his full, considerable size, towering over both his brothers.

Silence. Asher just stared at him. Edward looked down at the blood on the snow and cringed, eyes jumping between Derry and Asher.

Finally, one corner of Asher's mouth quirked up.

"That's not what her mother and sister told me."

Of all the words that could have poured out of Asher's mouth, those were the last he expected to hear.

A great numbness seized him, making him close his eyes and take a deep breath, the inhale so long he wondered if he could stretch it beyond eternity.

"What did Lilah and Marilyn say?" Edward asked, too naïve to realize the statement wasn't open for discussion. Now that he had given Asher an opportunity, of course he would go in for the kill.

Derry and Asher both looked at their youngest brother, who removed himself immediately from the situation, opening the glass door to return to the reception. As the door opened, the cacophony of joyous celebration made Derry's party heart leap with excitement at the same time that he hunkered down for the fight of his life.

Living in parallel was a given when you were a shifter.

Living two emotional lives simultaneously when it came to Asher was a price too high to pay.

"You really do not understand the gravity of the situation, do you?" Asher said slowly, his voice emerging like cracked ice. He ignored the slow trickle of one drop of blood that made its way from his nostril, pooling at the curve of his upper lip.

"I understand that you hate the fact that anyone else ever finds love."

Asher's left eyelid twitched, sunlight pinpointing his pupils, the white shine of light against the new snow making every detail harsher. Starker.

"This has nothing to do with love," Asher spat.

"This has everything to do with love, you fool."

The word came out at the end, tacked on like an afterthought, a term Asher had thrown at him hundreds of times in his life. Asher's face remained impassive, that damned drop of blood cresting over his lip's edge, now spreading at the crease of his mouth, as if filling in the chasm between them.

"Her humanity is our downfall."

"What?"

"Humans. You and Gavin fail to understand how much time and effort goes into shielding our kind from humans. How much of *my* time and effort. While you're globetrotting on your 'Around The World in Eighty Women' tour, I am here at the ranch performing constant damage control."

Derry bristled at the barb. "I have never jeopardized our kind. Not one woman. I have never revealed the secret. Jess learned from Lilah. Not me."

Asher's sigh finally made him crack, his lips licking the blood Derry had elicited, the edges of his teeth glowing pink with a nasty, predatory look that sped up Derry's pulse rate.

"I know that, McDermott." Oh. Getting formal now, were we?

Derry knew that trick. What would come next? His middle name?

"Then what the hell is wrong with humans?"

"The more they know about us, the more we become their target. Gavin made a mess of secrecy containment with that whole Mason Webb affair."

The conversation was detouring in directions Derry couldn't fathom. "What the hell does Mason Webb have to do with my being in love with Jess?" Webb had attacked Lilah last summer right here at the ranch. Gavin had shifted in a moment of protective rage, nearly killing Mason as he saved Lilah from being ravaged by the human piece of excrement.

"Mason Webb is one of many humans who represent a threat to our entire way of life. If he—and others like him—ever find out about the core shifter families, we'll be destroyed. Hunted. Ferreted out until bloodlines are destroyed." Asher closed his eyes and sighed, a long, winding sound of deep frustration. "Or worse."

"Worse? What could be worse?"

Asher's eyes gleamed with an intensity that made Derry feel two hundred pounds heavier, instantly, the burden so great his knees almost buckled.

"You do not want to know."

"Of course I want to know. You sound like a raving lunatic, Asher. Are you so desperate to ruin my happiness that you'll invent stories?" Calling Asher a liar would be tantamount to declaring World War III. He teetered on the edge.

Asher didn't take the bait. "Stay away from the humans, Derry. Dip your cock into them, take your pleasure, but don't fall in love. The more humans know about our truths, the more we're in danger. Falling in love with a human is just bringing us all one step closer to destruction."

"Gavin can love a human, but I can't?"

"Gavin is putting us all in danger. I've never sanctioned this marriage. In fact, I find the entire production akin to a funeral rather than a celebration of love."

"You would," Derry declared, the weight lifting as he realized what Asher was saying. "After all, *you* loved a human, too. And look what happened. Loving Claire destroyed you."

It was a relief, really, when his own nose snapped with the pain of Asher's punch. Bringing up Asher's late wife, who had died in childbirth before making the shift, taking their babe with her, was a low blow.

But a necessary one.

"Asher!" Sophia's high-pitched scream flooded his senses as he smelled her, all fire and disdain, the scent of lilies and shrimp mixed with her shower gel and the masculine odor of one of the catering staff ending as his nose filled with nothing but his own blood.

Her hands wrapped around Asher's forearm, steel against steel, and as the blinding lightning bolt of stinging pain made Derry's vision warble, he wondered who would win. Asher vs. Sophia.

That would be quite a show.

"Have you lost your mind?" she hissed, chiding Asher, who stared at Derry with deadly force that ought to have moved objects but instead left Derry with a cold, coiled sense that every molecule in the universe had just turned inside out. Blood dripped onto the white shirt of his tuxedo.

Asher shook her off as his head turned slightly left, slightly right, the reproach evident in his eyes. No, he said to Derry.

Just no.

And then he turned on his heel and walked out into the cold, cruel daylight, his shoulders broad and upright, body language clear.

Asher believed he was right.

Derry knew his eldest brother was wrong. And he would prove it.

"Did he hurt you? God, Derry, you're bleeding everywhere.

You always did have lots of nosebleeds when we were kids. You must have blood vessels close to the surface . . ." Sophia nattered on, reaching into her small clutch purse and pulling out a crumpled cocktail napkin, pressing it against his wet nostril. The words rolled over him like fog coming into a bay.

His mind became a blur.

"What was that all about? Why did Asher punch you in the face? What did you say, Derry? Why would he hit you? I've never seen him do that to you. Ever. Even when we were kids I—"

"I punched him first."

As the words came out of his mouth, mingled with the taste of his own blood, a light snow began. Under different circumstances, it would be romantic. It felt ominous now, a chill in the air that brought cover for events better left hidden.

"WHY?" Sophia screamed. "Why would you punch Asher?" Horror filled her features. He knew he was supposed to feel the same, to realize his transgression, but he was hollow. Drained.

Done.

"Because he told me I couldn't love Jess."

He had to reach out and grab his sister by the waist, for she reeled back at his words and her heels skittered on the slippery stones. "You *what*?"

"I love her. She's the One for me."

"Oh, Derry." Tears filled Sophia big brown eyes, and her muscles melted in his hands, going limp and soft, making him hold tighter in protection. She reached for the back of an iron chair and braced herself. "You're serious." The soft voice made his jaw loosen. He was rigid, on guard, and ready for battle.

Sophia was joining Derry. Was on his side.

"Yes."

"You love her that much?"

"Yes."

"She's not just a . . ."

Derry knew what she meant. "A piece of quim, like Asher just said?"

Sophia's eyes bugged out of her head. "He said that? About Lilah's sister?"

"Yes."

She nodded. "I see." He didn't have to explain.

"What are you doing here?" he asked, slowly coming to his senses. Dazed, he looked around the courtyard, marveling at the beauty. Fat, lazy flakes of snow fell all around, the air changing from an atmosphere of doom to one of intrigue. Of hope.

Of purpose.

"Edward found me. Said you and Asher were fighting. He was practically hyperventilating." She stood and reached for the napkin he still held to his nose, patting gently. "I can see why."

"Edward hates conflict."

"Until this moment, I'd have said the same of you." Her thick, shapely brows turned downward in question. "I've seen you spar with the guys, but this? Derry . . . what's happening to you?"

"Love." It sounded trite, but it was his truth.

"You're sure?"

"Why do you keep asking me that?" he growled.

The tears in her eyes swelled, clear orbs flowing over her lower lashes, unleashed and untamed. "Because I have no idea what you're feeling right now, and wish I could. How you can love someone so much that you risk everything for them. Is it a good feeling? Is it as wonderful as people say? I always thought it was a myth. Something that humans made up to feel better about their inferior little lives." Her breath hitched at the end, rendering her unable to speak as a small sob ended her words.

Derry nearly choked.

"Gavin feels it," he said softly, unable to give her the answers she wanted.

"Gavin's the exception."

"Funny. I think I am too. You gather enough exceptions, and you start to have a rule, Sophia."

Her eyes swam in tears. "You asshole." Sophia gave him a shaky, genuine smile, her broad face glowing with vicarious happiness even through the crying.

His lip curled up in amusement, making the pain in his nose worse. "I'm an asshole for realizing I'm deeply in love?"

"You're an asshole for changing, Derry. Don't change."

Lilah's murmured words as she fainted yesterday filled his mind.

"Jess, you can't. You can't change."

He closed his eyes slowly, the falling snow disappearing, felt only on the bones of his cheeks as flakes landed, then melted, turning into a facsimile of tears that matched his twin's real ones.

"It wasn't my decision, Sophia. I've changed already. I love her. She's my One. It was never a choice to begin with."

Twenty-Two

J ess drained her wine glass, ignoring her untouched food on
her plate, and fixed another fake smile on her face.

Next to Gavin at the long bridal table, Derry's seat was
empty.

He'd completely disappeared. In spite of her pleas, Sophia,
sitting to her right, wouldn't explain, although Jess could tell
she knew something. They all seemed to know why he wasn't
there—Edward, Sophia, Asher—but no one said a word to her or
made any announcements about the missing best man.

On display at the head table, seated between Lilah and Sophia,
she had to pretend that nothing was wrong and she was having
a wonderful, beautiful, unforgettable time.

Was it because she hadn't taken his arm? No, that was ridiculous. Maybe it was something with Asher. He'd been watching
them right before Derry went missing. Had the domineering
prick said something to drive him away? Was it possible that the
fresh bruise on his face was not, as he'd said, from walking into
the kitchen door, but from Derry's fist? Would Derry strike his
elder brother?

She picked up her fork and moved the lobster mac and cheese

around on her plate, her fake smile softening to a more authentic one.

"The mac had to be your idea," Jess said to Lilah. She'd always had a thing for mac and cheese. This luxurious version looked delicious, but her stomach was clenched too tightly.

"It was Gavin's, actually," Lilah said with a blissful sigh, then leaned back to accept another kiss from her husband while the guests cheered.

A dark idea was nagging at her: maybe Derry had slipped away to have sex with somebody else. That's certainly what the old Derry would've done. Hell, maybe he was in the middle of an orgy with six beautiful movie stars at this very minute, driven to it by the unfamiliar, unbearable trial of being celibate for an entire day.

During another kiss between the bride and groom, Sophia squeezed her hand. The gesture was so uncharacteristic, Jess had thought she'd been trying to grab the breadbasket or take her fork away. Before Jess could respond, Sophia had released her and turned to talk to Molly on her other side.

After a tense eternity, the meal was finally over, and Jess jumped up from the table to go looking for Derry. She didn't care what she'd find—and she knew it couldn't be her worst fear, she knew it—but she had to search anyway.

Sophia stopped her with a vise grip on her wrist. "They're doing the cake."

"I'm not hungry."

"He's giving the toast," Sophia said, gesturing over Jess's shoulder.

Standing behind her, appearing out of nowhere at his seat next to Gavin, Derry held a microphone—and his face was as battered as Asher's. It was impossible that both of them had such terrible luck with the kitchen door, wasn't it? Hair disheveled, cheeks flushed, and eyes shining, Derry now raised a glass and began to give a speech about Gavin's ugliness as a child, his pathological love of New England football, and his undeserved good fortune in having Lilah ever speak to him, let alone agree to—here he paused suggestively and let the crowd hoot and cheer—marry him.

"Where has he been?" Jess whispered to Sophia.

Sophia simply shook her head

Had he been fighting with Asher because of her? Had Asher found him in an orgy of beautiful, slutty wedding guests? In spite of the angry bruise on his face, he was smiling like the cat with a few gallons of cream—

No, she wouldn't believe he'd been in any orgies tonight. Given the circumstances, he was rising to the occasion and giving a lively, entertaining toast to the groom, putting on as much of an act as she was. And before . . .

She'd just have to ask him.

She tried to catch his eye, but he sat down on Gavin's far side and leaned away. There was cake and more speeches, and finally it was over. The groomsmen and bridesmaids were invited to dance with Gavin and Lilah, the lights dimmed, and the music grew louder and faster. Soon dozens of guests were on their feet, either headed to the dance floor or over to one of the several bars set up around the perimeter of the ballroom.

And Derry had disappeared again. While she'd been distracted by Gavin and Lilah's first dance, he'd slipped away without a word.

She looked around and found Molly standing next to her chair, holding two delicate glasses and a bottle of Champagne. "Come with me."

Shaking her head, Jess scanned the room again. "I need to find—"

"He's not here. I saw him leave."

"Which way was he walk—"

Molly leaned closer. "Look, I don't know what's going on with him, but I think you should take a minute to think before you do anything." She straightened, waving the bottle again. "Carl told me this stuff is two thousand bucks a bottle. You and I are going to drink it before anyone else gets it or either one of us does something stupid."

"But won't drinking it make it more likely that we would do something stupid?"

"Then we can blame it on the Champagne," Molly said triumphantly.

Warming to their blossoming friendship, Jess followed Molly out of the ballroom, slowly making their way around the sea of emptying tables and servers with trays of more drink and seconds of cake. In another large room across the hall, they found a spot tucked away in a nook behind a freestanding brick fireplace. They could barely hear the music, just the crackling of the fire and the hum of conversation. Luckily, most people had stayed in the ballroom for the dancing, and Jess felt herself unwinding in the peaceful, quiet spot.

She accepted the first glass of Champagne with a smile. "Thank you so much," she said, tapping her glass against Molly's. "I owe you one."

Grinning, Molly brought her glass to her mouth. "I figure each gulp is about fifty bucks." After her first sip, she licked her lips. "And worth it," she added with a sigh.

From the sound of voices, they could hear more guests come into the room, but they were hidden out of sight around the corner of the fireplace. A huge oil painting of a rolling green landscape—England?—hung on the wall behind them. Jess wondered if Derry ever painted landscapes or if he only did women.

She suspected the latter.

"Don't think about him," Molly said, elbowing her in the ribs, tightly bound by the bridesmaid dress bodice that Jess would be happy to take off as soon as possible. "At least not when you're angry. I'm sure there's nothing to worry about. He's crazy about you. Anybody can see that."

"I'm not angry at him."

"You seem angry," Molly said.

"I'm angry at his family. They've done something to him and now he's . . . I don't know what. That's why I'm a little tiny bit annoyed."

"Yeah, you were such a little bit annoyed, I was afraid you were going to smash cake into Asher's face," Molly said.

"I wasn't sitting anywhere near Asher."

Molly laughed and took another drink. "You were glaring at him like you had laser beams in your eyeballs. I thought he was going to burst into smoke."

"Like the demon he is," Jess muttered.

"I wouldn't know. I've never spent much time with him. He doesn't visit the club very often."

"Take it from me. He's bad news."

"And now he's part of your family," Molly said.

Jess finished her drink and held it out for a refill. "Let's not talk. Let's just drink."

Shrugging, Molly poured and fell silent. Jess stared at the painting, searching for a signature. Did Derry sign his work, or was he so private that he left them anonymous? Unwillingly, she wondered if he had slept with every model, or painted every lover, if he displayed his favorites in his bedroom so that he could relive his happiest, most sensual moments?

Would she have to make love to him with other women looking on?

". . . and the sister, the fat blonde," a man's voice said, carrying over the crackling of the fire, "she's another gold digger."

Molly and Jess locked eyes on one another, both instantly on the alert. Jess felt her face start to burn. The voice was familiar, but she couldn't place it.

"A social climber," the man's voice continued. He was the kind of man to talk high and loud, as if he were on stage and doing everyone a favor by projecting his voice into the far corners of the room. Like manspreading on the subway, only with his mouth. "Just saw her on campus, trying to suck up to my prof for a job. She's not really a student, of course. Just wants people to think she is."

Hand shaking, Jess set down her glass. Otherwise, she might've snapped its delicate stem in her grip.

Archibald Rumsey. Here. The bastard was here at the wedding, only several feet away. First at Professor Jane Lethbridge's office at Harvard, now here.

His father was a senator in this state. The Stantons must've felt obligated to invite their family.

Another man asked, "She thought she could seduce her?"

Archie laughed. "Professor Lethbridge has been known to swing both ways, but she'd never touch that townie cow. No, the bitch probably just wanted to say she 'went' to Harvard. You know how it is."

His companion made a grunt of agreement. "You called her a gold digger. I thought she'd hit on your professor."

"I'd love to see her try. Even if she dropped fifty pounds, Lethbridge would never stoop to that level. The girl was grateful to be invited to a pig party. I would know. I'm the one who invited her."

The other guy grunted like a real pig. "Come on."

"No shit. Today's maid of honor, the bride's sister, now the legal sister-in-law to the obscenely rich asshole Gavin Stanton, was my date to my frat's pig party a few years ago," Archie said. "She had no fucking idea. She actually thought I found her attractive. That I would bring her to a real party where other guys would see her with me."

"Well, it's not like she's ugly," his companion said. "I mean, she's kind of pretty, you've got to admit. Like you've always said about pig parties, *I'm not particular.*"

Jess's entire body flushed like ice water being pumped into her veins. Archie had said that the night he humiliated her. She was reliving every painful second.

"That's what a billion dollars can do for a girl," Archie said. "I'm sure the makeover cost a fortune. But it won't last. How could it?"

The other man didn't seem to agree, which obviously annoyed Archie. Raising his voice, he went on with even more malice. "They're cocktail waitresses, the both of them. What the hell is Stanton thinking? I mean, fuck her if you must, but . . . marry?" He snorted. "I hope he's got an ironclad prenup, the stupid bastard."

"You might want to keep your voice down, Arch. His family's all over this place. Your dad's a senator, but you're not. They'll kick your skinny ass out of here if you keep talking like that."

"The fuck they will. I'm friends with the best man," Archie said, laughing again.

Jess put her fist over her stomach, afraid she was going to throw up.

"Which one was that? I kind of dozed off during the ceremony."

"Dozed, my ass," Archie said. "You were still drunk from last night. Lucky for you the fake snow woke you up before you passed out in the aisle."

"I was not drunk. I was hungover."

"Same difference." Archie was getting impatient with his companion's change of subject. "I'm talking about the big guy, Derry. Gavin's brother. Now *he's* a man who knows how to have a good time. You're not going to see him stupid enough to let a fat waitress tie him down."

"I wouldn't mind letting that one tie me down for a little while," the guy said.

Archie groaned in disgust. "Not you too. You *are* drunk."

"Now I am," the man agreed. "Not letting expensive booze go to waste. But I wasn't earlier."

"Shut up and listen to me. I'm telling you something."

"When aren't you?"

"Derry Stanton was there," Archie said. "That's what I was trying to get through that thick, proletariat, alcoholic brain of yours."

"Of course he was there, he's the best man."

"Not the wedding, you stupid fuck. The pig party. At the frat house that night." Archie let out his breath, satisfied at finally delivering his bombshell. "And here he has to walk around with her all weekend, pretending he didn't remember how much fun we'd had with her a few years ago."

"Man, that's awkward."

"He doesn't care. He slipped away with some hot chick or two before things got messy at the party," Archie said. "Hold on, there he is. You've got to meet this guy. Hang out with him and you're sure to get laid."

"He's cute, but I'm not interested," the man said. There was a thump and a shout. "Hey, you spilled my drink."

"You were being an idiot," Archie said. He raised his already-loud voice to a bellow. "Derry! Derry Stanton! Over here!"

"Dude, you're hurting my ears."

"Shut up and act cool," Archie said. "He'll know which girls are extra fuckable. You don't want to go to bed alone tonight, do you?"

"I'm kind of tired—"

"Derry!" Archie shouted again.

The man groaned.

Jess felt a sharp pain on her wrist and realized it was Molly, gripping her arm. "Let's get out of here."

In a daze, Jess shook her head and removed Molly's fingers. She had to know it all. She had to. And besides, they couldn't get away without walking right by Archie and his drunk, slightly less hateful pal.

"Good evening," came Derry's voice, cheerful and sociable. "I trust you fine men are having a good time?"

Jess closed her eyes and began to tremble. Derry, so close. And he didn't sound like he was faking his happiness or his enjoyment of the evening. Wherever he'd been, whatever he'd been doing, he'd loved it.

"Derry, it's been too long," Archie said. "Remember your old pal, Archie Rumsey? And here's my associate, Benjamin Tanner. He's a stupid fuck but not too bad."

Jess held her breath.

"Of course I remember you, my fine man," Derry said with loud enthusiasm. He knew him. It was true. "Pleasure to meet you, Benjamin Tanner. You might want to talk to Archie about his introductions."

"I'm used to it," Benjamin said.

"Beautiful day, isn't it? I trust you're having a lovely time," Derry said.

"We sure are, Der," Archie said. "As I'm sure you are."

Derry's voice warmed. "I certainly am," he said, chuckling. "The finest of my life. And that's saying something."

The other men guffawed. Jess's blood drained out of her body. She waited, cold and stiff as ice, to learn the truth about the man she thought she loved.

"I was just telling Benji about that party a few years ago," Archie said. "You must remember that one, at my frat? With the girls?"

"How could I forget? You college men certainly know how to have a good time. Shame so many of you forget how to enjoy yourselves after you graduate," Derry said. "Not a mistake I've ever made, thank God. Which is why you excellent fellows must excuse me. I've got a lady waiting for me and too little time to prepare for her."

Jess put a hand over her mouth to muffle her cry.

Archie laughed. "Hear that, Benji? I told you. Any chance we could—"

"Find me at the Plat back in Boston sometime," Derry said, his voice drifting away. "We'll catch up. Bring your friend."

"I'll do that," Archie called after him. Then, "Shit, he's already got some pussy waiting for him. We'll have to catch him earlier next time, see if he'll share. Last time I saw him, he had four strippers on a trampoline. The man knows how to live."

"What's the Plat?" Benjamin asked. His voice came from a distance. They were leaving.

"My club in Boston," Archie said. "Very exclusive. I'll take you . . ."

As his words faded away, Jess got to her feet, her legs trembling. "Derry was at the party," she whispered.

"He was just being polite," Molly said. "I doubt he even re-membered those guys."

"He didn't deny it. And Archie wasn't making it up. He was proud of it." Jess's hands clenched into fists. "He was there. All this time, I thought he was . . ." She'd thought he was different. She'd thought he was better than the Archibald Rumseys of the world. But he wasn't.

He was the same.

No. He was worse. He hadn't only taken her to a party, he'd taken her to bed. He hadn't only taken her pride, he'd taken her heart.

The Champagne roiled in her gut. "I'm going to be sick."

"You need some fresh air," Molly said, grabbing her elbow and pulling her around the fireplace to a pair of French doors overlooking the deck.

Teeth clenched, Jess cast a sideways glance at the room as she let Molly pull her outside. No sign of Archie, his friend, or Derry.

No doubt he was having a wonderful time somewhere. A fucking wonderful time.

"Come on, let's walk," Molly said. "Breathe, Jess. Breathe."

The sun was setting behind the mountains, casting the lake into shadow. A film of ice and a dusting of snow had formed on its surface. Jess's nausea was fading, but crippling shame was taking its place. "I've been such a fool."

"We can't get to our rooms without walking by a bunch of people," Molly said. "How about those little houses near the pool? Isn't your mom staying in one of those?"

"Yeah, but it'll be locked."

"Why would it be locked? This isn't a hotel. The Stantons would make sure her spot was safe." Molly pulled her along the path. "Is that one hers? She was telling me about how cute it was."

"Yes, that's it, but—"

"The light is on." Molly dragged her over to the door and knocked. "You can be alone here for a minute until you feel—" Just as she was reaching for the handle, the door swung open to reveal Marilyn.

The sight of her mother's kind, loving face unraveled Jess completely. "Oh, Mom," she said, reaching out for her.

"What's the matter? What—"

Not able to speak, Jess clung to her and inhaled her familiar scent. Tears that she'd held inside since first hearing Archie's horrible voice now poured out of her.

As she sobbed, she heard Molly say, "Derry."

"I knew it," Marilyn said, holding her tightly. Her hand came down on Jess's head, stroking her hair as she made soothing noises. "Thanks for bringing her to me."

"I thought she might just need a minute to get away from everything."

"I'm glad I was here. I had to change my shoes. They were beautiful, but I was silly to think I could wear them for more

THE BILLIONAIRE SHIFTER'S *Virgin Mate*   269

than an hour. Come in." Marilyn drew Jess inside, wiped her tears with her thumbs, and led her over to the sofa. "Let it out, baby. Just let it out."

"He was there, Mom. At that . . . party. The p-p—" Jess couldn't make herself say it. Overwhelmed with old, hot humiliation, she began to cry again. "That party. And tonight he disappeared, and I'm pretty sure . . . you know . . ."

"Which party?" Marilyn asked. When Jess didn't explain, she turned to Molly.

"Something at Harvard a few years ago?" Molly replied uncertainly.

"Oh no," Marilyn said. She'd been the one to drive Jess home that night. Her hysterical, nonverbal, broken daughter. "No," she said again, this time with steel in her voice.

"What happened?" Molly asked. She lowered her voice. "Was she assaulted?"

"Emotionally, yes. Absolutely she was." Marilyn gave Jess a fierce hug before rising to her feet. "Stay with her, Molly. I'll be back as soon as I can."

In alarm, Jess realized her mother was going off to confront him. She grabbed her mom's wrist. "No, you can't. He's gone off somewhere. You won't find him."

"Don't you worry about a thing." Marilyn patted her hand and released herself. "I'm sure you're right. I just want to let Lilah know there's nothing to worry about, that we're both fine."

"She and Gavin are going to slip away soon," Jess said. "They're not doing a big departure. They warned everyone they're just going to take off on their honeymoon when they're ready."

"And I'll be sure to kiss her good-bye for both of us." Marilyn shoved her feet into a pair of flats by the door. "I'll be back in a few minutes. Don't you worry," she said again, then was gone.

Jess closed her eyes and fell back against the sofa.

Don't you worry.

Why would she? What did she have to worry about? Her life was over.

Impulsive. Asher had thrown that descriptor at him thousands of times throughout his life, and he'd chafed against it, but right now, he reveled in it. The thought had hit him like Cupid's arrow through his soul:

Wife.

He knew Jess was the One, knew it with a timeless sense of eternity that ran through the universe, a frequency that pervaded each cell, each membrane, every molecule that made up our known world, and even the unknown dimensions that Derry's heart-swelled mind could not fathom. He was both larger than life and oh, so delicately focused on the tiniest of details as he created a haven for him and Jess, one in which they would be husband and wife.

The plans required too much of him, he knew, as he dashed to and fro, making furtive phone calls and seeking expert assistance for the whirlwind elopement he would unveil momentarily. He'd spent the better part of the reception thus far scheduling travel, a ring, an officiant, and making certain no luxury would be spared. It had to be perfect.

Perfect.

For Jess deserved no less.

"The jet's arranged?" he hissed into his phone. "Amsterdam?" Chosen on a whim based entirely on Jess's appreciation of his use of light in his paintings, he'd selected Amsterdam as their starting point. The Dutch masters held an appeal for him, and that she could see that—sense it from a simple examination of his work—made the destination all the more meaningful. He'd called a contact at the State Department earlier, chagrined to find that Jessica Eileen Murphy possessed no passport, but his friend assured him the orderly gears of the federal government could be cranked up a notch to get her a passport by morning.

"Yes, sir," Roger answered. The stalwart pilot had flown the Stanton family around the world for years, one of a batch of three pilots who knew their secret, each paid three times the normal rate for their work—and happy for it. "We have the plane here at the landing strip in Montana, ready to go at a moment's notice."

"Thank you." Derry readied to finish the call, the jeweler on the other line. He'd requested an express delivery here, to the ranch, for the hastily chosen diamond ring. They could resize it later, but he had to have a ring.

"And Mr. Stanton?"

"Yes, Roger?"

"Congratulations."

Derry beamed into the telephone. "Thank you."

Eva appeared, eyes wide and head tilted in question, judgment written all over her smooth face. "What are you doing on the telephone, Derry? You are the best man. Get in there and do your job!" Her hands were on his shoulders, shooing him before he could protest, the conversation with the jeweler cut off with a hurried apology and promise to call back in five minutes.

"I've already mingled," he groused. "I spoke with Senator Rumsey's little jerky son. Such a frat boy, that one. Blabbering on about some ridiculous party from ages ago that I don't even remember attending. I gave a lovely best man toast and complimented the bride, which is not a difficult task. Lilah's amazing and a perfect fit for Gavin. What more do I need to do, Eva?"

"I've never, ever known you to avoid a party, Derry," Eva said in a recriminating tone, as if he were violating a social norm by not expressing his bacchanalian side.

His head swam. "You're chiding me for *not* being a wild and hedonistic rake?"

She blinked, the slow, sly smile spreading across her face.

"You have a point."

Electricity shot through his every pore. Two more calls, and it would be set. He needed the ring and an officiant to perform the wedding.

And there was one minor detail he needed to remember:

To propose.

Eva came to an abrupt halt as that thought rang out in his brain like the bells of Notre Dame. Her own smartphone buzzed in her hand, and she looked at a text message, then up at Derry, then back at the screen.

"No!" she hissed.

He frowned.

"You're—I can't—Derry, what do you think you're doing!" she said, her voice going low and smoky at the end, the change far worse than being screeched at like a child caught doing something horrible.

"I am mingling?"

"You're planning to elope with Jessica Murphy?" She held up her phone. "I'm being asked to stock Champagne for your flight to Amsterdam."

It wasn't her words that made the thick hair at the base of his skull begin to stand on end, the gooseflesh rippling across his upper back and scalp, spreading like an undulating wave in a wheat field. Eva's face morphed from unmitigated horror to her cool, sophisticated mask as her eyes darted to something behind him.

That was the source of his unease.

He turned, half knowing what he would see before his eyes landed on her, the scent of Marilyn Murphy already in his nose.

Based on the look on her face, she had heard every word Eva had just said.

And was not pleased.

"You!" she said through gritted teeth, the end of her finger jabbing the middle of his chest. She wore flat shoes and looked up—way up—to meet his eyes. He was at least a foot taller and more than one hundred pounds heavier, but by God she made him feel like a church mouse.

"Marilyn! I can explain—"

"You will not! How dare you? How *dare you?*" The last two words came out like molten lava being poured over flesh. Eva gave him a sympathetic look and departed smoothly, leaving him utterly alone and in a state of abject horror.

"How dare I, what?" He tried to laugh it off, turning on his charm like a fire hose, reaching for her shoulder and bending down with a warm, conspirator's touch. "You heard what Eva said about the elopement? I assure you, Marilyn, I planned to find you and ask permission for your lovely daughter's hand."

"I wouldn't give my permission if you held a gun to my head, you sick bastard."

He shattered, his body jolting as if made of glass, her words like a baseball bat.

"Excuse me?" His phone rang in his pocket. Likely the jeweler or the Amsterdam authorities, helpfully navigating red tape for him to find an official. The buzz in his pocket was like a signal from another planet.

"You hurt Jessica like no one else has ever hurt her. I've had to pick up the shards of her poor little heart because of you." That finger poked over and over, like a jackhammer driving pain into his core.

She was so angry. But it wasn't the fury he saw in Marilyn Murphy's eyes that made his heart break in half.

It was the disgust.

He paused, breath hitching as the words he needed didn't appear. What was this? Did the Murphy family always communicate their feelings so bluntly? Had he been right about Lilah not wanting Jess with him? A thousand doubts ripped through him like a herd of startled gazelles.

"Marilyn, I don't understand."

She snorted. "Men like you say that. You make women fall in love with you for sport. For fun. So you can trifle with their emotions and sit back and watch them twist into pretzels over you, and then you brush them aside like a piece of used-up garbage."

"What? Me?"

"You," she said emphatically. "I've known men like you. Hell, turns out I married one. Did Jess ever tell you about the last time I ever saw her father?"

His throat went dry. "No."

"He was in bed. With another woman."

A dreadful sense of understanding washed over him. "Oh, Marilyn. I assure you—"

She held out her palm, flat to him. He stopped speaking. "You're the worst of them all. Smooth and friendly on the out- side, but all you care about are the notches on your belt. Keeping score. Getting drunk and having your way with anyone who you can manipulate. You're a male whore. A rich, male whore who takes good, decent, beautiful women like my Jessica and breaks them. Well, I won't have it. Not again!"

Poke.

"You stay away from my daughter! I can't undo what's hap- pened with Gavin and Lilah marrying, so we're 'family' whether we like it or not." Marilyn's mouth twisted into a sneer at the word "family."

"Marilyn, there's a big misunderstanding here." He flushed deeply, trying to find words. They slipped out of his mouth like tadpoles in a small pool, so elusive. "Please, can't we talk about this so I can—"

"There is nothing to talk about. And God help Lilah if Gavin turns out to be like you." She practically spat out the words. "I have no idea how you could be twins with such a lovely, compas- sionate young woman like Sophia." She shook her head slowly, revulsion reeking off her. The odor was so overwhelming he nearly gagged, pinching his nostrils internally, resorting to breathing through his mouth.

"Let me be crystal clear here, Derry: don't you ever, *ever* go near Jess again. Don't look at her. Don't call her. And certainly don't you dare touch her!"

And with that, Marilyn Murphy turned on one foot and stormed off, leaving him breathless. Literally. He couldn't breathe, because if he inhaled he would inject himself with nothing but the scent of his rotting heart.

Twenty-Three

J ess sent Molly away so she could sit alone for a few minutes in her mother's cabin and get a grip on herself.

She'd known what she was getting into with Derry when she took off her clothes the first time. She'd known who he was, what he was, just hadn't let herself accept all its implications. How had she convinced herself an infamous womanizer would've always been a sensitive, considerate man underneath all the sexual posturing?

Drying her eyes for the third time, she took a deep breath and headed for the door. Getting angry at Derry for being a shallow playboy was idiotic. Of course he went to frat parties and enjoyed himself the way those men always did—taking, laughing, fucking, never looking back, never getting close enough to see if they were hurting somebody. The question was, could he change? Could anyone?

Perhaps she was as cynical as Lilah had always said she was, but she didn't think so. Any man who could enjoy the mob-driven, premeditated humiliation of a young, vulnerable woman just hadn't inherited a conscience. It wasn't sexual promiscuity that bothered her. It was the cruelty.

She stepped outside and sucked in more cold, bracing air.

Instead of going back into the house the way she'd come, she decided to walk around the back and return to her bedroom through a side door. Crossing her arms over her chest, shivering in the cold, she strode past the old stairs to Derry's cabin.

Lilah was slipping away with Gavin any minute now. In fact, she probably had already. Jess could climb into bed alone and leave the big thoughts until tomorrow. Curled up in bed, she'd sleep off the stress of the day and decide what to do about Derry tomorrow.

But then she imagined him laughing in his cabin with a woman or two from the reception. No, he wasn't really doing that, was he? She just couldn't believe it. Even after what he'd said to Archie, she just didn't feel that he could fake his feelings for her so well. The way he'd looked at her, showed her his paintings . . .

Give me a break, she thought. Maybe that was his line. *Come see my art up in my room. I never show anyone my work, only you. You're special.*

Damn it, this couldn't wait until tomorrow. She had to know. Shivering in the cold, she turned and returned to the steps that led to his cabin, jogging up them two at a time, catching her heel on the uneven stone and falling to her knees.

She stopped for a moment and swiped at the clumps of earth on her dress, her heart pounding. The silk was torn. Lilah was going to kill her . . .

No, the wedding was over. It didn't matter. Nothing mattered anymore.

She climbed the remaining steps and paused at the top to catch her breath. A strange glow was coming from the path to her left. To the right, Derry's cabin waited with its secrets she didn't want but had to find.

Nevertheless, the glow was pulling at her. She sniffed the air and was alarmed to smell smoke. What if Lilah and Gavin had slipped away to change for their honeymoon and there'd been some kind of accident? Lilah had always loved candles too much, sticking them on bookshelves and beneath curtains, and never remembered to blow them out. With everyone partying at the house, nobody would notice a fire until it was too late.

Derry could wait. She turned and began to hurry through the trees toward Gavin's cabin, rubbing her bare arms for warmth. But as she drew closer, she realized she wasn't cold anymore. The air was noticeably warmer here. Thoughts of a fire made her break into a run.

Then she came out of the trees into broad clearing and saw the bonfire. A huge one. Not a forest fire, but completely contained. And around it stood several familiar figures—she recognized Sophia's statuesque form and Edward's bearded head next to hers. Staring intently at something, they didn't see her arrive.

Curious, Jess followed the direction of their gaze. Apart from the others stood another couple, holding hands.

Lilah and Gavin. And holy mother of *fuckmenow*, they were naked. The glow of the fire cast red streaks of light on their bare skin.

Every hair on Jess's body stood on end. What was going on?

As the fire crackled, Gavin took Lilah's face in his hands and kissed her. Unlike the wedding, nobody sighed, cheered, and applauded. The people witnessing this scene were as silent as the moon.

Except they weren't people. The thin veneer of this family she'd come to know was suddenly stripped away as each man and each woman took their other form. First was a man farthest from her—Asher, she realized—who fell to his hands and knees and morphed into a sleek gray creature with gleaming teeth and shining eyes.

Seconds later it was Gavin, after another kiss to his bride, who dropped to the ground and shifted like a man pulling a cape over his shoulders, quick and smooth. And then another wolf stood there, head turned up to Lilah, who reached down and stroked his head.

Heart pounding, Jess scanned the clearing for—

Yes, there he was. On the other side of the fire, mostly hidden from her, stood Derry. But as he lowered to the ground, she lost sight of him.

Just then Sophia shifted too, rejoining the earth as a brown grizzly bear that somehow looked like her. How could a bear look like a woman? Jess had no idea, but she was positive that if she'd seen the bear surrounded by a dozen others, she could've identified Sophia instantly.

Edward bowed to Lilah, said "Congratulations," and fell to the ground as a lion, powerfully built and sleek with the coloring of a mountain cat.

All the Stantons had taken their other form. It was almost like some kind of ceremony—no, no, that's *exactly* what it was, a ritual honoring the marriage. The hot, crackling air was thick with supernatural meaning. This was as important to them as the wedding earlier, if not more.

The wolves, bears, and lion gathered around Lilah, forming a loose ring around her. Tears on Lilah's cheeks reflected the firelight. Sucking in a deep breath, she bent down and embraced Gavin in his wolf form, her wet cheek stroking his fur.

Jess took a step backward, belatedly afraid to intrude. She shouldn't have seen this. This was for Lilah, not for her.

Not yet, a voice said. Again she didn't know if it was her own fears, her own wishes, or something, somebody else.

Him.

Her hands were shaking and not from the cold. The mysteries of this were deeper than anything she'd ever known. It was like trying to count the stars. She could try, but from the beginning she knew it was impossible for her to comprehend it. Only vaguely, with faith, could she attempt to understand.

Like the stars in the universe, some scientific explanation had to exist. They just hadn't found it yet. Humans weren't technologically advanced enough to decipher the biological mystery, or socially advanced enough to accept the unknown without trying to fear, kill, or destroy it.

The Stantons had inherited something in their DNA that linked them to other animals, like a gene mutation or fork in the evolutionary tree. Gavin owned a biotech company, and she dimly remembered something about genetic research at LupiNex.

Jess was telling herself this as she moved farther away, slowly stepping backward into the darkness out of range of the bonfire, when Lilah lifted her hands to the sky and then fell to her knees.

Jess's heart stopped. No, it couldn't be. She couldn't. It wasn't—

Before her eyes, her own sister began turning into a wolf. The nose, the ears, the teeth. The fur, the shoulders, the chest, the tail, the paws. Only the eyes were the same. Only the eyes were her sister's.

Mouth open in a silent scream, Jess fled.

Fueled by adrenaline, Jess managed to jog down the path to the old steps without making a sound. She wanted to shout, cry, demand answers—but the last thing she wanted was to talk to Lilah right now. Not that she *could* talk, being a wolf and everything—

Jess slapped her hand over her mouth to stifle the hysterical giggle that was bubbling out of her. What was the big deal? She'd seen Derry as a bear. She knew this was how it was. Had accepted it. So why freak out now?

Because Lilah hadn't told her, damn it! All these months, and she'd never said a thing. How was it possible? How could Lilah hide this from her? Of course their mother couldn't know, but Jess was in on the secret. Why hadn't she said anything?

"Jessica."

It was a man's voice, right behind her, but not the man she wanted to see.

No, she didn't want to see him either. She didn't want to see anyone.

"There's something you need to see," the man said. It was Asher, and he was a man again, in black trousers but shirtless and barefoot. Some woman might find his perfect chest appealing, but she wanted to claw his eyes out.

Claw . . .

Would she . . . could she . . .

"I've seen it all," Jess said coldly. "But don't worry, I won't tell anyone." Like Lilah hadn't told *her*.

"Don't be childish. You've seen nothing. But maybe if you see it all before it's too late, you'll act more wisely than your sister."

Jess clasped her hands together to stop them from shaking. "Fine. Go ahead. Show me. You're going to turn into an elephant?"

Asher unfurled a white shirt she realized he'd been holding in his fist and pulled it on. As he buttoned it, he pivoted on his heel. His fingers were impossibly long, on hands that looked regal, powerful. "Follow me."

"We're going to Derry's?"

He didn't answer. When they drew near the path to Gavin's cabin, he veered to the right and escorted her down another narrow path through the trees. Moodily following, she lifted the skirt of her gown in an attempt to stop it from catching on the undergrowth, but it dragged and stuck on the branches. Even Goodwill wouldn't want this sucker now.

After several minutes, they arrived at yet another cabin, far grander than the others. As they walked up to the front door, a porch light flickered on, revealing an oversized, carved door. It wasn't a cabin. It was a mansion, with two stories and a vast wraparound deck.

He led her into the dark house without turning on any more

lights. She had to reach out to feel for the wall to stop herself from bumping into anything. Just ahead of her, he disappeared into a room, finally turned on a lamp, and she saw the shelves of a large personal library.

"Sit," he said, claiming the chair behind an enormous oak desk.

"I'm not the puppy here," she replied.

He peered up from a big golden book he was shoving across the desk. It looked like one of those gigantic old dictionaries they have at libraries that need a magnifying glass. "I beg your pardon?" His voice was as icy as the water she'd fallen into that morning.

"I thought Englishmen had good manners."

"I thought you wanted to know our secrets," he said, not missing a beat.

"I never said that."

He put his hands on the book and began to pull it back toward him. "I see. My mistake."

Oh, damn it. "Fine, fine." Rearranging the skirt of her dress, she took the chair in front of the desk. "I'm sitting."

"You're certainly an infuriating female," he said. "I'm tempted to let Derry have you. It would be an appropriate form of justice."

"It's not your decision to let anyone have me. What century are you from, anyway?"

"Ah, finally we have returned to the point." He shoved the book closer to her. "Open that up, and tell me what you see."

She lifted the heavy cover and thick pages and peered inside. The writing was in a language she'd never seen before. She didn't even recognize the alphabet. "What country is this from?"

"Not a country," he said. "A family. Ours."

The chill that hadn't left her since she'd left the main house settled more deeply into her bones. "What does it say?"

"You can't read it?" he asked.

"Of course I can't read it. It's in a different language or something."

"Your sister could," he said softly.

"What?"

"Immediately," he continued. "As if born to us."

Jess recoiled, unexpected tears burning in her eyes. She moved her hands into her lap so he wouldn't see them trembling.

Lilah had been fated to be with Gavin. He was her One. She was his.

"What's your point?" Jess asked, proud she'd kept her voice steady.

"You know what my point is. You want what your sister has," he said. "But you can't have it. I have my doubts about Lilah, and I will always have them, but you, well, there is no doubt. You are not Derry's One. Humans and shifters do not belong together. Your sister is an outlier." His face went sour at the words.

She jumped to her feet. "It's not for you to—"

"Don't blame me. I'm showing you what you already know. You have doubt, as you should. Now you need to find the courage within yourself to accept it."

"You're just trying to stop Derry from being with—with anyone—"

"On the contrary. I'll rejoice if he finds his mate among his own kind, though bears don't mate for life. Surely you can feel this. If you care for him, and I think you do, please accept the truth of this." Asher rose and walked past her to the door. He raised his voice. "Edward, we're in the library."

His own kind . . .

You can feel this . . .

If you care for him . . .

Tears streaming down her cheek, she opened the book again and strained to understand the cryptic lettering. She was a great student. There was nothing she couldn't master if she studied hard enough. But these words were gibberish. Scribbles.

"Edward will escort you home," Asher said behind her.

"Lilah could read this?" Her voice wasn't steady anymore.

"Yes." His had grown softer, gentler.

"What does it say?" she asked.

He put a hand on her shoulder. "If you need me to tell you, you're not the One."

The hard truth struck her so hard, her knees buckled. Strong hands came up and supported her. Edward. He wrapped a blanket around her shoulders.

"You looked cold," Edward said.

Asher was pushing them toward the front door. "Get her to the helicopter. Her things are already packed and ready. I'll talk to the mother."

Before answering, Edward dipped his head to Jess. "Is that all right? Would you like to go home?"

The thought of home, safe and normal, was a siren's song. "Boston?" she asked weakly.

"The jet's waiting for us," Edward said.

"Us?"

"I'll go with you," he said. "So you're not alone."

Jess turned and looked into Edward's kind face. Lilah was right. This was the type of guy she should've fallen in love with. Too late now.

"Yes," she said. "I'd like to go home."

The cool autumn air whistled through his thick, coarse fur, moonlight glittering on soft, thin snow like the crackle of fire, the ebb and flow of embers made by humans. Scent magnified by thousands of standard deviations, he felt the blood pound through his enormous form, eyes taking in his pack.

His pack.

Wolves, bears, and the lonely lion made for a motley crew, but one that was his no matter what. As his brain spiraled from bear to human, he felt the shift take place, the true mating ritual now complete, one forged by a new approach. Asher had explained to them all that there was, in more than a thousand years of shifter documentation, no written instructions for how to bring a human shifter into a pack—unless she'd borne her shifter mate an heir.

What they had just done with Gavin and Lilah was wholly original, without precedent, and yet it felt oddly perfect. Complete and true.

Ears perking, he heard the skitter of creatures in the woods, caught the remnants of partygoers via scent, and swore he could smell Jess closer than she should be.

Her. His true pack would never be complete without her.

The ache in his bones was not only from the change in his physical stature, but a yearning need for her that came undefined. The shock of her mother's attack had barely registered before Gavin had come to him, insisting he join the secret gathering to witness the true joining of Gavin and Lilah. He'd gone, of course, but with a spinning mind and a pained heart, his body tingling with fury, his soul a whirling dervish.

In the dark, under a blanket of crisp stars, he'd joined his siblings and watched the impossible—a human turning into a wolf through the simple force of love. The metaphysics of it were, of course, far more complex, but at its most basic foundation, that was the answer.

Love.

As he inhaled, he smelled Jess, her strong feminine scent light on his nose, his brow furrowed and his frown deepening as the scent elongated, the color of it turning from a pale gray to a darker, demonic brown tinged with a burning, sickly odor. She was distraught. He needed to find her. Help her. The mess with Marilyn would fix itself, for surely her mother was mistaken.

Was Jess hurt? Where was she? The odor came on a breeze, carried too far for him to locate quickly.

He looked down.

And of all the times to be in human form, naked. If only she were here and her scent were happy.

Sprinting, he bounded through the woods and down the steps to his cabin, the route memorized by his muscles even in human form. Slowed by his awkward bones, wishing briefly he were still in bear form to make this trip speedier, he threw on a pair of old jeans and a sweatshirt, shoving his feet into loafers and running out the door, following her scent.

A handful of partying guests lingered at the reception, too drunk to notice him or too tired to care. Her scent should have strengthened along the path to her guest cottage, but instead, it detoured.

To Asher's.

No.

No, no, no.

The fury drove him to run like the wind, his hands eager to drop to the ground and move on all fours, faster if he were bear but achingly sluggish now. Asher's home was the oldest building on the ranch, made with a carved oak door that bore scratches from earlier battles that Derry did not have the luxury to think about. With one mighty shove of his shoulder, he cracked the door open, not bothering with the preliminaries, already half-mad with the grief and pure rage that made a polite knock announcing his presence impossible.

"Asher!" he bellowed, her scent filling him. Champagne, roses, baby powder, musk, excitement, sweat—and Jess's fear, disappointment, anxiety, and a scent he couldn't name, but he could imitate.

It was the scent that matched the ragged feeling in his chest.

She had just been here, and Asher had put all the negativity into her.

"ASHER!" he screamed, the word no longer articulate, indiscernible from the roar that came from his jutting jaw, the bones crunching for the second time in under an hour, the popping sounds of tendons changing place and the vague sound of his skin stretching, like a wet parchment scroll being unrolled. Clothes became rags. Shoes became annoyances. His spine cracked, and his hair grew thick and lustrous, converting back to fur in seconds, his jaw narrowing as his head grew, and then—

He smelled his oldest brother.

And he was human.

"Derry," said Asher in a low, calm voice, one that was so sonorous it could put overcaffeinated college students to sleep. "She is gone."

One sniff, and he knew that. Throwing the large oak partner's desk aside like a child's toy in the way, Derry heard the crack of wood against the wall, but it did not matter.

He wanted her.

"She is gone," Asher repeated, the words clear, his face a stone that needed to have the emotion clawed out of it. "She asked to go home."

Just as his arm reached for Asher, his brother unflinching, the *snick-snick-snick* of a familiar machine filled his ears with too much sound.

He knew that sound.

But it was the scent that saved Asher's life.

Oil. Machine gears. Gasoline. Petroleum and Jess and *her her her*, and he loped through the open, crooked front door, flurries dotting the path he'd just been on, speeding through the fluffy flakes toward the sound of the machine that would turn her into a bird and make her leave him.

No.

He couldn't let that happen, and as he rounded the corner at the main stone gate, he lumbered across the field to the landing strip, his eyes unfocused, his heart pumping in his chest so hard the blood pounded behind his eyes, the snow keeping him cool as his internal engine matched the helicopter in its rhythm.

Snick-snick-snick.

He was close. So close, her forlorn scent nearly halting him in his tracks to howl in shared pain with her, to pull Jess into his arms and make it better, to explain and understand and forgive and reconnect and—

The scent began to break.

He looked up, eyes laser sharp, and saw the helicopter lift.

"Noooooooooooooooo!" he yelled.

It came out like a ferocious growl, a groan and roar that shook him so deeply inside he would still hear that sound in death, ringing in his ears forever.

Two pairs of eyes glowed in the dark as he reached the ground where the chopper's landing gear had just rested, the machine now a few hundred feet away and up to the east.

Jess and Edward.

Her eyes met his, and the pain seared him, surely made his fur and thick skin shed until he was naked and mewling before her, the hatred in her look making him wish for words. He leapt into the air, knowing full well it would not work, the ungroomed rocks mingled with dirt beneath his feet scraping against him.

"JESS!!" he called out, the word sounding like the caterwaul of a wild beast.

Because it was.

He kept his eyes on hers until he could only imagine he saw those beautiful mirrors to his own soul.

And then he could see them no longer.

His heart folded in on itself, and he collapsed right there.

Everyone had always been right.

He really was a fool.

Twenty-Four

Her apartment back in Waltham was cramped, cold, and gloomy, but blessedly empty. Finally, after traveling all night via the generosity of the Stanton private transit system, she could be alone. When she'd dragged all her bags over the threshold, Jess kicked the door shut behind her and flung her keys to the side, not caring that they missed the little table and fell on the floor.

"Are you sure you don't want me to escort you inside? I can carry—" Edward had asked on the street downstairs, but she'd refused. He'd held her hand and offered her tissues and tea for hours during the journey back—she'd appreciated every kindness, but now it was time to nurse her wounds in private. He'd assured her that his chauffeur would retrieve and deliver Smoky, her dog, in the morning.

Shock had settled in like ice over a mountain lake. She was cold, her hands shivering, but she barely noticed. Without turning on the lights, moving through her apartment merely by the glow of the dawn, she pushed off her shoes and climbed into bed, still in her clothes.

What day was it? What month? What year? Her life had taken a surreal turn into the unknown, like a disorienting dream.

A dream that had turned into a nightmare.

Derry. Derry.

Neither was each other's One. It was all an illusion.

Too tired to cry anymore, she fell into a fitful sleep filled with shape-shifting men and women who picnicked on a warm, sunny beach while she thrashed and drowned in the icy water just offshore. No matter how she cried out, shouting each of their names, none turned her way, none stopped laughing. Even Edward, as kind as he'd been to her, was playing cards with Molly. What was she doing there? Why was she allowed to be on the beach and Jess wasn't?

Asher sat in the lifeguard chair, not on the picnic blanket, but he didn't move to save her. Lilah and Gavin were walking away, arm in arm, both in their wedding clothes. Sophia was eating and laughing at something the big man next to her was saying. The big man had a woman in his lap—Molly, it was Molly—and she knew the man was Derry, and that he was kissing Molly, stroking her back and thighs, taking off her clothes, oblivious to Jess out in the perilous water.

"No!" Jess cried, waking up with a start, her heart pounding so hard her ribs ached. Still wearing her winter coat under the thick comforter, she was drenched in sweat. She kicked off the covers and unzipped her coat, sucking in calming breaths as she rolled to one side.

Was Molly a shifter? Was she destined to belong to the Stantons in a way Jess never would? If Asher had shown Molly the book, would *she* have been able to read it?

Maybe her dream was showing her a truth she couldn't bear to acknowledge when she was awake: it was Molly and Derry who were destined for each other, and Jess was only a brief detour. The catalyst for their true love.

Oh fuck. She crawled out of bed and tore off her coat. Fuck it all. Her dreams might torture her, but she wasn't going to let her waking mind do it too. She could control her thoughts. If she didn't, she'd kill herself. How could she go on, thinking about him, remembering him, imagining what could've been?

Her mind drove on, pursuing more forbidden thoughts: *If it were up to her, she'd be a bear shifter like Derry . . . She never had liked wolves or lions, too aggressive . . . but bears . . . they were strong and warm and clever . . .*

Giving her head a violent shake, she marched to the shower and climbed in before the water got warm. *Ah, there. Ice. Remember that. Your heart needs it. Embrace the cold. That's where you'll live from now on if you want to survive.*

I wasn't the One. He isn't the One. It's all bullshit. It's just sex and lust and fucking like it always is.

She was going to be a doctor. Those were the dreams to remember.

As always, it wasn't about pleasure. It was about work. And she was going to return to the habits that had made her who she was—hard work, solitude, and a guarded heart. As soon as she got dressed and had some coffee and toast, she was going to call Professor Lethbridge again about that job. Earlier she'd let herself be intimidated. Now she would take advantage of a job and a connection that could propel her career. And as a bonus, she would have the opportunity to destroy Archie Rumsey.

She let the cold water chill her too-hot blood.

The only dreams she would pay attention to were the ones about the future. Her future. Alone, the way she'd always imagined it.

"This whole lovesick act is making me just plain old sick," Sophia declared, shoving back the heavy curtains to his loft, making certain a shaft of light as sharp as a needle struck him right in the eyes.

He groaned in response, rolled over in bed, and settled his

face between two down pillows.

Which reminded him of Jess's thighs.

Which made him think of Jess.

Jess.

And . . . now he was hard as a fucking rock.

He remained on his belly, a prisoner of his own erection.

"Go away," he muttered.

"I am not leaving until you shower and shave and pretend to be a decent human being," Sophia insisted. "Or, at least, a partial human being."

I was speaking to my cock, he thought.

As much as he hated what Sophia was doing, she was his first shred of company in over a week, since he'd come home from the wedding, livid and destroyed at the same time. He'd left the ranch on his own, without a word to anyone. Ignored texts and phone calls. Eschewed all social events.

Gavin would have come long before Sophia, but he and Lilah were in Paris, doing what honeymooners do in Paris.

Which reminded him of his cock again.

Damn it.

"Why do I need to shower?" he asked his pillow, sighing deeply. As he inhaled afterward, his own nose gave him the answer.

Oh God. When *had* he last managed basic hygiene? His own scent offended him, which meant his sister was right.

He sat up and said, "Turn away."

"Why? I've seen you naked thousands of times. Are you afraid you'll poke my eye out?" Sofia laughed, using the end of her closed umbrella to stab a stack of pizza boxes, making a disgusted face.

"Fine. Suit yourself." He slithered out of bed and headed for the shower, his dick deflating instantly. Between the cool Massachusetts late-autumn air and his sister's joke about his penis, he was quite limp by the time the hot water kicked in on his shower's jets.

As he soaped up, he made quick work, using two rounds of shampoo on his long, greasy hair, scrubbing his body with a washcloth, his skin prickling with the hot water and the friction of simple attention. Leaning against the marbled wall after the basics had been met, he pressed his forehead into the tile and let the rivers of hot water wash over his tense back, willing the muscles to relax.

They refused.

One week of self-imposed isolation doing nothing but drinking and painting, with the occasional takeout order for sustenance, had left him weak and hollow.

The pain had not abated.

Not one bit.

He wasn't lovesick. Sophia was wrong.

Derry was *heartsick*.

If he were the type of man who cried, he would be sobbing uncontrollably by now. But he wasn't. Stanton men didn't cry. It wasn't in their DNA, or something like that, he'd been told. They punched things and fought fellow animals and men. They purchased businesses and squashed competitors. They ridiculed and cajoled.

A Stanton man never, ever cried.

What the other Stanton men didn't know, though, was that Derry painted his pain away.

And how.

He finished the shower and walked into the main loft area wearing a robe, toweling his long black hair.

"Feel better?" Sophia asked, her hands covered in hospital gloves, a large trash bag in one hand.

"Yes," he admitted reluctantly. "What the hell are you doing?"

"Cleaning this pigsty." She shoved a takeout container into the giant black bag, nose wrinkling.

He bristled. "Don't refer to me as a pig."

Her brow lowered in confusion, then raised. "Right. That's why I'm here."

"To call me a pig? Have you joined Marilyn Murphy's team?"

She sighed and set down the trash bag, snapping off the gloves and tossing them in. "No. I've come here to talk to you. Got any coffee?"

He pointed to the espresso machine, which looked like a small coffee bomb had gone off around it, grounds scattered in little piles all over the counter.

"Jesus, Derry. You really are a p—mess."

He growled.

She shrugged.

Five minutes later, coffee in hand, she stood behind him and brushed his long hair.

"This really isn't necessary," he insisted.

"You haven't let me do this since we were eleven."

"Because it's juvenile." Sophia used the wide-toothed comb with a precision that a hairdresser would envy, separating his thick locks into three strong cords.

"It's fun. You always had the better head of hair of the two of us. Mine is just a dull color, like dark construction paper. Yours shines like obsidian."

He smiled in spite of himself and indulged her, but he wasn't letting her off the hook. "What do you want to talk about?"

"Marilyn and Jess."

"Did they ask you to convey a message? Am I to be called a pig yet again? Because message received from them both. I am staying away." *Even if it kills me*, he thought.

Sophia pulled the thick hair tie along the base of the braid she'd just made and dropped it against his back, the bottom thwacking between his shoulder blades. She moved around the couch and sat across from him in a red Bauhaus chair.

"No. But I understand why Marilyn said what she said to you.

And it's all an enormous misunderstanding."

"Really?" One side of his mouth quirked up. "So I'm not a pig?"

"You're not. Jess was."

He slammed his cup of coffee onto the melamine table, the scalding liquid burning the web of his hand. "What the fuck, Sophia? Why would you say that?"

"Easy, Derry," she snapped back. "I'm trying to explain."

Both went from zero to sixty so quickly.

Why?

"Explain without calling Jess a pig."

"That's the point. Archie Rumsey made her one."

"Quit speaking in ciphers."

"Archie Rumsey. The senator's son. You were talking to him at the party."

"I remember. That little twit? What about him? I was making chitchat only because Gavin finds his father useful for some business reason, and Asher told me to play nice. Archie blathered on about some party . . ." His voice tapered off as he remembered the exchange, his eyes narrowing as he looked at Sophia. "That . . . that little piece of shit has something to do with all this?"

"Do you remember the pig party he talked about with you?"

"Pig party? What pig party?" A bell began to ding deep inside him, an alarm he couldn't quite name.

"Archie talked about you and a party a few years ago."

"I was distracted. He's just an overprivileged drunk little gnat. I said the least possible to get him off my back." The inner alarm sounded louder.

Sophia took a delicate sip of her coffee and met his eyes. "Turns out Jess overheard you and Archie. That party he mentioned was a pig party. Do you know what that is?"

"Oh God," he groaned. He knew exactly what a pig party was, and he'd never attended one on purpose. A gross, sick violation of the loveliness of the female form. He'd always considered such events to be disgusting—and the men who participated in them to be vile, spineless creatures who could only lift themselves up by bringing others down. "I remember that. Once I found out what those little shits were doing, I backed out quietly."

"Jess was Archie's 'date.'" Sophia used finger quotes to dig the truth in.

Deep.

So deep he began to shake.

"No." Oh, that little bastard. The pain he must have caused Jess, to be paraded and degraded and by a worthless asshole like Archie, all to be the butt of such a cruel joke.

Fury poured into his veins.

"Yes, Derry," she said with a sigh, leaning forward and putting her hand over his, either as a show of compassion or to stop his shaking. "When Jess overheard you at the wedding reception, talking with Archie, she thought you were—"

"NO!" he bellowed, standing, pacing like a caged animal. "NO!" he shouted. "Dear God, no! I would never—I could never—Oh, my sweet Jess thought that of me?"

"She assumed you were part of Archie's nasty crowd, just trifling with her. That you thought the same of her as Archie. That you convinced her to fall in love with you and it was all a game. Like the pig party."

"And she left the ranch."

"Yes."

"Why didn't she come and talk to me? At least try?"

"Would you? After thinking you'd been played with, ridiculed and considered ugly, batted around like a cat toy for fun? Talked about behind your back?"

"I did none of those things!" he roared.

"But *she* doesn't know that. She saw you with Archie, reminiscing and laughing, and . . ." Sophia's face crumpled with sympathy. "I'm so sorry, Derry."

His eyes bugged out of his head, and a dull throb began his temples, his hands clenching and releasing in time with his heartbeat. No.

No. No. No.

Storming across the room, he threw off his robe and began shoving his legs into the first pair of pants he found, a filthy, paint-covered pair strewn across a chair in front of his covered canvas.

"What are you doing?" she asked.

"Going to see Jess."

"Now? No way. She was escorted home by Edward and doesn't want anything to do with our family. She's done, Derry. Marilyn told me to keep you away."

"Then why tell me this? How do you know?"

"Marilyn asked me if I was part of the whole ruse to convince Jess you were really in love with her. I told her absolutely not and tried to explain that your feelings are real."

"You did?" Shock made him stop dressing, the jerk of his arm through a cotton Oxford shirt tearing the cloth at the seam. "What did she say?"

Sophia's eyes turned down, the gesture making Derry's alarm inside turn into a hollow scream.

"She said that it was probably for the best anyhow, because Jess would always wonder if any expression of love from you was true."

The scream inside him poured out. Ripping the shirt off his back, he picked up anything within reach, flinging it at the ground, the exposed brick walls, at the support beams and the ductwork. A small wooden statue he'd collected on a trip to Zimbabwe years ago bounced off the canvas covering his painting, sending the easel and painting to the ground. Ranting and grunting, he let the emotion out of him the only way he knew how.

Just short of shifting.

Sophia watched him with the detached pain of a loved one who cannot help. Her peaceful presence meant something to him, even as he avoided harming her.

"Damn Archie Rumsey and damn Asher and damn Marilyn and damn the fucking world!" he growled.

His sister no longer watched him. She bent to the ground and righted the easel, carefully placing the painting on it, her eyes wide and narrow at the same time, darting over the eight-by-eight-foot canvas, which she'd picked up as easily as if it had been a playing card.

Rage pumped through him, self-righteous and loathing, as the truth sank in.

This was all one big, fat misunderstanding. One he couldn't fix.

"Derry?" Sophia's voice was choked with emotion, her eyes welling with tears, nose twitching and her hand at her chin, fingers resting lightly against her lips. The emotionality of her countenance made him look at her sharply.

"Yes," he sighed, breathing harshly through his nose, trying to resume control.

"Is this—Did you—Derry?" She began to weep, a soft, panting sound that made him cross the room and put one hand on her shoulder.

Her eyes remained on the painting.

His painting of Jess.

"Derry, did you paint that?"

"Yes."

He couldn't help himself, watching his sister take in the warm lines of his memory of Jess's curves, the serious look on her face in profile, the drape of an imagined silk shawl about her bare back. The light, in his dream world, kissed her shoulders and nose and cheeks just so, giving her an ethereal glow. For the past week, he'd taken the shards of their shattered relationship and reconstructed what he could, giving him the faintest imitation of her company the only way he knew how.

His eyelids closed slowly, unable to continue to look at what he could never have.

Sophia grabbed his face, forcing him to open his eyes and confront her fierce look.

"Derry!" Now she *was* panting, her eyes stormy and troubled, tears streaking her face. "Derry, if that painting represents even one one-hundredth of what you feel for Jess, then go to her. Now."

"But you said—"

"Forget what I said." Sophia turned to the painting, back to the Derry, then pinged to the painting again, looking at it as she added, "Anyone who can capture love like that with just paint and canvas and memory . . . Oh, Derry. Try again. Try for her again. You just painted your One."

Twenty-Five

"I was surprised to hear from you," Dr. Lethbridge said to Jess, offering her the chair in front of her desk. None of the other students were there that day, for which Jess was extremely grateful. The new semester was about to start, and the halls were empty as people enjoyed every last drop of their break. Her eventual confrontation with Archie was better held on its own. "Pleased but surprised. What changed your mind, my dear?"

Jess clasped her hands in her lap. Unlike her first visit, she wasn't nervous. What did she have to lose? What she'd been through with Derry and the Stantons had changed her forever.

She'd decided to be honest. Shockingly so. "I was a virgin then. I'm not anymore."

The professor's eyes widened with delight. Then she laughed. "Is that so? How wonderful for you. And your lucky partner." Her smile grew. "Or was it more than one?"

Part of Jess wanted to snap back that it was none of her business. But that wasn't how she'd decided to play this. "He was big enough to feel like it," she said, crossing her legs.

The professor flinched but was obviously amused. "Perhaps it was just because it was your first time—"

"Oh, no. He's huge all over." With effort, Jess kept her voice cool and controlled. "Rather, he was. I won't be seeing him again."

"How tragic if one little roll in the hay has soured you forever, Jessica."

"Oh, there was a lot more than one. We hardly did anything else for days." Jess shook her head. "But the party's over. I'm ready to get back to work."

"And so you called me?"

"I was intimidated before by my own lack of experience. Now I know there's nothing to it. Sex is easy. It's the other—" She cut herself off, not wanting to reveal too much. "Sex can be wonderful, but it's nothing to be afraid of. I'm fascinated more than ever by your research, Professor. I'll work my butt off for you. I've had to work twice as hard as your other assistants have had to, just to be sitting here. I've had to overcome more than they have. I promise you won't be sorry if you hire me."

The professor leaned back in her chair, bringing her fingers together in a steeple as she smiled. "I'm quite sure I won't be," she said. "How about you start tonight, around seven?"

Jess took another deep breath. "That's one thing we'll have to talk about," she said carefully. "I waitress most nights, but I'm free every day from noon until six, and weekends all day. Will that be a problem?" She had to leave some free hours during the day for classes.

"You're working at the Platinum Club, isn't that right?"

"Yes, Professor."

"And you like it? You see yourself continuing to work there indefinitely?"

Jess had been asking herself the same thing but couldn't abandon the best paying job she'd ever had, even if it would be socially painful. Medical school would cost a fortune. She refused to beg for Stanton money to pay for it. "I have to support myself, and it's the best way right now."

"Wise. Very wise." Dr. Lethbridge got to her feet and held out her hand. "Then I'll see you at noon tomorrow, Jessica. So glad to have you aboard."

Tension Jess hadn't realized she was holding drained out of her. "Thank you. I'm glad too." Smiling, she shook the professor's hand, then gathered her things and moved to the door. Just as she was stepping outside, her new boss called out to her.

"If something comes up—someone, rather—don't be afraid to ask for the day off. I'd hate to be the one to spoil your first love affair."

Blood rushed to Jess's face. She turned. "That's not going to happen."

"I'm just saying, if the impossible happens, I'll understand. And you won't even have to tell me all about it afterward, although I'd certainly enjoy every word if you did."'

"It's not—He won't—I—"

"Have a lovely afternoon, Jessica." Waving her hand in a friendly dismissal, the professor turned away and opened a file drawer on the wall behind her.

It was remarkably simple, really, to take out the trash that called itself Archibald Rumsey.

A little too easy.

Then again, narcissistic, overprivileged little dickheads left behind a nasty trail of injured parties who could easily be turned against them as long as one provided the right tools.

Tools like money and power, both of which Derry possessed.

In spades.

After one quick, apologetic phone call to Gavin, Derry had permission to perform whatever scorched earth policy he needed to unleash, Gavin's political connections for his business be damned. In a solemn oath between brothers, Gavin promised he wouldn't tell Lilah any details about the mess with Jess, and in return, Derry swore to leave the honeymooners alone, even if a two-month-long honeymoon did seem a bit excessive.

All in all, a reasonable arrangement.

His first step had been to call a certain Professor Lethbridge at Harvard, the director of many of the school's largest sexuality research projects on campus, and Archie Rumsey's thesis advisor. A thirty-minute in-person meeting in which Derry had poured out every drop of charm and venom in his body led to the professor's outraged promise to terminate Rumsey's fellowship and destroy his academic career.

The trigger?

A three-minute-and-ten-second video that Derry had procured from one of Rumsey's fraternity brothers, a guy named Tanner, taken the night of the infamous pig party.

"Rumsey's view of women is abundantly clear in even a brief clip of his alcohol-sodden life," Derry had told Dr. Lethbridge as he held the video out for her to see. "Don't you agree?"

"Abundantly disgusting," she'd said, taking the tablet from him and scrolling the video back to watch it again. And then again. "I must admit, I'm impressed."

"By the depths of his depravity?" Derry had asked.

She handed him the tablet, her expression thoughtful. "By Jessica Murphy's guts in coming back here. Not only the first time but the second."

"She's the most remarkable woman I've ever known." And then he'd corrected himself. "The most remarkable being of all." And given his family, that was saying something.

He'd finally extracted himself from the conversation with the professor with a promise of a Stanton family donation to fund a new arts exhibit devoted to celebrating the nude form, with one condition: that the exhibition include a very special painting.

And that Jessica Murphy work at opening night.

"I assure you," the professor had said, her voice warm, "I'll make it so." Then she'd given him a head tilt and a studied expression that made him wonder, briefly, if she was flirting with him.

He'd fled quickly without the slightest regret.

The *coup de grace*, though, had been a second video, one that even Derry had been discreet enough to keep from the lovely professor and had, instead, turned over to the authorities. Whatever favors Archie's senator father had granted Gavin paled in comparison to the cover-ups Senator Rumsey must have engaged in over the years regarding his son.

Archie was, at best, a cad.

At worst, a serial date rapist.

The police would sort it all out.

After leaving the Cambridge police station, he paused in the crisp night air, his phone buzzing uncharacteristically against his breast pocket.

A text.

From Sophia.

The Plat? it read.

Nearly two months had passed since he'd last seen Jess, the winter holidays lonely and unyielding. Avoiding the Platinum Club had become a sport. All the fun he used to experience was gone. Long gone. No longer out on the prowl for pussy and tits, he felt a wave of nostalgia, nonetheless, for the old place.

As he stared at the screen, a second text arrived.

She's not working tonight, Sophia elaborated.

Ah.

He'd been holding his breath without realizing it, the large puffs of chilled air surrounding him like disciples. The coast was clear. Perhaps he should drop in for a brief drink.

Just one.

Then home.

Manny delivered him to the club within ten minutes, and as

he walked through the lobby to the elevators, the area bustling with midafternoon business activity, he heard a familiar, loathsome voice call for him.

"Derry!"

Blood fled to his extremities, nature's alarm system for readying the body to fight to the death.

That voice belonged to Archie Rumsey.

Stoic and furious, Derry watched the color of the air change as blood flowed to the surface of his skin, his body a pillar, the elevator achingly slow in its arrival.

"Stanton! It's me, Archie. From your brother's wedding? I'm a member at the Plat Club too." He sounded friendly, looking around the lobby, making sure other people heard him brag about his club membership. Eager but condescending to everyone but Derry.

Just like the social-climbing sociopathic degenerate Archie was.

Clearly the man had no idea that Derry had just distributed videos that would destroy his life, videos that captured only a few of Archie's own actions but would be more than enough to ruin him.

All it had taken was a nudge from Derry to get the videos in the right hands.

"Stanton!" This time, Rumsey's voice held a warning, a tone that said he would not be ignored. If that were all Archie had done, he would have escaped unharmed.

But he touched Derry's arm, pulling hard to get his full attention.

And he got it.

That touch triggered Derry's reaction, a stunningly straightforward right hook that flattened the weak little worm, his head cracking on shined marble, onlookers gasping at the sight and stepping back, forming a perfect circle of shock around the moaning, whimpering piece of excrement.

"Don't you ever touch me or anyone I love," Derry said in a low voice, Archie's eyes rolling up and catching Derry's with a satisfactory panic. "You little pig."

Ding!

The elevator opened, and Derry took five steps forward, ignoring the increasingly agitated murmur of the crowd, facing the back wall of the lift, his eyes glossy and cool with the frank knowledge that revenge, a dish best served cold, was one that also tasted quite sweet when served steaming hot.

But not as sweet as Jess.

Jess wasn't supposed to work tonight, but Eva's last-minute call had included words that sounded as close to begging as Eva was capable of expressing. A virulent stomach virus was felling servers at the club, and if Jess could please come in, she would be paid double time.

The bus to the train had been late, her panty hose had snagged on the turnstile to enter the T, and the Red Line was running late—par for the course. So by the time she reached the front lobby of the building that held the Platinum Club, not only was she late, she had a throbbing headache.

It reminded her of the kind she had with—

No.

Impossible.

Rubbing her temple, she ran up the steps, flew through a door to the marble-floored lobby, and hoped an elevator would be open, but—

An enormous man's arm pulled back and threw a punch. A woman screamed. Another man dropped like a sack of potatoes, his head cracking against the ground. More screams.

And Jess froze.

Him.

Eyes flitting to the injured party, she was doubly shocked to find herself staring at the face of Archie Rumsey, a trickle of blood running from where he'd bitten his lip, a pool of fluid darkening the front of his pants where he'd obviously just pissed himself.

"Don't you ever touch me or anyone I love," Derry growled, the words barely audible, but she heard them in stereo, with her ears and her heart. "You little pig," he added.

Holding back an impulse to help, she stood in place, transfixed, as Derry walked away coolly from the scene, stepping into an elevator, his broad back cloaked in a tailored black wool coat.

Slow motion captured time in that instant.

Derry hadn't seen her. Archie hadn't seen her.

Flooded with emotions she couldn't sift through while she was there in the lobby with the agitated crowd and the two men who had each unbalanced her life, she turned on her heel and fled back out to the street. Blindly she made her way back to the subway, where she texted Eva with shaking hands that she couldn't possibly come in after all because she was sick, she was barely able to think, she was about to collapse.

And then she went to her mother's.

By the time she arrived, she'd formed a theory about what had happened. Derry had punched Archie for interfering in his life with Jess, for scaring her away from the wedding where they were having such a good time. That was it. That was his only motivation.

And if Derry thought he loved her . . . well, he didn't know what love was. He hadn't admitted to himself that what they'd had wasn't enough. It wasn't like Lilah and Gavin.

She couldn't read the book. He wasn't the type to mate for life.

But she kept coming back to the image of Archie's battered, humiliated form on the marble floor of the foyer and feeling a smile tug at the corners of her mouth. Hugging herself, trying to calm down, but almost smiling.

He'd pissed himself, the bastard. There in front of the most powerful men and women in New England.

It was almost ten when she reached her mother's house, quite late by her mother's schedule. As she climbed the front steps, she was relieved to see lights on inside.

"Mom?" she called from the front door, hearing the TV playing in the living room. "Mom, it's Jess." She was a little embarrassed to come running to cry on her shoulder again, but Lilah was on her never-ending honeymoon and Jess needed somebody who loved her. This made her think of Derry, his strong shoulders under that tailored black coat, the waves of his glossy hair falling to his shoulders as he walked away from Archie's whimpering body.

Somebody who loved her . . .

Her mother started to rise from her recliner as Jess entered the room. "You saw the news?" Marilyn cried, reaching out to her, tears in her eyes. "Oh, baby. My baby."

"Don't get up," Jess said, bending over to steal a hug. She lingered in the embrace, tears burning again. Seeing Derry had hit her hard. Her soul, her heart, her body were aching for him. Forcing the thoughts aside, she stood and wiped her eyes. "What's happened now? Why are you crying?" she asked, even though the last thing she wanted to hear about was another tragedy on the news.

Lilah appeared in the doorway to the kitchen. "Jess, I'm so glad you came over. I was about to call you."

"But why? What's happened?" Jess's worried glance darted between her mother and sister. "And Lilah! When did you get back from your honeymoon?"

"Two hours ago. I wanted to check on Mom," Lilah said.

"But didn't you come over because of the news?" Marilyn pointed at the TV. "They've arrested him!"

"Oh no! For hitting Archie?" Jess spun around to look at the screen, instantly horrified to think of Derry being cuffed and locked up in a cell.

"What? Who hit him?" her mother asked.

Lilah put a hand on Jess's shoulder. "I think you'd better sit down."

The headline on the television was shocking: SENATOR'S SON ARRESTED FOR SEXUAL ASSAULT.

Suddenly weak in the knees, she sagged against the arm of the recliner.

Derry wasn't arrested for hitting Archie. Archie was arrested for . . .

Rape?

"But . . . how?" Jess whispered, afraid to believe her own eyes.

"There's video," her mother said. "Not just of those awful parties, which is bad enough. But now they've got some video of him doing far worse—assault, they're saying. The police said it was more than enough to bring him in."

"But I just saw him at the Platinum Club. Derry"—Jess was too overwhelmed to describe the punch or the aftermath—"Derry punched him."

"That must've been nice to see," Lilah said.

Her mother pointed at the TV again. "That monster assaulted other girls, the police said. It's all on the video."

Shaking, Jess fell onto the sofa. "It's all happening so fast."

"Somebody wanted him to get what he deserved," Lilah said, joining her. "The video will help them put him away, Jess. His father won't be able to get him off. Not with so many women coming forward."

In spite of herself, for all her gratitude that the evil SOB was finally facing justice, Jess's heart went out to the poor women in the video. It seemed like another horrible violation. "I hope those women get some justice. Thank God somebody was decent enough to turn it in."

"Somebody, indeed," Marilyn said. "They think it was an

orchestrated effort by a women's rights group. But that group is saying they didn't know anything about it. Maybe one of his buddies discovered a conscience and turned it in."

One of his buddies . . .

"I need to see Derry," Jess said suddenly.

Marilyn shook her head. "You think it was him? Oh, no, I can't imagine he'd bother doing something like that. I'm sure he's partying in Monte Carlo right now. You need to put that man out of your—"

"No," Jess said. For the first time in weeks, her heart took the wheel, telling her brain to get in the backseat. "He's here. I just saw him." She jumped to her feet and headed for the front door. She had to find him right away.

"After what he did to you?" Marilyn asked. "You shouldn't have gone anywhere near him. Of course you're feeling—"

"I'm feeling all kinds of things." Jess didn't know if Derry really loved her, didn't know if he'd done more than just punch Archie in the face, but she had to find out.

Lilah was at her heels. "I'll talk to her, Mom."

"Jess, wait! Listen to your sister!" Marilyn called out. "Don't do anything you're going to regret."

Jess shook off her sister's grip and strode outside. "I need to find out if I already have."

Twenty-Six

J ess felt Lilah grab her arm again, trying to pull her back to the house. "Don't try to stop me, Lilah. I've got to talk to him. I've got to."

"You are going to talk to him," Lilah said. "But you're going to talk to me first." Her grip tightened.

Feeling the pressure of her sister's fingers and hearing the steel in her voice, Jess stopped walking. The clear night was cold, filling her lungs with shards of icy air. After a moment, Jess said, "I think Derry did this to Archie. Somehow he found that video and got the police to do something about it."

"If that's true, will everything be all right?" Lilah asked. "Between the two of you?"

Jess frowned. "What do you mean?"

"Was Archie the only reason you ran away from the wedding and refused to see Derry again?"

Caught by the serious tone in her sister's question, Jess was forced to think about the night she'd fled Montana. Yes, overhearing the conversation with Archie had upset her, but she'd already been worried about what she'd been doing with Derry, whatever it was.

Archie wasn't the only reason she'd left him. She looked at

her sister, at her smooth, human skin.

Her small, human teeth.

"No," she said softly, zipping up her coat. "I had other reasons."

Lilah pulled out her key fob and pointed it at the gleaming white SUV parked in the driveway, the Land Rover that Gavin had given her as an engagement present. The horn chirped. "Get in. We've got a lot to talk about."

———

"I knew you'd come," Eva said as Derry lounged in the subterranean Novo Club, rooted in place by the fire for hours, slowly drinking his way into what he hoped would be an escapist dreamland. Lord knew, the day had been a nightmare. Passing out in the safest place in the world was about the best way to end this particularly odious day.

He'd felt Jess, behind him, as the elevator doors had closed.

And then she'd fled.

His violence scared her. His presence made her seek escape. Perhaps his very existence was too much for Jess, who had left the ranch without saying good-bye and who would not respond to outreach. Eva had said she was not working tonight, but that had clearly not been true, and as his half-drunk mind tried to piece it all together, he kept coming back to one thought:

Never, not once, had she recoiled from his shifter status.

For most human women, that alone would be a showstopper, a hard line that could not be crossed. Jess had taken his shifting in stride. Shocked, for sure—but her acceptance had spoken to his heart, a beat between the two of them that had been interrupted by . . .

What?

Fate had brought them together.

And it ripped them apart.

Derry had done good deeds when it came to Archie Rumsey.

Hidden in the stone-arched club, he knew only that he'd handed those videos over to the police and needed more scotch to get drunk.

Properly.

"Derry." Eva's voice held a note of concern. "Morgan told me you requested a room. Why?" The Novo Club had a series of pleasantly decorated overnight rooms in a catacomb that twisted through long stretches, the rooms totaling more than thirty in all, designed as a bunker for a worst-case scenario. The marauding shifter hunts in the Old World centuries ago had shaped the Novo Club founders' vision for the club.

Now the rooms served as a luxurious bed-and-breakfast for wealthy shifters like Derry.

Who drank themselves into oblivion and needed a place to hide.

"I don't want to go home," he answered, his own truth surprising even him. "After the day I've had, I don't even want to know my own damn name within the next hour."

Morgan delivered another glass of scotch. Derry reached over the tray, grabbed the bottle, and just started drinking from the neck.

"That's one way to accomplish your goal," she said as Morgan's eyes met hers. With a few eyebrow twitches and lip quirks, some vast communications network was triggered.

"Don't bother Gavin. Or Asher, God forbid. And Edward is terrified of cities."

"Then it's a pity all you have left is me," Sophia said, stepping out from the shadows. Morgan's face lit up like the moon, the eerie change in his expression like watching a cadaver come to life. He hugged Sophia with vigor and left them to privacy.

Eva remained.

Here it came. The motherly lecture.

"Are you my drinking buddy tonight, Sophia?"

"I'm your sister. And you've had a harrowing day. They caught him."

"Caught?"

"The police. A detective has been looking at Archie for quite some time, assembling evidence behind the scenes. Archie's father suppressed it. Your video was the lynchpin. He's already been arrested."

"For what? Pig parties?"

"Serial rape. DNA tests will likely confirm it."

"Jess!" He sat bolt upright, his mind clearing like a cannonball shot through fog.

"She wasn't a victim."

"You're certain?"

"I spoke with Marilyn already."

"Give her my regards," he said coldly. The freeze was tempered by his dancing heart, the adrenaline injection of fear making it do the jitterbug behind his ribs. If that worthless piece of shit had touched Jess—had *violated* her—he'd tear him apart with his bear hands.

Human hands would be too weak.

"I suspected you gave them the videos."

His chill returned, but with a different emotion attached. "You said nothing about me, I assume."

She nodded.

He swigged more scotch, the alcohol doing its job, making him sleepy.

"Good."

"They could charge you for assault against Archie for that punch. Senator Rumsey's threatening it. The blow is on video, and—"

"Any video you watch shows him touching me first. And the press won't give one whit about me. They'll sink their fangs into the juicy Archie story. Besides," he said with a toothful grin, extending his arm around the room. "Why do you think I'm hiding here?"

"Stay as long as you need, of course," Eva said, reaching out for his hand and squeezing it. The affection in the gesture made his chest ache.

"I'm lying low. It serves multiple purposes for me. Besides, Morgan needs to do something other than hang upside down in the corner of the pantry ceiling all night."

"I heard that, Mr. Stanton," Morgan intoned from around the corner.

"Good. You were meant to." Derry could feel his mouth slurring the words, wishing he could pickle his heart and make it stop wanting Jess.

"We will take good care of you," Eva promised, letting go of his hand and standing.

"But only for a few days. You can mope, but you can't become a hermit," Sophia chided.

"I could hibernate, you know? It's that time." He yawned, the motion contagious, leaving Sophia with a wide mouth and a sleepy growl.

"You could," Sophia conceded. "The ranch would be better for that."

"Live with Asher full time? I'd rather shave Morgan's back with my teeth."

"That can be arranged," Eva joked as she stood and walked to the elevators. "Just be careful, Derry. I don't know exactly what happened with Jess Murphy, but I know she's been subdued and withdrawn since Gavin and Lilah's wedding. She's a good worker and a . . ." Her words faded, like a radio dial turning the volume down, his eyelids closing until he was blissfully asleep.

And dreaming of Jess.

Lilah drove them to Walden Pond. For the first ten minutes, neither of them spoke. Lilah maneuvered through the mess to get to Route 126 while Jess thought about the sight of her embracing Gavin at the bonfire, then taking the shape of her new husband's other nature.

Why hadn't Jess been horrified to see her sister turn into a wolf? She'd been shocked, yes, but that hadn't been the dominant emotion.

Her sister had hidden it from her. Was it because she'd known Jess would never understand? Would never *need* to understand, since she and Derry wouldn't have that bond together?

Or was it something else? Maybe turning into a wolf meant she wouldn't want to be her sister anymore, that she'd slowly withdraw from their family and join the Stantons in all ways.

"Why didn't you tell me?" Like a gunshot, Jess's voice shattered the silence.

Her words hung there between them, huge and potent.

"Let me park first. I can't talk about this while I'm driving on Route 2."

Jess waited, exhaustion pouring over her. The thrill at seeing Archie brought down had faded, leaving only grief at what he'd done and an empty ache for who she'd lost.

Derry. My One.

My God, if he wasn't the One for her, who would be?

It had to be Derry. She had to be his.

But there was so much she didn't understand and was afraid to believe.

Finally Lilah parked the car on the side of the road, the water peeking through the leafless trees, and shut off the engine. "There." Inhaling deeply, she gripped the steering wheel and looked out at the view.

"I wonder if Thoreau was a shifter," Lilah finally said, a tiny chuckle piercing the tension.

"No way," Jess answered, eyeing the Land Rover. "He was too poor."

Lilah groaned at the bad joke and descended into an uneasy pause.

After another deep breath, she finally began to speak. "This is why I came back from the honeymoon early. Gavin let it slip that you'd been there at the fire. Tonight, when I went to Mom's, I was working up my courage to talk to you about what you'd seen."

"I saw you turn into a wolf."

"Yes. I know."

"I was annoyed you hadn't told me about that earlier," Jess added.

"Annoyed? That's it?"

"Well, maybe a little freaked out too," Jess said.

"It certainly freaked me out the first time it happened. You see—"

"But it proved you and Gavin were fated for each other," Jess said. "That had to be nice. You don't have the agony of doubting—"

"There was plenty of doubt."

"But the book settled things. Even Asher has to admit he was wrong about you two," Jess said.

Lilah slapped her hands against the wheel. "You spoke to Asher. Of course that's what happened. Of course! I knew it couldn't just be because of me and my shifting." She hit the wheel again. "That man needs a woman. He's out of control."

"Don't blame Asher. At least he explained things to me. You were hiding—"

"I don't know what he said, but don't you believe it, whatever it was. He doesn't know any more than I do, or Gavin does, about why I became a shifter when I did. It broke all tradition, all myth, all law."

"But the book—"

"Listen to me, Jess. Don't interrupt. Just listen to me. That book is old and strange, and not even the Stantons really understand it. What they expect is for a human mate to maybe—sometimes, not always—become a shifter after bearing a child with one. There have been centuries of humans and shifters loving and bearing children with one another, but they aren't very good about keeping records. And each of those families were so damn secretive, hiding their origins and histories as if their survival depended on it, which of course it does, with the world being what it is."

Jess clung to one of the little things Lilah had said. "Humans only sometimes become a shifter when they have kids with one?"

"Until me, the Stantons assumed it was the only way for a human to become a shifter, ever. And hardly a sure thing. My turning into a wolf really messed up Asher's worldview, let me tell you. And that man's worldview needs messing up."

"I hate him." Jess spat out the words.

"Oh, no, don't say that," Lilah said quickly, then her voice softened. "I've seen inside him, Jess. The damage. The pain. The grief. What we see is just a shadow of who he used to be. Deep down, he's a wonderfully loving, caring man. Whatever he did to you and to me, it was only to protect the brothers he loves so much."

"What did he do to you?"

"Made Gavin choose between us." Lilah sighed. "Poor Asher."

"Poor *Asher*? How can you say that?"

Lilah gave her a sad smile. "Because Gavin chose me, of course. I'm his One."

"And then Asher took it back. Figures. He's all bluff."

"No," Lilah said, "he's all grief. Don't you hear me? He's mourning the loss of his own One. Imagine if you lost Derry—"

"I've already lost Derry."

"You know you haven't. You just have to fight for him. But

Asher . . . well, his wife is lost forever. She died in childbirth. A human, like us, she couldn't survive the transition to live with the shifters." Lilah shuddered. "He feels responsible. If not for him, if not for his love, she'd be alive. Alone, but alive. It gnaws at him. I can feel it when I look into his eyes."

The chill sank into Jess's blood. She hugged her arms over her chest. "She died giving birth?"

"To his son. Who also died." Lilah's voice cracked. "Later Gavin told me how Asher buried their ashes with his bare hands at the house in Montana, in the winter, his fingers and knees bleeding into the snow, the frozen ground, almost killing himself from exposure."

Jess's eyes filled with tears. She couldn't speak for a moment. "Up near his cabin?"

"Where we had the bonfire," Lilah whispered. "Our commitment ceremony. That was sacred ground."

Tears began to flow freely now. "Asher didn't mind?"

Turning in her seat, Lilah reached up, cupped Jess's cheek, and gazed intently into her eyes. "It was his idea."

Jess shook free. "I don't believe it. Right afterward, he was trying to get rid of me. He practically flew me home himself."

"It's what he does," Jess said. "He thinks he's protecting his siblings. If you and Derry let him break you, then you deserve to be broken."

"Is that you talking or him?"

Lilah gave her a look, then started the car. The moon reappeared as the wind blew smoky clouds out of its way, the sudden luminescence glittering on Walden Pond like a dance. The SUV's engine rumbled in Jess's head, a soothing whine smoothing out as Lilah backed up.

"Where are we going?"

"I don't know. I just need to wander."

Jess had to admit to herself that being in motion was easier than standing still. Something troubled Lilah, though, her fingers tapping nervously on the steering wheel.

"Spit it out," Jess demanded.

Lilah didn't even try to pretend. "Are you really sure Derry's the One for you? He's such a smooth talker, and his reputation as a party animal isn't undeserved."

Jess snorted. Lilah frowned.

"What's so funny?"

"'Party animal' fits Derry on so many, many levels."

The two shared a laugh. As the tension lifted, Jess felt she could be more open. It felt so good to be with Lilah, spending time together. Just the two of them.

And now they had even more in common.

"I hear him in my head. I feel him in my heart. Not like a crush or wishful thinking. It's real," Jess said.

Lilah nodded, her head bobbing in quick agreement. "Then it's true."

"Plus the sex is so damn good. Oh my God, Lilah, why didn't you tell me sex could be like that?"

Lilah began coughing uncontrollably. Then she laughed like a hyena.

"Don't tell Gavin any of that, ever!" Lilah rasped. "He's incensed that Derry hooked up with you."

Jess bristled. "It's not just a hookup."

"I know. Truly." Jess realized Lilah was driving them back to her apartment.

"What are you doing? I want to go to Derry's loft to see if he's there."

"He's not."

Lilah's tone spoke thousands of words. "You know where he is?"

"Yes."

"It must be the club."

"You know about it?"

Jess gave Lilah a sour look. "Do I know about it? I work there, Lilah."

"Oh." Lilah wiggled in her seat and tapped her fingers again. Secrets. Her sister was hiding more secrets from her.

"Then take me to the club."

"He doesn't want company."

"How do you know?"

"Eva and Sophia. They're with him. He's fine. He just . . . He's been through a lot."

"Haven't we all?" Jess huffed. This didn't make sense. Lilah's nerves, Derry's seclusion. Was he hurt? Was he involved in some problem?

And then it hit her.

"Derry's the one who turned in those videos, isn't he? I saw him punch Archie in the foyer at the club, and—oh, Lilah." She could tell she was right from the look on Lilah's face.

"Let him be, Jess. It's been a long day for him."

"I want to see him! Apologize. Hell, grovel at his feet and tell him what a fool I've been!" Jess's voice cracked, and a sob captured her throat.

Lilah's hand lifted from the steering wheel and went to Jess's knee. "You'll have time. Plenty of time. But tonight let me hang out with you at the old apartment."

Jess just nodded, too overwhelmed to speak.

Too overwhelmed to *anything*. All she heard was her own heart, chiming like a tower clock.

A deep beat.

The Beat?

And then she heard him. He said one simple word.

Yes.

Twenty-Seven

D erry was so close to excusing himself from the gallery floor and banging his head against a brick wall until he passed out.

Not the best approach to being social, but it was a tempting option. A fine publicity stunt as well, if he were seeking attention.

Instead, he reached for his second tiny glass of Champagne and hoped for the best.

The mixed media art show featuring nudes had a simple title: *Her.*

Professor Lethbridge had suggested the title, raving like a fawning loon about the size of the Stanton family donation, insisting on three art exhibits devoted to nudes: *Her, Him* and *They.*

All Derry cared about was knowing that his own "Her" would be in attendance. As he finished his mouthful of drink, he caught a flash of purple dress from the doorway, then a familiar calf, loose hair in waves cascading down her back.

Her.

And she would soon be all his.

"Jess!" Professor Lethbridge called out. "We're unveiling the final painting. You simply must gather 'round with the rest of the interns and see this beauty!" Clapping like a schoolmarm, the professor collected a motley crew of students. He could tell they were students by the way they shoveled free alcohol down their throats.

He stepped to the right, half-hidden by a long, red curtain that bisected the enormous gallery, and watched from afar. Jess reached up to her temple and rubbed the spot right above her cheekbone.

I'm here, he thought.

She jolted visibly, her hand shaking as it fluttered down to her lips. Jess looked around the room, eyes like a predator's.

But the prey hid behind the red velvet curtain.

"Derry." A firm hand on his shoulder made him reel back out of instinct, caught off guard by the interruption, his elbow catching someone's belly as he pushed back and pivoted, turning around to find himself staring at a very pale, gasping, and quite angry Edward.

Derry rubbed his eyes, for surely he was hallucinating. What they hell was in that Champagne? Edward couldn't be here. He hated the city.

Sophia popped up behind Edward, her hands on his shoulders, urging him to take deep breaths, eyes on Derry, blazing with anger. "Why did you hit him?"

"He surprised me!" Derry said. "I was deep in thought!"

"How deep? The earth's core?"

Sophia's eyes flitted across the room until she clearly saw Jess. "Have you spoken with her?" Standing on the edge of the crowd, a few feet from the throng of students, he saw the woman from the Plat, Molly, Lilah's friend. Molly turned and gave Edward a dazzling smile. The buffoon didn't notice, but then again, he was still recovering.

"No," Derry said. "And what the hell are you two doing here?"

Edward finally unfolded himself and stood upright, giving thanks for the water Sophia handed him. He took a sip and said, "Sophia told me about your painting. Gavin couldn't be here, and—"

"You told everyone?" he growled at Sophia, his heart pounding so hard he could feel it in his bulging eyes.

"Not Asher, silly. Of course not. But I told Gavin and Edward. You have a gift, Derry. We're here to support you," Sophia replied, giving him a kiss on the cheek, reaching up with her thumb to smear off the lipstick mark she must have left.

I miss you.

The words shot through his mind like a bullet, piercing every part of him that formed his sense of self, and he closed one eye, wincing in pain.

Edward's brow folded in concern, and Derry heard Sophia call out his name, but then, oh then, a cloth was whisked away from the eight-by-eight-foot painting of Jess that was the show's centerpiece, the crowd around it gasping, small, intimate sounds of appreciation bubbling up to make the static of community in his ears.

"Jesus," Edward whispered, and Sophia linked one of her arms through each of theirs and just stared at the painting of beautiful, gorgeous, achingly authentic Jessica Murphy immortalized by paint, sweat, compassion, hope, lust, faith, fear and knowing.

"Isn't it amazing?" Sophia murmured, tears spilling down her cheeks, the sight of her emotional reaction gutting Derry.

"I had no idea you could do this," Edward said.

"Paint?" Derry joked.

Edward's face remained serious, his eyes troubled. "No, Derry. This isn't just painting. You take emotion and give it an image."

Derry's heart skipped a beat.

Jess's back was to him, her body frozen, head tipped up just enough for him to know she was taking in every square inch, her eyes missing nothing. What was she thinking?

More important—what did she *feel*?

I love you.

When Professor Lethbridge, with a dramatic flourish, removed the cover from the last painting, Jess froze in shock.

It was her. Dominating the center of the room, reaching up to the ceiling, was an eight-foot-high painting of *her*. In the nude. Every inch of skin, every hair, every nipple—right there.

A shared gasp whistled through the crowd. Two of the people standing next to her turned to stare, their eyes wide, before returning their gaze to the painting. They'd recognized her. There was no mistaking her. He'd captured her perfectly.

The other paintings and sculptures in the show were also of nudes, of course, but she'd barely noticed them. Mixed media had made Cubism seem boring. But this . . .

Since the moment she'd walked into the gallery, her birthmark had throbbed like a brand-new tattoo, so intensely she'd dipped into the bathroom to take a look. The mark had disappeared a while ago, then reappeared.

She frowned.

It disappeared when she and Derry were together. A couple.

And it had reappeared when they had split up.

There was no time to contemplate the meaning of *that*, just as Professor Lethbridge waved her over to a group of students urgently struggling with a six-foot labia sculpture made from recycled tires.

She'd felt him, been sure he was there—he was the artist, and this was his show—but she'd been unable to find him.

But all of a sudden, it didn't matter. She knew where he was.

Right there. On the canvas.

I love you, the paint said, caressed by his brushes, by his soul.

Her heart was pounding. *I love you too, Derry.*

She had to find him. Now.

Ignoring the curious looks of those around her, she turned

away from the painting and maneuvered through the crowd to an empty corner. Feeling weightless, she wrapped her arms around her chest and squeezed, trying to keep herself from flying apart completely. Nothing seemed to matter anymore: the other students, the professor, her job, her future. The material universe faded away. All that mattered was finding Derry as soon as possible.

Where are you?

For some unfathomable reason, he was hiding from her. The man who had created that painting—more than a man, more than a painting—had nothing to fear from her but the force of her own love. Was that it? Was he afraid of where their feelings would lead?

Simply looking hadn't found him; perhaps she had to use deeper senses. With her birthmark aching, she closed her eyes and cast out her thoughts and feelings, searching for a hint of his powerful physique, his charming spirit, his irresistible vitality.

He was so close she could almost taste him. Inhaling, but keeping her eyes closed, she pivoted on one heel and turned to face the spot where she felt his presence.

Come to me, my love, she thought. Beneath closed eyelids, tears pooled. Perhaps he wasn't afraid of her loving him too much; he was afraid she couldn't love him enough. Hadn't she left him without a word? Wiping the escaping tears off her cheeks, she added, *Forgive me.*

The form she sensed was silent and came no closer.

She turned back to face the wall again, not wanting the others to see her cry. Shame washed over her, leaving her hot and shaky. Maybe it was too late. The painting wasn't an expression of his love. Maybe it was a good-bye. Like the other paintings of women, it was nothing more than a memento. Woman of the month, not of his life.

Oh no. She was sobbing in the middle of an art show right

in front of her professor and dozens of other students. With that painting on the wall, she'd never get out of here without completely humiliating herself.

"For God's sake, my darling, forgive you for what?"

His deep, familiar voice surrounded her, forming a fortress of love that shut out the world. Without turning around, she inhaled deeply and wiped her cheeks with shaking hands, suddenly aware that she probably looked terrible, with melting mascara and swollen eyes.

"For leaving you," she whispered.

"You had cause," he said roughly. "More than enough."

"No, I was wrong. I assumed—" she finally turned around and looked up into his midnight-blue eyes, the gallery lights reflecting in the irises like stars. Her explanation died on her lips. The only words she could remember were *I love you, I love you, I love you.*

He was so beautiful, so good. Seeing him again made her knees weak, and she had to lean against the wall behind her for support.

"Whatever you believed, I'd given you cause to believe it," he said.

"No, it wasn't fair, just because you knew Archie didn't mean—" But she couldn't talk about that infamous prick here where they might be overheard. She glanced past Derry to the crowd. Several faces were indeed pointedly aimed in their direction. "Oh, Derry, I really need to explain, but not here."

Just a hint of his former rakish grin flickered across his lips. "And I need to touch you, but not here."

Flushing, she grinned back at him. "Pity."

His mirth faded, leaving a seriously ravenous look on his face. His gaze dropped to her lips. She realized that both of them were breathing heavily.

"Oh, to hell with it," he said, taking her in his arms. When she snaked up her arms and slid them around his neck, he growled, pinned her against the wall, buried his hands in her hair, and lowered his mouth to hers for a hard, hungry, desperate kiss.

Through the sound of rushing blood in her brain, she was vaguely aware of whistles, bubbling laughter, and then applause from the other side of the room. The show attendees continued like this for the full length of the kiss—the first kiss, and then the second—cheering and clapping, but Jess was too enraptured in the strong, euphoric sweetness of Derry's embrace to care. Let them do whatever they wanted. As long as she had Derry, she didn't give a damn what they thought.

In fact, if it had been up to her, they would've stripped and done it right there in front of everyone: her boss, her peers, the painted eyes of his former lovers. But he was a gentleman, and he loved her, and so he captured her hands before they unbuttoned his pants and, smiling against her mouth, took a step back.

"Come," he said, entwining his fingers in hers. He turned to the door.

"I almost did," she said under her breath as he pulled her across the floor. "Just now."

He stopped abruptly and looked back. His gaze burned. "I love you, Jess."

"I love you, Derry."

They started to move together again, but suddenly Sophia was there, pushing them like a snowplow. "For God's sake, finish up outside," she muttered. "This is an art show, not a peep show."

"Ironically, unlike the show, we're both fully dressed," Jess said, giddy now to have Derry's hand in hers and the fresh taste of his lips on her tongue.

"The limo's waiting," Sophia said, giving a final shove toward the door. "We'll call for another." Edward smiled from over Sophia's shoulder, eyes filled with a quiet mirth.

They hurried out of the gallery to the street and into the car, which was waiting only several steps from the entrance. Derry waved aside Manny's help and flung open the back door for Jess himself. As she bent over to climb in, one hand caressed her bottom, claiming her body the way she'd missed so desperately in the past weeks.

He piled in after her and tapped on the window behind Manny. "My place, as fast as you possibly can." As the limo peeled out into traffic, he fell against Jess's side. "Curse me. Are you hurt, sweetheart? I have the grace of a drunken elephant in a rowboat. I probably broke your arm. Let me—"

Smiling, she caught him by his broad, seductive shoulders and pulled him close. "I'm fine. You didn't hurt me."

"You're lying. You shouldn't ever forgive me." He sighed and moved away, turning his head away. "I really don't deserve it."

She knew he meant it as a joke, but there was a faint thread of sincere self-loathing in his voice. This man who had single-handedly brought the hateful Archibald Rumsey to justice—which he'd obviously done for her sake—even after she'd left him without telling him why.

She put her hand on his leg, trying to tune out the way the muscles of his thigh flexed under her palm because they reminded her of how his skin felt naked, hot, and sweaty, and right now she wanted to talk seriously. Thinking about his body would make keeping a clear head impossible. "I need to explain—"

He stopped her words by suddenly catching her in his arms and hauling her into his lap. While he bent her head back with a fierce kiss, his hands slid her skirt up to her waist, exploring her upper thighs gently, then roughly, pushing them apart. Cupping her damp panties, he spoke into her mouth, his voice low and ravenous. "I need you," he growled, pressing and circling her mound with too-clever fingers. "I can't wait."

"I don't want to wait," she gasped, twisting around and getting onto her knees to straddle him, the streets of Boston a blur outside the tinted windows. "Derry, Derry." She attacked the coat he wore, the tie, the button-down shirt, hungry for the feel of warm skin, dark hair, powerful muscle and bone. Between her thighs, she felt the bulge of his erection straining at his trousers. As her fingers unbuttoned his shirt, she sank down and rubbed against him through the wool and the nylon, tormenting them both.

With another growl, he ripped her panties off and stroked his hand over her bare, wet, aching flesh while at the same time his tongue pushed past her teeth and tangled with hers in a dance she'd dreamed of every night.

Oh, to be in his arms again. To have him in *her* arms.

When he'd unfastened his pants, she reached down to free his cock, glorying in how hard it was, how it throbbed in her hand.

Pressing her open mouth against his, she guided his erection between her legs and impaled herself down on it, deep and fast, all the way. He groaned and threw his head back, grabbing her hips, trembling from their union, and then began to pump her up and down.

She'd explain later.

I'm home.

He felt her lips twitch with a smile against his neck as the words flowed between the two of them, his cock rising up into her, the limousine's motion an afterthought as he rocketed up, planting himself where he needed to grow and bloom.

Inside her.

Her fingers dug into his wide back, the tips dragging along his skin as if she were writing her name across his shoulders, etching herself in his body, claiming him. Long waves of honey hair hovered over him, creating a curtain, the heat of their wild, ragged breath filling the space between them. He tasted her as he took her mouth with his, the slant of lips and tongues alive and seeking, making him groan.

"You," he rasped, thrusting up so hard that she clenched,

pinning him against her core, her pussy a hot, wet vise grip that made him growl, the sound like months of pain being exorcised from a heart that once wept with grief and now with joy.

Her body moved against his with a kind of violent surrender that consumed him, his hands ripping the thin fabric of her dress, his fingers sliding just so against the creamy curves of her ass, skimming up over her hips, cupping breasts that were sadly bound by the undeniable injustice of that most barbaric of binding devices.

He tore off her bra with his teeth, a few snaps between her breasts and a fine grind of tooth against tooth just enough to dispatch with the worthless device, and his mouth found the rosy nipple that tasted like nirvana, his tongue suckling her as she tipped back, hands splayed on his knees, and rode him like a wild animal.

Which was so fitting.

"God, I've missed you," she moaned, her tongue finding his ear as she moved her hips against his thick rod, pulling up just enough to make this deliciously drawn out, then plunging down to encase him in the sweet juice of lust.

"You've missed me so much you've forgotten my name, sweetheart. I'm Derry. Not God."

A low, smoky laugh was her response. "You keep doing this," she whispered, biting his earlobe, "and you'll become my god. We're about as close to heaven as I've ever been."

"Then by all means, Jessica, let's get you all the way to nirvana." He'd been holding back, but her words released a primal madness in him, his mind shutting down as instinct took over, a singular goal to extract and provide as much sensual pleasure his sole mission now. His nose tingled with the scent of her lemon soap, the odor of the coffee she drank minutes before their first kiss, the sweet, delicious tang of her pussy, the light musk of his own sweating skin, the old leather of the limo's seats, and the new-to-him scent that combined everything Derry and everything Jess and created a signature, like a fingerprint, that made words irrelevant.

Yours, her voice echoed. *I'm yours. Take me.*

And so he did.

"Derry!" she cried as the sublime feeling of their bodies communing made him stroke up, thrusting hard, controlling her body, forcing her to his own rhythm, making her fingernails rake his back with the writhing of a woman on the cusp of, well . . .

Nirvana.

The Beat throbbed between them, making their flesh unite, their blood burn hot and cold with a tempo of their own.

"I—oh—oh, what is this? I—" The low, feral sound that emerged from Jess's delicate throat was a war cry of passion, her thighs widening, wrapping hard around his midsection, knees digging into the leather seat, as she matched him stroke for stroke, thrust for thrust, the slam of body against body a carnal ceremony, his blood racing with a pulse that matched some chant inside him that was sound without words, tone without reproach, meaning without form.

She rammed against him so hard she shoved him back against the seat, his powerful thighs thickening and ass tightening to dominate her, and then he flipped her, needing to tower above her, wanting to protect her from a world that tried to tell them this was wrong.

He would prove, in the flesh, how very right this was.

Lick by lick, stroke by stroke.

And then she *bit* him.

The bite was so hard he roared, impaling her with his cock. His skin seared with the piercing of her teeth into his chest, her mouth moving with tiny bites, her pussy walls clenching him so hard he had to fight for his thrusts, his own climax so close.

So damned close.

Her heels slapped against his ass, thighs tightening as she let her lips part, his eyes catching her in the throes of passion, fascinated by the pure, unadulterated rawness she expressed, the complete abandon of propriety as Jessica Murphy unraveled before his eyes, giving him the privilege of letting his body and heart do this to her.

She became nothing but untamed instinct.

Then he came right with her, his pounding untenable, the mounting wave of rapturous desire too much to hold back. His instinct to protect her from his own rutting need was overcome by the unarticulated realization that she was causing him pain, with bites and scratches and shouts and calls to join him in ecstasy and the savage ritual of fusing into one soul, one life, one love.

Just . . . One.

He wanted to call out her name but lost the word in the rush of his seed, filling her, hot and needy, his mouth against her precious neck, his chin gliding along her collarbone, his panting an echo that turned him into nothing but the animal he was. Human, still, yet . . . more.

When he finally opened his eyes, he found himself the subject of her own stare right back, pupils so dilated they might as well have been black moons, a drop of his own blood at the edge of her mouth.

Derry sank to her, ear against her breast, the intimate comfort of her samba-dance heartbeat the best symphony he could ever experience, and then in Jess's arms, McDermott Stanton gave himself permission for one final, illicit pleasure.

He let the tears come.

Her body played out its electrical impulses as he allowed himself the luxury of falling to pieces in tiny ways, his breathing controlled by the wellspring of emotion too much for his eyes, which insisted on filling with this cursed fluid and leaking out. A drop landed on her nipple, then another, and as her little twitches and groans steadied, and her heart stopped its racing, he felt her smooth his hair back from his forehead, the cool, steady hand of grace and love making the bridge of his nose ache.

"Are you crying?" she asked softly.

"What? No. Of course not." He cleared his throat, horrified to find it filled with salty tears as well. "Stanton men don't cry."

"Then you're leaking."

"The only fluid I am leaking, my dear, just went into your body." Relief filled him, his voice rough with emotion. He could only keep up the ruse for so long. Letting himself give in to the tidal wave of emotion inside was one thing.

Admitting it was quite another.

She laughed but reached to caress his brow, her fingertips finding wetness at the edge of one eye.

"It's all right, you know," she said, her own voice thick with feelings. "I want to cry too."

"Was the sex that bad?"

She batted at him, her hands useless against his back, though her skin hit open scratches from earlier, the sting a reminder of how lost they'd been in each other, moments ago.

"Quit joking," she admonished.

The limo halted.

Hurrying into their clothes, Derry chagrined as Jess pointed to a series of popped buttons on her dress, he offered her his jacket, and they made their way to his loft, pausing only to kiss a thousand times along the way.

He needed even more.

As he punched the key code and the enormous wooden door slid open, he escorted Jess inside, ready for anything but tears.

She turned around, clutching the sides of his jacket, which

was so big on her that she looked shrunken. Ethereal beauty glowed from within as she looked up at him. He reached for her.

Jess stepped back, out of his grasp, and took a deep, soulful sigh.

"Derry, we need to talk."

Twenty-Eight

J ess could see the panic in her One's eyes and rushed to soothe it away.

"Don't look so worried," she said, smiling at him, hoping that every bit of her love shone in her eyes. "I need to explain why I left. Before I lose my guts."

He frowned. "You don't need to explain. You saw Lilah shift. And then, adding insult to injury, my intolerable brother Asher filled your head with rubbish."

"He showed me a book."

"Rubbish," he said.

"Lilah could read it, he said. But all I saw was scribbles. I thought it meant . . . but I don't care anymore about your stupid myths or rules or legends. I love you, you love me. That's enough." She stiffened her spine. "More than enough."

"That book, my darling, doesn't mean a thing. Or we don't know what it means. Asher was . . . wrong"—his jaw clenched as he seemed to swallow a harsher word or two—"to show it to you and suggest it meant anything."

"Lilah could read it. I can't."

"Reading is overrated," he said.

"Lilah shifts into a wolf just like Gavin, as if she was always meant to be with him."

"Lilah's shifting is a mystery to everyone. For whatever reason, she is unique. You, my love, are unique in other, much more important ways." He moved to touch her, but Jess arched out of reach.

"I get that now. But that night—"

"I should've sensed you and explained everything. I should've—"

"I wouldn't have listened. I was already upset about Archie."

He let out a disgusted sound. "I should never have spoken to that walking pile of fetid rat entrails."

"I shouldn't have run off without talking to you. I assumed you guys were old pals, that you were one of them. That you enjoyed hurting people." She looked down at her feet, ashamed to remember how quickly she'd jumped to conclusions. "I'm so sorry. More than anything, I'm sorry for ever thinking that of you. Not once have I ever seen you be cruel. Not once."

"You saw me greet him as a friend," Derry said. "What else would you think?"

"That you were being polite, as you always are—"

He snorted.

"In your own way," she said. "It was your brother's wedding. You couldn't insult a guest, let alone a senator's son."

"Absolutely I could have. I should have. If I'd known—"

She hugged her arms around herself, his enormous coat wrapping her in a Derry-scented embrace. "But you didn't know, honey. I was wrong to think you did. That party—" Her voice caught.

"We're not going to talk about that."

"Yes, yes, we have to." She took a deep breath. "It . . . fucked me up. Being humiliated like that, when I was so young and stupid—"

"Don't insult yourself," he said fiercely. "Never, ever insult the woman I love."

Her knees wobbled a little. But she overcame the urge to throw herself at him just yet. "All right, then. I was naïve. I thought . . . I thought I was hot, in my own way—"

"You were right." Now he sounded angry.

Oh, Derry. He wasn't making this easy. She took another step backward to lessen the temptation of flinging her arms around his neck and kissing him silly. "Thank you," she said, swallowing a smile. She was trying to describe the most humiliating, devastating moment of her life, but she felt like laughing. This. This is what he'd done for her. "I never imagined that those successful, intelligent guys would stoop so low, be so cruel—"

"Losers," Derry growled. "Idiots."

She gave him a nod of her head, acknowledging the correction. "Like I said, I was wrong. And they really, really hurt me, inside. My self-worth. I was so vulnerable then. It took me a long time to get over it." *Until you*, she thought. Someday she'd tell him how much he'd done for her. Not quite yet, though—he was cocky enough tonight. "Learning that you were at the party that night—"

"I had no idea what it was," he said quickly. "I left as soon as I realized. With a pair of the loveliest—" He cleared his throat. "Memories. Of how beautiful the women—I mean, you, how beautiful *you* were."

Now she let herself move to him. Stepping just inches away, she tilted her head back, eyebrows raised. "You remember seeing me back then? Seriously?"

He bit his lip. Nodded.

Holding his gaze, she flung the jacket off her shoulders, leaving her exposed in the unbuttoned dress. "That's your story, and you're sticking to it?"

His eyelids fell as he took in the sight of her breasts peeking through her open dress. "I'm sticking really, really hard."

"But why didn't you say anything then when you saw me in the elevator?" She knew he was shining her on. It was sweet but unnecessary.

"Elevator?"

"When we met," she said. "At the Plat. My first day at the club. Or, rather, were reunited, since you're saying we met at Archie's lovely social event years earlier." Jess wanted to see how far he would take this ruse.

But he seemed to have lost all interest in the conversation. Instead, he was bending over to lick the tip of one increasingly erect nipple that had escaped the drape of thin fabric. At the feel of his tongue on this sensitive point, she found herself losing interest in talking as well.

"You're right," he admitted, bending over as he kissed his way along the curve of her breast. "I didn't see you then. I doubt we were even there at the same time, because I would have *felt* you. If I had, I would never have wasted the years since, squeezing out the weakest excuse of a pathetic existence without you." He wrapped his arms around her waist and lifted her off the ground. In another second, she was flung over his shoulder, her butt in the air and her head hanging down his back.

When she was done squealing in surprise, she reached down and slapped his ass. He patted hers in return as he hauled her, laughing harder, down a dark hallway into a room she hoped, beyond hope, had a very large, sturdy bed.

She was not disappointed. Lit faintly by wall sconces, the sleeping chamber was obviously that of a passionate, artistic, and wealthy man. There were rich fabrics draping the windows and mattress, and diverse paintings and drawings of all eras and styles covering the walls. A bronze female figure—elegant, not tacky—perched on a pedestal near the window, arms outstretched like a goddess greeting the sun.

But she didn't notice any of those details until the morning, hours and hours later. Right now she was feeling her passions build inside her again, unbound from their years of youthful loneliness and, more recently, the past months of heartbreak. Feeling equal and permanently bound to this man, her One, gave her a joy in the moment she'd never known.

This curve of muscled hip was hers. This thick, strong neck was hers. This skin, these lips, those eyes. The sound of his low, urgent voice in her ear as he tore off the last of her clothing. The fingertips that stroked up her thigh and buried themselves into her slippery, wet need, demanding she unlock the last of her secrets and give him all her treasure, every scrap of her soul.

"Derry, Derry," she moaned, the words coming in time to a third pulse that took over. Was this the Beat that Lilah mentioned? Jess wanted to believe it, and then suddenly it didn't matter.

He mattered. Derry mattered.

The rest wasn't worth another thought.

The duvet beneath her shoulders was as thick and billowy as a cloud in heaven. She could barely feel the mattress beneath it. The enormous man looming above with his hairy chest and thickly muscled shoulders didn't seem to belong in such an elegantly comfortable bed, but then she realized, as she stroked the hard lines of his abdomen, the broad and flexing chest, that of course her Derry, her One, belonged in decadent, baroque luxury, not plain, cold, Scandinavian austerity.

"So much to learn about you," he said softly, his lips tickling the hollow of her throat.

Because of the deft motions of his hands, she could only choke out one gasp after another. She arched up, powerless to stop the reaction of her body.

"So much to learn," he murmured again, sounding amused.

She smiled in a daze, having no interest whatsoever in stopping the reactions of her body. And more than that, she had no interest in stopping anything that happened with Derry. This was their fate. They belonged together. No brother, no book, no past could ever stand between them. Sealed together from this moment on,

Derry and Jess were One.

Well, not quite yet. He was still chuckling at the way her body was bucking off the bed under his skilled hands.

She was too aroused to laugh with him. But if he thought he'd won some game by teasing her this way, he was very wrong. By surrendering to this passion he was insisting she accept, her heart expanded and overflowed with love, acceptance, hope. By surrendering, she had won everything.

She'd won *him*.

With the skills he'd learned over his many years of practice—she would think of them that way, merely as skill-building exercises for being with her—he pulled her back from the edge of orgasm again and again until she was finally pounding his shoulders with frustration.

"Now," she gasped.

But he withdrew, sitting back on his knees, regarding her with mock-confusion. "Now what?"

"You know what, you—" She stopped when she saw how much he was enjoying her torment. Closing her eyes, she sucked in deep breaths, her heart pounding so hard it had almost become a steady, unbroken roar in her ears. "Fine. I'll do it myself." And with that, she reached between her legs.

His laughter died. The dark pools of his eyes told her how aroused he, too, had become. He'd been teasing her, but he'd been torturing himself even more. With his gaze locked on every move of her hand, he shuddered, swallowing hard, and began to reach for her.

She slapped his hand. "You had your turn."

A growl rumbled deep in his throat. "You're killing me."

"Just you wait," she said, her voice thick from the tightening pleasure.

"I beg your pardon," he said, bending down and kissing her feet in supplication. "Please, allow me to pleasure you. My darling.

My love."

The feel of his wet mouth around her toes only sent her higher on the wave of passion she was riding. She was seconds from coming. But did she really want to come with her foot in his mouth instead of—

"You may continue," she gasped.

He was on top of her before the words were out of her mouth. "Thank you, thank you—"

Out of her mind, she dug her fingernails into his shoulders. "Now!"

At last he entered her, and the unbearable tightness snapped, breaking her into shards and fragments and nothingness. And as he joined her, wave after wave of sweet, hot pleasure washed over her, tearing her apart from the inside out, blacking out her vision.

Minutes later, when they were both spent and limp, just crying. No—he wasn't crying this time, it was her. Tears streamed down her cheeks, but she was too tired to care, too happy to stop.

As she drifted into a mindless sleep, she felt a gentle mouth kissing each one of them away.

And then, from deep inside her own soul, she heard his voice. *I love you.*

And she felt it.

The Beat. As if it had always been there, just waiting for her to finally hear it.

<hr />

Startled awake by a dream that was marked by scent more than image, Derry sat up, propping his sore body on one large palm, his nose working overtime to recapture the unconscious mind's scent story. There had been a moon, a clearing, a placid lake and mists filled with Jess, naked and half-submerged, her shoulders back and hair skimming the water, breasts calling out for him, the strange birthmark on her neck glowing like a beacon, emanating a scent that only he could smell.

As that dream scent faded, he picked up the odor of coffee. Ah, the blessings of the twenty-first century. For as cheap and gaudy as this age could be, programmable coffeemakers were some tool of the gods that Derry found worthy of gratitude.

Pale, lush skin greeted his gaze as he looked down to find her warming his bed. His free hand touched her bare hip, palm greedy to caress every inch of her.

Mine.

She was his, and he was hers, and they were each other's One.

He sat up, watching Jess's face in slumber, tension gone from a face that last night he'd found rapturous. Her brow smooth, her lips lush, her slow breath even and sweet, he greedily watched this woman, naked and in his bed, covered in their blended juices.

The red birthmark on her neck was gone.

Brushing aside a stray lock of hair with a hand so big it could cover her entire face, he paused, blinking at the contrast. While Jess was not a small-boned woman, compared to him she was tiny. Vulnerable. Trusting.

His.

The sense of peace inside him had not left with the morning. As they'd drifted off last night after making love with a frenzy that turned him inside out, he'd felt a centered calm. A Oneness. The call of his name, of a silent language between the two of them that he knew was private. Unique.

Exclusive.

And the thought had floated through him as consciousness dissolved.

Here it was again.

Peeling himself from her prone body, he covered her with the thick duvet and stood, stretching, holding back the contented growl that threatened to emanate from him as blood flooded his aching muscles. Waking her would defeat the purpose of the next few minutes.

A smile tickled his lips as he padded naked into the kitchen, pouring two cups of coffee, filling hers with so much milk that the coffee turned the color of pale beige.

He set the coffee on a small tray, then walked to his studio, finding the tiny box easily. A flick of one thumb and there it was.

The dazzling diamond engagement ring he'd ordered at the ranch.

Before.

Before the confusion and fear, before the misunderstanding and the escape. Before the pain of abandonment and the terror of humiliation.

Before they'd understood that being each other's One had nothing to do with any external rules.

Sunlight peeked through the heavy velvet curtains that covered the soaring, old warehouse windows of his loft. The diamond sent dancing sunbeams into the ceiling, bounding off support beams and painted ductwork, a visual feast that promised a lifetime of play and boundless joy.

Peering through the open door to his bed, he smiled.

No ring could guarantee that.

But love could.

Come here, she said without words.

On impulse, he started to hide the ring, finding a long expanse of bare ass where his back pocket should be.

Oh, dear.

Instead, Derry set the ring on the tray and decided to face this head on. The sooner she was his in every way possible—body, soul, mind, heart, and in marriage—the better.

"Is that coffee I smell?" she called out. Her nude backside appeared as he walked into the room, carrying the tray, her hair pushed back over one shoulder, the vision so close to his painting he groaned. Too much beauty.

Too, too much beauty.

A man needed more than one lifetime to appreciate a woman like Jess.

Even a lifetime as long as his.

"Mmmmmm," she purred as he set the tray on the bed. "Coffee in bed. You're a dream man, Derry. Where did you come fr—" Her eyes froze on the small black velvet box. She said nothing, but held her breath.

He did too. Plucking it off the tray, he looked at her and opened it slowly.

This time, it was not sunlight that danced.

It was his heart.

She sat on the bed, legs forward and flat on the wide pine floor, and he dipped to one knee, making her gasp and throw her hands to her mouth, the gesture so universally enacted by women in proposals that he let out a burst of deep laughter. Nervousness never entered the picture, replaced instead by a rooted sense of eternity. He was not just proposing.

He was righting a wrong.

At some point throughout the ages, he and Jessica Murphy had been One, then lost each other.

Now they were One again.

"Will you, Jessica, marry—"

She tackled him before he could finish the sentence. Jess was far stronger than he'd imagined, pushing his body to the floor, covering him with kisses and squeals of joy, his hand fumbling for hers, sliding the ring on her left finger.

There was nothing more to say, but he needed her to say it.

Say yes, he told her, but his mouth was currently occupied by hers, tongues dancing with their hearts.

Yes, oh yes, she answered, the drag of her ring kissing his skin as she buried her hand in his long hair, his own hands cupping her jaw.

You're mine.

He wasn't sure who said it, the words echoing a thousand times, like the peal of church bells so loud they linger in the mind long after the actual sound is gone.

And then there were no more words.

The End

Thank you so much for reading *The Billionaire Shifter's Virgin Mate*! Please leave a review and tell your friends about this new series.

Get the next book in the series, *The Billionaire Shifter's Second Chance*, now. Join my New Releases email list to learn about future books.

Loved Derry and Jess's story? Go back and read about Lilah and Gavin and enter a whole new love story . . . and watch for new books in the series!

Books by Diana Seere

THE BILLIONAIRE SHIFTERS CLUB SERIES

The Billionaire Shifter's Curvy Match

The Billionaire Shifter's Virgin Mate

The Billionaire Shifter's Second Chance

The Billionaire Shifter's Secret Baby

About the Author

Diana Seere was raised by wolves in the forests outside San Francisco and Boston. The only time she spends in packs these days is at romance writing conventions. In truth, Diana is two New York Times and USA Today bestselling authors who decided to write shifter romance and have more fun. You can find "her" on Facebook at Diana Seere's Facebook Page: : *www.facebook.com/dianaseere*

Sign up for her New Releases and Sales email newsletter here: *eepurl.com/beUZnr*

Made in the USA
Columbia, SC
24 April 2023